Emperor in Exile

Simon Firth

"Uneasy lies the head that wears a crown"

Henry IV, Part II, Act III, Scene I
William Shakespeare 1597

First Published in Great Britain by Ammon Press 2015

ISBN   978-0-993-27920-1

For Goatu

CHAPTER I

AN EXILE IN LONDON

The May sunlight streamed in through the window, making curious patterns of the curtains upon the carpet. Outside, the tide of life was flowing fast; the green leaves of the Park were already offering agreeable shade to early strollers; the noise of cabs and omnibuses had set in steadily for the day. Outside, Knightsbridge was awake and active; inside, sleep reigned with quiet. The room was one of the best bedrooms in Paulo's Hotel; it was really tastefully furnished, soberly decorated, in the style of the fifteenth French Louis. A very good copy of Watteau was over the mantel-piece, the only picture in the room. There had been a fire in the hearth overnight, for a grey ash lay there. Outside on the ample balcony stood a laurel in a big blue pot, an emblematic tribute on Paulo's part to honourable defeat which might yet turn to victory.

There were books about the room: a volume of Napoleon's maxims, a French novel, a little volume of Sophocles in its original Greek. A uniform-case and a sword-case stood in a corner. A map of South America lay partially unrolled upon a chair. The dainty gilt clock over the mantel-piece, a genuine heritage from the age of Louis Quinze, struck eight briskly. The Emperor stirred in his sleep.

Presently there was a tapping at the door to the left of the bed, a door communicating with the Emperor's private sitting-room. Still the Emperor slept, undisturbed by the slight sound. The sound was not repeated, but the door was softly opened, and a young man put his head into the room and looked at the slumbering Emperor. The young man was dark, smooth-shaven, with a look of quiet alertness in his face. He seemed to be about thirty years of age. His dark eyes watched the sleeping figure affectionately for a few seconds. 'It seems a pity to wake him,' he muttered; and he was about to draw his head back and close the door, when the Emperor stirred again, and suddenly waking swung himself round in the bed and faced his visitor. The visitor smiled pleasantly. 'Buenos dias, Escelencia,' he said.

The Emperor propped himself up on his left arm and looked at him.

'Good morning, Hamilton,' he answered. 'What's the good of talking Spanish here? Better fall back upon simple Saxon until we can see the sun rise again in Surmer. And as for the Excellency, don't you think we had better drop that too?'

'Until we see the sun rise in Surmer,' said Hamilton. He had pushed the door open now, and entered the room, leaning carelessly against the door-post. 'Yes; that may not be so far off, please Heaven; and, in the meantime, I think we had better stick to the title and all forms, Excellency.'

The Emperor laughed again. 'Very well, as you please. The world is governed by form and title, and I suppose such dignities lend a decency even to exile in men's eyes. Is it late? I was tired, and slept like a dog.'

'Oh no; it's not late,' Hamilton answered. 'Only just struck eight. You wished to be called, or I shouldn't have disturbed you.'

'Yes, yes; one must get into no bad habits in London. All right; I'll get up now, and be with you in twenty minutes.'

'Very well, Excellency.' Hamilton bowed as he spoke in his most official manner, and withdrew. The Emperor looked after him, laughing softly to himself.

'L'excellence malgré lui,' he thought. 'An excellency in spite of myself. Well, I dare say Hamilton is right; it may serve to fill my sails when I have any sails to fill. In the meantime let us get up and salute London. Thank goodness it isn't raining, at all events.'

He did his dressing unaided. 'The best master is his own man' was an axiom with him. In the most splendid days of Surmer he had always valeted himself; and in Surmer, where assassination was always a possibility, it was certainly safer. His body-servant filled his bath and brought him his brushed clothes; for the rest he waited upon himself.

He did not take long in dressing. All his movements were quick, clean, and decisive; the movements of a man to whom moments are precious, of a man who has learnt by long experience how to do everything as shortly and as well as possible. As soon as he was finished he stood for an instant before the long looking-glass and surveyed himself. A man of rather more than medium height, strongly built, of soldierly carriage, wearing his dark frock-coat like a uniform. His left hand seemed to miss its familiar sword-hilt. The face was bronzed by Southern suns; the brown eyes were large, and bright, and keen; the hair was a fair brown, faintly touched here and there with grey. His full moustache and beard were trimmed to a point, almost in the Elizabethan fashion. Any serious student of humanity would at once have been attracted by the face. Habitually it wore an expression of gentle gravity, and it could smile very sweetly, but it was the face of a strong man, nevertheless, of a stubborn man, of a man ambitious, a man with clear resolve, personal or otherwise, and prompt to back his resolve with all he had in life, and with life itself.

He put into his buttonhole the green-and-yellow button which represented the order of the Sword and Myrtle, the great Order of La Surmer, which in Surmer was invested with all the splendour of the Golden Fleece; the order which could only be worn by those who had actually ruled in the Empire. That, according to satirists, did not greatly limit the number of persons who had the right to wear it. Then he formally saluted himself in the looking-glass. 'Excellency,' he said again, and laughed again. Then he opened his double windows and stepped out upon the balcony.

London was looking at its best just then, and his spirits stirred in grateful response to the sunlight. How dismal everything would have seemed, he was thinking, if the streets had been soaking under a leaden sky, if the trees had been dripping dismally, if his glance directed to the street below had rested only upon distended umbrellas glistening like the backs of gigantic crabs! Now everything was bright, and London looked as it can look sometimes, positively beautiful. Paulo's Hotel stands, as everybody knows, in the pleasantest part of Knightsbridge, facing Kensington Gardens. The sky was brilliantly blue, the trees were deliciously green; Knightsbridge below him lay steeped in a pure gold of sunlight. The animation of the scene cheered him sensibly. May is seldom summery in England, but this might have been a royal day of June.

Opposite to him he could see the green-grey roofs of Kensington Palace. At his left he could see a public-house which bore the name and stood upon the site of the hostelry where the Pretender's friends gathered on the morning when they expected to see Queen Anne succeeded by the heir to the House of Stuart. Looking from the one place to the other, he reflected upon the events of that morning when those gentlemen waited in vain for the expected tidings, when Bolingbroke, seated in the council chamber at yonder palace, was so harshly interrupted. It pleased the stranger for a moment to trace a resemblance between the fallen fortunes of the Stuart Prince and his own fallen fortunes, as dethroned Emperor of the South American Empire of Surmer. 'London is my St. Germain's,' he said to himself with a laugh, and he drummed the national hymn of Surmer upon the balcony-rail with his fingers.

His gaze, wandering over the green bravery of the Park, lost itself in the blue sky. He had forgotten London; his thoughts were with another place under a sky of stronger blue, in the White House of a white square in a white town. He seemed to hear the rattle of rifle shots, shrill trumpet calls, angry party cries, the clatter of desperate charges across the open space, the angry despair of repulses, the piteous pageant of civil war. Knightsbridge knew nothing of all that. Danes may have fought there, the chivalry of the White Rose or the Red Rose ridden there, gallant Cavaliers have spurred along it to fight for their king. All that was past; no troops moved there now in hostility to brethren of their blood. But to that one Englishman standing there, moody in spite of the sunlight, the scene which his eyes saw was not the tranquil London street, but the Plaza Nacional of Surmer, red with blood, and 'cut up,' in the painter's sense, with corpses.

'Shall I ever get back? Shall I ever get back?' that was the burden to which his thoughts were dancing. His spirit began to rage within him to think that he was here, in London, helpless, almost alone, when he ought to be out there, sword in hand, dictating terms to rebels repentant or impotent. He gave a groan at the contrast, and then he laughed a little bitterly and called himself a fool. 'Things might be worse,' he said. 'They might have shot me. Better for them if they had, and worse for Surmer. Yes, I am sure of it—worse for Surmer!'

His mind was back in London now, back in the leafy Park, back in Knightsbridge. He looked down into the street, and noted that a man was loitering on the opposite side. The man in the street saw that the Emperor noted him. He looked up at the Emperor, looked up above the Emperor, and, raising his hat, pointed as if towards the sky. The Emperor, following the direction of the gesture, turned slightly and looked upwards, and received a sudden thrill of pleasure, for just above him, high in the air, he could see the flutter of a mass of green and yellow, the colours of the national flag of Surmer. Mr Paulo, mindful of what was due even to exiled sovereignty, had flown the Surmer flag in honour of the illustrious guest beneath his roof. When that guest looked down again the man in the street had disappeared.

'That is a good omen. I accept it,' said the Emperor. 'I wonder who my friend was?' He turned to go back into his room, and in doing so noticed the laurel.

'Another good omen,' he said. 'My fortunes feel more summerlike already. The old flag still flying over me, an unknown friend to cheer me, and a laurel to prophesy victory—what more could an exile wish? His breakfast, I think,' and on this reflection he went back into his bedroom, and, opening the door through which Hamilton had talked to him, entered the sitting-room.

CHAPTER II

A GENTLEMAN ADVENTURER

The room which the Emperor entered was an attractive room, bright with flowers, which Miss Paulo had been pleased to arrange herself—bright with the persevering sunshine. It was decorated, like his bedroom, with the restrained richness of the mid-eighteenth century. With discretion, Paulo had slightly adapted the accessories of the room to please by suggestion the susceptibilities of its occupant. A marble bust of Caesar stood upon the dwarf bookcase. A copy of a famous portrait of Napoleon was on one of the walls; on another an engraving of Dr Francia still more delicately associated great leaders with South America. At a table in one corner of the room—a table honeycombed with drawers and pigeon-holes, and covered with papers, letters, documents of all kinds—Hamilton sat writing rapidly. Another table nearer the window, set apart for the Emperor's own use, had everything ready for business—had, moreover, in a graceful bowl of tinted glass, a large yellow carnation, his favourite flower, the flower which had come to be the badge of those of his inclining. This, again, was a touch of Miss Paulo's sympathetic handiwork.

The Emperor, whose mood had brightened, smiled again at this little proof of personal interest in his welfare. As he entered, Hamilton dropped his pen, sprang to his feet, and advanced respectfully to greet him. The Emperor pointed to the yellow carnation.

'The way of the exiled autocrat is made smooth for him here, at least,' he said.

Hamilton inclined his head gravely. 'Mr Paulo knows what is due,' he answered, 'to John Ericson, to the victor of San Felipe and the Emperor of Surmer. He knows how to entertain one who is by right, if not in fact, a reigning sovereign.'

'He hangs out our banner on the outer wall,' said Ericson, with an assumed gravity as great as Hamilton's own. Then he burst into a laugh and said, 'My dear Hamilton, it's all very well to talk of the victor of San Felipe and the Emperor of Surmer. But the victor of San Felipe is the victim of the Plaza Nacional, and the Emperor of Surmer is at present but one inconsiderable item added to the exile world of London, one more of the many refugees who hide their heads here, and are unnoted and unknown.'

His voice had fallen a little as his sentences succeeded each other, and the mirth in his voice had a bitter ring in it when he ended. His eye ranged from the bust to the picture, and from the picture to the engraving contemplatively.

Something in the contemplation appeared to cheer him, for his look was brighter, and his voice had the old joyous ring in it when he spoke again. It was after a few minutes' silence deferentially observed by Hamilton, who seemed to follow and to respect the course of his leader's thoughts.

'Well,' he said, 'how is the old world getting on? Does she roll with unabated energy in her familiar orbit, indifferent to the fall of states and the fate of rulers? Stands Surmer where she did?'

Hamilton laughed. 'The world has certainly not grown honest, but there are honest men in her. Here is a telegram from Surmer which came this morning. It was sent, of course, as usual, to our City friends, who sent it on here immediately.' He handed the despatch to his chief, who seized it and read it eagerly. It seemed a commonplace message enough—the communication of one commercial gentleman in Surmer with another commercial gentleman in Farringdon Street. But to the eyes of Hamilton and of Ericson it meant a great deal. It was a secret communication from one of the most influential of the Emperor's adherents in Surmer. It was full of hope, strenuously encouraging. The Emperor's face lightened.

'Anything else?' he asked.

'These letters,' Hamilton answered, taking up a bundle from the desk at which he had been sitting. 'Five are from money-lenders offering to finance your next attempt. There are thirty-three requests for autographs, twenty-two requests for interviews, one very pressing from "The Catapult," another from "The Moon"—Society papers, I believe; ten invitations to dinner, six to luncheon; an offer from a well-known lecturing agency to run you in the United States; an application from a publisher for a series of articles entitled "How I Governed Surmer," on your own terms; a letter from a certain Oisin Stewart Sarrasin, who calls himself Captain, and signs himself a soldier of fortune.'

'What does *he* want?' asked Ericson. 'His seems to be the most interesting thing in the lot.'

'He offers to lend you his well-worn sword for the re-establishment of your rule. He hints that he has an infallible plan of victory, that in a word he is your very man.'

The Emperor smiled a little grimly. 'I thought I could do my own fighting,' he said. 'But I suppose everybody will be wanting to help me now, every adventurer in Europe who thinks that I can no longer help myself. I don't think we need trouble Captain Stewart. Is that his name?'

'Stewart Sarrasin.'

'Sarrasin—all right. Is that all?'

'Practically all,' Hamilton answered. 'A few other letters of no importance. Stay; no, I forgot. These cards were left this morning, a little after nine o'clock, by a young lady who rode up attended by her groom.'

'A young lady,' said Ericson, in some surprise, as he extended his hand for the cards.

'Yes, and a very pretty young lady too,' Hamilton answered, 'for I happened to be in the hall at the time, and saw her.'

Ericson took the cards and looked at them. They were two in number; one was a man's card, one a woman's. The man's card bore the legend 'Sir Rupert Langley,' the woman's was merely inscribed 'Helena Langley.' The address was a house at Prince's Gate.

The Emperor looked up surprised. 'Sir Rupert Langley, the Foreign Secretary?'

'I suppose it must be,' Hamilton said, 'there can't be two men of the same name. I have a dim idea of reading something about his daughter in the papers some time ago, just before our revolution, but I can't remember what it was.'

'Very good of them to honour fallen greatness, in any case,' Ericson said. 'I seem to have more friends than I dreamed of. In the meantime let us have breakfast.'

Hamilton rang the bell, and a man brought in the coffee and rolls which constituted the Emperor's simple breakfast. While he was eating it he glanced over the letters that had come. 'Better refuse all these invitations, Hamilton.'

Hamilton expostulated. He was Ericson's intimate and adviser, as well as secretary.

'Do you think that is the best thing to do?' he suggested. 'Isn't it better to show yourself as much as possible, to make as many friends as you can? There's a good deal to be done in that way, and nothing much else to do for the present. Really I think it would be better to accept some of them. Several are from influential political men.'

'Do you think these influential political men would help me?' the Emperor asked, good-humouredly cynical. 'Did they help Kossuth? Did they help Garibaldi? What I want are war-ships, soldiers, a big loan, not the agreeable conversation of amiable politicians.'

'Nevertheless——' Hamilton began to protest.

His chief cut him short. 'Do as you please in the matter, my dear boy,' he said. 'It can't do any harm, anyhow. Accept all you think it best to accept; decline the others. I leave myself confidently in your hands.'

'What are you going to do this morning?' Hamilton inquired. 'There are one or two people we ought to think of seeing at once. We mustn't let the grass grow under our feet for one moment.'

'My dear boy,' said Ericson good-humouredly, 'the grass shall grow under my feet today, so far as all that is concerned. I haven't been in London for ten years, and I have something to do before I do anything else. Tomorrow you may do as you please with me. But if you insist upon devoting this day to the cause——'

'Of course I do,' said Hamilton.

'Then I graciously permit you to work at it all day, while I go off and amuse myself in a way of my own. You might, if you can spare the time, make a call at the Foreign Office and say I should be glad to wait on Sir Rupert Langley there, any day and hour that suit him—we must smooth down the dignity of these Foreign Secretaries, I suppose?'

'Oh, of course,' Hamilton said, peremptorily. Hamilton took most things gravely; the Emperor usually did not. Hamilton seemed a little put out because his chief should have even indirectly suggested the possibility of his not waiting on Sir Rupert Langley at the Foreign Office.

'All right, boy; it shall be done. And look here, Hamilton, as we are going to do the right thing, why should you not leave cards for me and for yourself at Sir Rupert Langley's house? You might see the daughter.'

'Oh, she never heard of me,' Hamilton said hastily.

'The daughter of a Foreign Secretary?'

'Anyhow, of course I'll call if you wish it, Excellency.'

'Good boy! And do you know I have taken a fancy that I should like to see this soldier of fortune, Captain——'

'Sarrasin?'

'Sarrasin—yes. Will you drop him a line and suggest an interview—pretty soon? You know all about my times and engagements.'

'Certainly, your Excellency,' Hamilton replied, with almost military formality and precision; and the Emperor departed.

CHAPTER III

AT THE GARDEN GATE

Londoners are so habituated to hear London abused as an ugly city that they are disposed too often to accept the accusation humbly. Yet the accusation is singularly unjust. If much of London is extremely unlovely, much might fairly be called beautiful. The new Chelsea that has arisen on the ashes of the old might well arouse the admiration even of the most exasperated foreigner. There are recently created regions in that great tract of the earth's surface known as South Kensington which in their quaintness of architectural form and braveness of red brick can defy the gloom of a civic March or November. Old London is disappearing day by day, but bits of it remain, bits dear to those familiar with them, bits worth the enterprise of the adventurous, which call for frank admiration and frank praise even of people who hated London as fully as Heinrich Heine did. But of all parts of the great capital none perhaps deserve so fully the title to be called beautiful as some portions of Hampstead Heath.

Some such reflections floated lightly through the mind of a man who stood, on this May afternoon, on a high point of Hampstead Hill. He had climbed thither from a certain point just beyond the Regent's Park, to which he had driven from Knightsbridge. From that point out the way was a familiar way to him, and he enjoyed walking along it and noting old spots and the changes that time had wrought. Now, having reached the highest point of the ascent, he paused, standing on the grass of the heath, and turning round, with his back to the country, looked down upon the town.

There is no better place from which to survey London. To impress a stranger with any sense of the charm of London as a whole, let him be taken to that vantage-ground and bidden to gaze. The great city seemed to lie below and around him as in a hollow, tinged and glorified by the luminous haze of the May day. The countless spires which pointed to heaven in all directions gave the vast agglomeration of buildings something of an Italian air; it reminded the beholder agreeably of Florence. To right and to left the gigantic city spread, its grey wreath of eternal smoke resting lightly upon its fretted head, the faint roar of its endless activity coming up distinctly there in the clear windless air. The beholder surveyed it and sighed slightly, as he traced meaningless symbols on the turf with the point of his stick.

'What did Caesar say?' he murmured. 'Better be the first man in a village than the second man in Rome! Well, there never was any chance of my being the second man in Rome; but, at least, I have been the first man in my village, and that is something. I suppose I reckon as about the last man there now. Well, we shall see.'

He shrugged his shoulders, nodded a farewell to the city below him, and, turning round, proceeded to walk leisurely across the Heath. The grass was soft and springy, the earth seemed to answer with agreeable elasticity to his tread, the air was exquisitely clear, keen, and exhilarating. He began to move more briskly, feeling quite boyish again. The years seemed to roll away from him as rifts of sea fog roll·away before a wind.

Even Surmer seemed as if it had never been—aye, and things before Surmer was, events when he was still really quite a young man.

He cut at the tufted grasses with his stick, swinging it in dexterous circles as if it had been his sword. He found himself humming a tune almost unconsciously, but when he paused to consider what the tune was he found it was the national march of Surmer. Then he stopped humming, and went on for a while silently and less joyously. But the gladness of the fine morning, of the clear air, of the familiar place, took possession of him again. His face once more unclouded and his spirits mounted.

'The place hasn't changed much,' he said to himself, looking around him while he walked. Then he corrected himself, for it had changed a good deal. There were many more red brick houses dotting the landscape than there had been when he last looked upon it some seven years earlier.

In all directions these red houses were springing up, quaintly gabled, much verandahed, pointed, fantastic, brilliant. They made the whole neighbourhood of the Heath look like the Merrie England of a comic opera. Yet they were pretty in their way; many were designed by able architects, and pleased with a balanced sense of proportion and an impression of beauty and fitness. Many, of course, lacked this, were but cheap and clumsy imitations of a prevailing mode, but, taken all together, the effect was agreeable, the effect of the varied reds, russet, and scarlet and warm crimson against the fresh green of the grass and trees and the pale faint blue of the May sky.

To the observer they seemed to suit very well the place, the climate, the conditions of life. They were infinitely better than suburban and rural cottages people used to build when he was a boy. His mind drifted away to the kind of houses he had been more familiar with of late years, houses half Spanish, half tropical; with their wide courtyards and gaily striped awnings and white walls glaring under a glaring sun.

'Yes, all this is very restful,' he thought—'restful, peaceful, wholesome.' He found himself repeating softly the lines of Browning, beginning, 'Oh to be in England now that April's here,' and the transitions of thought carried him to that other poem beginning, 'It was roses, roses, all the way,' with its satire on fallen ambition. Thinking of it, he first frowned and then laughed.

He walked a little way, cresting the rising ground, till he came to an open space with an unbroken view over the level country to Barnet. Here, the last of the houses that could claim to belong to the great London army stood alone in its own considerable space of ground. It was a very old-fashioned house; it had been half farmhouse, half hall, in the latter days of the last century, and the dull red brick of its walls, and the dull red tiles of its roof showed warm and attractive through the green of the encircling trees. There was a small garden in front, planted with pine trees, through which a winding path led up to the low porch of the dwelling. Behind the house a very large garden extended, a great garden which he knew so well, with its lengths of undulating russet orchard wall, and its divisions into flower garden and fruit garden and vegetable garden, and the field beyond, where successive generations of ponies fed, and where he had loved to play in boyhood.

He rested his hand on the upper rim of the garden gate, and looked with curious affection at the inscription in faded gold letters that ran along it. The inscription read, 'Blarulfsgarth,' and he remembered ever so far back asking what that inscription meant, and being told that it was Icelandic, and that it meant the Garth, or Farm, of the Blue Wolf. And he remembered, too, being told the tale from which the name came, a tale that was related of an ancestor of his, real or imaginary, who had lived and died centuries ago in a grey northern land. It was curious that, as he stood there, so many recollections of his childhood should come back to him. He was a man, and not a very young man, when he last laid his hand upon that gate, and yet it seemed to him now as if he had left it when he was quite a little child, and was returning now for the first time with the feelings of a man to the place where he had passed his infancy.

His hand slipped down to the latch, but he did not yet lift it. He still lingered while he turned for a moment and looked over the wide extent of level smiling country that stretched out and away before him. The last time he had looked on that sweep of earth he was going off to seek adventure in a far land, in a new world. He had thought himself a broken man; he was sick of England; his thoughts in their desperation had turned to the country which was only a name to him, the country where he was born. Now the day came vividly back to him on which he had said good-bye to that place, and looked with a melancholy disdain upon the soft English fields. It was an earlier season of the year, a day towards the end of March, when the skies were still but faintly blue, and there was little green abroad. Ten years ago: how many things had passed in those ten years, what struggles and successes, what struggles again, all ending in that three days' fight and the last stand in the Plaza Nacional of Valdorado! He turned away from the scene and pressed his hand upon the latch.

As he touched the latch someone appeared in the porch. It was an old lady dressed in black. She had soft grey hair, and on that grey hair she wore an old-fashioned cap that was almost coquettish by very reason of its old fashion. She had a very sweet, kind face, all cockled with wrinkles like a sheet of crumpled tissue paper, but very beautiful in its age. It was a face that a modern French painter would have loved to paint—a face that a sculptor of the Renaissance would have delighted to reproduce in faithful, faultless bronze or marble.

At sight of the sweet old lady the Emperor's heart gave a great leap, and he pressed down the latch hurriedly and swung the gate wide open. The sound of the clicking latch and the swinging gate slightly grinding on the path aroused the old lady's attention. She saw the Emperor, and, with a little cry of joy, running with an almost girlish activity to meet the bearded man who was coming rapidly along the pathway, in another moment she had caught him in her arms and was clasping him and kissing him enthusiastically. The Emperor returned her caresses warmly. He was smiling, but there were tears in his eyes. It was so odd being welcomed back like this in the old place after all that had passed.

'I knew you would come today, my dear,' the old lady said half sobbing, half laughing. 'You said you would, and I knew you would. You would come to your old aunt first of all.'

'Why, of course, of course I would, my dear,' the Emperor answered, softly touching the grey hair on the forehead below the frilled cap.

'But I didn't expect you so early,' the old lady went on. 'I didn't think you would get up so soon on your first morning. You must be so tired, my dear, so very tired.'

She was holding his left hand in her right now, and they were walking slowly side by side up by the little path through the fir trees to the house.

'Oh, I'm not so very tired as all that comes to,' he said with a laugh. 'A long voyage is a restful thing, and I had time to get over the fatigue of the——' he seemed to pause an instant for a word; then he went on, 'the trouble, while I was on board the "Almirante Cochrane." Do you know they were quite kind to me on board the "Almirante Cochrane"?'

The old lady's delicate face flushed angrily. 'The wretches, the wicked wretches!' she said quite fiercely, and the thin fingers closed tightly upon his and shook, agitating the lace ruffles at her wrists.

The Emperor laughed again. It seemed too strange to have all those wild adventures quietly discussed in a Hampstead garden with a silver-haired elderly lady in a cap.

'Oh, come,' he said, 'they weren't so bad; they weren't half bad, really. Why, you know, they might have shot me out of hand. I think if I had been in their place I should have shot out of hand, do you know, aunt?'

'Oh, surely they would never have dared—you an Englishman?'

'I am a citizen of Surmer, aunt.'

'You who were so good to them.'

'Well, as to my being good to them, there are two to tell that tale. The gentlemen of the Congress don't put a high price upon my goodness, I fancy.' He laughed a little bitterly. 'I certainly meant to do them some good, and I even thought I had succeeded. My dear aunt, people don't always like being done good to. I remember that myself when I was a small boy. I used to fret and fume at the things which were done for my good; that was because I was a child. The crowd is always a child.'

They had come to the porch by this time, and had stopped short at the threshold. The little porch was draped in flowers and foliage, and looked very pretty.

'You were always a good child,' said the old lady affectionately.

Ericson looked down at her rather wistfully.

'Do you think I was?' he asked, and there was a tender irony in his voice which made the playful question almost pathetic. 'If I had been a good child I should have been content and had no roving disposition, and have found my home and my world at Hampstead, instead of straying off into another hemisphere, only to be sent back at last like a bad penny.'

'So you would,' said the old lady, very softly, more as if she were speaking to herself than to him. 'So you would if——'

She did not finish her sentence. But her nephew, who knew and understood, repeated the last word.

'If,' he said, and he, too, sighed.

The old lady caught the sound, and with a pretty little air of determination she called up a smile to her face.

'Shall we go into the house, or shall we sit awhile in the garden? It is almost too fine a day to be indoors.'

'Oh, let us sit out, please,' said Ericson. He had driven the sorrow from his voice, and its tones were almost joyous. 'Is the old garden-seat still there?'

'Why, of course it is. I sit there always in fine weather.'

They wandered round to the back by a path that skirted the house, a path all broidered with rose-bushes. At the back, the garden was very large, beginning with a spacious stretch of lawn that ran right up to the wide French windows. There were several noble old trees which stood sentinel over this part of the garden, and beneath one of these trees, a very ancient elm, was the sturdy garden-seat which the Emperor remembered so well.

'How many pleasant fairy tales you have told me under this tree, aunt,' said the Emperor, as soon as they had sat down. 'I should like to lie on the grass again and listen to your voice, and dream of Njal, and Grettir, and Sigurd, as I used to do.'

'It is your turn to tell me stories now,' said the old lady. 'Not fairy stories, but true ones.'

The Emperor laughed. 'You know all that there is to tell,' he said. 'What my letters didn't say you must have found from the newspapers.'

'But I want to know more than you wrote, more than the newspapers gave—everything.'

'In fact, you want a full, true, and particular account of the late remarkable revolution in Surmer, which ended in the deposition and exile of the alien tyrant. My dear aunt, it would take a couple of weeks at the least computation to do the theme justice.'

'I am sure that I shouldn't tire of listening,' said Miss Ericson, and there were tears in her bright old eyes and a tremor in her brave old voice as she said so.

The Emperor laughed, but he stooped and kissed the old lady again very affectionately.

'Why, you would be as bad as I used to be,' he said. 'I never was tired of your *sagas*, and when one came to an end I wanted a new one at once, or at least the old one over again.'

He looked away from her and all around the garden as he spoke. The winds and rains and suns of all those years had altered it but little.

'We talk of the shortness of life,' he said; 'but sometimes life seems quite long. Think of the years and years since I was a little fellow, and sat here where I sit now, then, as now, by your side, and cried at the deeds of my forbears and sighed for the gods of the North. Do you remember?'

'Oh, yes; oh, yes. How could I forget? You, my dear, in your bustling life might forget; but I, day after day in this great old garden, may be forgiven for an old woman's fancy that time has stood still, and that you are still the little boy I love so well.'

She held out her hand to him, and he clasped it tenderly, full of an affectionate emotion that did not call for speech.

There were somewhat similar thoughts in both their minds. He was asking himself if, after all, it would not have been just as well to remain in that tranquil nook, so sheltered from the storms of life, so consecrated by tender affection. What had he done that was worth rising up to cross the street for, after all? He had dreamed a dream, and had been harshly awakened. What was the good of it all? A melancholy seemed to settle upon him in that place, so filled with the memories of his childhood. As for his companion, she was asking herself if it would not have been better for him to stay at home and live a quiet English life, and be her help and solace.

Both looked up from their reverie, met each other's melancholy glances, and smiled.

'Why,' said Miss Ericson, 'what nonsense this is! Here are we who have not met for ages, and we can find nothing better to do than to sit and brood! We ought to be ashamed of ourselves.'

'We ought,' said the Emperor, 'and for my poor part I am. So you want to hear my adventures?'

Miss Ericson nodded, but the narrative was interrupted. The wide French windows at the back of the house opened and a man entered the garden. His smooth voice was heard explaining to the maid that he would join Miss Ericson in the garden.

The new-comer made his way along the garden, with extended hand, and blinking amiably. The Emperor, turning at his approach, surveyed him with some surprise. He was a large, loosely made man, with a large white face, and his somewhat ungainly body was clothed in loose light material that was almost white in hue. His large and slightly surprised eyes were of a kindly blue; his hair was a vague yellow; his large mouth was weak; his pointed chin was undecided. He dimly suggested some association to the Emperor; after a few seconds he found that the association was with the Knave of Hearts in an ordinary pack of playing-cards.

'This is a friend of mine, a neighbour who often pays me a visit,' said the old lady hurriedly, as the white figure loomed along towards them. 'He is a most agreeable man, very companionable indeed, and learned, too—extremely learned.'

This was all that she had time to say before the white gentleman came too close to them to permit of further conversation concerning his merits or defects.

The new-comer raised his hat, a huge, white, loose, shapeless felt, in keeping with his ill-defined attire, and made an awkward bow which at once included the old lady and the Emperor, on whom the blue eyes beamed for a moment in good-natured wonder.

'Good morning, Miss Ericson,' said the new-comer. He spoke to Miss Ericson; but it was evident that his thoughts were distracted. His vague blue eyes were fixed in benign bewilderment upon the Emperor's face.

Miss Ericson rose; so did her nephew. Miss Ericson spoke.

'Good morning, Mr Sarrasin. Let me present you to my nephew, of whom you have heard so much. Nephew, this is Mr Gilbert Sarrasin.'

The new-comer extended both hands; they were very large hands, and very soft and very white. He enfolded the Emperor's extended right hand in one of his, and beamed upon him in unaffected joy.

'Not your nephew, Miss Ericson—not the hero of the hour? Is it possible; is it possible? My dear sir, my very dear and honoured sir, I cannot tell you how rejoiced I am, how proud I am, to have the privilege of meeting you.'

The Emperor returned his friendly clasp with a warm pressure. He was somewhat amused by this unexpected enthusiasm.

'You are very good indeed, Mr Sarrasin.' Then, repeating the name to himself, he added, 'Your name seems to be familiar to me.'

The white gentleman shook his head with something like playful repudiation.

'Not my name, I think; no, not my name, I feel sure.' He accentuated the possessive pronoun strongly, and then proceeded to explain the accentuation, smiling more and more amiably as he did so. 'No, not my name; my brother's—my brother's, I fancy.'

'Your brother's?' the Emperor said inquiringly. There was some association in his mind with the name of Sarrasin, but he could not reduce it to precise knowledge.

'Yes, my brother,' said the white gentleman. 'My brother, Oisin Stewart Sarrasin, whose name, I am proud to think, is familiar in many parts of the world.'

The recollection he was seeking came to the Emperor. It was the name that Hamilton had given to him that morning, the name of the man who had written to him, and who had signed himself 'a soldier of fortune.' He smiled back at the white gentleman.

'Yes,' he said truthfully, 'I have heard your brother's name. It is a striking name.'

The white gentleman was delighted. He rubbed his large white hands together, and almost seemed as if he might purr in the excess of his gratification. He glanced enthusiastically at Miss Ericson.

'Ah!' he went on. 'My brother is a remarkable man. I may even say so in your illustrious presence; he is a remarkable man. There are degrees, of course,' and he bowed apologetically to the Emperor; 'but he is remarkable.'

'I have not the least doubt of that,' said the Emperor politely.

The white gentleman seemed much pleased. At a sign from Miss Ericson he sat down upon a garden-chair, still slowly and contentedly rubbing his white hands together. Miss Ericson and her nephew resumed their seats.

'Captain Sarrasin is a great traveller,' Miss Ericson said explanatorily to the Emperor. The Emperor bowed his head. He did not quite know what to say, and so, for the moment, said nothing. The white gentleman took advantage of the pause.

'Yes,' he said, 'yes, my brother is a great traveller. A wonderful man, sir; all parts of the wide world are as familiar as home to him. The deserts of the nomad Arabs, the Prairies of the great West, the Steppes of the frozen North, the Pampas of South America; why, he knows them all better than most people know Piccadilly.'

'South America?' questioned the Emperor; 'your brother is acquainted with South America?'

'Intimately acquainted,' replied Mr Sarrasin. 'I hope you will meet him. You and he might have much to talk about. He knew Surmer in the old days.'

The Emperor expressed courteously his desire to have the pleasure of meeting Captain Sarrasin. 'And you, are you a traveller as well?' he asked.

Mr Sarrasin shook his head, and when he spoke there was a certain accent of plaintiveness in his reply.

'No,' he said, 'not at all, not at all. My brother and I resemble each other very slightly. He has the wanderer's spirit; I am a confirmed stay-at-home. While he thinks nothing of starting off at any moment for the other ends of the earth, I have never been outside our island, have never been much away from London.'

'Isn't that curious?' asked Miss Ericson, who evidently took much pleasure in the conversation of the white gentleman. The Emperor assented. It was very curious.

'Yet I am fond of travel, too, in my way,' Mr Sarrasin went on, delighted to have found an appreciative audience. 'I read about it largely. I read all the old books of travel, and all the new ones, too, for the matter of that. I have quite a little library of voyages, travels, and explorations in my little home. I should like you to see it some time if you should so far honour me.'

The Emperor declared that he should be delighted. Mr Sarrasin, much encouraged, went on again.

'There is nothing I like better than to sit by my fire of a winter's evening, or in my garden of a summer afternoon, and read of the adventures of great travellers. It makes me feel as if I had travelled myself.'

'And Mr Sarrasin tells me what he has read, and makes me, too, feel travelled,' said Miss Ericson.

'Perhaps you get all the pleasure in that way with none of the fatigue,' the Emperor suggested.

Mr Sarrasin nodded. 'Very likely we do. I think it was à Kempis who protested against the vanity of wandering. But I fear it was not à Kempis's reasons that deterred me; but an invincible laziness and unconquerable desire to be doing nothing.'

'Travelling is generally uncomfortable,' the Emperor admitted. He was beginning to feel an interest in his curious, whimsical interlocutor.

'Yes,' Mr Sarrasin went on dreamily. 'But there are times when I regret the absence of experience. I have tramped in fancy through tropical forests with Stanley or Cameron, dwelt in the desert with Burton, battled in Nicaragua with Walker, but all only as it were in dreams.'

'We are such stuff as dreams are made of,' the Emperor observed sententiously.

'And our little lives are rounded by a sleep,' Miss Ericson said softly, completing the quotation.

'Yes, yes,' said Mr Sarrasin; 'but mine are dreams within a dream.' He was beginning to grow quite communicative as he sat there with his big stick between his knees, and his amorphous felt hat pushed back from his broad white forehead.

'Sometimes my travels seem very real to me. If I have been reading Ford or Kinglake, or Warburton or Lane, I have but to lay the volume down and close my eyes, and all that I have been reading about seems to take shape and sound, and colour and life. I hear the tinkling of the mule-bells and the guttural cries of the muleteers, and I see the Spanish market-place, with its arcades and its ancient cathedral; or the delicate pillars of the Parthenon, yellow in the clear Athenian air; or Stamboul, where the East and West join hands; or Egypt and the desert, and the

Nile and the pyramids; or the Holy Land and the walls of Jerusalem—ah! it is all very wonderful, and then I open my eyes and blink at my dying fire, and look at my slippered feet, and remember that I am a stout old gentleman who has never left his native land, and I yawn and take my candle and go to my bed.'

There was something so curiously pathetic and yet comic about the white gentleman's case, about his odd blend of bookish knowledge and personal inexperience, that the Emperor could scarcely forbear smiling. But he did forbear, and he spoke with all gravity.

'I am not sure that you haven't the better part after all,' he said. 'I find that the chief pleasure of travel lies in recollection. *You* seem to get the recollection without the trouble.'

'Perhaps so,' said Mr Sarrasin; 'perhaps so. But I think I would rather have had the trouble as well. Believe me, my dear sir, believe a dreamer, that action is better than dreams. Ah! how much better it is for you, sir, to sit here, a disappointed man for the moment it may be, but a man with a glowing past behind him, than, like me, to have nothing to look back upon! My adventures are but compounded out of the essences of many books. I have never really lived a day; you have lived every day of your life. Believe me, you are much to be envied.'

There was genuine conviction in the white gentleman's voice as he spoke these words, and the note of genuine conviction troubled the Emperor in his uncertainty whether to laugh or cry. He chose a medium course and smiled slightly.

'I should think, Mr Sarrasin, that you are the only one in London today who looks upon me as a man much to be envied. London, if it thinks of me at all, thinks of me only as a disastrous failure, as an unsuccessful exile—a man of no account, in a word.'

Mr Sarrasin shook his head vehemently. 'It is not so,' he protested, 'not so at all. Nobody really thinks like that, but if everybody else did, my brother Oisin Stewart Sarrasin certainly does not think like that, and his opinion is better worth having than that of most other men. You have no warmer admirer in the world than my brother, Mr Ericson.'

The Emperor expressed much satisfaction at having earned the good opinion of Mr Sarrasin's brother.

'You would like him, I am sure,' said Mr Sarrasin. 'You would find him a kindred spirit.'

The Emperor graciously expressed his confidence that he should find a kindred spirit in Mr Sarrasin's brother. Then Mr Sarrasin, apparently much delighted with his interview, rose to his feet and declared that it was time for him to depart. He shook hands very warmly with Miss Ericson, but he held the Emperor's hands with a grasp that was devoted in its enthusiasm. Then, expressing repeatedly the hope that he might soon meet the Emperor again, and once more assuring him of the kinship between the Emperor and Captain Oisin Stewart Sarrasin, the white gentleman took himself off, a pale bulky figure looming heavily across the grassy lawn and through the French window into the darkness of the sitting-room.

When he was quite out of sight the Emperor, who had followed his retreating figure with his eyes, turned to Miss Ericson with a look of inquiry. Miss Ericson smiled.

'Who is Mr Sarrasin?' the Emperor asked. 'He has come up since my time.'

'Oh, yes; he first came to live here about six years ago. He is one of the best souls in the world; simple, good-hearted, an eternal child.'

'What is he?' The Emperor asked.

'Well, he is nothing in particular now. He was in the City, his father was the head of a very wealthy firm of tea merchants, Sarrasin, Jermyn,& Co. When the father died a few years ago he left all his property to Mr Gilbert, and then Mr Gilbert went out of business and came here.'

'He does not look as if he would make a very good business man,' said the Emperor.

'No; but he was very patient and devoted to it for his father's sake. Now, since he has been free to do as he likes, he has devoted himself to folk-lore.'

'To folk-lore?'

'Yes, to the study of fairy tales, of comparative mythology. I am quite learned in it now since I have had Mr Sarrasin for a neighbour, and know more about "Puss in Boots" and "Jack and the Beanstalk" than I ever did when I was a girl.'

'Really,' said the Emperor, with a kind of sigh. 'Does he devote himself to fairy tales?' It crossed his mind that a few moments before he had been thinking of himself as a small child in that garden, with a taste for fairy tales, and regretting that he had not stayed in that garden. Now, with the dust of battle and the ashes of defeat upon him, he came back to find a man much older than himself, who seemed still to remain a child, and to be entranced with fairy tales. 'I wish I were like that,' the Emperor said to himself, and then the veil seemed to lift, and he saw again the Plaza Nacional of Surmer, and the Imperial Palace, where he had laboured at laws for a free people. 'No,' he thought, 'no; action, action.'

'What are you thinking of?' asked Miss Ericson softly. 'You seem to be quite lost in thought.'

'I was thinking of Mr Sarrasin,' answered the Emperor. 'Forgive me for letting my thoughts drift. And the brother, what sort of man is this wonderful brother?'

'I have only seen the brother a very few times,' said Miss Ericson dubiously. 'I can hardly form an opinion. I do not think he is as nice as his brother, or, indeed, as nice as his brother believes him to be.'

'What is his record?'

'He didn't get on with his father. He was sent against his will to China to work in the firm's offices in Shanghai. But he hated the business, and broke away and entered the Chinese army, I believe, and his father was furious and cut him off. Since then he has been all over the world, and served all sorts of causes. I believe he is a kind of soldier of fortune.'

The Emperor smiled, remembering Captain Sarrasin's own words.

'And has he made his fortune?'

'Oh, no; I believe not. But Gilbert behaved so well. When he came into the property he wanted to share it all with his disinherited brother, for whom he has the greatest affection.'

'A good fellow, your Gilbert Sarrasin.'

'The best. But the brother wouldn't take it, and it was with difficulty that Gilbert induced him to accept so much as would allow him a small certainty of income.'

'So. A good fellow, too, your Oisin Stewart Sarrasin, it would seem; at least in that particular.'

'Yes; of course. The brothers don't meet very often, for Captain Sarrasin——'

'Where does he take his title from?'

'He was captain in some Turkish irregular cavalry.'

'Turkish irregular cavalry? That must be a delightful corps,' the Emperor said with a smile.

'At least he was captain in several services,' Miss Ericson went on; 'but I believe that is the one he prefers and still holds. As I was going to say, Captain Sarrasin is almost always abroad.'

'Well, I feel curious to meet him. They are a strange pair of brothers.'

'They are, but we ought to talk of nothing but you today. Ah, my dear, it is so good to have you with me again.'

'Dear old aunt!'

'Let me see much of you now that you have come back. Would it be any use asking you to stop here?'

'Later, every use. Just at this moment I mustn't. Till I see how things are going to turn out I must live down there in London. But my heart is here with you in this green old garden, and where my heart is I hope to bring my battered old body very often. I will stop to luncheon with you if you will let me.'

'Let you? My dear, I wish you were always stopping here.' And the grey old lady put her arms round the neck of the Emperor and kissed him again.

CHAPTER IV

THE LANGLEYS

That same day there was a luncheon party at the new town house of the Langleys, Prince's Gate. The Langleys were two in number all told, father and daughter.

Sir Rupert Langley was a remarkable man, but his daughter, Helena Langley, was a much more remarkable woman. The few handfuls of people who considered themselves to constitute the world in London had at one time talked much about Sir Rupert, but now they talked a great deal more about his daughter. Sir Rupert was once grimly amused, at a great party in a great house, to hear himself pointed out by a knowing youth as Helena Langley's father.

There was a time when people thought, and Sir Rupert thought with them, that Rupert Langley was to do great deeds in the world. He had entered political life at an early age, as all the Langleys had done since the days of Anne, and he made more than a figure there. He had travelled in Central Asia in days when travel there or anywhere else was not so easy as it is now, and he had published a book of his travels before he was three-and-twenty, a book which was highly praised, and eagerly read. He was saluted as a sort of coming authority upon Eastern affairs in a day when the importance of Eastern affairs was beginning to dawn dimly upon the insular mind, and he made several stirring speeches in the House of Commons' which confirmed his reputation as a coming man. He was very dogmatic, very determined in his opinions, very confident of his own superior knowledge, and possessed of a degree of knowledge which justified his confidence and annoyed his antagonists. He formed a little party of his own, a party of strenuous young Tories who recognized the fact that the world was out of joint, but who rejoiced in the conviction that they were born for the express purpose of setting it right. In Sir Rupert they found a leader after their own heart, and they rallied around him and jibed at their elders on the Treasury Bench in a way that was quite distressing to the sensitive organs of the party.

Sir Rupert and his adherents preached the new Toryism of that day—the new Toryism which was to work wonders, which was to obliterate Radicalism by doing in a practical Tory way, and conformably to the best traditions of the kingdom, all that Radicalism dreamed of. Toryism, he used to say in those hot-blooded, hot-headed days of his youth, Toryism is the triumph of Truth, and the phrase became a catchword and a watchword, and frivolous people called his little party the T. T.s— the Triumphers of Truth. People versed in the political history of that day and hour will remember how the newspapers were full of the T. T.s, and what an amazing rejuvenescence of political force was supposed to be behind them.

Then came a general election which carried the Tory Party into power, and which proved the strength of Langley and his party. He was offered a place in the new Government, and accepted it—the Under-Secretaryship for India. Through one brilliant year he remained the most conspicuous member of the

Administration, irritating his colleagues by daring speeches, by innovating schemes; alarming timid party-men by a Toryism which in certain aspects was scarcely to be distinguished from the reddest radicalism. One brilliant year there was in which he blazed the comet of a season. Then, thwarted in some enterprise, faced by a refusal for some daring reform of Indian administration, he acted, as he had acted always, impetuously.

One morning the 'Times' contained a long, fierce, witty, bitter letter from Rupert Langley assailing the Government, its adherents, and, above all, its leaders in the Lords. That same afternoon members coming to the Chamber found Langley sitting, no longer on the Treasury Bench, but in the corner seat of the second row below the gangway. It was soon known all over the House, all over town, all over England, that Rupert Langley had resigned his office. The news created no little amazement, some consternation in certain quarters of the Tory camp, some amusement among the Opposition sections. One or two of the extreme Radical papers made overtures to Langley to cross the floor of the House, and enter into alliance with men whose principles so largely resembled his own. These overtures even took the form of a definite appeal on the part of Mr Wynter, M. P., then a rising Radical, who actually spent half an hour with Sir Rupert on the terrace, putting his case and the case of youthful radicalism.

Sir Rupert only smiled at the suggestion, and put it gracefully aside. 'I am a Tory of the Tories,' he said; 'only my own people don't understand me yet. But they have got to find me out.' That was undoubtedly

Sir Rupert's conviction, that he was strong enough to force the Government, to coerce his party, to compel recognition of his opinions and acceptance of his views. 'They cannot do without me,' he said to himself in his secret heart. He was met by disappointment. The party chiefs made no overtures to him to reconsider his decision, to withdraw his resignation. Another man was immediately put in his place, a man of mediocre ability, of commonplace mind, a man of routine, methodical, absolutely lacking in brilliancy or originality, a man who would do exactly what the Government wanted in the Government way. There was a more bitter blow still for Sir Rupert. There were in the Government certain members of his own little Adullamite party of the Opposition days, T. T.s who had been given office at his insistence, men whom he had discovered, brought forward, educated for political success.

It is certain that Sir Rupert confidently expected that these men, his comrades and followers, would endorse his resignation with their own, and that the Government would thus, by his action, find itself suddenly crippled, deprived of its young blood, its ablest Ministers. The confident expectation was not realised. The T. T.s remained where they were. The Government took advantage of the slight readjustment of places caused by Sir Rupert's resignation to give two of the most prominent T. T.s more important offices, and to those offices the T. T.s stuck like limpets.

Sir Rupert was not a man to give way readily, or readily to acknowledge that he was defeated. He bided his time, in his place below the gangway, till there came an Indian debate. Then, in a House which had been roused to intense excitement by vague rumours of his intention, he moved a resolution which was practically a vote of censure upon the Government for its Indian policy. Always a fluent, ready, ornate speaker, Sir Rupert was never better than on that desperate night. His attack upon the Government was merciless; every word seemed to sting like a poisoned arrow; his exposure of the imbecilities and ineptitudes of the existing system of administration was complete and cruel; his scornful attack upon 'the Limpets' sent the Opposition into paroxysms of delighted laughter, and roused a storm of angry protest from the crowded benches behind the Ministry. That night was the memorable event of the session. For long enough after those who witnessed it carried in their memories the picture of that pale, handsome young man, standing up in that corner seat below the gangway and assailing the Ministry of which he had been the most remarkable Minister with so much cold passion, so much fierce disdain. 'By Jove! he's smashed them!' cried Wynter, M.P., excitedly, when Rupert Langley sat down after his speech of an hour and a quarter, which had been listened to by a crowded House amidst a storm of cheering and disapproval. Wynter was sitting on a lower gangway seat, for every space of sitting room in the chamber was occupied that night, and he had made this remark to one of the Opposition leaders on the front bench, craning over to call it into his ear. The leader of the Opposition heard Wynter's remark, looked round at the excited Radical, and, smiling, shook his head. The excitement faded from Wynter's face. His chief was never wrong.

The usual exodus after a long speech did not take place when Rupert sat down. It was expected that the leader of the House would reply to Sir Rupert, but the expectation was not realised. To the surprise of almost everyone present the Government put up as their spokesman one of the men who had been most allied with Sir Rupert in the old T.T. party, Sidney Blenheim. Something like a frown passed over Sir Rupert's face as Blenheim rose; then he sat immovable, expressionless, while Blenheim made his speech. It was a very clever speech, delicately ironical, sharply cutting, tinged all through with an intolerable condescension, with a gallingly gracious recognition of Langley's merits, an irritating regret for his errors. There was a certain languidness in Blenheim's deportment, a certain air of sweetness in his face, which made his satire the more severe, his attack the more telling. People were as much surprised as if what looked like a dandy's cane had proved to be a sword of tempered steel. Whatever else that night did, it made Blenheim's reputation.

Langley did not carry a hundred men with him into the lobby against the Government. The Opposition, as a body, supported the Administration; a certain proportion of Radicals, a much smaller number of men from his own side, followed him to his fall. He returned to his seat after the numbers had been read out, and sat there as composedly as if nothing had happened, or as if the ringing cheers which greeted the Government triumph were so many tributes to his own success. But those who knew, or thought they knew, Rupert Langley well said that the hour in which he sat there must have been an hour of terrible suffering. After that great debate, the business of the rest of the evening fell rather flat, and was conducted in a House which rapidly thinned down to little short of emptiness. When it was at its emptiest, Rupert Langley rose, lifted his hat to the Speaker, and left the Chamber.

It would not be strictly accurate to say that he never returned to it that session; but practically the statement would be correct. He came back occasionally during the short remainder of the session, and sat in his new place below the gangway. Once or twice he put a question upon the paper; once or twice he contributed a short speech to some debate. He still spoke to his friends, with cold confidence, of his inevitable return to influence, to power, to triumph; he did not say how this would be brought about—he left it to be assumed.

Then paragraphs began to appear in the papers announcing Sir Rupert Langley's intention of spending the recess in a prolonged tour in India. Before the recess came Sir Rupert had started upon this tour, which was extended far beyond a mere investigation of the Indian Empire. When the House met again, in the February of the following year, Sir Rupert was not among the returned members. Such few of his friends as were in communication with him knew, and told their knowledge to others, that Sir Rupert was engaged in a voyage round the world. Not a voyage round the world in the hurried sense in which people occasionally made then, and frequently make now—

a voyage round the world, scampering, like the hero of Jules Verne, across land and sea, fast as steam-engine can drag and steamship carry them. Sir Rupert intended to go round the world in the most leisurely fashion, stopping everywhere, seeing everything, setting no limit to the time he might spend in any place that pleased him, fixing beforehand no limit to chain him to any place that did not please him. He proposed, his friends said, to go carefully over his old ground in Central Asia, to make himself a complete master of the problems of Australasian colonisation, and especially to make a very profound and exhaustive study of the strange civilisations of China and Japan. He intended further to give a very considerable time to a leisurely investigation of the South American Empires. 'Why,' said Wynter, M.P., when one of Sir Rupert's friends told him of these plans, 'why, such a scheme will take several years.' 'Very likely,' the friend answered; and Wynter said, 'Oh, by Jove!' and whistled.

The scheme did take several years. At various intervals Sir Rupert wrote to his constituents long letters spangled with stirring allusions to the Empire, to England's meteor flag, to the inevitable triumph of the New Toryism, to the necessity a sincere British statesman was under of becoming a complete master of all the possible problems of a daily-increasing authority. He made some sharp thrusts at the weakness of the Government, but accused the Opposition of a lack of patriotism in trading upon that weakness; he almost chaffed the leader in the Lower House and the leader in the Lords; he made no allusion to Sidney Blenheim, then rapidly advancing along the road of success. He concluded each letter by offering to resign his seat if his constituents wished it.

His constituents did not wish it—at least, not at first. The Conservative committee returned him a florid address assuring him of their confidence in his statesmanship, but expressing the hope that he might be able speedily to return to represent them at Westminster, and the further hope that he might be able to see his way to reconcile his difficulties with the existing Government. To this address Sir Rupert sent a reply duly acknowledging its expression of confidence, but taking no notice of its suggestions. Time went on, and Sir Rupert did not return. He was heard of now and again; now in the court of some rajah in the North-West Provinces; now in the khanate of some Central Asian despot; now in South America, from which continent he sent a long letter to the 'Times,' giving an interesting account of the latest revolution in the Surmer Empire, of which he had happened to be an eye-witness; now in Java; now in Pekin; now at the Cape. He did not seem to pursue his idea of going round the world on any settled consecutive plan.

Of his large means there could be no doubt. He was probably one of the richest, as he was certainly one of the oldest, baronets in England, and he could afford to travel as if he were an accredited representative of the Queen—almost as if he were an American Midas of the fourth or fifth class. But as to his large leisure people began to say things. It began to be hinted in leading articles that it was scarcely fair that Sir Rupert's constituents should be disfranchised because it pleased a disappointed politician to drift idly about the world. These hints had their effect upon the disfranchised constituents, who began to grumble. The Conservative Committee was goaded almost to the point of addressing a remonstrance to Sir Rupert, then in the interior of Japan, urging him to return or resign, when the need for any such action was taken out of their hands by a somewhat unexpected General Election. Sir Rupert telegraphed back to announce his intention of remaining abroad for the present, and of not, therefore, proposing to seek just then the suffrages of the electors. Sidney Blenheim succeeded in getting a close personal friend of his own, who was also his private secretary, accepted by the Conservative Committee, and he was returned at the head of the poll by a slightly decreased majority.

Sir Rupert remained away from England for several years longer. After he had gone round the world in the most thorough sense, he revisited many places where he had been before, and stayed there for longer periods. It began to seem as if he did not really intend to return to England at all. His communications with his friends grew fewer and shorter, but wandering Parliamentarians in the recess occasionally came across him in the course of an extended holiday, and always found him affable, interested to animation in home politics, and always suggesting by his manner, though never in his speech, that he would some day return to his old place and his old fame. Of Sidney Blenheim he spoke with an equable, impartial composure.

At last one day he did come home. He had been in the United States during the closing years of the

American Civil War, and in Washington, when peace was concluded, he had met at the English Ministry a young girl of great beauty, of a family that was old for America, that was wealthy, though not wealthy for America. He fell in love with her, wooed her, and was accepted. They were married in Washington, and soon after the marriage they returned to England. They settled down for a while at the old home of the Langleys, the home whose site had been the home of the race ever since the Conquest. Part of an old Norman tower still held itself erect amidst the Tudor, Elizabethan, and Victorian additions to the ancient place. It was called Queen's Langley now, had been so called ever since the days when, in the beginning of the Civil War, Henrietta Maria had been besieged there, during her visit to the then baronet, by a small party of Roundheads, and had successfully kept them off. Queen's Langley had been held during the Commonwealth by a member of the family, who had declared for the Parliament, but had gone back to the head of the house when he returned with his king at the Restoration.

At Queen's Langley Sir Rupert and his wife abode for a while, and at Queen's Langley a child was born to them, a girl child, who was christened after her mother, Helena. Then the taste for wandering, which had become almost a passion with Sir Rupert, took possession of Sir Rupert again. If he had expected to re-enter London in any kind of triumph he was disappointed. He had allowed himself to fall out of the race, and he found himself almost forgotten. Society, of course, received him almost rapturously, and his beautiful wife was the queen of a resplendent season. But politics seemed to have passed him by. The New Toryism of those youthful years was not very new Toryism now. Sidney Blenheim was a settled reactionary and a recognised celebrity. There was a New Toryism, with its new cave of strenuous, impetuous young men, and they, if they thought of Sir Rupert Langley at all, thought of him as old-fashioned, the hero or victim of a piece of ancient history.

Nevertheless, Sir Rupert had his thoughts of entering political life again, but in the meantime he was very happy. He had a steam yacht of his own, and when his little girl was three years old he and his wife went for a long cruise in the Mediterranean. And then his happiness was taken away from him. His wife suddenly sickened, died, unconscious, in his arms, and was buried at sea. Sir Rupert seemed like a broken man. From Alexandria he wrote to his sister, who was married to the Duke of Magdiel's third son, Lord Edmond Herrington, asking her to look after his child for him—the child was then with her aunt at Herrington Hall, in Argyllshire—in his absence. He sold his yacht, paid off his crew, and disappeared for two years.

During those two years he was believed to have wandered all over Egypt, and to have passed much of his time the hermit-like tenant of a tomb on the lovely, lonely island of Phylæ, at the first cataract of the Nile. At the end of the two years he wrote to his sister that he was returning to Europe, to England, to his own home, and his own people. His little girl was then five years old.

He reappeared in England changed and aged, but a strong man still, with a more settled air of strength of purpose than he had worn in his wild youth. He found his little girl a pretty child, brilliantly healthy, brilliantly strong. The wind of the mountain, of the heather, of the woods, had quickened her with an enduring vitality very different from that of the delicate fair mother for whom his heart still grieved. Of course the little Helena did not remember her father, and was at first rather alarmed when Lady Edmond Herrington told her that a new papa was coming home for her from across the seas. But the feeling of fear passed away after the first meeting between father and child. The fascination which in his younger days Rupert Langley had exercised upon so many men and women, which had made him so much of a leader in his youth, affected the child powerfully. In a week she was as devoted to him as if she had never been parted from him.

Helena's education was what some people would call a strange education. She was never sent to school; she was taught, and taught much, at home, first by a succession of clever governesses, then by carefully chosen masters of many languages and many arts. In almost all things her father was her chief instructor. He was a man of varied accomplishments; he was a good linguist, and his years of wandering had made his attainments in language really colloquial; he had a rich and various store of information, gathered even more from personal experience than from books. His great purpose in life appeared to be to make his daughter as accomplished as himself. People had said at first when he returned that he would marry again, but the assumption proved to be wrong. Sir Rupert had made up his mind that he would never marry again, and he kept to his determination. There was an intense sentimentality in his strong nature; the sentimentality which led him to take his early defeat and the defection of Sidney Blenheim so much to heart had made him vow, on the day when the body of his fair young wife was lowered into the sea, changeless fidelity to her memory. Undoubtedly it was somewhat of a grief to him that there was no son to carry on his name; but he bore that grief in silence. He resolved, however, that his daughter should be in every way worthy of the old line which culminated in her; she should be a woman worthy to surrender the ancient name to some exceptional mortal; she should be worthy to be the wife of some great statesman.

In those years in which Helena Langley was growing up from childhood to womanhood, Sir Rupert returned to public life. The constituency in which Queen's Langley was situated was a Tory constituency which had been represented for nearly half a century by the same old Tory squire. The Tory squire had a grandson who was as uncompromisingly Radical as the squire was Tory; naturally he could not succeed, and would not contest the seat. Sir Rupert came forward, was eagerly accepted, and successfully returned. His reappearance in the House of Commons after so considerable an interval made some small excitement in Westminster, roused some comment in the press. It was fifteen years since he had left St. Stephen's; he thought curiously of the past as he took his place, not in that corner seat below the gangway, but on the second bench behind the Treasury Bench. His Toryism was now of a settled type; the Government, which had been a little apprehensive of his possible antagonism, found him a loyal and valuable supporter. He did not remain long behind the Treasury Bench. An important vacancy occurred in the Ministry; the post of Foreign Secretary was offered to and accepted by Sir Rupert. Years ago such a place would have seemed the highest goal of his ambition. Now he—accepted it. Once again he found himself a prominent man in the House of Commons, although under very different conditions from those of his old days.

In the meantime Helena grew in years and health, in beauty, in knowledge. Sir Rupert, as an infinite believer in the virtues of travel, took her with him every recess for extended expeditions to Europe, and, as she grew older, to other continents than Europe. By the time that she was twenty she knew much of the world from personal experience; she knew more of politics and political life than many politicians. After she was seventeen years old she began to make frequent appearances in the Ladies' Gallery, and to take long walks on the Terrace with her father. Sir Rupert delighted in her companionship, she in his; they were always happiest in each other's society. Sir Rupert had every reason to be proud of the graceful girl who united the beauty of her mother with the strength, the physical and mental strength, of her father.

It need surprise no one, it did not appear to surprise Sir Rupert, if such an education made Helena Langley what ill-natured people called a somewhat eccentric young woman. Brought up on a manly system of education, having a man for her closest companion, learning much of the world at an early age, naturally tended to develop and sustain the strongly marked individuality of her character. Now, at three-and-twenty, she was one of the most remarkable girls in England, one of the best-known girls in London. Her independence, both of thought and of action, her extended knowledge, her frankness of speech, her slightly satirical wit, her frequent and vehement enthusiasms for the most varied pursuits and pleasures, were much commented on, much admired by some, much disapproved of by others. She had many friends among women and more friends among men, and these were real friendships, not flirtations, nor love affairs of any kind. Whatever things Helena Langley did there was one thing she never did—she never flirted. Many men had been in love with her and had declared their love, and had been laughed at or pitied according to the degree of their deserts, but no one of them could honestly say that Helena had in any way encouraged him, or tempted him with false hopes, unless indeed the masculine frankness of her friendship was an encouragement and a treacherous temptation. One and all, she unhesitatingly refused her adorers. 'My father is the most interesting man I know,' she once said to a discomfited and slightly despairing lover. 'Till I find some other man as interesting as he is, I shall never think of marriage. And really I am sure you will not take it in bad part if I say that I do not find you as interesting a man as my father.' The discomfited adorer did not take it amiss; he smiled ruefully, and took his departure; but, to his credit be it spoken, he remained Helena's friend.

CHAPTER V

'MY GREAT DEED WAS TOO GREAT'

The luncheon hour was an important epoch of the day in the Langley house in Prince's Gate. The Langley luncheons were an institution in London life ever since Sir Rupert bought the big Queen Anne house and made his daughter its mistress. As he said himself good-humouredly, he was a mere Roi Fainéant in the place; his daughter was the Mayor of the Palace, the real ruling power.

Helena Langley ruled the great house with the most gracious autocracy. She had everything her own way and did everything in her own way. She was a little social Queen, with a Secretary of State for her Prime Minister, and she enjoyed her sovereignty exceedingly. One of the great events of her reign was the institution of what came to be known as the Langley luncheons.

These luncheons differed from ordinary luncheons in this, that those who were bidden to them were in the first instance almost always interesting people— people who had done something more than merely exist, people who had some other claim upon human recognition than the claim of ancient name or of immense wealth. In the second place, the people who were bidden to a Langley luncheon were of the most varied kind, people of the most different camps in social, in political life. At the Langley table statesmen who hated each other across the floor of the House sat side by side in perfect amity. The heir to the oldest dukedom in England met there the latest champion of the latest phase of democratic socialism; the great tragedian from the Acropolis met the low comedian from the Levity on terms of as much equality as if they had met at the Macklin or the Call-Boy clubs; the President of the Royal Academy was amused by, and afforded much amusement to, the newest child of genius fresh from Paris, with the slang of the Chat Noir upon his lips and the scorn of *les vieux* in his heart. Whig and Tory, Catholic and Protestant, millionaire and bohemian, peer with a peerage old at Runnymede and the latest working-man M.P., all came together under the regal Empireanism of Langley House. Someone said that a party at Langley House always suggested to him the Day of Judgment.

On the afternoon of the morning on which Sir Rupert's card was left at Paulo's Hotel, various guests assembled for luncheon in Miss Langley's Japanese drawing-room. The guests were not numerous—the luncheons at Langley House were never large parties. Eight, including the host and hostess, was the number rarely exceeded; eight, including the host and hostess, made up the number in this instance. Mr and Mrs Selwyn, the distinguished and thoroughly respectable actor and actress, just returned from their tour in the United States; the Duke and Duchess of Deptford—the Duchess was a young and pretty American woman; Mr Soame Rivers, Sir Rupert's private secretary; and Mr Hiram Borringer, who had just returned from one expedition to the South Pole, and who was said to be organising another.

When the ringing of a chime of bells from a Buddhist's temple announced luncheon, and everyone had settled down in the great oak room, where certain of the ancestral Langleys, gentlemen and ladies of the last century, whom Reynolds and Gainsborough and Romney and Raeburn had painted, had been brought up from Queen's Langley at Helena's special wish, the company seemed to be under special survey. There was one vice-admiral of the Red who was leaning on a Doric pillar, with a spy-glass in his hand, apparently wholly indifferent to a terrific naval battle that was raging in the background; all his shadowy attention seemed to be devoted to the mortals who moved and laughed below him. There was something in the vice-admiral which resembled Sir Rupert, but none of the lovely ladies on the wall were as beautiful as Helena.

Mrs Selwyn spoke with that clear, bell-like voice which always enraptured an audience. Every assemblage of human beings was to her an audience, and she addressed them accordingly. Now, she practically took the stage, leaning forward between the Duke of Deptford and Hiram Borringer, and addressing Helena Langley.

'My dear Miss Langley,' she said, 'do you know that something has surprised me today?'

'What is it?' Helena asked, turning away from Mr Selwyn, to whom she had been talking.

'Why, I felt sure,' Mrs Selwyn went on, 'to meet someone here today. I am quite disappointed— quite.'

Everyone looked at Mrs Selwyn with interest. She had the stage all to herself, and was enjoying the fact exceedingly. Helena gazed at her with a note of interrogation in each of her bright eyes, and another in each corner of her sensitive mouth.

'I made perfectly sure that I should meet him here today. I said to Harry first thing this morning, when I saw the name in the paper, "Harry," I said, "we shall be sure to meet him at Sir Rupert's this afternoon." Now did I not, Harry?'

Mr Selwyn, thus appealed to, admitted that his wife had certainly made the remark she now quoted.

Mrs Selwyn beamed gratitude and affection for his endorsement. Then she turned to Miss Langley again.

'Why isn't *he* here, my dear Miss Langley, why?' Then she added, 'You know you always have everybody before anybody else, don't you?'

Helena shook her head.

'I suppose it's very stupid of me,' she said, 'but, really, I'm afraid I don't know who your "he" is. Is your "he" a hero?'

Mrs Selwyn laughed playfully. 'Oh, now your very words show that you do know whom I mean.'

'Indeed I don't.'

'Why, that wonderful man whom you admire so much, the illustrious exile, the hero of the hour, the new Napoleon.'

'I know whom you mean,' said Soame Rivers. 'You mean the Emperor of Surmer?'

'Of course. Whom else?' said Mrs Selwyn, clapping her hands enthusiastically. The Duke gave a sigh of relief, and Hiram Borringer, who had been rather silent, seemed to shake himself into activity at the mention of Surmer. Mr Selwyn said nothing, but watched his wife with the wondering admiration which some twenty years of married life had done nothing to diminish.

The least trace of increased colour came into Helena's cheeks, but she returned Mrs Selwyn's smiling glances composedly.

'The Emperor,' she said. 'Why did you expect to see him here today?'

'Why, because I saw his name in the "Morning Post" this very morning. It said he had arrived in London last night from Paris. I felt morally certain that I should meet him here today.'

'I am sorry you should be disappointed,' Helena said, laughing, 'but perhaps we shall be able to make amends for the disappointment another day. Papa called upon him this morning.'

Sir Rupert, sitting opposite his daughter, smiled at this. 'Did I really?' he asked. 'I was not aware of it.'

'Oh, yes, you did, papa; or, at least, I did for you.'

Sir Rupert's face wore a comic expression of despair. 'Helena, Helena, why?'

'Because he is one of the most interesting men existing.'

'And because he is down on his luck, too,' said the Duchess. 'I guess that always appeals to you.' The beautiful American girl had not shaken off all the expressions of her fatherland.

'But, I say,' said Selwyn, who seemed to think that the subject called for statesmanlike comment, 'how will it do for a pillar of the Government to be extending the hand of fellowship——'

'To a defeated man,' interrupted Helena. 'Oh, that won't matter one bit. The affairs of Surmer are hardly likely to be a grave international question for us, and in the meantime it is only showing a courtesy to a man who is at once an Englishman and a stranger.'

A slightly ironical 'Hear, Hear,' came from Soame Rivers, who did not love enthusiasm.

Sir Rupert followed suit good-humouredly.

'Where is he stopping?' asked Sir Rupert.

'At Paulo's Hotel, papa.'

'Paulo's Hotel,' said Mrs Selwyn; 'that seems to be quite the place for exiled potentates to put up at. The ex-King of Capri stopped there during his recent visit, and the chiefs from Mashonaland.'

'And Don Herrera de la Mancha, who claims the throne of Spain,' said the Duke.

'And the Rajah of Khandur,' added Mrs Selwyn, 'and the Herzog of Hesse-Steinberg, and ever so many more illustrious personages. Why do they all go to Paulo's?'

'I can tell you,' said Soame Rivers. 'Because Paulo's is one of the best hotels in London, and Paulo is a wonderful man. He knows how to make coffee in a way that wins a foreigner's heart, and he understands the cooking of all sorts of eccentric foreign dishes; and, though he is as rich as a Chicago pig-dealer, he looks after everything himself, and isn't in the least ashamed of having been a servant himself. I think he was a Portuguese originally.'

'And our Emperor went there?' Mrs Selwyn questioned.

Soame Rivers answered her, 'Oh, it is the right thing to do; it poses a distinguished exile immediately. Quite the right thing. He was well advised.'

'If only he had been as well advised in other matters,' said Mr Selwyn.

Then Hiram Borringer, who had hitherto kept silent, after his wont, spoke.

'I knew him,' he said, 'some years ago, when I was in Surmer.'

Everybody looked at once and with interest at the speaker. Hiram seemed slightly embarrassed at the attention he aroused; but he was not allowed to escape from explanation.

'Did you really?' said Sir Rupert. 'How very interesting! What sort of man did you find him?'

Helena said nothing, but she fixed her dark eyes eagerly on Hiram's face and listened, with slightly parted lips, all expectation.

'I found him a big man,' Hiram answered. 'I don't mean big in bulk, for he's not that; but big in nature, the man to make an empire and boss it.'

'A splendid type of man,' said Mrs Selwyn, clasping her hands enthusiastically. 'A man to stand at Cæsar's side and give directions.'

'Quite so,' Hiram responded gravely; 'quite so, madam. I met him first just before he was offered the throne , and that's five years ago.'

'Rather a curious thing making an Englishman Emperor, wasn't it?' Mr Selwyn inquired. At Sir Rupert's Mr Selwyn always displayed a profound interest in all political questions.

'Oh, he is a naturalised citizen of Surmer, of course,' said Soame Rivers, deftly insinuating his knowledge before Hiram could reply.

'But I thought,' said the Duke, 'that in those South American nations, as in the United States, a man has to be born in the country to be head of state.'

'That is so,' said Hiram. 'Though I fancy his friends in Surmer wouldn't have stuck at a trifle like that just then. But as a matter of fact he was actually born in Surmer.'

'Was he really?' said Sir Rupert. 'How curious!' To which Mr Selwyn added, 'And how convenient;' while Mrs Selwyn inquired how it happened.

'Why, you see,' said Hiram, 'his father was English Consul at Valdorado long ago, and he married a Spanish woman there, and the woman died, and the father seems to have taken it to heart, for he came home, bringing his baby boy with him. I believe the father died soon after he got home.'

Sir Rupert's face had grown slightly graver. Soame Rivers guessed that he was thinking of his own old loss. Helena felt a new thrill of interest in the man whose personality already so much attracted her. Like her, he had hardly known a mother.

'Then was that considered enough?' the Duke asked. 'Was the fact of his having been born there, although the son of an English father, enough, with subsequent naturalisation, to qualify him for the throne?'

'It was a peculiar case,' said Hiram. 'The point had not been raised before. But, as he happened to have the army at his back, it was concluded then that it would be most convenient for all parties to yield the point. But a good deal has been made of it since by his enemies.'

'I should imagine so,' said Sir Rupert. 'But it really is a very curious position, and I should not like to say myself off-hand how it ought to be decided.'

'The big battalions decided it in his case,' said Mrs Selwyn.

'Are they big battalions in Surmer?' inquired the Duke.

'Relatively, yes,' Hiram answered. 'It wasn't very much of an army at that time, even for Surmer; but it went solid for him. Now, of course, it's different.'

'How is it different?' This question came from Mr Selwyn, who put it with an air of profound curiosity.

Hiram explained. 'Why, you see, he introduced the conscription system. He told me he was going to do so, on the plan of some Prussian statesman.'

'Stein,' suggested Soame Rivers.

'Very likely. Every man to take service for a certain time. Well, that made pretty well all Surmer soldiers; it also made him a heap of enemies, and showed them how to make themselves unpleasant. I thought it wasn't a good plan for him or them at the time.'

'Did you tell him so?' asked Sir Rupert.

'Well, I did drop him a hint or two of my ideas, but he wasn't the sort of man to take ideas from anybody. Not that I mean at all that my ideas were of any importance, but he wasn't that sort of man.'

'What sort of man was he, Mr Borringer?' said Helena impetuously. 'What was he like, mentally, physically, every way? That's what we want to know.'

Hiram knitted his eyebrows, as he always did when he was slightly puzzled. He did not greatly enjoy haranguing the whole company in this way, and he partly regretted having confessed to any knowledge of the Emperor. But he was very fond of Helena, and he saw that she was sincerely interested in the subject, so he went on:

'Well, I seem to be spinning quite a yarn, and I'm not much of a hand at painting a portrait, but I'll do my best.'

'Shall we make it a game of twenty questions?' Mrs Selwyn suggested. 'We all ask you leading questions, and you answer them categorically.'

Everyone laughed, and Soame Rivers suggested that they should begin by ascertaining his age, height, and fighting weight.

'Well,' said Hiram, 'I guess I can get out my facts without cross-examination.' He had lived a great deal in America, and his speech was full of American colloquialisms. For which reason the beautiful Duchess liked him much.

'He's not very tall, but you couldn't call him short; rather more than middling high; perhaps looks a bit taller than he is, he carries himself so straight. He would have made a good soldier.'

'He did make a good soldier,' the Duke suggested.

'That's true,' said Hiram thoughtfully. 'I was thinking of a man to whom soldiering was his trade, his only trade.'

'But you haven't half satisfied our curiosity,' said Mrs Selwyn. 'You have only told us that he is a little over the medium height, and that he bears him stiffly up. What of his eyes, what of his hair—his beard? Does he discharge in either your straw-colour beard, your orange tawny beard, your purple-in-grain beard, or your French crown-coloured beard, your perfect yellow?'

Hiram looked a little bewildered. 'I beg your pardon, ma'am,' he said. The Duke came to the rescue.

'Mrs Selwyn's Shakespearean quotation expresses all our sentiments, Mr Borringer. Give us a faithful picture of the hero of the hour.'

'As for his hair and beard,' Hiram resumed, 'why, they are pretty much like most people's hair and beard—a fairish brown—and his eyes match them. He has very much the sort of favour you might expect from the son of a very fair-haired man and a dark woman. His father was as fair as a Scandinavian, he told me once. He was descended from some old Danish Viking, he said.'

'That helps to explain his belligerent Berserker disposition,' said Sir Rupert.

'A fine type,' said the Duke pensively, and Mr Selwyn caught him up with 'The finest type in the world. The sort of men who have made our empire what it is;' and he added somewhat confusedly, for his wife's eyes were fixed upon him, and he felt afraid that he was overdoing his part, 'Hawkins, Frobisher, Drake, Rodney, you know.'

'But,' said Helena, who had been very silent, for her, during the interrogation of Hiram, 'I do not feel as if I quite know all I want to know yet.'

'The noble thirst for knowledge does you credit, Miss Langley,' said Soame Rivers pertly.

Miss Langley laughed at him.

'Yes, I want to know all about him. He interests me. He has done something; he casts a shadow, as somebody has said somewhere. I like men who do something, who cast shadows instead of sitting in other people's shadows.'

Soame Rivers smiled a little sourly, and there was a suggestion of acerbity in his voice as he said in a low tone, as if more to himself than as a contribution to the general conversation, 'He has cast a decided shadow over Surmer.' He did not quite like Helena's interest in the dethroned Emperor.

'He made Surmer worth talking about!' Helena retorted. 'Tell me, Mr Borringer, how did he happen to get to Surmer at all? How did it come in his way to be Emperor and all that?'

'Rebellion lay in his way and he found it,' Mrs Selwyn suggested, whereupon Soame Rivers tapped her playfully upon the wrist, carrying on the quotation with the words of Prince Hal, 'Peace, chewit, peace.' Mr Soame Rivers was a very free-and-easy young gentleman, occasionally, and as he was a son of Lord Riverstown, much might be forgiven to him.

Hiram, always slightly bewildered by the quotations of Mrs Selwyn and the badinage of Soame Rivers, decided to ignore them both, and to address himself entirely to Miss Langley.

'Sorry to say I can't help you much, Miss Langley. When I was in Surmer five years ago I found him there, as I said, commanding the army. He had been a naturalised citizen there for some time, I reckon, but how he got so much to the front I don't know.'

'Doesn't a strong man always get to the front?' the Duchess asked.

'Yes,' said Hiram, 'I guess that's so. Well, I happened to get to know him, and we became a bit friendly, and we had many a pleasant chat together. He was as frank as frank, told me all his plans. "I mean to make this little old place move," he said to me.'

'Well, he has made it move,' said Helena. She was immensely interested, and her eyes dilated with excitement.

'A little too fast, perhaps,' said Hiram meditatively. 'I don't know. Anyhow, he had things all his own way for a goodish spell.'

'What did he do when he had things his own way?' Helena asked impatiently.

'Well, he tried to introduce reforms——'

'Yes, I knew he would do that,' the girl said, with the proud air of a sort of ownership.

'You seem to have known all about him,' Mrs Selwyn said, smiling loftily, sweetly, as at the romantic enthusiasm of youth.

'Well, so I do somehow,' Helena answered almost sharply; certainly with impatience. She was not thinking of Mrs Selwyn.

'Now, Mr Borringer, go on—about his reforms.'

'He seemed to have gotten a kind of notion about making things English or American. He abolished flogging of criminals and all sorts of old-fashioned ways; and he tried to reduce taxation; and he put down a sort of remnant of slavery that was still hanging round; and he wanted to give free land to all the emancipated folks; and he wanted to have an equal suffrage to all men, and to do away with corruption in the public offices and the civil service; and to compel the judges not to take bribes; and all sorts of things. I am afraid he wanted to do a good deal too much reform for what you folks would call the governing classes out there. I thought so at the time. He was right, you know,' Hiram said meditatively, 'but, then, I am mightily afraid he was right in a wrong sort of way.'

'He was right, anyhow,' Helena said, triumphantly.

'S'pose he was,' said Hiram; 'but things have to go slow, don't you see?'

'Well, what happened?'

'I don't rightly know how it all came about exactly; but I guess all the privileged classes, as you call them here, got their backs up, and all the officials went dead against him——'

'My great deed was too great,' Helena said.

'What is that, Helena?' her father asked.

'It's from a poem by Mrs Browning, about another Emperor; but more true of my Emperor than of hers,' Helena answered.

'Well,' Hiram went on, 'the opposition soon began to grumble——'

'Some people are always grumbling,' said Soame Rivers. 'What should we do without them? Where should we get our independent opposition?'

'Where, indeed,' said Sir Rupert, with a sigh of humorous pathos.

'Well,' said Helena, 'what did the opposition do?'

'Made themselves nasty,' answered Hiram. 'Stirred up discontent against the foreigner, as they called him. He found his congress hard to handle. There were votes of censure and talk of forced abdication, and I don't know what else. He went right ahead, his own way, without paying them the least attention. Then they took to refusing to vote his necessary supplies for the army and navy. He managed to get the money in spite of them; but whether he lost his temper, or not, I can't say, but he took it into his head to declare that the constitution was endangered by the machinations of unscrupulous enemies, and to declare himself Dictator.'

'That was brave,' said Helena, enthusiastically.

'Rather rash, wasn't it?' sneered Soame Rivers.

'It may have been rash, and it may not,' Hiram answered meditatively. 'I believe he was within the strict letter of the constitution, which does empower the head of state to take such a step under certain conditions. But the opposition meant fighting. So they rebelled against the Emperor, and that's how the bother began. How it ended you all know.'

'Where were the people all this time?' Helena asked eagerly.

'I guess the people didn't understand much about it then,' Hiram answered.

'My great deed was too great,' Helena murmured once again.

'The usual thing,' said Soame Rivers. 'Victory to begin with, and the confidence born of victory; then defeat and disaster.'

'The story of those three days' fighting in Valdorado is one of the most rattling things in recent times,' said the Duke.

'Was it not?' said Helena. 'I read every word of it every day, and I did want him to win so much.'

'Nobody could be more sorry that you were disappointed than he, I should imagine,' said Mrs Selwyn.

'What puzzles me,' said Mr Selwyn, 'is why when they had got him in their power they didn't shoot him.'

'Ah, you see he was an Englishman by family,' Sir Rupert explained; 'and though, of course, he had changed his nationality, I think the Congressionalists were a little afraid of arousing any kind of feeling in England.'

'As a matter of fact, of course,' said Soame Rivers, 'we shouldn't have dreamed of making any row if they had shot him or hanged him, for the matter of that.'

'You can never tell,' said the Duke. 'Somebody might have raised the Civis Romanus cry——'

'Yes, but he wasn't any longer Civis Romanus,' Soame Rivers objected.

'Do you think that would matter much if a cry was wanted against the Government?' the Duke asked, with a smile.

'Not much, I'm afraid,' said Sir Rupert. 'But whatever their reasons, I think the victors did the wisest thing possible in putting their man on board their big ironclad, the "Almirante Cochrane," and setting him ashore at Cherbourg.

'With a polite intimation, I presume, that if he again returned to the territory of Surmer he would be shot without form of trial,' added Soame Rivers.

'But he will return,' Helena said. 'He will, I am sure of it, and perhaps they may not find it so easy to shoot him then as they think now. A man like that is not so easily got rid of.'

Helena spoke with great animation, and her earnestness made Sir Rupert smile.

'If that is so,' said Soame Rivers, 'they would have done better if they had shot him out of hand.'

Helena looked slightly annoyed as she replied quickly, 'He is a strong man. I wish there were more men like him in the world.'

'Well,' said Sir Rupert, 'I suppose we shall all see him soon and judge for ourselves. Helena seems to have made up her mind already. Shall we go upstairs?'

'My great deed was too great' held possession that day of the mind and heart of Helena Langley.

CHAPTER VI

'HERE IS MY THRONE—BID KINGS COME BOW TO IT'

London, eager for a lion, lionised Ericson. That royal sport of lion-hunting, practised in old times by kings in Babylon and Nineveh, as those strange monuments in the British Museum bear witness, is the favourite sport of fashionable London today. And just at that moment London lacked its regal quarry. The latest traveller from Darkest Africa, the latest fugitive pretender to authority in France, had slipped out of the popular note and the favours of the Press. Ericson came in good time. There was a gap, and he filled it.

He found himself, to his amazement and his amusement, the hero of the hour. Invitations of all kinds showered upon him; the gates of great houses yawned wide to welcome him; had he been gifted like Kehama with the power of multiplying his personality, he could scarcely have been able to accept every invitation that was thrust upon him. But he did accept a great many; indeed, it might be said that he had to accept a great many. Had he had his own way, he might, perhaps, have buried himself in Hampstead, and enjoyed the company of his aunt and the mild society of Mr Gilbert Sarrasin. But the impetuous, indomitable Hamilton would hear of no inaction. He insisted copying a famous phrase of Lord Beaconsfield's, that the key of Surmer was in London. 'We must make friends,' he said; 'we must keep ourselves in evidence; we must never for a moment allow our claim to be forgotten, or our interests to be ignored. If we are ever to get back to Surmer we must make the most of our inevitable exile.'

The Emperor smiled at the enthusiasm of his young henchman. Hamilton was tremendously enthusiastic. A young Englishman of high family, of education, of some means, he had attached himself to Ericson years before at a time when Hamilton, fresh from the University, was taking that complement to a University career—a trip round the world, at a time when Ericson was just beginning that course of reform which had ended for the present in London and Paulo's Hotel. Hamilton's enthusiasm often proved to be practical. Like Ericson, he was full of great ideas for the advancement of mankind; he had swallowed all Socialisms, and had almost believed, before he fell in with Ericson, that he had elaborated the secret of social government. But his wide knowledge was of service; and his devotion to the Emperor showed itself of sterling stuff on that day in the Plaza Nacional when he saved his life from the insurgents. If the Emperor sometimes smiled at Hamilton's enthusiasm, he often allowed himself to yield to it. Just for the moment he was a little sick of the whole business; the inevitable bitterness that tinges a man's heart who has striven to be of service, and who has been misunderstood, had laid hold of him; there were times when he felt that he would let the whole thing go and make no further effort. Then it was that Hamilton's enthusiasm proved so useful; that Hamilton's restless energy in keeping in touch with the friends of the fallen man roused him and stimulated him.

He had made many friends now in London. Both the great political parties were civil to him, especially, perhaps, the Conservatives. Being in power, they could not make an overt declaration of their interest in him, but just then the Tory Party was experiencing one of those emotional waves which at times sweep over its consciousness, when it feels called upon to exalt the banner of progress; to play the old Roman part of lifting up the humble and casting down the proud; of showing a paternal interest in all manner of schemes for the redress of wrong and suffering everywhere. Somehow or other it had got it into its head that Ericson was a man after its own heart; that he was a kind of new Gordon; that his gallant determination to make the people of Surmer happy in spite of themselves was a proof of the application of Tory methods. Sir Rupert encouraged this idea. As a rule, his party was a little afraid of his advanced ideas; but on this occasion they were willing to accept them, and they manifested the friendliest interest in the Emperor's defeated schemes. Indeed, so friendly were they that many of the Radicals began to take alarm, and think that something must be wrong with a man who met with so cordial a reception from the ruling party.

Ericson himself met these overtures contentedly enough. If it was for the good of Surmer that he should return some day to carry out his dreams, then anything that helped him to return was for the good of Surmer too, and undoubtedly the friendliness of the Ministerialists was a very important factor in the problem he was engaged upon. He did not know at first how much Tory feeling was influenced by Sir Rupert; he did not know until later how much Sir Rupert was influenced by his daughter.

Helena had aroused in her father something of her own enthusiasm for the exiled Emperor. Sir Rupert had looked into the whole business more carefully, had recognised that it certainly would be very much better for the interests of British subjects under the green and yellow banner that Surmer should be ruled by an Englishman like Ericson than by the wild and reckless Junta, who at present upheld uncertain authority by martial law. England had recognised the Junta, of course; it was the *de facto* Government, and there was nothing else to be done. But it was not managing its affairs well; the credit of the country was shaken; its trade was gravely impaired; the very considerable English colony was loud in its protests against the defects of the new *régime*. Under these conditions Sir Rupert saw no reason for not extending the hand of friendship to the Emperor.

He did extend the hand of friendship. He met the Emperor at a dinner-party given in his honour by Mr Wynter, M. P.: Mr Wynter, who had always made it a point to know everybody, and who was as friendly with Sir Rupert as with the chieftains of his own party. Sir Rupert had expressed to Wynter a wish to meet Ericson; so when the dinner came off he found himself placed at the right-hand side of Ericson, who was at his host's right-hand side. The two men got on well from the first. Sir Rupert was attracted by the fresh unselfishness of Ericson, by something still youthful, still simple, in a man who had done and endured so much, and he made himself agreeable, as he only knew how, to his neighbour. Ericson, for his part, was frankly pleased with Sir Rupert. He was a little surprised, perhaps, at first to find that Sir Rupert's opinions coincided so largely with his own; that their views of government agreed on so many important particulars. He did not at first discover that it was Ericson's unconstitutional act in enforcing his reforms, rather than the actual reforms themselves, that aroused Sir Rupert's admiration. Sir Rupert was a good talker, a master of the manipulation of words, knowing exactly how much to say in order to convey to the mind of his listener a very decided impression without actually committing himself to any pledged opinion. Ericson was a shrewd man, but in such delicate dialectic he was not a match for a man like Sir Rupert.

Sir Rupert asked the Emperor to dinner, and the Emperor went to the great house in Queen's Gate and was presented to Helena, and was placed next to her at dinner, and thought her very pretty and original and attractive, and enjoyed himself very much. He found himself, to his half-unconscious surprise, still young enough and human enough to be pleased with the attention people were paying him—above all, that he was still young enough and human enough to be pleased with the very obvious homage of a charming young woman. For Helena's homage was very obvious indeed. Accustomed always to do what she pleased, and say what she pleased, Helena, at three-and-twenty, had a frankness of manner, a straightforwardness of speech, which her friends called original and her detractors called audacious. She would argue, unabashed, with the great leader of the party on some high point of foreign policy; she would talk to the great chieftain of Opposition as if he were her elder brother. People who did not understand her said that she was forward, that she had no reserve; even people who understood her, or thought they did, were sometimes a little startled by her careless directness. Soame Rivers once, when he was irritated by her, which occasionally happened, though he generally kept his irritation to himself, said that she had a 'slap on the back' way of treating her friends. The remark was not kind, but it happened to be fairly accurate, as unkind remarks sometimes are.

But from the first Helena did not treat the Emperor with the same brusque spirit of *camaraderie* which she showed to most of her friends. Her admiration for the public man, if it had been very enthusiastic, was very sincere. She had, from the first time that Ericson's name began to appear in the daily papers, felt a keen interest in the adventurous Englishman who was trying to introduce free institutions and advanced civilisation into one of the worm-eaten nations of the New World. As time went on, and Ericson's doings became more and more conspicuous, the girl's admiration for the lonely pioneer waxed higher and higher, till at last she conjured up for herself an image of heroic chivalry as romantic in its way as anything that could be evolved from the dreams of a sentimental schoolgirl. To reform the world—was not that always England's mission, if not especially the mission of her own party?—and here was an Englishman fighting for reform in that feverish place, and endeavouring to make his people happy and prosperous and civilised, by methods which certainly seemed to have more in common with the benevolent despotism of the Tory Party than with the theories of the Opposition. Bit by bit it came to pass that Helena Langley grew to look upon Ericson over there in that queer, ebullient corner of new Spain, as her ideal hero; and so it happened that when at last she met her hero in the flesh for the first time her frank audacity seemed to desert her.

Not that she showed in the slightest degree embarrassment when Sir Rupert first presented to her the grave man with the earnest eyes, whose pointed beard and brown hair were both slightly touched with grey. Only those who knew Helena well could possibly have told that she was not absolutely at her ease in the presence of the Emperor. Ericson himself thought her the most self-possessed young lady he had ever met, and to him, familiar as he was with the exquisite effrontery belonging to the New Castilian dames of Surmer, self-possession in young women was a recognised fact. Even Sir Rupert himself scarcely noticed anything that he would have called shyness in his daughter's demeanour as she stood talking to the Emperor, with her large fine eyes fixed in composed gaze upon his face. But Soame Rivers noticed a difference in her bearing; he was not her father, and he was accustomed to watch every tone of her speech and every movement of her eyes, and he saw that she was not entirely herself in the company of the 'new man,' as he called Ericson; and seeing it he felt a pang, or at least a prick, at the heart, and sneered at himself immediately in consequence. But he edged up to Helena just before the pairing took place for dinner, and said softly to her, so that no one else could hear, 'You are shy tonight. Why?'— and moved away smiling at the angry flash of her eyes and the compression of her mouth.

Possibly the words of Rivers may have affected her more than she was willing to admit; but she certainly was not as self-composed as usual during that first dinner. Her wit flashed vivaciously; the Emperor thought her brilliant, and even rather bewildering. If anyone had said to him that Helena Langley was not absolutely at her ease with him, he would have stared in amazement. For himself, he was not at all dismayed by the brilliant, beautiful girl who sat next to him. The long habit of intercourse with all kinds of people, under all kinds of conditions, had given him the experience which enabled him to be at his ease under any circumstances, even the most unfamiliar, and certainly talking to Helena Langley was an experience that had no precedent in the Emperor's life. But he talked to her readily, with great pleasure; he felt a little surprise at her obvious willingness to talk to him and accept his judgment upon many things; but he set this down as one of the few agreeable conditions attendant upon being lionised, and accepted it gratefully. 'I am the newest thing,' he thought to himself, 'and so this child is interested in me and consequently civil to me. Probably she will have forgotten all about me the next time we meet; in the meanwhile she is very charming.' The Emperor had even been about to suggest to himself that he might possibly forget all about her; but somehow this did not seem very likely, and he dismissed it.

He did not see very much of Helena that night after the dinner. Many people came in, and Helena was surrounded by a little court of adorers, men of all ages and occupations, statesmen, soldiers, men of letters, all eagerly talking a kind of talk which was almost unintelligible to the Emperor. In that bright Babel of voices, in that conversation which was full of allusions to things of which he knew nothing, and for which, if he had known, he would have cared less, the Emperor felt his sense of exile suddenly come strongly upon him like a great chill wave. It was not that he could feel neglected. A great statesman was talking to him, talking at much length confidentially, paying him the compliment of repeatedly inviting his opinion, and of deferring to his judgment. There was not a man or woman in the room who was not anxious to be introduced to Ericson, who was not delighted when the introduction was accorded, and when he or she had taken his hand and exchanged a few words with him. But somehow it was Helena's voice that seemed to thrill in the Emperor's ears; it was Helena's face that his eyes wandered to through all that brilliant crowd, and it was with something like a sense of serious regret that he found himself at last taking her hand and wishing her good-night. Her bright eyes grew brighter as she expressed the hope that they should meet soon again. The Emperor bowed and withdrew. He felt in his heart that he shared the hope very strongly.

The hope was certainly realised. So notable a lion as the Emperor was asked everywhere, and everywhere that he went he met the Langleys. In the high political and social life in which the Emperor, to his entertainment, found himself, the hostilities of warring parties had little or no effect. In that rarefied air it was hard to draw the breath of party passion, and the Emperor came across the Langleys as often in the houses of the Opposition as in Ministerial mansions. So it came to pass that something almost approaching to an intimacy sprang up between John Ericson on the one part and Sir Rupert and Helena Langley on the other. Sir Rupert felt a real interest in the adventurous man with the eccentric ideas; perhaps his presence recalled something of Sir Rupert's own hot youth when he had had eccentric ideas and was looked upon with alarm by the steady-going. Helena made no concealment of her interest in the exile. She was always so frank in her friendships, so off-hand and boyish in her air of comradeship with many people, that her attitude towards the Emperor did not strike any one, except Soame Rivers, as being in the least marked—for her. Indeed, most of her admirers would have held that she was more reserved with the Emperor than with others of her friends. Soame Rivers saw that there was a difference in her bearing towards the Emperor and towards the courtiers of her little court, and he smiled cynically and pretended to be amused.

Ericson's acquaintance with the Langleys ripened into that rapid intimacy which is sometimes possible in London. At the end of a week he had met them many times and had been twice to their house. Helena had always insisted that a friendship which was worth anything should declare itself at once, should blossom quickly into being, and not grow by slow stages. She offered the Emperor her friendship very frankly and very graciously, and Ericson accepted very frankly the gracious gift. For it delighted him, tired as he was of all the strife and struggle of the last few years, to find rest and sympathy in the friendship of so charming a girl; the cordial sympathy she showed him came like a balm to the humiliation of his overthrow. He liked Helena, he liked her father; though he had known them but for a handful of days, it always delighted him to meet them; he always felt in their society that he was in the society of friends.

One evening, when Ericson had been little more than a month in London, he found himself at an evening party given by Lady Seagraves. Lady Seagraves was a wonderful woman—'the fine flower of our modern civilisation,' Soame Rivers called her. Everybody came to her house; she delighted in contrasts; life was to her one prolonged antithesis. Soame Rivers said of her parties that they resembled certain early Italian pictures, which gave you the mythological gods in one place, a battle in another, a scene of pastoral peace in a third. It was an astonishing amalgam.

Ericson arrived at Lady Seagraves' house rather late; the rooms were very full—he found it difficult to get up the great staircase. There had been some great Ministerial function, and the clothes of many of the men in the crowd were as bright as the women's. Court suits, ribands, and orders lent additional colour to a richly coloured scene. But even in a crowd where everybody bore some claim to distinction the arrival of the Emperor aroused general attention. Ericson was not yet sufficiently hardened to the experience to be altogether indifferent to the fact that everyone was looking at him; that people were whispering his name to each other as he slowly made his way from stair to stair; that pretty women paused in their upward or downward progress to look at him, and invariably with a look of admiration for his grave, handsome face.

When he got to the top of the stairs Ericson found his hostess, and shook hands with her. Lady Seagraves was an effusive woman, who was always delighted to see any of her friends; but she felt a special delight at seeing the Emperor, and she greeted him with a special effusiveness. Her party was choking with celebrities of all kinds, social, political, artistic, legal, clerical, dramatic; but it would not have been entirely triumphant if it had not included the Emperor. Lady Seagraves was very glad to see him indeed, and said so in her warm, enthusiastic way.

'I'm so glad to see you,' Lady Seagraves murmured. 'It was so nice of you to come. I was beginning to be desperately afraid that you had forgotten all about me and my poor little party.'

It was one of Lady Seagraves' graceful little affectations to pretend that all her parties were small parties, almost partaking of the nature of impromptu festivities. Ericson glanced around over the great room crammed to overflowing with a crowd of men and women who could hardly move, men and women most of whose faces were famous or beautiful, men and women all of whom, as Soame Rivers said, had their names in the play-bill;

there was a smile on his face as he turned his eyes from the brilliant mass to Lady Seagraves' face.

'How could I forget a promise which it gives me so much pleasure to fulfil?' he asked. Lady Seagraves gave a little cry of delight.

'Now that's perfectly sweet of you! How did you ever learn to say such pretty things in that dreadful place? Oh, but of course; I forgot Spaniards pay compliments to perfection, and you have learnt the art from them, you frozen Northerner.'

Ericson laughed. 'I am afraid I should never rival a Spaniard in compliment,' he said. He never knew quite what to talk to Lady Seagraves about, but, indeed, there was no need for him to trouble himself, as Lady Seagraves could at all times talk enough for two more.

So he just listened while Lady Seagraves rattled on, sending his glance hither and thither in that glittering assembly, seeking almost unconsciously for one face. He saw it almost immediately; it was the face of Helena Langley, and her eyes were fixed on him. She was standing in the throng at some little distance from him, talking to Soame Rivers, but she nodded and smiled to the Emperor.

At that moment the arrival of the Duke and Duchess of Deptford set Ericson free from the ripple of Lady Seagraves' conversation. She turned to greet the new arrivals, and the Emperor began to edge his way through the press to where Helena was standing. Though she was only a little distance off, his progress was but slow progress. The rooms were tightly packed, and almost every person he met knew him and spoke to him, or shook hands with him, but he made his way steadily forward.

'Here comes the illustrious exile!' said Soame Rivers, in a low tone. 'I suppose nobody will have a chance of saying a word to you for the rest of the evening?'

Miss Langley glanced at him with a little frown. 'I am afraid I can scarcely hope that Mr Ericson will consent to be monopolised by me for the whole of the evening,' she said; 'but I wish he would, for he is certainly the most interesting person here.'

Soame Rivers shrugged his shoulders slightly. 'You always know someone who is the most interesting man in the world—for the time being,' he said.

Miss Langley frowned again, but she did not reply, for by this time Ericson had reached her, and was holding out his hand. She took it with a bright smile of welcome. Soame Rivers slipped away in the crowd, after nodding to Ericson.

'I am so glad that you have come,' Helena said. 'I was beginning to fear that you were not coming.'

'It is very kind of you,' the Emperor began, but Miss Langley interrupted him.

'No, no; it isn't kind of me at all; it is just natural selfishness. I want to talk to you about several things; and if you hadn't come I should have been disappointed in my purpose, and I hate being disappointed.'

The Emperor still persisted that any mark of interest from Miss Langley was kindness. 'What do you want to talk to me about particularly?' he asked.

'Oh, many things! But we can't talk in this awful crush. It's like trying to stand up against big billows on a stormy day. Come with me. There is a quieter place at the back, where we shall have a chance of peace.'

She turned and led the way slowly through the crowd, the Emperor following her obediently. Once again the progress was a slow one, for every man had a word for Miss Langley, and he himself was eagerly caught at as they drifted along. But at last they got through the greater crush of the centre rooms and found themselves in a kind of lull in a further saloon where a piano was, and where there were fewer people. Out of this room there was a still smaller one with several palms in it, and out of the palms arising a great bronze reproduction of the Hermes of Praxiteles. Lady Seagraves playfully called this little room her Pagan parlour. Here people who knew the house well found their way when they wanted quiet conversation. There was nobody in it when Miss Langley and the Emperor arrived. Helena sat down on a sofa with a sigh of relief, and Ericson sat down beside her.

'What a delightful change from all that awful noise and glare!' said Helena. 'I am very fond of this little corner, and I think Lady Seagraves regards it as especially sacred to me.'

'I am grateful for being permitted to cross the hallowed threshold,' said the Emperor. 'Is this the tutelary divinity?' And he glanced up at the bronze image.

'Yes,' said Miss Langley; 'that is a copy of the Hermes of Praxiteles which was discovered at

Olympia some years ago. It is the right thing to worship.'

'One so seldom worships the right thing—at least, at the right time,' he said.

'I worship the right thing, I know,' she rejoined, 'but I don't quite know about the right time.'

'Your instincts would be sure to guide you right,' he answered, not indeed quite knowing what he was talking about.

'Why?' she asked, point blank.

'Well, I suppose I meant to say that you have nobler instincts than most other people.'

'Come, you are not trying to pay me a compliment? I don't want compliments; I hate and detest them. Leave them to stupid and uninteresting men.'

'And to stupid and uninteresting women?'

'Another try at a compliment!'

'No; I felt that.'

'Well, anyhow, I did not entice you in here to hear anything about myself; I know all about myself.'

'Indeed,' he said straightforwardly, 'I do not care to pay compliments, and I should never think of wearying you with them. I believe I hardly quite knew what I was talking about just now.'

'Very well; it does not matter. I want to hear about you. I want to know all about you. I want you to trust in me and treat me as your friend.'

'But what do you want me to tell you?'

'About yourself and your projects and everything. Will you?'

The Emperor was a little bewildered by the girl's earnestness, her energy, and the perfect simplicity of her evident belief that she was saying nothing unreasonable. She saw reluctance and hesitation in his eyes.

'You are very young,' he began.

'Too young to be trusted?'

'No, I did not say *that*.'

'But your look said it.'

'My look then mistranslated my feeling.'

'What did you feel?'

'Surprise, and interest, and gratitude.'

She tossed her head impatiently.

'Do you think I can't understand?' she asked, in her impetuous way—her imperial way with most others, but only an impetuous way with him. For most others with whom she was familiar she was able to control and be familiar with, but she could only be impetuous with the Emperor. Indeed, it was the high tide of her emotion which carried her away so far as to fling her in mere impetuousness against him.

The Emperor was silent for a moment, and then he said: 'You don't seem much more than a child to me.'

'Oh! Why? Do you not know?—I am twenty-three!'

'I am twenty-three,' the Emperor murmured, looking at her with a kindly and half-melancholy interest. 'You are twenty-three! Well, there it is—do you not see, Miss Langley?'

'There what is?'

'There is all the difference. To be twenty-three seems to you to make you quite a grown-up person.'

'What else should it make me? I have been of age for two years. What am I but a grown-up person?'

'Not in my sense,' he said placidly. 'You see, I have gone through so much, and lived so many lives, that I begin to feel quite like an old man already. Why, I might have had a daughter as old as you.'

'Oh, stuff!' the audacious young woman interposed.

'Stuff? How do you know?'

'As if I hadn't read lives of you in all the papers and magazines and I don't know what. I can tell you your birthday if you wish, and the year of your birth. You are quite young—in my eyes.'

'You are kind to me,' he said, gravely, 'and I am quite sure that I look at my very best in your eyes.'

'You do indeed,' she said fervently, gratefully.

'Still, that does not prevent me from being twenty years older than you.'

'All right; but would you refuse to talk frankly and sensibly about yourself?—sensibly, I mean, as one talks to a friend and not as one talks to a child. Would you refuse to talk in that way to a young man merely because you were twenty years older than he?'

'I am not much of a talker,' he said, 'and I very much doubt if I should talk to a young man at all about my projects, unless, of course, to my friend Hamilton.'

Helena turned half away disappointed. It was of no use, then—she was not his friend. He did not care to reveal himself to her; and yet she thought she could do so much to help him. She felt that tears were beginning to gather in her eyes, and she would not for all the world that he should see them.

'I thought we were friends,' she said, giving out the words very much as a child might give them out—and, indeed, her heart was much more as that of a little child than she herself knew or than he knew then; for she had not the least idea that she was in love or likely to be in love with the Emperor. Her free, energetic, wild-falcon spirit had never as yet troubled itself with thoughts of such kind. She had made a hero for herself out of the Emperor—she almost adored him; but it was with the most genuine hero-worship—or fetish-worship, if that be the better and harsher way of putting it—and she had never thought of being in love with him. Her highest ambition up to this hour was to be his friend and to be admitted to his confidence, and—oh, happy recognition!—to be consulted by him. When she said 'I thought we were friends,' she jumped up and went towards the window to hide the emotion which she knew was only too likely to make itself felt.

The Emperor got up and followed her. 'We are friends,' he said.

She looked brightly round at him, but perhaps he saw in her eyes that she had been feeling a keen disappointment.

'You think my professed friendship mere girlish inquisitiveness—you know you do,' she said, for she was still angry.

'Indeed I do not,' he said earnestly. 'I have had no friendship since I came back an outcast to England—no friendship like that given to me by you——'

She turned round delightedly towards him.

'And by your father.'

And again, she could not tell why, she turned partly away.

'But the truth is,' he went on to say, 'I have no clearly defined plans as yet.'

'You don't mean to give in?' she asked eagerly.

He smiled at her impetuosity. She blushed slightly as she saw his smile.

'Oh I know,' she exclaimed, 'you think me an impertinent schoolgirl, and you only laugh at me.'

'I do nothing of the kind. It is only too much of a pleasure to me to talk to you on terms of friendship. Look here, I wish we could do as people used to do in the old melodramas, and swear an eternal friendship.'

'I swear an eternal friendship to you,' she exclaimed, 'whether you like it or not,' and, obeying the wild impulse of the hour, she held out both her hands.

He took them both in his, held them for just one instant, and then let them go.

'I accept the friendship,' he said, with a quiet smile, 'and I reciprocate it with all my heart.'

Helena was already growing a little alarmed at her own impulsiveness and effusiveness. But there was something in the Emperor's quiet, grave, and protecting way which always seemed to reassure her. 'He will be sure to understand me,' was the vague thought in her mind.

Assuredly the Emperor now thought he did understand her. He felt satisfied that her enthusiasm was the enthusiasm of a generous girl's friendship, and that she thought about him in no other way. He had learned to like her companionship, and to think much of her fresh, courageous intellect, and even of her practical good sense. He had no doubt that he should find her advice on many things worth having. His battlefield just now and for some time to come must be in London—in the London of finance and diplomacy.

'Come and sit down again,' the Emperor said; 'I will tell you all I know—and I don't know much. I do not mean to give up, Miss Langley. I am not a man who gives up—I am not built that way.'

'Of course I knew,' Helena exclaimed triumphantly; 'I knew you would never give up. You couldn't.'

'I couldn't—and I do not believe I ought to give up. I am sure I know better how to provide for the future of Surmer than—than—well, than Surmer knows herself—just now. I believe Surmer will want me back.'

'Of course she will want you back when she comes to her senses,' Helena said with sparkling eyes.

'I don't blame her for having a little lost her senses under the conditions—it was all too new, and I was too hasty. I was too much inspired by the ungoverned energy of the new broom. I should do better now if I had the chance.'

'You will have the chance—you must have it!'

'Do you promise it to me?' he asked with a kindly smile.

'I do—I can—I know it will come to you!'

'Well, I can wait,' he said quietly. 'When Surmer calls me to go back to her I will go.'

'But what do you mean by Surmer? Do you want a *plébiscite* of the whole population in your favour?'

'Oh no! I only mean this, that if the large majority of the people whom I strove to serve are of opinion they can do without me—well, then, I shall do without them. But if they call me I shall go to them, although I went to my death and knew it beforehand.'

'One may do worse things,' the girl said proudly, 'than go knowingly to one's death.'

'You are so young,' he said. 'Death seems nothing to you. The young and the generous are brave like that.'

'Oh,' she exclaimed, 'let my youth alone!'

She would have liked to say, 'Oh, confound my youth!' but she did not give way to any such unseemly impulse. She felt very happy again, her high spirits all rallying round her.

'Let your youth alone!' the Emperor said, with a half-melancholy smile. 'So long as time lets it alone—and even time will do that for some years yet.'

Then he stopped and felt a little as if he had been preaching a sermon to the girl.

'Come,' she broke in upon his moralisings, 'if I am so dreadfully young, at least I'll have the benefit of my immaturity. If I am to be treated as a child, I must have a child's freedom from conventionality.' She dragged forward a heavy armchair lined with the soft, mellowed, dull red leather which one sees made into cushions and sofa-pillows in the shops of Nuremberg's more artistic upholsterers, and then at its side on the carpet she planted a footstool of the same material and colour. 'There,' she said, 'you sit in that chair.'

'And you, what are you going to do?'

'Sit first, and I will show you.'

He obeyed her and sat in the great chair. 'Well, now?' he asked.

'I shall sit here at your feet.' She flung herself down and sat on the footstool.

'Here is my throne,' she said composedly; 'bid kings come bow to it.'

'Kings come bowing to a banished Empirean?'

'You are my King,' she answered, 'and so I sit at your feet and am proud and happy. Now talk to me and tell me some more.'

But the talk was not destined to go any farther that night. Rivers and one or two others came lounging in. Helena did not stir from her lowly position. The Emperor remained as he was just long enough to show that he did not regard himself as having been disturbed. Helena flung a saucy little glance of defiance at the principal intruder.

'I know you were sent for me,' she said. 'Papa wants me?'

'Yes,' the intruder replied; 'if I had not been sent I should never have ventured to follow you into this room.'

'Of course not—this is my special sanctuary. Lady Seagraves has dedicated it to me, and now I dedicate it to Mr Ericson. I have just been telling him that, for all he is a Empirean, he is *my* King.'

The Emperor had risen by this time.

'You are sent for?' he said.

'Yes—I am sorry.'

'So am I—but we must not keep Sir Rupert waiting.'

'I shall see you again—when?' she asked eagerly.

'Whenever you wish,' he answered. Then they shook hands, and Soame Rivers took her away.

Several ladies remarked that night that really Helena Langley was going quite beyond all bounds, and was overdoing her unconventionality quite too shockingly. She was actually throwing herself right at

Mr Ericson's head. Of course Mr Ericson would not think of marrying a chit like that. He was quite old enough to be her father.

One or two stout dowagers shook their heads sagaciously, and remarked that Sir Rupert had a great deal of money, and that a large fortune got with a wife might come in very handy for the projects of a dethroned Emperor. 'And men are all so vain, my dear,' remarked one to another. 'Mr Ericson doesn't look vain,' the other said meditatively. 'They are all alike, my dear,' rejoined the one. And so the matter was settled—or left unsettled.

Meanwhile the Emperor went home, and began to look over maps and charts of Surmer. He buried himself in some plans of street improvement, including a new and splendid opera house, of which he had actually laid the foundation before the crash came.

CHAPTER VII

THE PRINCE AND CLAUDIO

Why did the Emperor bury himself in his maps and his plans and his improvements in the street architecture of a city which in all probability he was never to see again?

For one reason. Because his mind was on something else tonight, and he did not feel as if he were acting with full fidelity to the cause of Surmer if he allowed any subject to come even for an hour too directly between him and that. Little as he permitted himself to put on the airs of a patriot and philanthropist—much as he would have hated to exhibit himself or be regarded as a professional patriot—yet the devotion to that cause which he had himself created—the cause of a regenerated Surmer—was deep down in his very heart. Surmer and her future were his day-dream—his idol, his hobby, or his craze, if you like; he had long been possessed by the thought of a redeemed and regenerated Surmer. Tonight his mind had been thrown for a moment off the track—and it was therefore that he pulled out his maps and was endeavouring to get on to the track again.

But he could not help thinking of Helena Langley. The girl embarrassed him—bewildered him. Her upturned eyes came between him and his maps. Her frank homage was just like that of a child. Yet she was not a child, but a remarkably clever and brilliant young woman, and he did not know whether he ought to accept her homage. He was, for all his strange career, somewhat conservative in his notions about women. He thought that there ought to be a sweet reserve about them always. He rather liked the pedestal theory about woman. The approaches and the devotion, he thought, ought to come from the man always. In the case of Helena Langley, it never occurred to him to think that her devotion was anything different from the devotion of Hamilton; but then a young man who is one's secretary is quite free to show his devotion, while a young woman who is not one's secretary is not free to show her devotion. Ericson kept asking himself whether Sir Rupert would not feel vexed when he heard of the way in which his dear spoiled child had been going on—as he probably would from herself—for she evidently had not the faintest notion of concealment. On the other hand, what could Ericson do? Give Helena Langley an exposition of his theories concerning proper behaviour in unmarried womanhood? Why, how absurd and priggish and offensive such a course of action would be? The girl would either break into laughter at him or feel herself offended by his attempt to lecture her. And who or what had given him any right to lecture her? What, after all, had she done? Sat on a footstool beside the chair of a public man whose cause she sympathised with, and who was quite old enough—or nearly so, at all events—to be her father. Up to this time Ericson was rather inclined to press the 'old enough to be her father,' and to leave out the 'nearly so.' Then, again, he reminded himself that social ways and manners had very much changed in London during his absence, and that girls were allowed, and even encouraged, to do all manner of things now which would have been thought tomboyish, or even improper, in his younger days. Why, he had glanced at scores of leading articles and essays written to prove that the London girl of the close of the century was free to do things which would have brought the deepest and most comprehensive blush to the cheeks of the meek and modest maidens of a former generation.

Yes—but for all this change of manners it was certain that he had himself heard comments made on the impulsive unconventionality of Miss Langley. The comments were sometimes generous, sympathetic, and perhaps a little pitying—and of course they were sometimes ill-natured and spiteful. But, whatever their tone, they were all tuned to the one key—that Miss Langley was impulsively unconventional.

The Emperor was inclined to resent the intrusion of a woman into his thoughts. For years he had been in the habit of regarding women as trees walking. He had had a love disappointment early in life. His true love had proved a false true love, and he had taken it very seriously—taken it quite to heart. He was not enough of a modern London man to recognise the fact that something of the kind happens to a good many people, and that there are still a great many girls left to choose from. He ought to have made nothing of it, and consoled himself easily, but he did not. So he had lost his ideal of womanhood, and went through the world like one deprived of a sense. The man is, on the whole, happiest whose true love dies early, and leaves him with an ideal of womanhood which never can change. He is, if he be at all a true man, thenceforth as one who walks under the guidance of an angel. But Ericson's mind was put out by the failure of his ideal. Happily he was a strong man by nature, with deep impassioned longings and profound convictions; and going on through life in his lonely, overcrowded way, he soon became absorbed in the entrancing egotism of devotion to a great cause. He began to see all things in life first as they bore on the regeneration of Surmer—now as they bore on his restoration to Surmer. So he had been forgetting all about women, except as ornaments of society, and occasionally as useful mechanisms in politics.

The memory of his false true love had long faded. He did not now particularly regret that she had been false. He did not regret it even for her own sake—for he knew that she had got on very well in life—had married a rich man—held a good position in society, and apparently had all her desires gratified. It was probable—it was almost certain—that he should meet her in London this season—and he felt no interest or curiosity about the meeting—did not even trouble himself by wondering whether she had been following his career with eyes in which old memories gleamed. But after her he had never again felt inclined for romance. His ideal, as has been said, was gone—and he did not care for women without an ideal to pursue.

Every night, however late, when the Emperor had got back to his rooms, Hamilton came to see him, and they read over letters and talked over the doings of the next day. Hamilton came this night in the usual course of things, and Ericson was delighted to see him. He was sick of trying to study the street improvements of the metropolis of Surmer, and he was vexed at the intrusion of Helena Langley into his mind—for he did not suspect in the least that she had yet made any intrusion into his heart.

'Well, Hamilton, I hope you have been enjoying yourself?'

'Yes, Excellency—fairly enough. Do you know I had a long talk with Sir Rupert Langley about you?'

'Aye, aye. What does Sir Rupert say about me?'

'Well, he says,' Hamilton began distressedly, 'that you had better give up all notions of Surmer and go in for English politics.'

The Emperor laughed; and at the same time felt a little touched. He could not help remembering the declaration of his life's policy he had just been making to Sir Rupert Langley's daughter.

'What on earth do I know about English politics?'

'Oh, well; of course you could get it all up easily enough, so far as that goes.'

'But doesn't Sir Rupert see that, so far as I understand things at all, I should be in the party opposed to him?'

'Yes, he sees that; but he doesn't seem to mind. He thinks you would find a field in English politics; and he says the life of the House of Commons is the life to which the ambition of every true Englishman ought to turn—and, you know—all that sort of thing.'

'And does he think that I have forgotten Surmer?'

'No; but he has a theory about all South American States. He thinks they are all rotten, and that sort of thing. He insists that you are thrown away on Surmer.'

'Fancy a man being thrown away upon a country,' the Emperor said, with a smile. 'I have often heard and read of a country being thrown away upon a man, but never yet of a man being thrown away upon a country. I should not have wondered at such an opinion from an ordinary Englishman, who has no idea of a place the size of Surmer, where we could stow away England, France, and Germany in a little unnoticed corner. But Sir Rupert—who has been there! Give us out the cigars, Hamilton—and ring for some drinks.'

Hamilton brought out the cigars, and rang the bell.

'Well—anyhow—I have told you,' he said hesitatingly.

'So you have, boy, with your usual indomitable honesty. For I know what you think about all this.'

'Of course you do.'

'You don't want to give up Surmer?'

'Give up Surmer? Never—while grass grows and water runs!'

'Well, then, we need not say any more about that. Tell me, though, where was all this? At Lady Seagraves'?'

'No; it was at Sir Rupert's own house.'

'Oh, yes, I forgot; you were dining there?'

'Yes; I was dining there.'

'This was after dinner?'

'Yes; there were very few men there, and he talked all this to me in a confidential sort of way. Tell me, Excellency, what do you think of his daughter?'

The Emperor almost started. If the question had come out of his own inner consciousness it could not have illustrated more clearly the problem which was perplexing his heart.

'Why, Hamilton, I have not seen very much of her, and I don't profess to be much of a judge of young ladies. Why on earth do you want my opinion? What is your own opinion of her?'

'I think she is very beautiful.'

'So do I.'

'And awfully clever.'

'Right again—so do I.'

'And singularly attractive, don't you think?'

'Yes; very attractive indeed. But you know, my boy, that the attractions of young women have now little more than a purely historical interest for me. Still, I am quite prepared to go as far with you as to admit that Miss Langley is a most attractive young woman.'

'She thinks ever so much of *you*,' Hamilton said dogmatically.

'She has great sympathy with our cause,' the Emperor said.

'She would do anything *you* asked her to do.'

'My boy, I don't want to ask her to do anything.'

'Excellency, I want you to advise her to do something—for *me*.'

'For you, Hamilton? Is that the way?' The Emperor asked the question with a tone of infinite sympathy, and he stood up as if he were about to give some important order. Hamilton, on the other hand, collapsed into a chair.

'That is the way, Excellency.'

'You are in love with this child?'

'I am madly in love with this child, if you call her so.'

Ericson made some strides up and down the room with his hands behind him. Then he suddenly stopped.

'Is this quite a serious business?' he asked, in a low, soft voice.

'Terribly serious for me, Excellency, if things don't turn out right. I have been hit very hard.'

The Emperor smiled.

'We get over such things,' he said.

'But I don't want to get over this; I don't mean to get over it.'

'Well,' Ericson said good-humouredly, and with quite recovered composure, 'it may not be necessary for you to get over it. Does the young lady want you to get over it?'

'I haven't ventured to ask her yet.'

'What do you mean to ask her?'

'Well, of course—if she will—have me.'

'Yes, naturally. But I mean when——'

'When do I mean to ask her?'

'No; when do you propose to marry her?'

'Well, of course, when we have settled ourselves again in Surmer, and all is right there. You don't fancy I would do anything before we have made that all right?'

'But all that is a little vague,' the Emperor said; 'the time is somewhat indefinite. One does not quite know what the young lady might say.'

'She is just as enthusiastic about Surmer as I am, or as you are.'

'Yes, but her father. Have you said anything to him about this?'

'Not a word. I waited until I could talk of it to you, and get your promise to help me.'

'Of course I'll help you, if I can. But tell me, how can I? What do you want me to do? Shall I speak to Sir Rupert?'

'If you would speak to him after, I should be awfully glad. But I don't so much mind about him just yet; I want you to speak to her!'

'To Miss Langley? To ask her to marry you?'

'That's about what it comes to,' Hamilton said courageously.

'But, my dear love-sick youth, would you not much rather woo and win the girl for yourself?'

'What I am afraid of,' Hamilton said gravely, 'is that she would pretend not to take me seriously. She would laugh and turn me into ridicule, and try to make fun of the whole thing. But if you tell her that it is positively serious and a business of life and death with me, then she will believe you, and she *must* take it seriously and give you a serious answer, or at least promise to give me a serious answer.'

'This is the oddest way of wooing a lady, Hamilton.'

'I don't know,' Hamilton said; 'we have Shakespeare's authority for it, haven't we? Didn't Don Pedro arrange for Claudio and Hero?'

'Well, a very good precedent,' Ericson said with a smile. 'Tell me about this tomorrow. Think over it and sleep over it in the meantime, and if you still think that you are willing to make your proposals through the medium of an envoy, then trust me, Hamilton, your envoy will do all he can to win for you your heart's desire.'

'I don't know how to thank you,' Hamilton exclaimed fervently.

'Don't try. I hate thanks. If they are sincere they tell their tale without words. I know you—everything about you is sincere.'

Hamilton's eyes glistened with joy and gratitude. He would have liked to seize his chief's hand and press it to his lips; but he forbore. The Emperor was not an effusive man, and effusiveness did not flourish in his presence. Hamilton confined his gratitude to looks and thoughts and to the dropping of the subject for the present.

'I have been pottering over these maps and plans,' the Emperor said.

'I am so glad,' Hamilton exclaimed, 'to find that your heart is still wholly absorbed in the improvement of Surmer.'

The Emperor remained for a few moments silent and apparently buried in thought. He was not thinking, perhaps, altogether of the projected improvements in the capital of Surmer. Hamilton had often seen him in those sudden and silent, but not sullen, moods, and was always careful not to disturb him by asking any question or making any remark. The Emperor had been sitting in a chair and pulling the ends of his moustache. At once he got up and went to where Hamilton was seated.

'Look here, Hamilton,' he said, in a tone of positive sternness, 'I want to be clear about all this. I want to help you—of course I want to help you—if you can really be helped. But, first of all, I must be certain—as far as human certainty can go—that you really know what you do want. The great curse of life is that men—and I suppose women too—I can't say—do not really know or trouble to know what they do positively want with all their strength and with all their soul. The man who positively knows what he does want and sticks to it has got it already. Tell me, do you really want to marry this young woman?'

'I do—with all my soul and with all my strength!'

'But have you thought about it—have you turned it over in your mind—have you come down from your high horse and looked at yourself, as the old joke puts it?'

'It's no joke for me,' Hamilton said dolefully.

'No, no, boy; I didn't mean that it was. But I mean, have you really looked at yourself and her? Have you thought whether she could make you happy?—have you thought whether you could make her happy? What do you know about her? What do you know about the kind of life which she lives? How do you know whether she could do without that kind of life—whether she could live any other kind of life? She is a London Society girl, she rides in the Row at a certain hour, she goes out to dinner parties and to balls, she dances until all hours in the morning, she goes abroad to the regular place at the regular time, she spends a certain part of the winter visiting at the regulation country houses. Are you prepared to live that sort of life—or are you prepared to bear the responsibility of taking her out of it? Are you prepared to take the butterfly to live in the camp?'

'She isn't a butterfly——'

'No, no; never mind my bad metaphor. But she has been brought up in a kind of life which is second nature to her. Are you prepared to live that life with her? Are you sure—are you quite, quite sure—that she would be willing, after the first romantic outburst, to put up with a totally different life for the sake of you?'

'Excellency,' Hamilton said, smiling somewhat sadly, 'you certainly do your best to take the conceit out of a young man.'

'My boy, I don't think you have any self-conceit, but you may have a good deal of self-forgetfulness. Now I want you to call a halt and remember yourself. In this business of yours—supposing it comes to what you would consider at the moment a success——'

'At the moment?' Hamilton pleaded, in pained remonstrance.

'At the moment—yes. Supposing the thing ends successfully for you, one plan of life or other must necessarily be sacrificed—yours or hers. Which is it going to be? Don't make too much of her present enthusiasm. Which is it going to be?'

'I don't believe there will be any sacrifice needed,' Hamilton said, in an impassioned tone. 'I told you she loves Surmer as well as you or I could do.'

The Emperor shook his head and smiled pityingly.

'But if there is to be any sacrifice of any life,' Hamilton said, driven on perhaps by his chief's pitying smile, 'it shan't be hers. No, if she will have me after we have got back to Surmer, I'll live with her in London every season and ride with her in the Row every morning and afternoon, and take her, by Jove! to all the dinners and balls she cares about, and she shall have her heart's desire, whatever it be.'

The Emperor's face was crossed by some shadows. Pity was there, and sympathy was there—and a certain melancholy pleasure, and, it may be, a certain disappointment. He pulled himself together very quickly, and was cool, genial, and composed, according to his usual way.

'All right, my boy,' he said, 'this is genuine love at all events, however it may turn out. You have answered my question fairly and fully. I see now that you do know what you want. That is one great point, anyhow. I will do my very best to get for you what

you want. If it only rested with me, Hamilton!'
There was a positive note of tenderness in his voice
as he spoke these words; and yet there was a kind of
forlorn feeling in his heart, as if the friend of his
heart was leaving him. He felt a little as the brother
Vult in Richter's exquisite and forgotten novel might
have felt when he was sounding on his flute that
final morning, and going out on his cold way never
to see his brother again. The brother Walt heard the
soft, sweet notes, and smiled tranquilly, believing
that his brother was merely going on a kindly errand
to help him, Walt, to happiness. But the flute-player
felt that, come what might, they were, in fact, to be
parted for ever.

CHAPTER VIII

'I WONDER WHY?'

The Emperor had had a good deal to do with marrying and giving in marriage in the Empire of Surmer. One of the social and moral reforms he had endeavoured to bring about was that which should secure to young people the right of being consulted as to their own inclinations before they were formally and finally consigned to wedlock. The ordinary practice in Surmer was very much like that which prevails in certain Indian tribes—the family on either side arranged for the young man and the maiden, made it a matter of market bargain, settled it by compromise of price or otherwise, and then brought the pair together and married them. Ericson set his face against such a system, and tried to get a chance for the young people. He carried his influence so far that the parents on both sides among the official classes in the capital consulted him generally before taking any step, and then he frankly undertook the mediator's part, and found out whether the young woman liked the young man or not—whether she liked someone better or not. He had a sweet and kindly way with him which usually made both the youths and the maidens confidential—and he learned many a quiet heart-secret; and where he found that a suggested marriage would really not do, he told the parents as much, and they generally yielded to his influence and his authority. He had made happy many a pair of young lovers who, without his beneficent intervention, would have been doomed to 'spoil two houses,' as the old saying puts it.

Therefore, he did not feel much put out at the mere idea of intervening in another man's love affairs, or even the idea of carrying a proposal of marriage from another man.

Yet the Emperor was in somewhat thoughtful mood as he drove to Sir Rupert Langley's. He had taken much interest in Helena Langley. She had an influence over him which he told himself was only the influence of a clever child—told himself of this again and again. Yet there was a curious feeling of unfitness or dissatisfaction with the part he was going to play. Of course, he would do his very best for Hamilton. There was no man in the world for whom he cared half so much as he did for Hamilton. No—that is not putting it strongly enough—there was now no man in the world for whom he really cared but Hamilton. The Emperor's affections were curiously narrowed. He had almost no friends whom he really loved but Hamilton—and acquaintances were to him just all the same, one as good as another, and no better. He was a philanthropist by temperament, or nature, or nerve, or something; but while he would have risked his life for almost any man, and for any woman or child, he did not care in the least for social intercourse with men, women, and children in general. He could not talk to a child—children were a trouble to him, because he did not know what to say to them. Perhaps this was one reason why he was attracted by Helena Langley; she seemed so like the ideal child to whom one can talk. Then came up the thought in his mind—must he lose Hamilton if Miss Langley should consent to take him as her husband? Of course, Hamilton had declared that he would never marry until the Emperor and he had won back Surmer; but how long would that resolve last if Helena were to answer, Yes—and Now? The Emperor felt lonely as his cab stopped at Sir Rupert Langley's door.

'Is Miss Langley at home?'

Yes, Miss Langley was at home. Of course, the Emperor knew that she would be, and yet in his heart he could almost have wished to hear that she was out. There is a mood of mind in which one likes any postponement. But the duty of friendship had to be done—and the Emperor was sorry for everybody.

The Emperor was met in the hall by the footman, and also by To-to. To-to was Helena's black poodle. The black poodle took to all Helena's friends very readily. Whom she liked, he liked. He had his ways, like his mistress—and he at once allowed Ericson to understand not only that Helena was at home, but that Helena was sitting just then in her own room, where she habitually received her friends. The footman told the Emperor that Miss Langley was at home—To-to told him what the footman could not have ventured to do, that she was waiting for him in her own drawing-room, and ready to receive him.

Now, how did To-to contrive to tell him that? Very easily, in truth. To-to had a keen, healthy curiosity. He was always anxious to know what was going on. The moment he heard the bell ring at the great door he wanted to know who was coming in, and he ran down the stairs and stood in the hall to find out. When the door was opened, and the visitor appeared, To-to instantly made up his mind. If it was an unfamiliar figure, To-to considered it an introduction in which he had no manner of interest, and, without waiting one second, he scampered back to rejoin his mistress, and try to explain to her that there was some very uninteresting man or woman coming to call on her. But if it was somebody he knew, and whom he knew that his mistress knew, then there were two courses open to him. If Helena was not in her sitting room, To-to welcomed the visitor in the most friendly and hospitable way, and then fell into the background, and took no further notice, but ranged the premises carelessly and on his own account. If, however, his mistress were in her drawing room, then To-to invariably preceded the visitor up the stairs, going in front even of the footman, and ushered the new-comer into my lady's chamber. The process of reasoning on To-to's part must have been somewhat after this fashion. 'My business is to announce my lady's friends, the people whom I, with my exquisite intelligence, know to be people whom she wants to see. If I know that she is in her drawing-room ready to see them, then, of course, it is my duty and my pleasure to go before, and announce them. But if I know, having just been there, that she is not yet there, then I have no function to perform. It is the business of some other creature—her maid very likely—to receive the news from the footman that someone is waiting to see her. That is a complex process with which I have nothing to do.' The favoured visitor, therefore—the visitor, that is to say, whom To-to favoured, believing him or her to be favoured by To-to's mistress—had to pass through what may be called two portals, or ordeals. First, he had to ask of the servant whether Miss Langley was at home. Being informed that she was at home, then it depended on To-to to let the visitor know whether Miss Langley was actually in her drawing-room waiting to receive him, or whether he was to be shown into the drawing-room and told that Miss Langley would be duly informed of his presence, and asked if he would be good enough to take a chair and wait for a moment. Never was To-to known to make the slightest mistake about the actual condition of things. Never had he run up in advance of the Emperor when his mistress was not seated in her drawing-room ready to receive her visitor. Never had he remained lingering in the hall and the passages when Miss Langley was in her room, and prepared for the reception. Evidently, To-to regarded himself as Helena's special functionary. The other attendants and followers—footmen, maids, and such like—might be allowed the privilege of saying whether Miss Langley was or was not at home to receive visitors; but the special and quite peculiar function of To-to was to make it clear whether Miss Langley was or was not at that very moment waiting in her own particular drawing-room to welcome them.

So the Emperor, who had not much time to spare, being pressed with various affairs to attend to, was much pleased to find that To-to not merely welcomed him when the door was opened—a welcome which the Emperor would have expected from To-to's undisguised regard and even patronage—but that To-to briskly ran up the stairs in advance of the footman, and ran before him in through the drawing-room door when the footman had opened it. The Emperor loved the dog because of the creature's friendship for him and love for its mistress. The Emperor did not know how much he loved the dog because the dog was devoted to Helena Langley. On the stairs, as he went up, a sudden pang passed through the Emperor's heart. It might, perhaps, have brought him even clearer warning than it did. 'If I succeed in my mission'—it might have told him—'what is to become of *me*?' But, although the shot of pain did pass through him, he did not give it time to explain itself.

Helena was seated on a sofa. The moment she heard his name announced she jumped up and ran to meet him.

'I ought to have gone beyond the threshold,' she said, blushing, 'to meet my king.'

'So kind of you,' he said, rather stiffly, 'to stay in for me. You have so many engagements.'

'As if I would not give up any engagement to please you! And the very first time you expressed any wish to see me!'

'Well, I have come talk to you about something very serious.'

She looked up amazed, her bright eyes broadening with wonder.

'Something that concerns the happiness of yourself, perhaps—of another person certainly.'

She drooped her eyes now, and her colour deepened and her breath came quickly.

The Emperor went to the point at once.

'I am bad at prefaces,' he said, 'I come to speak to you on behalf of my dear young friend and comrade, Ernest Hamilton.'

'Oh!' She drew herself up and looked almost defiantly at him.

'Yes; he asked me to come and see you.'

'What have I to do with Mr Hamilton?'

'That you must teach me,' said Ericson, smiling rather sadly, and quoting from 'Hamlet.'

'I can teach you that very quickly—Nothing.'

'But you have not heard what I was going to say.'

'No. Well, you were quoting from Shakespeare—let me quote too. "Had I three ears I'd hear thee."' She drew herself back into her sofa. They were seated on the sofa side by side. He was leaning forward—she had drawn back. She was waiting in a sort of dogged silence.

'Hamilton is one of the noblest creatures I ever knew. He is my very dearest friend.'

A shade came over her face, and she shrugged her shoulders.

'I mean amongst men. I was not thinking of you.'

'No,' she answered, 'I am quite sure you were not thinking of me.'

She perversely pretended to misunderstand his meaning. He hardly noticed her words. 'Please go on,' she said, 'and tell me about Mr Hamilton.'

'He is in love with you,' the Emperor said in a soft low-voice, and as if he envied the man about whom that tale could be told.

'Oh!' she exclaimed impatiently, turning on the sofa as if in pain, 'I am sick of all this! Why can't a young man like one without making an idiot of himself and falling in love with one? Why can't we let each other be happy all in our own way? It is all so horribly mechanical! You meet a man two or three times, and you dance with him, and you talk with him, and perhaps you like him—perhaps you like him ever so much—and then in a moment he spoils the whole thing by throwing his ridiculous offer of marriage right in your face! Why on earth should I marry Mr Hamilton?'

'Don't take it too lightly, dear young lady—I know Hamilton to the very depth of his nature. This is a serious thing with him—he is not like the commonplace young masher of London society; when he feels, he feels deeply—I know what has been his personal devotion to myself.'

'Then why does he not keep to that devotion? Why does he desert his post? What does he want of me? What do I want of him? I liked him chiefly because he was devoted to you—and now he turns right round and wants to be devoted to me! Tell him from me that he was much better employed with his former devotion—tell him my advice was that he should stick to it.'

'You must give a more serious answer,' the Emperor said gravely.

'Why didn't he come himself?' she asked somewhat inconsequently, and going off on another tack at once. 'I can't understand how a man of any spirit can make advances by deputy.'

'Kings do sometimes,' the Emperor said.

Helena blushed again. Some thought was passing through her mind which was not in his. She had called him her king.

'Mr Hamilton is not a king,' she said almost angrily. She was on the point of blurting out, 'Mr Hamilton is not *my* king,' but she recovered herself in good time. 'Even if he were,' she went on, 'I should rather be proposed to in person as Katherine was by Henry the Fifth.'

'You take this all too lightly,' Ericson pleaded. 'Remember that this young man's heart and his future life are wrapped up in your answer, and in *you*.'

'Tell him to come himself and get his answer,' she said with a scornful toss of her head. Something had risen up in her heart which made her unkind.

'Miss Langley,' Ericson said gravely, 'I think it would have been much better if Hamilton had come himself and made his proposal, and argued it out with you for himself. I told him so, but he would not be advised. He is too modest and fearful, although, I tell you, I have seen more than once what pluck he has in danger. Yes, I have seen how cool, how elate he can be with the bullets and the bayonets of the enemy all at work about him. But he is timid with *you*—because he loves you.'

'"He either fears his fate too much——"' she began.

'You can't settle this thing by a quotation. I see that you are in a mood for quotations, and that shows that you are not very serious. I shall tell you why he asked me, and prevailed upon me, to come to you and speak for him. There is no reason why I should not tell you.'

'Tell me,' she said.

'I am old enough to have no hesitation in telling a girl of your age anything.'

'Again!' Helena said. 'I do wish you would let my age alone? I thought we had come to an honourable understanding to leave my age out of the question.'

'I fear it can't well be left out of this question. You see, what I was going to tell you was that Hamilton asked me to break this to you because he believes that I have great influence with you.'

'Of course, you know you have.'

'Yes—but there was more.'

'What more?' She turned her head away.

'He is under the impression that you would do anything I asked you to do.'

'So I would, and so I will!' she exclaimed impetuously. 'If you ask me to marry Mr Hamilton I will marry him! Yes—I *will*. If you, knowing what you do know, can wish your friend to marry me, and me to become his wife, I will accept his condescending offer! You know I do not love him—you know I never felt one moment's feeling of that kind for him—you know that I like him as I like twenty other young men—and not a bit more. You know this—at all events, you know it now when I tell you—and will you ask me to marry Mr Hamilton now?'

'But is this all true? Is this really how you feel to him?'

'Zwischen uns sei Wahrheit,' Helena said scornfully. 'Why should I deceive you? If I loved Mr Hamilton I could marry him, couldn't I?—seeing that he has sent you to ask me? I do not love him—I never could love him in that way. Now what do you ask me to do?'

'I am sorry for my poor young friend and comrade,' the Emperor answered sadly. 'I thought, perhaps, he might have had some reason to believe——'

'Did he tell you anything of the kind?'

'Oh, no, no; he is the last man in the world to say such a thing, or even to think it. One reason why he wished me to open the matter to you was that he feared, if he spoke to you about it himself, you would only laugh at him and refuse to give him a serious answer. He thought you would give me a serious answer.'

'What a very extraordinary and eccentric young man!'

'Indeed, he is nothing of the kind—although, of course, like myself, he has lived a good deal outside the currents of English feeling.'

'I should have thought,' she said gravely, 'that that was rather a question of the currents of common human feeling. Do the young women in Surmer like to be made wooed by delegation?'

'Would it have made any difference if he had come himself?'

'No difference in the world—now or at any other time. But remember, I am a very loyal subject, and I admit the right of my king to hand me over in marriage. If you tell me to marry Mr Hamilton, I will.'

'You are only jesting, Miss Langley, and this is not a jest.'

'I don't feel much in the mood for jesting,' she answered. 'It would rather seem as if I had been made the subject of a jest——'

'Oh, you must not say that,' he interposed in an almost angry tone. 'You can't, and don't, think that either of him or of me.'

'No, I don't; I could not think it of *you*—and no, I could not think it of him either. But you must admit that he has acted rather oddly.'

'And I too, I suppose?'

'Oh, you—well, of course, you were naturally thinking of the interest, or, at least, the momentary wishes, of your friend.'

'Of my two friends—you are my friend. Did we not swear an eternal friendship the other night?'

'Now you *are* jesting.'

'I am not; I am profoundly serious. I thought perhaps this might be for the happiness of both.'

'Did you ever see anything in me which seemed to make such an idea likely?'

'You see, I have known you but for so short a time.'

'People who are worth knowing at all are known at once or never known,' she said promptly and very dogmatically.

'Young ladies do not wear their hearts upon their sleeves.'

'I am afraid I do sometimes—too much,' she said.

'I thought it at least possible.'

'Now you *know*. Well, are you going to ask me to marry your friend Mr Hamilton?'

'No, indeed, Miss Langley. That would be a cruel injustice and wrong to him and to you. He must marry someone who loves him; you must marry someone whom you love. I am sorry for my poor friend—this will hurt him. But he cannot blame you, and I cannot blame you. He has some comfort—he has Surmer to fight for some day.'

'Put it nicely—*very* nicely to him,' Helena said, softening now that all was over. 'Tell him—won't you?—that I am ever so fond of him; and tell him that this must not make the least difference in our friendship. No one shall ever know from me.'

'I will put it all as well as I can,' said the Emperor; 'but I am afraid it must make a difference to him. It made a difference to me—when I was a young man of about his age.'

'You were disappointed?' Helena asked, in rather tremulous tone.

'More than that; I think I was deceived. I was ever so much worse off than Hamilton, for there was bitterness in my story, and there can be none in his. But I have survived—as you see.'

'Is—she—still living?'

'Oh, yes; she married for money and rank, and has got both, and I believe she is perfectly happy.'

'And have you recovered—quite?'

'Quite; I fancy it must have been an unreal sort of thing altogether. My wound is quite healed—does not give me even a passing moment of pain, as very old wounds sometimes do. But I am not going to lapse into the sentimental. It was only the thought of Hamilton that brought all this up.'

'You are not sentimental?' Helena asked.

'I have not had time to be. Anyhow, no woman ever cared about me—in that way, I mean—no, not one.'

'Ah, you never can tell,' Helena said gently. He seemed to her somehow, to have led a very lonely life; it came into her thoughts just then; she could not tell why. She was relieved when he rose to go, for she felt her sympathy for him beginning to be a little too strong, and she was afraid of betraying it. The interview had been a curious and a trying one for her. The Emperor left the room wondering how he could ever have been drawn into talking to a girl about the story of his lost love. 'That girl has a strange influence over me,' he thought. 'I wonder why?'

CHAPTER IX

THE PRIVATE SECRETARY

Soame Rivers was in some ways, and not a few, a model private secretary for a busy statesman. He was a gentleman by birth, bringing-up, appearance, and manners; he was very quick, adroit and clever; he had a wonderful memory, a remarkable faculty for keeping documents and ideas in order; he could speak French, German, Italian, and Spanish, and conduct a correspondence in these languages. He knew the political and other gossip of most or all of the European capitals, and of Washington and Cairo just as well. He could be interviewed on behalf of his chief, and could be trusted not to utter one single word of which his chief could not approve. He would see any undesirable visitor, and in five minutes talk him over into the belief that it was a perfect grief to the Minister to have to forego the pleasure of seeing him in person. He was to be trusted with any secret which concerned his position, and no power on earth could surprise him into any look or gesture from which anybody could conjecture that he knew more than he professed to know. He was a younger son of very good family, and although his allowance was not large, it enabled him, as a bachelor, to live an easy and gentlemanly life. He belonged to some good clubs, and he always dined out in the season. He had nice little chambers in the St. James's Street region, and, of course, he spent the greater part of every day in Sir Rupert's house, or in the lobby of the House of Commons. It was understood that he was to be provided with a seat in Parliament at the earliest possible opportunity, not, indeed, so much for the good of the State as for the convenience of his chief, who, naturally, found it unsatisfactory to have to go out into the lobby in order to get hold of his private secretary. Rivers was devoted to his chief in his own sort of way. That way was not like the devotion of Hamilton to the Emperor; for it is very likely that, in his own secret soul, Rivers occasionally made fun of Sir Rupert, with his Quixotic ideas and his sentimentalisms, and his views of life. Rivers had no views on the subject of life or of anything else. But Hamilton himself could not be more careful of his chief's interests than was Rivers. Rivers had no beliefs and no prejudices. He was not an immoral man, but he had no prejudice in favour of morality; he was not cruel, but he had no objection to other people being as cruel as they liked, as cruel as the law would allow them to be, provided that their cruelty was not exercised on himself, or any one he particularly cared about. He never in his life professed or felt one single impulse of what is called philanthropy. It was to him a matter of perfect indifference whether ten thousand people in some remote place did or did not perish by war, or fever, or cyclone, or inundation. Nor did he care in the least, except for occasional political purposes, about the condition of the poor in our rural villages or in the East End of London. He regarded the poor as he regarded the flies—that is, with entire indifference so long as they did not come near enough to annoy him. He did not care how they lived, or whether they lived at all. For a long time he could not bring himself to believe that Helena Langley really felt any strong interest in the poor. He could not believe that her professed zeal for their welfare was anything other than the graceful affectation of a pretty and clever girl.

But we all have our weaknesses, even the strongest of us, and Soame Rivers found, when he began to be much in companionship with Helena Langley, where the weak point was to be hit in his panoply of pride. To him love and affection and all that sort of thing were mere sentimental nonsense, encumbering a rising man, and as likely as not, if indulged in, to spoil his whole career. He had always made up his mind to the fact that, if he ever did marry, he must marry a woman with money. He would not marry at all unless he could have a house and entertain as other people in society were in the habit of doing. As a bachelor he was all right. He could keep nice chambers; he could ride in the Row; he could have a valet; he could wear good clothes—and he was a man whom Nature had meant, and tailor recognised, for one to show off good clothes. But if he should ever marry it was clear to him that he must have a house like other people, and that he must give dinner parties. He did not reason this out in his mind—he never reasoned anything out in his mind—it was all clear and self-evident to him. Therefore, after a while, the question began to arise—why should he not marry Helena Langley? He knew perfectly well that if she wished to be married to him Sir Rupert would not offer the slightest objection. Any man whom his daughter really loved Sir Rupert would certainly accept as a son-in-law. Rivers even fancied, not, perhaps, altogether without reason, that Sir Rupert personally would regard it as a convenient arrangement if his daughter were to fall in love with his secretary and get married to him. But above and beyond all this, Rivers, as a practical philosopher, had broken down, and he found himself in love with Helena Langley. For herself, Helena never suspected it. She had grown to be very fond of Soame Rivers. He seemed to fill for her exactly the part that a good-tempered brother might have done. Indeed, not any brother, however good-natured, would have been as attentive to a sister as Rivers was to her. He had a quiet, unobtrusive way of putting his personal attentions as part of his official duty which absolutely relieved Helena's mind of any idea of lover-like consideration. At many a dinner party or evening party her father had to leave her prematurely, and go down to the House of Commons. It became to her a matter of course that in such a case Rivers was always sure to be there to put her into her carriage and see that she got safely home. There was nothing in it. He was her father's secretary—a gentleman, to be sure; a man of social position, as good as the best; but still, her father's secretary looking after her because of his devotion to her father. She began to like him every day more and more for his devotion to her father. She did not at first like his cynical ways—his trick of making out that every great deed was really but a small one, that every seemingly generous and self-sacrificing action was actually inspired by the very principle of selfishness; that love of the poor, sympathy with the oppressed, were only with the better classes another mode of amusing a weary social life. But she soon made out a generous theory to satisfy herself on that point. Soame Rivers, she felt sure, put on that panoply of cynicism only to guard himself against the weakness of yielding to a futile sensibility. He was very poor, she thought. She had lordly views about money, and she thought a man without a country house of his own must needs be wretchedly poor, and she knew that Soame Rivers passed all his holiday seasons in the country houses of other people. Therefore, she made out that Soame Rivers was very poor; and, of course, if he was very poor, he could not lend much practical aid to those who, in the East End or otherwise, were still poorer than he. So she assumed that he put on the mask of cynicism to hide the flushings of sensibility. She told him as much; she said she knew that his affected indifference to the interests of humanity was only a disguise put on to conceal his real feelings. At first he used to laugh at her odd, pretty conceits. After a while he came to encourage her in the idea, even while formally assuring her that there was nothing in it, and that he did not care a straw whether the poor were miserable or happy.

Chance favoured him. There were some poor people whom Helena and her father were shipping off to New Zealand. Sir Rupert, without Helena's knowledge, asked his secretary to look after them the night of their going aboard, as he could not be there himself. Helena, without consulting her father, drove down to the docks to look after her poor friends, and there she found Rivers installed in the business of protector. He did the work well—as he did every work that came to his hand. The emigrants thought him the nicest gentleman they had ever known. Helena said to him, 'Come now! I have found you out at last.' And he only said, 'Oh, nonsense! this is nothing.' But he did not more directly contradict her theory, and he did not say her father had sent him—for he knew Sir Rupert would never say that of himself.

Rivers found himself every day watching over Helena with a deepening interest and anxiety. Her talk, her companionship, were growing to be indispensable to him. He did not pay her compliments—indeed, sometimes they rather sparred at one another in a pleasant schoolboy and schoolgirl sort of way. But she liked his society, and felt herself thoroughly companionable and comrade-like with him, and she never thought of concealing her liking. The result was that Soame Rivers began to think it quite on the cards that, if nothing should interpose, he might marry Helena Langley—and that, too, before very long. Then he should have in every way his heart's desire.

If nothing should interpose? Yes, but there was where the danger came in! If nothing should interpose? But was it likely that nothing and nobody would interpose? The girl was well known to be a rich heiress; she was the only child of a most distinguished statesman; she would be very likely to have Dukes and Marquises competing for her hand, and where might Soame Rivers be then? The young man sometimes thought that, if through her unconventional and somewhat romantic nature he could entangle her in a love affair, he might be able to induce her to get secretly married to him—before any of the possible Dukes and Marquises had time to put in a claim. But, of course, there would be always the danger of his turning Sir Rupert hopelessly against him by any trick of that kind, and he saw no use in having the daughter on his side if he could not also have the father. Besides, he had a sore conviction that the girl would not do anything to displease her father. So he gave up the idea of the romantic elopement, or the secret marriage, and he reminded himself that, after all, Helena Langley, with all her unconventional ways, was not exactly another Lydia Languish.

Then the Emperor and Hamilton came on the scene, and Rivers had many an unhappy hour of it. At first he was more alarmed about Hamilton than about the Emperor. He could easily understand an impulsive girl's hero-worship for the Emperor, and he did not think much about it. The Emperor, he assured himself, must seem quite an elderly sort of person to a girl of Helena's age; but Hamilton was young and handsome, of good family, and undoubtedly rich. Hamilton and Helena fraternised very freely and openly in their adoration for Ericson, and Rivers thought moodily that that partnership of admiration for a third person might very well end in a partnership of still closer admiration for each other. So, although from the very first he disliked the Emperor, yet he soon began to detest Hamilton a great deal more.

His dislike of Ericson was not exclusively and altogether because of Helena's hero-worship. According to his way of thinking, all foreign adventure had something more or less vulgar in it, but that was especially objectionable in the case of an Englishman. What business had an Englishman—one who claims apparently to be an

English gentleman—what business had he with a lot of South American Empireans? What did he want among such people? Why should he care about them? Why should he want to govern them? And if he did want to govern them, why did he not stay there and govern? The thing was in any case mere bravado, and melodramatic enterprise.

It was the morning after the day when the Emperor had proposed to Helena for poor Hamilton. Soame Rivers met Helena on the staircase.

'Of course,' he said, with an emphasis, '*you* will be at luncheon today?'

'Why, of course?' she asked, carelessly.

'Well—your hero is coming—didn't you know?'

'I didn't know; and who is my hero?'

'Oh, come now!—the Emperor, of course.'

'*Is* he coming?' she asked, with a sudden gleam of genuine emotion flashing over her face.

'Yes; your father particularly wants him to meet Sir Lionel Rainey.'

'Oh, I didn't know. Well, yes—I shall be there, I suppose, if I feel well enough.'

'Are you not well?' Rivers asked, with a tone of somewhat artificial tenderness in his voice.

'Oh, yes, I am all right; but I might not feel quite up to the level of Sir Lionel Rainey. Only men, of course?'

'Only men.'

'Well, I shall think it over.'

'But you can't want to miss your Emperor?'

'My Emperor will probably not miss me,' the girl said in scornful tones which brought no comfort to the heart of Soame Rivers.

'You would be very sorry if he did not miss you,' Soame Rivers said blunderingly. Your cynical man of the world has his feelings and his angers.

'Very sorry!' Helena defiantly declared.

The Emperor came punctually at two—he was always punctual. To-to was friendly, but did not conduct him. He was shown at once into the dining-room, where luncheon was laid out. The room looked lonely to the Emperor. Helena was not there.

'My daughter is not coming down to luncheon,' Sir Rupert said.

'I am so sorry,' the Emperor said. 'Nothing serious, I hope?'

'Oh, no!—a cold, or something like that—she didn't tell me. She will be quite well, I hope, tomorrow. You see how To-to keeps her place.'

Ericson then saw that To-to was seated resolutely on the chair which Helena usually occupied at luncheon.

'But what is the use if she is not coming?' the Emperor suggested—not to disparage the intelligence of To-to, but only to find out, if he could, the motive of that undoubtedly sagacious animal's taking such a definite attitude.

'Well, To-to does not like the idea of anyone taking Helena's place except himself. Now, you will see;

when we all settle down, and no one presumes to try for that chair, To-to will quietly drop out of it and allow the remainder of the performance to go undisturbed. He doesn't want to set up any claim to sit on the chair himself; all he wants is to assert and to protect the right of Helena to have that chair at any moment when she may choose to join us at luncheon.'

The rest of the party soon came in from various rooms and consultations. Soame Rivers was the first.

'Miss Langley not coming?' he said, with a glance at To-to.

'No,' Sir Rupert answered. 'She is a little out of sorts today—nothing much—but she won't come down just yet.'

'So To-to keeps her seat reserved, I see.'

The Emperor felt in his heart as if he and To-to were born to be friends.

The other guests were Lord Courtreeve and Sir Lionel Rainey, the famous Englishman, who had settled himself down at the Court of the King of Siam, and taken in hand the railway and general engineering and military and financial arrangements of that monarch; and, having been somewhat hurt in an expedition against the Black Flags, was now at home, partly for rest and recovery, and partly in order to have an opportunity of enlightening his Majesty of Siam, who had a very inquiring mind, on the immediate condition of politics and house-building in England. Sir Lionel said that, above all things, the King of Siam would be interested in learning something about Ericson and the condition of Surmer, for the King of Siam read everything he could get hold of about politics everywhere. Therefore, Sir Rupert had undertaken to invite the Emperor to this luncheon, and the Emperor had willingly undertaken to come. Soame Rivers had been showing Sir Lionel over the house, and explaining all its arrangements to him—for the King of Siam had thoughts of building a palace after the fashion of some first-class and up-to-date house in London. Sir Lionel was a stout man, rather above the middle height, but looking rather below it, because of his stoutness. He had a sharply turned-up dark moustache, and purpling cheeks and eyes that seemed too tightly fitted into the face for their own personal comfort.

Lord Courtreeve was a pale young man, with a very refined and delicate face. He was a member of the London County Council, and was a chairman of a County Council in his own part of the country. He was a strong advocate of Local Option, and wore at his courageous buttonhole the blue ribbon which proclaimed his devotion to the cause of temperance. He was an honoured and a sincere member of the League of Social Purity. He was much interested in the increase of open spaces and recreation grounds for the London poor. He was an unaffectedly good young man, and if people sometimes smiled quietly at him, they respected him all the same. Soame Rivers had said of him that Providence had invented him to be the chief living argument in favour of the principle of hereditary legislation.

Sir Lionel Rainey and Lord Courtreeve did not get on at all. Sir Lionel had too many odd and high-flavoured anecdotes about life in Siam to be a congenial neighbour for the champion of social purity. He had a way, too, of referring everything to the lower instincts of man, and roughly declining to reckon in the least idea of any of man's, or woman's, higher qualities. Therefore, the Emperor did not take to him any more than Lord Courtreeve did; and Sir Rupert began to think that his luncheon party was not well mixed. Soame Rivers saw it too, and was determined to get the company out of Siam.

'Do you find London society much changed since you were here last, Sir Lionel?' he asked.

'Didn't come to London to study society,' Sir Lionel answered, somewhat gruffly, for he thought there was much more to be said about Siam. 'I mean in that sort of way. I want to get some notions to take back to the King of Siam.'

'But might it not interest his Majesty to know of any change, if there were any, in London society during that time?' Rivers blandly asked.

'No, sir. His Majesty never was in England, and he could not be expected to take any interest in the small and superficial changes made in the tone or the talk of society during a few years. You might as well expect him to be interested in the fact that whereas when I was here last the ladies wore eel-skin dresses, now they wear full skirts, and some of them, I am told, wear a divided skirt.'

'But I thought such changes of fashion might interest the King,' Rivers remarked with an elaborate meekness.

'The King, sir, does not care about divided skirts,' Sir Lionel answered, with scorn and resentment in his voice.

'I must confess,' the Emperor said, glad to be free of Siam, 'that I have been much interested in observing the changes that have been made in the life of England—I mean in the life of London—since I was living here.'

'We have all got so Empirean,' Sir Rupert said sadly.

'And we all profess to be Socialists,' Soame Rivers added.

'There is much more done for the poor than ever there was before,' Lord Courtreeve pleaded.

'Because so many of the poor have got votes,' Rivers observed.

'Yes,' Sir Lionel struck in with a laugh, 'and you fellows all want to get into the House of Commons or the County Council, or some such place. By Jove! in my time a gentleman would not want to become a County Councillor.'

'I am not troubling myself about English politics,' the Emperor said. 'I do not care to vex myself about them. I should probably only end by forming opinions quite different from some of my friends here, and, as I have no mission for English political life, what would be the good of that? But I am much interested in English social life, and even in what is called Society. Now, what I want to know is how far does society in London represent social London, and still more, social England?'

'Not the least in the world,' Sir Rupert promptly replied.

'I am not quite so sure of that,' Soame Rivers interposed, 'I fancy most of the fellows try to take their tone from us.'

'I hope not,' the Emperor said.

'So do I,' added Sir Rupert emphatically; 'and I am quite certain they do not. What on earth do you know about it, Rivers?' he asked almost sharply.

'Why shouldn't I know all about it, if I took the trouble to find out?' Rivers answered languidly.

'Yes, yes. Of course you could,' Sir Rupert said benignly, correcting his awkward touch of anger as a painter corrects some sudden mistake in drawing. 'I didn't mean in the least to disparage your faculty of acquiring correct information on any subject. Nobody appreciates more than I do what you are capable of in that way—nobody has had so much practical experience of it. But what I mean is this—that I don't think you know a great deal of English social life outside the West End of London.'

'Is there anything of social life worth knowing to be known outside the West End of London?' Soame Rivers asked.

'Well, you see, the mere fact that you put the question shows that you can't do much to enlighten Mr Ericson on the one point about which he asks for some enlightenment. He has been out of England for a great many years, and he finds some fault with our ways—or, at least, he asks for some explanation about them.'

'Yes, quite so. I am afraid I have forgotten the point on which Mr Ericson desired to get information.' And Rivers smiled a bland smile without looking at Ericson. 'May I trouble you, Lord Courtreeve, for the cigarettes?'

'It was not merely a point, but a whole cresset of points—a cluster of points,' Ericson said, 'on every one of which I wished to have a tip of light. Is English social life to be judged of by the conversation and the canons of opinion which we find received in London society?'

'Certainly not,' Sir Rupert explained.

'Heaven forbid!' Lord Courtreeve added fervently.

'I don't quite understand,' said Soame Rivers.

'Well,' the Emperor explained, 'what I mean is this. I find little or nothing prevailing in London society but cheap cynicism—the very cheapest cynicism—cynicism at a farthing a yard or thereabouts. We all admire healthy cynicism—cynicism with a great reforming and purifying purpose—the cynicism that is like a corrosive acid to an evil system; but this West End London sham cynicism—what does that mean?'

'I don't quite know what you mean,' Soame Rivers said.

'I mean this, wherever you go in London society—at all events, wherever I go—I notice a peculiarity that I think did not exist, at all events to such an extent, in my younger days. Everything is taken with easy ridicule. A divorce case is a joke. Marriage is a joke. Love is a joke. Patriotism is a joke. Everybody is assumed, as a matter of course, to have a selfish motive in everything. Is this the real feeling of London society, or is it only a fashion, a sham, a grimace?'

'I think it is a very natural feeling,' Soame Rivers replied, with the greatest promptitude.

'And represents the true feeling of what are called the better classes of London?'

'Why, certainly.'

'I think the thing is detestable, anyhow,' Lord Courtreeve interposed, 'and I am quite sure it does not represent the tone of English society.'

'So am I,' Sir Rupert added.

'But you must admit that it is the tone which does prevail,' the Emperor said pressingly, for he wanted very much to study this question down to its roots.

'I am afraid it is the prevailing social tone of London—I mean the West End,' Sir Rupert admitted reluctantly. 'But you know what a fashion there is in these things, as well as in others. The fashion in a woman's gown or a man's hat does not always represent the shape of a woman's body or the size of a man's head.'

'It sometimes represents the shape of the man's mind, and the size of the woman's heart,' said Rivers.

'Well, anyhow,' Sir Rupert persevered, 'we all know that a great deal of this sort of talk is talked for want of anything else to say, and because it amuses most people, and because anybody can talk cheap cynicism; I believe that London society is healthy at the core.'

'But come now—let us understand?' Ericson asked; 'how can the society be healthy at the core for which you yourself make the apology by saying that it parrots the jargon of a false and loathsome creed because it has nothing better to say, or because it hopes to be thought witty by parroting it? Come, Sir Rupert, you won't maintain that?'

'I will maintain,' Sir Rupert said, 'that London society is not as bad as it seems.'

'Oh, well, I have no doubt you are right in that,' the Emperor hastily replied. 'But what I think so melancholy to see is that degeneracy of social life in England—I mean in London—which apes a cynicism it doesn't feel.'

'But I think it does feel it,' Rivers struck in; 'and very naturally and justly.'

'Then you think London society is really demoralised?' the Emperor spoke, turning on him rather suddenly.

'I think London society is just what is has always been,' Rivers promptly answered.

'Corrupt and cynical?'

'Well, no. I should rather say corrupt and candid.'

'If that is London society, that certainly is not English social life,' Lord Courtreeve declared emphatically, patting the table with his hand. 'It isn't even London social life. Come down to the East End, sir——'

'Oh, indeed, by Jove! I shall do nothing of the kind!' Rivers replied, as with a shudder. 'I think, of all the humbugs of London society, slumming is about the worst.'

'I was not speaking of that,' Lord Courtreeve said, with a slight flush on his mild face. 'Perhaps I do not think very differently from you about some of it—some of it—although, Heaven be praised, not about all; but what I mean and was going to say when I was interrupted'—and he looked with a certain modified air of reproach at Rivers—'what I was going to say when I was interrupted,' he repeated, as if to make sure that he was not going to be interrupted this time—'was, that if you would go down to the East End with me, I could show you in one day plenty of proofs that the heart of the English people is as sound and true as ever it was——'

'Very likely,' Rivers interposed saucily. 'I never said it wasn't.'

Lord Courtreevo gaped with astonishment.

'I don't quite grasp your meaning,' he stammered.

'I never said,' Soame Rivers replied deliberately, 'that the heart of the English people was not just as sound and true now as ever it was—I dare say it is just about the same—*même jeu*, don't you know?' and he took a languid puff at his cigarette.

'Am I to be glad or sorry of your answer?' Lord Courtreeve asked, with a stare.

'How can I tell? It depends on what you want me to say.'

'Well, if you mean to praise the great heart of the English people now, and at other times——'

'Oh dear, no; I mean nothing of the kind.'

'I say, Rivers, this is all bosh, you know,' Sir Rupert struck in.

'I think we are all shams and frauds in our set—in our class,' Rivers said, composedly; 'and we are well brought up and educated and all that, don't you know? I really can't see why some cads who clean windows, or drive omnibuses, or sell vegetables in a donkey-cart, or carry bricks up a ladder, should be any better than we. Not a bit of it—if we are bad, they are worse, you may put your money on that.'

'Well I think I have had my answer,' the Emperor said, with a smile.

'And what is your interpretation of the Oracle's answer?' Rivers asked.

'I should have to interpret the Oracle itself before I could be clear as to the meaning of its answer,' Ericson said composedly.

Soame Rivers knew pretty well by the words and by the tone that if he did not like the Emperor, neither did the Emperor very much like him.

'You must not mind Rivers and his cynicism,' Sir Rupert said, intervening somewhat hurriedly; 'he doesn't mean half he says.'

'Or say half he means,' Rivers added.

'But, as I was telling you, about the police organisation of Siam,' Sir Lionel broke out anew.

And this time the others went back without resistance to a few moments more of Siam.

CHAPTER X

A SOLDIER OF FORTUNE

Captain Oisin Sarrasin came one morning to see the Emperor by appointment.

Captain Oisin Sarrasin had described himself in his letter to the Emperor as a soldier of fortune. So he was indeed, but there are soldiers and soldiers of fortune. He was not the least in the world like the Orlando the Fearless, who is described in Lord Lytton's 'Rienzi,' and who cared only for his steed and his sword and his lady the peerless. Or, rather, he was like him in one respect—he did care for his lady the peerless. But otherwise Captain Oisin Sarrasin resembled in no way the traditional soldier of fortune, the Dugald Dalgetty, the Condottiere, the 'Heaven's Swiss' even. Captain Sarrasin was terribly in earnest, and would not lend the aid of his bright sword to any cause which he did not believe to be the righteous cause, and, owing to the nervous peculiarities of his organisation, it was generally the way of Captain Sarrasin to regard the weaker cause as the righteous cause. That was his ruling inclination. When he entered as a volunteer the Federal ranks in the great American war, he knew very well that he was entering on the side of the stronger. He was not blinded in the least, as so many Englishmen were, by the fact that in the first instance the Southerners won some battles. He knew the country from end to end, and he knew perfectly well what must be the outcome of such a struggle. But then he went in to fight for the emancipation of the negroes, and he knew that they were the weakest of all the parties engaged in the controversy, and so he struck in for them.

He was a man of about forty-eight years of age, and some six feet in height. He was handsome, strong, and sinewy—all muscles and flesh, and no fat. He had a deep olive complexion and dark-brown hair and eyes—eyes that in certain lights looked almost black.

He was a silent man habitually, but given anything to talk about in which he felt any interest and he could talk on for ever.

Unlike the ordinary soldier of fortune, he was not in the least thrasonical. He hardly ever talked of himself—he hardly ever told people of where he had been and what campaigns he had fought in. He looked soldierly; but the soldier in him did not really very much overbear the demeanour of the quiet, ordinary gentleman. At the moment he is a leader-writer on foreign subjects for a daily newspaper in London, and is also retained on the staff in order that he may give advice as to the meaning of names and places and allusions in late foreign telegrams. There is a revolution, say, in Burmah or Patagonia, and a late telegram comes in and announces in some broken-kneed words the bare fact of the crisis. Then the editor summons Captain Sarrasin, and Sarrasin quietly explains:—'Oh, yes, of course; I knew that was coming this long time. The man at the head of affairs was totally incompetent. I gave him my advice many a time. Yes, it's all right. I'll write a few sentences of explanation, and we shall have fuller news tomorrow.' And he would write his few sentences of explanation, and the paper he wrote for would come out next morning with the only intelligible account of what had happened in the far-off country.

The Emperor did not know it at the time, but it was certain that Captain Sarrasin's description of the rising in Surmer and the expulsion of Surmer's former chief had done much to secure a favourable reception of Ericson in London. The night when the news of the struggle and the defeat came to town no newspaper man knew anything in the world about it but Oisin Sarrasin. The tendency of the English Press is always to go in for foreign revolutions. It saves trouble, for one thing. Therefore, all the London Press except the one paper to which Oisin Sarrasin contributed assumed, as a matter of course, that the revolution in Surmer was a revolution against tyranny, or priestcraft, or corruption, or what not—and Oisin Sarrasin alone explained that it was a revolution against reforms too enlightened and too advanced—a revolution of corruption against healthy civilisation and purity—of stagnation against progress—of the system comfortable to corrupt judges and to wealthy suitors, and against judicial integrity. It was pointed out in Captain Sarrasin's paper that this was the sort of revolution which had succeeded for the moment in turning out the Englishman Ericson—and the other papers, when they came to look into the matter, found that Captain Sarrasin's version of the story was about right—and in a few days all the papers when they came out were glorifying the heroic Englishman who had endeavoured so nobly to reorganise the Empire of Surmer on the exalted principles of the British Constitution, and had for the time lost his place and his power in the generous effort. Then the whole Press of London rallied round the Emperor, and the Emperor became a splendid social success.

Oisin Sarrasin had been called to the English bar and to the American bar. He seemed to have done almost everything that a man could do, and to have been almost everywhere that a man could be. Yet, as we have said, he seldom talked of where he had been or what he had done. He did not parade himself—he was found out. He never paraded his intimate knowledge of Russia, but he happened at Constantinople one day to sit next to Sir Mackenzie Wallace at a dinner party, and to get into talk with him, and Sir Mackenzie went about everywhere the next day telling everybody that Captain Sarrasin knew more about the inner life of Russia than any other Englishman he had ever met. It was the same with Stanley and Africa—the same with Lesseps and Egypt—the same with South America and the late Emperor of Brazil, to whom Captain Sarrasin was presented at Cannes. There was a story to the effect that he had lived for some time among the Indian tribes of the Wild West—and Sarrasin had been questioned on the subject, and only smiled, and said he had lived a great many lives in his time—and people did not believe the story. But it was certain that at the time when the Wild West Show first opened in London, Oisin Sarrasin went to see it, and that Red Shirt, the fighting chief of the Sioux nations, galloping round the barrier, happened to see Sarrasin, suddenly wheeled his horse, and drew up and greeted Sarrasin in the Sioux dialect, and hailed him as his dear old comrade, and talked of past adventures, and that Sarrasin responded, and that they had for a few minutes an eager conversation. It was certain, too, that Colonel Cody (Buffalo Bill), noticing the conversation, brought his horse up to the barrier, and, greeting Sarrasin with the friendly way of an old comrade, said in a tone heard by all who were near, 'Why, Captain, you don't come out our way in the West as often as you used to do.' Sarrasin could talk various languages, and his incredulous friends sometimes laid traps for him. They brought him into contact with Richard Burton, or Professor Palmer, hoping in their merry moods to enjoy some disastrous results. But Burton only said in the end, 'By Jupiter, what a knowledge of Asiatic languages that fellow has!' And Palmer declared that Sarrasin ought to be paid by the State to teach our British officers all the dialects of some of the East Indian provinces. In a chance mood of talkativeness, Sarrasin had mentioned the fact that he spoke modern Greek. A good-natured friend invited him to a dinner party with Mr Gennadius, the Greek Minister in London, and presented him as one who was understood to be acquainted with modern Greek. The two had much conversation together after dinner was over, and great curiosity was felt by the sceptical friends as to the result. Mr Gennadius being questioned, said, 'Oh, well, of course he speaks Greek perfectly, but I should have known by his accent here and there that he was not a born Greek.'

The truth was that Oisin Sarrasin had seen too much in life—seen too much of life—of places, and peoples, and situations, and so had got his mind's picture painted out. He had started in life too soon, and overclouded himself with impressions. His nature had grown languorous under their too rich variety. His own extraordinary experiences seemed commonplace to him; he seemed to assume that all men had gone through just the like. He had seen too much, read too much, been too much. Life could hardly present him with anything which had not already been a familiar object or thought to him. Yet he was always on the quiet look-out for some new principle, some new cause, to stir him into activity. He had nothing in him of the used-up man—he was curiously the reverse of the type of the used-up man. He was quietly delighted with all he had seen and done, and he still longed to add new sights and doings to his experiences, but he could not easily discover where to find them. He did not crave merely for new sensations. He was on the whole a very self-sufficing man—devoted to his wife as she was devoted to him. He could perfectly well have done without new sensations. But he had a kind of general idea that he ought to be always doing something for some cause or somebody, and for a certain time he had not seen any field on which to develop his Don Quixote instincts. The coming of Ericson to London reminded him of the Empire of Surmer, and of the great reforms that were only too great, and, as we have said, he wrote Ericson up in his newspaper.

Captain Sarrasin had a home in the far southern suburbs, but he had lately taken a bedroom in Paulo's Hotel. The moment Captain Sarrasin entered the room the Emperor remembered that he had seen him before. The Emperor never forgot faces, but he could not always put names to them, and he was a little surprised to find that he and the soldier of fortune had met already.

He advanced to meet his visitor with the smile of singular sweetness which was so attractive to all those on whom it beamed. The Emperor's sweet smile was as much a part of his success in life—and of his failure, too, perhaps—as any other quality about him—as his nerve, or his courage, or his good temper, or his commander-in-chief sort of genius.

'We have met before, Captain Sarrasin,' he said. 'I remember seeing you in Surmer—I am not mistaken, surely?'

'I was in Surmer,' Captain Sarrasin answered, 'but I left long before the outbreak of the revolution. I remained there a little time. I think I saw even then what was coming. I am on your side altogether.'

'Yes, so you were good enough to tell me. Well, have you heard any late news? You know how my heart is bound up with the fortunes of Surmer?'

'I know very well, and I think I do bring you some news. It is all going to pieces in Surmer without you.'

'Going to pieces—how can that be?'

'The Empire is torn asunder by faction, and she is going to be annexed by her big neighbour.'

'The new Republic of Orizaba?'

This was a vast South American state which started into political existence as an empire and had shaken off its emperor—sent him home to Europe—and had set up as a Republic of a somewhat aggressive order.

'Yes, Orizaba, of course.'

'But do you really believe, Captain Sarrasin, that Orizaba has any actual intentions of that kind?'

'I happen to know it for certain,' Captain Sarrasin grimly replied.

'How do you know it, may I ask?'

'Because I have had letters offering me a command in the expedition to cross the frontier of Surmer.'

The Emperor looked straight into the eyes of Captain Sarrasin. They were mild, blue, fearless eyes. Ericson read nothing there that he might not have read in the eyes of Sarrasin's quiet, scholarly, untravelled brother.

'Captain Sarrasin,' he said, 'I am an odd sort of person, and always have been—can't help myself in fact. Do you mind my feeling your pulse?'

'Not in the least,' Sarrasin gravely answered, with as little expression of surprise about him as if Ericson had asked him whether he did not think the weather was very fine. He held out a strong sinewy and white wrist. Ericson laid his finger on the pulse.

'Your pulse as mine,' he said, 'doth temperately keep time, and makes as healthful music.'

Captain Sarrasin's face lighted.

'You are a Shakespearian?' he said eagerly. 'I am so glad. I am an old-fashioned person, and I love Shakespeare; that is only another reason why——'

'Go on, Captain Sarrasin.'

'Why I want to go along with you.'

'But do you want to go along with me, and where?'

'To Surmer, of course. You have not asked me why I refused to give my services to Orizaba.'

'No; I assumed that you did not care to be the mercenary of an invasion.'

'Mercenary? No, it wasn't quite that. I have been a mercenary in many parts of the world, although I never in my life fought on what I did not believe to be the right side. That's how it comes in here—in your case. I told the Orizaba people who wrote to me that I firmly believed you were certain to come back to Surmer, and that if the sword of Oisin Sarrasin could help you that sword was at your disposal.'

'Captain Sarrasin,' the Emperor said, 'give me your hand.'

Captain Sarrasin was a pretty strong man, but the grip of the Emperor almost made him wince.

'When you make up your mind to go back,' Captain Sarrasin said, 'let me know. I'll go with you.'

'If this is really going on,' the Emperor said meditatively—'if Orizaba is actually going to make war on Surmer—well, I *must* go back. I think Surmer would welcome me under such conditions—at such a crisis. I do not see that there is any other man——'

'There is no other man,' Sarrasin said. 'Of course one doesn't know what the scoundrels who are in office now might do. They might arrest you and shoot you the moment you landed—they are quite capable of it.'

'They are, I dare say,' the Emperor said carelessly. 'But I shouldn't mind that—I should take my chance,' And then the sudden thought went to his heart that he should dislike death now much more than he would have done a few weeks ago. But he hastened to repeat, 'I should take my chance.'

'Of course, of course,' said Sarrasin, quite accepting the Emperor's remark as a commonplace and self-evident matter of fact. 'I'll take *my* chance too. I'll go along with you, and so will my wife.'

'Your wife?'

'Oh, yes, my wife. She goes everywhere with me.'

The face of the Emperor looked rather blank. He did not quite see the appropriateness of petticoats in actual warfare—unless, perhaps, the short petticoats of a *vivandière*; and he hoped that Captain Sarrasin's wife was not a *vivandière*.

'You see,' Sarrasin said cheerily, 'my wife and I are very fond of each other, and our one little child is long since dead, and we have nobody else to care much about. And she is a tall woman, nearly as tall as I am, and she dresses up as my *aide-de-camp*; and she has gone with me into all my fights. And we find it so convenient that if ever I should get killed, then, of course, she would manage to get killed too, and *vice versâ—vice versâ*, of course. And that would be so convenient, don't you see? We are so used to each other, one of us couldn't get on alone.'

The Emperor felt his eyes growing a little moist at this curious revelation of conjugal affection.

'May I have the honour soon,' he asked, 'of being presented to Mrs Sarrasin?'

'Mrs Sarrasin, sir,' said her husband, 'will come whenever she is asked or sent for. Mrs Sarrasin will regard it as the highest honour of her life to be allowed to serve upon your staff with me.'

'Has she been with you in all your campaigns?' Ericson asked.

'In all what I may call my irregular warfare, certainly,' Captain Sarrasin answered. 'When first we married I was in the British service, sir; and of course they wouldn't allow anything of the kind there. But after that I gave up the English army—there wasn't much chance of any real fighting going on—and I served in all sorts of odd irregular campaignings, and Mrs Sarrasin found out that she preferred to be with me—and so from that time we fought, as I may say, side by side. She has been wounded more than once—but she doesn't mind. She is not the woman to care about that sort of thing. She is a very remarkable woman.'

'She must be,' the Emperor said earnestly. 'When shall I have the chance of seeing her? When may I call on her?'

'I hardly venture to ask it,' Captain Sarrasin said; 'but would you honour us by dining with us—any day you have to spare?'

'I shall be delighted,' the Emperor replied. 'Let us find a day. May I send for my secretary?'

Mr Hamilton was sent for and entered, bland and graceful as usual, but with a deep sore at his heart.

'Hamilton, how soon have I a free day for dining with Captain Sarrasin, who is kind enough to ask me?'

Hamilton referred to his engagement-book.

'Saturday week is free. That is, it is not filled up. You have seven invitations, but none of them has yet been accepted.'

'Refuse them all, please; I shall dine with Captain Sarrasin.'

'If Mr Hamilton will also do me the pleasure——' the kindly captain began.

'No, I am afraid I cannot allow him,' the Emperor answered. 'He is sure to have been included in some of these invitations, and we must diffuse ourselves as much as we can. He must represent me somewhere. You see, Captain Sarrasin, it is only in obedience to Hamilton's policy that I have consented to go to any of these smart dinner parties at all, and he must really bear his share of the burden which he insists on imposing upon me.'

'All right; I'm game,' Hamilton said.

'He likes it, I dare say,' Ericson said. 'He is young and fresh and energetic, and he is fond of mashing on to young and pretty women—and so the dinner parties give him pleasure. It will give me sincere pleasure to dine with Mrs Sarrasin and you, and we'll leave Hamilton to his countesses and marchionesses. But don't think too badly of him, Captain Sarrasin, for all that: he is so young. If there is a fight to go on in Surmer he'll be there with you and me—you may depend on that.'

'But is there any chance of a fight going on?' Hamilton asked, looking up from his papers with flushing face and sparkling eyes.

'Captain Sarrasin thinks that there is a good chance of something of the kind, and he offers to be with us. He has certain information that there is a scheme on foot in Orizaba for the invasion and annexation of Surmer.'

Hamilton leaped up in delight.

'By Jove!' he exclaimed, 'that would be the one chance to rally all that is left of the national and the patriotic in Surmer! Hip, hip, hurrah!—one cheer more—hurrah!' And the usually demure Hamilton actually danced then and there, in his exultation, some steps of a music-hall breakdown. His face was aflame with delight. The Emperor and Sarrasin both looked at him with an expression of sympathy and admiration. But there were different feelings in the breasts of the two sympathising men. Sarrasin was admiring the manly courage and spirit of the young man, and in his admiration there was that admixture of melancholy, of something like compassion, with which middle-age regards the enthusiasm of youth.

With the Emperor's admiration was blended the full knowledge that, amid all Hamilton's sincere delight in the prospect of again striking a blow for Surmer, there was a suffused delight in the sense of sudden lightening of pain—the sense that while fighting for Surmer he would be able, in some degree, to shake off the burden of his unsuccessful love. In the wild excitement of the coming struggle he might have a chance of now and then forgetting how much he loved Helena Langley and how she did not love him.

CHAPTER XI

HELENA

Love, according to the Greek proverb quoted by Plutarch, is the offspring of the rainbow and the west wind, that delicious west wind, so full of hope and youth in all its breathings—that rainbow that we may, if we will, pursue for ever, and which we shall never overtake. Helena Langley, although she was a fairly well-read girl, had probably never heard of the proverb, but there was something in her mood of mind at present that might seem to have sprung from the conjunction of the rainbow and the west wind. She was exalted out of herself by her feelings—the west wind breathed lovingly on her—and yet she saw that the rainbow was very far off. She was beginning to admit to herself that she was in love with the Emperor—at all events, that she was growing more and more into love with him; but she could not see that he was at all likely to be in love with her. She was a spoilt child; she had all the virtues and no doubt some of the defects of the spoilt child. She had always been given to understand that she would be a great match—that anybody would be delighted to marry her—that she might marry anyone she pleased provided she did not take a fancy to a royal prince, and that she must be very careful not to let herself be married for her money alone. She knew that she was a handsome girl, and she knew, too, that she had got credit for being clever and a little eccentric—for being a girl who was privileged to be unconventional, and to say what she pleased and whatever came into her head. She enjoyed the knowledge of the fact that she was allowed to speak out her mind, and that people would put up with things from her which they would not put up with from other girls. The knowledge did not make her feel cynical—it only made her feel secure. She was not a reasoning girl; she loved to follow her own impulses, and had the pleased conviction that they generally led her right.

Now, however, it seemed to her that things had not been going right with her, and that she had her own impulses all to blame. She had taken a great liking to Mr Hamilton, and she had petted him and made much of him, and probably got talked of with him, and all the time she never had the faintest idea that he was likely to misunderstand her feelings towards him. She thought he would know well enough that she admired him and was friendly and free with him because he was the devoted follower of the Emperor. And at first she regarded the Emperor himself only as the chief of a cause which she had persuaded herself to recognise and talked herself into regarding as *her* cause. Therefore it had not occurred to her to think that Hamilton would not be quite satisfied with the friendliness which she showed to him as the devoted follower of their common leader. She went on the assumption that they were sworn and natural comrades, Hamilton and herself, bound together by the common bond of servitude to the Emperor. All this dream had been suddenly shattered by the visit of Ericson, and the curious mission on which he had come. Helena felt her cheeks flushing up again and again as she thought of it. It had told her everything. It had shown her what a mistake she had made when she lavished so much of her friendly attentions on

Hamilton—and what a mistake she had made when she failed to understand her own feelings about the Emperor. The moment he spoke to her of Hamilton's offer she knew at a flash how it was with her. The burst of disappointment and anger with which she found that he had come there to recommend to her the love of another man was a revelation that almost dazzled her by its light. What had she said, what had she done? she now kept asking herself. Had she betrayed her secret to him, just at the very moment when it had first betrayed itself to her? Had she allowed him to guess that she loved him? Her cheeks kept reddening again and again at the terrible suspicion. What must he think of her? Would he pity her? Would he wonder at her—would he feel shocked and sorry, or only gently mirthful? Did he regard her only as a more or less precocious child? What had she said—how had she looked—had her eyes revealed her, or her trembling lips, or her anger, or the tone of her voice? A young man accustomed to ways of abstinence is tempted one sudden night into drinking more champagne than is good for him, and in a place where there are girls, where there is one girl in whose eyes above all others he wishes to seem an admirable and heroic figure. He gets home all right—he is apparently in possession of all his senses; but he has an agonised doubt as to what he may have said or done while the first flush of the too much champagne was still in his spirits and his brain. He remembers talking with her. He tries to remember whether she looked at all amazed or shocked. He does not think she did; he cannot recall any of her words, or his words; but he may have said something to convince her that he had taken too much champagne, and for her even to think anything of the kind about him would have seemed to him eternal and utter degradation in her eyes. Very much like this were the feelings of Helena Langley about the words which she might have spoken, the looks which she might have given, to the Emperor. All she knew was that she was not quite herself at the time: the rest was mere doubt and misery. And Helena Langley passed in society for being a girl who never cared in the least what she said or what she did, so long as she was not conventional.

To add to her concern, the Duchess of Deptford was announced. Now Helena was very fond of the beautiful and bright little Duchess, with her kindly heart, her utter absence of affectation, and her penetrating eyes. She gathered herself up and went to meet her friend.

'My! but you are looking bad, child!' the genial Duchess said. She may have been a year and a half or so older than Helena. 'What's the matter with you, anyway? Why have you got those blue semicircles round your eyes? Ain't you well?'

'Oh, yes, quite well,' Helena hastened to explain. 'Nothing is ever the matter with *me*, Duchess. My father says Nature meant to make me a boy and made a mistake at the last moment. I am the only girl he knows—so he tells me—that never is out of sorts.'

'Well, then, my dear, that only proves the more certainly that Nature distinctly meant you for a girl when she made you a girl.'

'Dear Duchess, how *do* you explain that?'

'Because you have got the art of concealing your feelings, which men have not got, anyhow,' the Duchess said, composedly. 'If you ain't out of sorts about something—and with these blue semicircles under your lovely eyes—well, then, a semicircle is not a semicircle, nor a girl a girl. That's so.'

'Dear Duchess, never mind me. I am really in the rudest health——'

'And no troubles—brain, or heart, or anything?'

'Oh, no; none but those common to all human creatures.'

'Well, well, have it your own way,' the Duchess said, good-humouredly. 'You have got a kind father to look after you, anyway. How is dear Sir Rupert?'

Helena explained that her father was very well, thank you, and the conversation drifted away from those present to some of those absent.

'Seen Mr Ericson lately?' the Duchess asked.

'Oh, yes, quite lately.' Helena did not explain how very lately it was that she had seen him.

'I like him very much,' said the Duchess. 'He is real sweet, I think.'

'He is very charming,' Helena said.

'And his secretary, young—what is his name?'

'Mr Hamilton?'

'Yes, yes, Mr Hamilton. Don't you think he is just a lovely young man?'

'I like him immensely.'

'But so handsome, don't you think? Handsomer than Mr Ericson, I think.'

'One doesn't think much about Mr Ericson's personal appearance,' Helena said, in a tone which distinctly implied that, according to her view of things, Mr Ericson was quite above personal appearance.

'Well, of course, he is a great man, and he did wonderful things; and he was an Emperor——'

'And will be again,' said Helena.

'What troubles me is this,' said the Duchess, 'I don't see much of the Emperor in him. Do you?'

'How do you mean, Duchess?' Helena asked evasively.

'Well, he don't seem to me to have much of a ruler of men about him. He is a charming man, and a brainy man, I dare say; but the sort of man that takes hold at once and manages things and puts things straight all of his own strength—well, he don't seem to be quite that sort of man—now, does he?'

'We haven't seen him tried,' Helena said.

'No, of course; we haven't had a chance that way, but it seems to me as if you could get some kind of notion about a man's being a great commander-in-chief without actually seeing him directing a field of battle. Now I don't appear to get that impression from Mr Ericson.'

'Mr Ericson wouldn't care to show off probably. He likes to keep himself in the background,' Helena said warmly.

'Dear child, I am not finding any fault with your hero, or saying that he isn't a hero; I am only saying that, so far, I have not discovered any of the magnetic force of the hero—isn't magnetic force the word? He is ever so nice and quiet and intellectual, and I dare say, as an all-round man, he's first-class, but I have not yet struck the Emperorship quality in him.'

The Duchess rose to go away.

'You see, there's nothing in particular for him to do in this country,' Helena said, still lingering on the subject which the Duchess seemed quite willing to put away.

'Is he going back to his own country?' the Duchess asked, languidly.

'His own country, Duchess? Why, *this* is his own country.' Wrapped as she was in the fortunes of Surmer, Helena, like a genuine English girl, could not help resenting the idea of any Englishman acknowledging any country but England. Especially she would not admit that her particular hero could be any sort of foreigner.

'Well—his adopted country I mean—the country where he was Emperor. Is he going back there?'

'When the people call him, he will go,' Helena answered proudly.

'Oh, my dear, if he wants to get back he had better go before the people call him. People forget so soon nowadays. We have all sorts of exiles over in the States, and it don't seem to me as if anybody ever called them back. Some of them have gone without being called, and then I think they mostly got shot.

But I hope your hero won't do that. Good-bye, dear; come and see me soon, or I shall think you as mean as ever you can be.' And the beautiful Duchess, bending her graceful head, departed, and left Helena to her own reflections.

Somehow these were not altogether pleasant reflections. Helena did not like the manner in which the Emperor had been discussed by the Duchess. The Duchess talked of him as if he were just some ordinary adventurer, who would be forgotten in his old domain if he did not keep knocking at the door and demanding readmittance even at the risk of being shot for his pains. This grated harshly on her ears. In truth, it is very hard to talk of the loved one to loving ears without producing a sound that grates on them. Too much praise may grate—criticism of any kind grates—cool indifferent comment, even though perfectly free from ill-nature, is sure to grate. The loved one, in fact, is not to be spoken of as other beings of earth may lawfully and properly be spoken of. On the whole, the loving one is probably happiest when the name of the loved one is not mentioned at all by profane or commonplace lips. But there was something more than this in Helena's case. The very thought which the Duchess had given out so freely and so carelessly had long been a lurking thought in Helena's own mind. Whenever it made its appearance too boldly she tried to shut it down and clap the hatches over it, and keep it there, suppressed and shut below. But it would come up again and again. The thought was, Where is the Emperor? She could recognise the bright talker, the intellectual thinker, the clever man of the world, the polished, grave, and graceful gentleman, but where were the elements of Emperorship? It was quite true, as she herself had said, had pleaded even, that some men never carry their great public qualities into civil life; and Helena raked together in her mind all manner of famous historical examples of men who had led great armies to victory, or had discovered new worlds for civilisation to conquer, and who appeared to be nothing in a drawing- or a dining-room but ordinary, well-behaved, undemonstrative gentlemen. Why should not the Emperor be one of these? Why, indeed? She was sure he must be one of these, but was it not to be her lot to see him in his true light—in his true self? Then the meeting of that other day gave her a keen pang. She did not like the idea of the Emperor coming to her to make advances as deputy for another man. It was not like him, she thought, to undertake a task such as that. It was done, of course, out of kindness and affection for Mr Hamilton— and that was, in its way, a noble and a generous act—but still, it jarred upon her feelings. The truth was that it jarred upon her feelings because it showed her, as she thought, how little serious consideration of her was in the Emperor's mind, and how sincere and genuine had been his words when he told her again and again that to him she seemed little more than a child. It was not that feeling which had brought up the wish that she could see the Emperor prove himself a man born to dictate. But that wish, or that doubt, or that questioning—whatever it might be—which was already in her mind was stirred to painful activity now by the consciousness which she strove to exclude, and could not help admitting, that she, after all, was nothing to the Emperor.

That night, like most nights when she did not herself entertain, Helena went with her father to a dinner party. She showed herself to be in radiant spirits the moment she entered the room. She was dressed bewitchingly, and everyone said she was looking more charming than ever. The fashion of lighting drawing-rooms and dining-rooms gives ample opportunity for a harmless deception in these days, and the blue half-circles were not seen round Helena's eyes, nor would any of the company in the drawing-room have guessed that the heart under that silken bodice was bleeding.

CHAPTER XII

DOLORES

Mr Paulo was perplexed. And as Mr Paulo was a cool-headed, clear-sighted man, perplexity was an unusual thing with him, and it annoyed him. The cause of his perplexity was connected almost entirely with the ex-Emperor of Surmer. Ericson had still kept his rooms in the hotel; he had said, and Hamilton agreed with him, that in remaining there they seemed more like birds of passage, more determined to regard return to Surmer as not merely a possible but a probable event, and an event in the near future. To take a house in London, the Emperor thought, and, of course, Hamilton thought with him, would be to admit the possibility of a lengthy sojourn in London, and that was a possibility which neither of the two men wished to entertain. 'It wouldn't look well in the papers,' Hamilton said, shaking his head solemnly. So they remained on at Paulo's, and Paulo kept the green and yellow flag of Surmer flying as if the guest beneath his roof were still a ruling potentate.

But it was not the stay of the Emperor that in any way perplexed Mr Paulo. Paulo was honestly proud of the presence of Ericson in his house. Paulo's father was a Spaniard who had gone out to Surmer as a waiter in a *café*, and who had entered the service of a young Englishman in the Legation, and had followed him to England and married an English wife. Mr Paulo—George Paulo—was the son of this international union. His father had been a 'gentleman's gentleman,' and Paulo followed his father's business and became a gentleman's gentleman too. George Paulo was almost entirely English in his nature, thanks to a strong-minded mother, who ruled the late Manuel Paulo with a kindly severity. The only thing Spanish about him was his face—smooth-shaven with small, black side whiskers—a face which might have seemed more appropriately placed in the bull rings of Madrid or Seville. George Paulo, in his turn, married an Englishwoman, a lady's-maid, with some economies and more ideas. They had determined, soon after their marriage, to make a start in life for themselves. They had kept a lodging-house in Sloane Street, which soon became popular with well-to-do young gentlemen, smart soldiers, and budding diplomatists, for both Paulo and his wife understood perfectly the art of making these young gentlemen comfortable.

Things went well with Paulo and his wife; their small economies were made into small investments; the investments, being judicious, prospered. A daring purchase of house property proved one stroke of success, and led to another. When he was fifty years of age Paulo was a rich man, and then he built Paulo's Hotel, and his fortune swelled yearly. He was a very happy man, for he adored his wife and he idolised his daughter, the handsome, stately, dark-eyed girl whom, for some sentimental reason, her mother had insisted upon calling Dolores. Dolores was, or at least seemed to be, that rarest creature among women—an unconscious beauty. She could pass a mirror without even a glance at it.

Dolores Paulo had everything she wanted. She was well taught; she knew several languages, including, first of all, that Spanish of which her father, for all his bull-fighter face, knew not a single syllable; she could play, and sing, and dance; and, above all things, she could ride. No one in the Park rode better than Miss Paulo; no one in the Park had better animals to ride. George Paulo was a judge of horseflesh, and he bought the best horses in London for Dolores; and when Dolores rode in the Row, as she did every morning, with a smart groom behind her, everyone looked in admiration at the handsome girl who was so perfectly mounted. The Paulos were a curious family. They had not the least desire to be above what George Paulo called their station in life. He and his wife were people of humble origin, who had honestly become rich; but they had not the least desire to force themselves upon a society which might have accepted them for their money, and laughed at them for their ambition. They lived in a suite of rooms in their own hotel, and they managed the hotel themselves. They gave all their time to it, and it took all their time, and they were proud of it. It was their business and their pleasure, and they worked for it with an artistic conscientiousness which was highly admirable. Dolores had inherited the sense and the business-like qualities of her parents, and she insisted on taking her part in the great work of keeping the hotel going. Paulo, proud of his hotel, was still prouder of the interest taken in it by his daughter.

Dolores came in from her ride one afternoon, and was hurrying to her room to change her dress, when she was met by her father in the public corridor.

'Dolores, my little girl'—he always called the splendidly proportioned young woman 'my little girl'—'I'm puzzled. I don't mind telling you, in confidence, that I am extremely puzzled.'

'Have you told mother?'

'Oh, yes, of course I've told mother, but she don't seem to think there is anything in it.'

'Then you may be sure there is nothing in it.' Mrs, or Madame, Paulo was the recognised sense-carrier of the household.

'Yes, I know. Nobody knows better than I what a woman *your* mother is.' He laid a kindly emphasis on the word 'your' as if to carry to the credit of Dolores some considerable part of the compliment that he was paying to her parent. 'But still, I thought I should like to talk to you, too, little girl. If two heads are better than one, three heads, I take it, are better than two.'

'All right, dear; go ahead.'

'Well, its about this Captain Sarrasin—in number forty-seven—you know.'

'Of course I know, dear; but what can puzzle you about him? He seems to me the most simple and charming old gentleman I have seen in this house for a long time.'

'Old gentleman,' Paulo said, with a smile. 'I fancy how much he would like to be described in that sort of way, and by a handsome girl, too! He don't think he is an old gentleman, you may be sure.'

'Why, father, he is almost as old as you; he must be fifty years old at least—more than that.'

'So you consider me quite an old party?' Paulo said, with a smile.

'I consider you an old darling,' his daughter answered, giving him a fervent embrace—they were alone in the corridor—and Paulo seemed quite contented.

'But now,' he said, releasing himself from the prolonged osculation, 'about this Captain Sarrasin?'

'Yes, dear, about him. Only what about him?'

'Well, that's exactly what I want to know. I don't quite see what he's up to. What does he have a room in this hotel for?'

'I suppose because he thinks it is a very nice hotel—and so it is, dear, thanks to you.'

'Yes, that's all right enough,' Paulo said, a little dissatisfied; the personal compliment did not charm away his discomfort in this instance, as the embrace had done in the other.

'I don't see where your trouble comes in, dear.'

'Well, you see, I have ascertained that this Captain Sarrasin is a married man, and that he has a house where he and his wife live down Clapham way,' and Paulo made a jerk with his hand as if to designate to his daughter the precise geographical situation of Captain Sarrasin's abode. 'But he sleeps here many nights, and he is here most of the day, and he gets his letters here, and all sorts of people come to see him here.'

'I suppose, dear, he has business to do, and it wouldn't be quite convenient for people to go out and see him in Clapham.'

'Why, my little girl, if it comes to that, it would be almost as convenient for people—City people for instance—to go to Clapham as to come here.'

'Dear, that depends on what part of Clapham he lives in. You see we are just next to a station here, and in parts of Clapham they are two miles off anything of the kind. Besides, all people don't come from the City, do they?'

'Business people do,' Mr Paulo replied sententiously.

'But the people I see coming after Captain Sarrasin are not one little bit like City people.'

'Precisely,' her father caught her up; 'there you have got it, little girl. That's what has set me thinking. What are your ideas about the people who come to see him? You know the looks of people pretty well by this time. You have a good eye for them. How do you figure them up?'

The girl reflected.

'Well, I should say foreign refugees generally, and explorers, and all that kind; Mr Hiram Borringer comes with his South Pole expeditions, and I see men who were in Africa with Stanley—and all that kind of thing.'

'Yes, but some of that may be a blind, don't you know. Have you ever, tell me, in all your recollection, seen a downright, unmistakable, solid City man go into Captain Sarrasin's room?'

'No, no,' said the girl, after a moment's thought; 'I can't quite say that I have. But I don't see what that matters to us. There are good people, I suppose, who don't come from the City?'

'I don't like it, somehow,' Paulo said. 'I have been thinking it over—and I tell you I don't like it!'

'What I can't make out,' the girl said, not impatiently but very gently, 'is what you don't like in the matter. Is there anything wrong with this Captain Sarrasin? He seems an old dear.'

'This is how it strikes me. He never came to this house until after his Excellency the Emperor made up his mind to settle here.'

'Oh!' Dolores started and turned pale. 'Tell me what you mean, dear—you frighten one.'

Paulo smiled.

'You are not over-easily frightened,' he said, 'and so I'll tell you all my suspicions.'

'Suspicions?' she said, with a drawing in of the breath that seemed as emphatic as a shudder. 'What is there to suspect?'

'Well, there is nothing more than suspicion at present. But here it is. I have it on the best authority that this Captain Sarrasin was out in Surmer. Now, he never told *me* that.'

'No? Well, go on.'

'He came back here to England long before his Excellency came, but he never took a room in this house until his Excellency had made up his mind to settle down here for all his time with Mr Hamilton. Now, what do you think his settling down here, and not taking a house, like General Boulanger—what do you think his staying on here means?'

'I suppose,' the girl said, slowly, 'it means that he has not given up the idea of recovering his position in Surmer.' She spoke in a low tone, and with eyes that sparkled.

'Right you are, girl. Of course, that's what it does mean. Mr Hamilton as good as told me himself; but I didn't want him to tell me. Now, again, if this Captain Sarrasin has been out in Surmer, and if he is on the right side, why didn't he call on his Excellency and prove himself a friend?'

'Dear, he has called on him.'

'Yesterday, yes; but not before.'

'Yes, but don't you see, dear,' Dolores said eagerly, 'that would cut both ways. You think that he is not a friend, but an enemy?'

'I begin to fear so, Dolores.'

'But, don't you see, an enemy might be for that very reason all the more anxious to pass himself off as a friend?'

'Yes, there's something in that, little girl; there's something in that, to be sure. But now you just hear me out before you let your mind come to any conclusion one way or the other.'

'I'll hear you out,' said Dolores; 'you need not be afraid about that.'

Dolores knew her father to be a cool-headed and sensible man; but still, even that fact would hardly in itself account for the interest she took in suspicions which appeared to have only the slightest possible foundation. She was evidently listening with breathless anxiety.

'Now, of course, I never allow revolutionary plotting in this house,' Paulo went on to say. 'I may have *my* sympathies and you may have *your* sympathies, and so on; but business is business, and we can't have any plans of campaign carried on in Paulo's Hotel. Kings are as good customers to me when they're on a throne as when they're off it—better maybe.'

'Yes, dear, I know all about that.'

'Still, one must assume that a man like his Excellency will see his friends in private, in his own rooms, and talk over things. I don't suppose he and Mr Hamilton are talking about nothing but the play and the opera and Hurlingham, and all that.'

'No, no, of course not. Well?'

'It would get out that they were planning a return to Surmer. Now I know—and I dare say you know— that a return to Surmer by his Excellency would mean the stopping of the supplies to hundreds of rascals there, who are living on public plunder, and who are always living on it as long as he is not there, and who never will be allowed to live upon it as long as he is there—don't you see?'

'Oh yes, dear; I see very plainly.'

'It's all true what I say, isn't it?'

'Quite true—quite—quite true.'

'Well, now, I dare say you begin to take my idea. You know how little that gang of scoundrels care about the life of any man.'

'Oh, father, please don't!' She had her riding-whip in her hand, and she made a quick movement with it, expressively suggesting how she should like to deal with such scoundrels.

'My child, my child, it has to be talked about. You don't seem quite in your usual form today——'

'Oh, yes; I'm all right. But it sounds so dreadful. You don't really think people are plotting to kill—him?'

'I don't say that they are; but from what I know of the scoundrels out there who are opposed to him, it wouldn't one bit surprise me.'

'Oh!' The girl shuddered, and again the riding-whip flashed.

'But it may not be quite that, you know, little girl; there are shabby tricks to be done short of that—there's spying and eavesdropping, to find out, in advance, all he is going to do, and to thwart it——'

'Yes, yes, there might be that,' Dolores said, in a tone of relief—the tone of one who, still fearing for the worst, is glad to be reminded that there may, after all, be something not so bad as the very worst.

'I don't want his Excellency spied on in Paulo's Hotel,' Mr Paulo proudly said. 'It has not been the way of this hotel, and I do not mean that it ever should be the way.'

'Not likely,' Dolores said, with a scornful toss of her head. 'The idea, indeed, of Paulo's Hotel being a resort of *mouchards* and spies, to find out the secrets of illustrious exiles who were sheltered as guests!'

'Well, that's what I say. Now I have my suspicions of this Captain Sarrasin. I don't know what he wants here, and why, if he is on the side of his Excellency, he don't boldly attend him every day.'

'I think you are wrong about him, dear,' Dolores quietly said. 'You may be right enough in your general suspicions and alarms and all that, and I dare say you *are* quite right; but I am sure you are wrong about him. Anyhow, you keep a sharp look-out everywhere else, and leave me to find out all about *him.*'

'Little girl, how can you find out all about him?'

'Leave that to me. I'll talk to him, and I'll make him talk to me. I never saw a man yet whose character I couldn't read like a printed book after I have had a little direct and confidential talk with him.' Miss Dolores tossed her head with the air of one who would say, 'Ask me no questions about the secret of my art; enough for you to know that the art is there.'

'Well, some of you women have wonderful gifts, I know,' her father said, half admiringly, half reflectively, proud of his daughter, and wondering how women came to have such gifts.

While they were speaking, Hamilton and Sir Rupert Langley came out of the Emperor's rooms together. Dolores knew that the Emperor had been out of the hotel for some hours. Mr Paulo disappeared. Dolores knew Sir Rupert perfectly well by sight, and knew who he was, and all about him. She had spoken now and again to Hamilton. He took off his hat in passing, and she, acting on a sudden impulse, asked if he could speak to her for a moment.

Hamilton, of course, cheerfully assented, and asked Sir Rupert to wait a few seconds for him. Sir Rupert passed along the corridor and stood at the head of the stairs.

'Only a word, Mr Hamilton. Excuse me for having stopped you so unceremoniously.'

'Oh, Miss Paulo, please don't talk of excuses.'

'Well, it's only this. Do you know anything about a Captain Sarrasin, who stays here a good deal of late?'

'Captain Sarrasin? Yes, I know a little about him; not very much, certainly; why do you ask?'

'Do you think he is a man to be trusted?'

She spoke in a low tone; her manner was very grave, and she fixed her deep, dark eyes on Hamilton. Hamilton read earnestness in them. He was almost startled.

'From all I know,' he answered slowly, 'I believe him to be a brave soldier and a man of honour.'

'So do I!' the girl said emphatically, and with relief sparkling in her eyes.

'But why do you ask?'

'I have heard something,' she said; 'I don't believe it; but I'll soon find out about his being here as a spy.'

'A spy on whom?'

'On his Excellency, of course.'

'I don't believe it, but I thank you for telling me.'

'I'll find out and tell you more,' she said hurriedly. 'Thank you very much for speaking to me; don't keep Sir Rupert waiting any longer. Good-morning, Mr Hamilton,' and with quite a princess-like air she dismissed him.

Hamilton hastily rejoined Sir Rupert, and was thinking whether he ought to mention what Dolores had been saying or not. The subject, however, at once came up without him giving it a start.

'See here, Hamilton,' Sir Rupert said as he was standing on the hotel steps, about to take his leave, 'I don't think that, if I were you, I would have Ericson going about the streets at nights all alone in his careless sort of fashion. It isn't common sense, you know. There are all sorts of rowdies—and spies, I fancy—and very likely hired assassins—here from all manner of South American places; and it can't be safe for a marked man like him to go about alone in that free and easy way.'

'Do you know of any danger?' Hamilton asked eagerly.

'How do you mean?'

'Well, I mean have you had any information of any definite danger—at the Foreign Office?'

'No; we shouldn't be likely to get any information of that kind at the Foreign Office. It would go, if there were any, to the Home Office.

'Have you had any information from the Home Office?'

'Well, I may have had a hint—I don't know what ground there was for it—but I believe there was a hint given at the Home Office to be on the look-out for some fellows of a suspicious order from Surmer.'

Hamilton started. The words concurred exactly with the kind of warning he had just received from Dolores Paulo.

'I wonder who gave the hint,' he said meditatively. 'It would immensely add to the value of the information if I were to know who gave the hint.'

'Oh! So, then, you have had some information of your own?'

'Yes, I may tell you that I have; and I should be glad to know if both hints came from the same man.'

'Would it make the information more serious if they did?'

'To my mind, much more serious.'

'Well, I may tell you in confidence—I mean, not to get into the confounded papers, that's all—the Home Secretary in fact, made no particular mystery about it. He said the hint was given at the office by an odd sort of person who called himself Captain Oisin Sarrasin.'

'That's the man,' Hamilton exclaimed.

'Well, what do you make of that and of him?'

'I believe he is an honest fellow and a brave soldier,' Hamilton said. 'But I have heard that some others have thought differently, and were inclined to suspect that he himself was over here in the interests of his Excellency's enemies. I don't believe a word of it myself.'

'Well, he will be looked after, of course,' Sir Rupert said decisively. 'But in the meantime I wouldn't let Ericson go about in that sort of way—at night especially. He never ought to be alone. Will you see to it?'

'If I can; but he's very hard to manage.'

'Have you tried to manage him on that point?' 'I have—yes—quite lately.'

'What did he say?'

'Wouldn't listen to anything of the kind. Said he proposed to go about where he liked. Said it was all nonsense. Said if people want to kill a man they can do it, in spite of any precautions he takes. Said that if anyone attacks him in front he can take pretty good care of himself, and that if fellows come behind no man can take care of himself.'

'But if someone walks behind him—to take care of him——'

'Oh, police protection?' Hamilton asked.

'Yes; certainly. Why not?'

'Out of the question. His Excellency never would stand it. He would say, "I don't choose to run life on that principle," and he would smile a benign smile on you, and you couldn't get him to say another word on the subject.'

'But we can put it on him, whether he likes it or not. Good heavens! Hamilton, you must see that it isn't only a question of him; it is a question of the credit and the honour of England, and of the London police system.'

'That's a little different from a question of the honour of England, is it not?' Hamilton asked with a smile.

'I don't see it,' Sir Rupert answered, almost angrily. 'I take it that one test of the civilisation of a society is the efficiency of its police system. I take it that if a metropolis like London cannot secure the personal safety of an honoured and distinguished guest like Ericson—himself an Englishman, too—by Jove! it forfeits in so far its claim to be considered a capital of civilisation. I really think you might put this to Ericson.'

'I think you had better put it to him yourself, Sir Rupert. He will take it better from you than he would from me. You know I have some of his own feeling about it, and if I were he I fancy I should feel as he feels. I wouldn't accept police protection against those fellows.'

'Why don't you go about with him yourself? You two would be quite enough, I dare say. *He* wouldn't be on his guard, but *you* would, for *him*.'

'Oh, if he would let *me*, that would be all right enough. I am always pretty well armed, and I have learned, from his very self, the way to use weapons. I think I could take pretty good care of him. But then, he won't always let me go with him, and he will persist in walking home from dinner parties and studying, as he says, the effect of London by night.'

'As if he were a painter or a poet,' Sir Rupert said in a tone which did not seem to imply that he considered painting and poetry among the grandest occupations of humanity.

'Why, only the other night,' Hamilton said, 'I was dining with some fellows from the United States at the Buckingham Palace Hotel, and I walked across St. James's Park on my way to look in at the Voyagers' Club, and as I was crossing the bridge I saw a man leaning on it and looking at the pond, and the sky, and the moon—and when I came nearer I saw it was his Excellency—and not a policeman or any other human being but myself within a quarter of a mile of him. It was before I had had any warning about him; but, by Jove! it made my blood run cold.'

'Did you make any remonstrance with him?'

'Of course I did. But he only smiled and turned it off with a joke—said he didn't believe in all that subterranean conspiracy, and asked whether I thought that on a bright moonlight night like that he shouldn't notice a band of masked and cloaked conspirators closing in upon him with daggers in their hands. No, it's no use,' Hamilton wound up despondingly.

'Perhaps I might try,' Sir Rupert said.

'Yes, I think you had better. At all events, he will take it from you. I don't think he would take it from me. I have worried him too much about it, and you know he can shut one up if he wants to.'

'I tell you what,' Sir Rupert suddenly said, as if a new idea had dawned upon him. 'I think I'll get my daughter to try what she can do with him.'

'Oh—yes—how is that?' Hamilton asked, with a throb at his heart and a trembling of his lips.

'Well, somehow I think my daughter has a certain influence over him—I think he likes her—of course, it's only the influence of a clever child and all that sort of thing—but still I fancy that something might be made to come of it. You know she professes such open homage for him, and she is all devoted to his cause—and he is so kind to her and puts up so nicely with all her homage, which, of course, although she *is* my daughter and I adore her, must, I should say, bore a man of his time of life a good deal when he is occupied with quite different ideas—don't you think so, Hamilton?'

'I can't imagine a man at any time of life or with any ideas being bored by Miss Langley,' poor Hamilton sadly replied.

'That's very nice of you, Hamilton, and I am sure you mean it, and don't say it merely to please me—and she likes you ever so much, that I know, for she has often told me—but I think I could make some use of her influence over him. Don't you think so? If she were to ask him as a personal favour—to her and to me, of course—leaving the Government altogether out of the question—as a personal favour to her and to me to take some care of himself—don't you think he could be induced? He is so chivalric in his nature that I don't think he would refuse anything to a young woman like her.'

'What is there that I could refuse to her,' poor Hamilton thought sadly within himself. 'But she will not care to plead to me that I should take care of my life. She thinks my poor, worthless life is safe enough—as indeed it is—who cares to attack me?—and even if it were not safe, what would that be to her?' He thought at the moment that it would be sweetness and happiness to him to have his life threatened by all the assassins and dynamiters in the world if only the danger could once induce Helena Langley to ask him to take a little better care of his existence.

'What do you think of my idea?' Sir Rupert asked. He seemed to find Hamilton's silence discouraging.

Perhaps Hamilton knew that the Emperor would not like being interfered with by any young woman. For the fondest of fathers can never quite understand why the daughter, whom he himself adores, might not, nevertheless, seem sometimes a little of a bore to a man who is not her father.

Hamilton pulled himself together.

'I think it is an excellent idea, Sir Rupert—in fact, I don't know of any other idea that is worth thinking about.'

'Glad to hear you say so, Hamilton,' Sir Rupert said, greatly cheered. 'I'll put it in operation at once. Good-bye.'

CHAPTER XIII

DOLORES ON THE LOOK-OUT

Captain Sarrasin when he was in the hotel always had breakfast in his little sitting-room. A very modest breakfast it was, consisting invariably of a cup of coffee and some dry toast with a radish. Of late, when he emerged from his bedroom he always found a little china jar on his breakfast-table with some fresh flowers in it. He thought this a delightful attention at first, and assumed that it would drop after a day or two, like other formal civilities of a hotel-keeper. But the days went on and the flowers came, and Captain Sarrasin thought that at least he ought to make it known that he received and appreciated them, and was grateful.

So he took care to be in the breakfast-room one day while the waiter was laying out the breakfast things, and crowning the edifice metaphorically with the little china jar and its fresh flowers—roses this time. Sarrasin knew enough to know that the deftest-handed waiter in the world had never arranged that cluster of roses and moss and leaves.

'Now, look here, dear boy,' he asked of the waiter in his beaming way—Sarrasin hardly ever addressed any personage of humbler rank without some friendly and encouraging epithet, 'to whom am I indebted for these delightful morning gifts of flowers?'

'To Miss Dolores—Miss Paulo,' the man said. He was a Swiss, and spoke with a thick, Swiss accent.

'Miss Paulo—the daughter of the house?'

'Yes, sir; she arranges them herself every day.'

'Is that the tall and handsome young lady I sometimes see with Mr Paulo in his room?'

'Yes; that is she.'

'But I want to thank her for her great kindness. Will you take a card from me, my dear fellow, and ask her if she will be good enough to see me?'

'Willingly, sir; Miss Dolores has her own room on this floor—No. 25. She is there every morning after she comes back from her early ride and until luncheon time.'

'After she comes back from her ride?'

'Yes, sir; Miss Dolores rides in the Park every morning and afternoon.'

This news somewhat dashed the enthusiasm of Captain Sarrasin. He liked a girl who rode, that was certain. Mrs Sarrasin rode like that rarest of creatures, except the mermaid, a female Centaur, and if he had had a dozen daughters, they would all have been trained to ride, one better than the other. The riding, therefore, was clearly in the favour of Dolores, so far as Captain Sarrasin's estimate was concerned. But then the idea of a hotel-keeper's daughter riding in the Row and giving herself airs! He did not like that. 'When I was young,' he said, 'a girl wasn't ashamed of her father's business, and did not try to put on the ways of a class she did not belong to.' Still, he reminded himself that he was growing old, and that the world was becoming affected—and that girls now, of any order, were not like the girls in the dear old days when Mrs Sarrasin was young. And in any case the morning flowers were a charming gift and a most delightful attention, and a gentleman must offer his thanks for them to the most affected young woman in the world. So he told the waiter that after breakfast he would send his card to Miss Paulo's room, and ask her to allow him to call on her.

'Miss Paulo will see you, of course,' the man replied. 'Mr Paulo is generally very busy, and sees very few people, but Miss Paulo—she will see everybody for him.'

'Everybody? What about, my good young man?'

'But, monsieur, about everything—about paying bills—and complaints of gentlemen, and ladies who think they have not had value for their money, and all that sort of thing—monsieur knows.'

'Then the young lady looks after the business of the hotel?'

'Oh, yes, monsieur—always.'

That piece of news was a relief to Captain Sarrasin. Miss Dolores went up again high in his estimation, and he felt abashed at having wronged her even by the misconception of a moment. He consumed his coffee and his radish and dry toast, and he selected from the china jar a very pretty moss rose, and put it in his gallant old buttonhole, and then he rang for his friend the waiter, and sent his card to Miss Paulo. In a moment the waiter brought back the intimation that Miss Paulo would be delighted to see Captain Sarrasin at once.

Miss Paulo's door stood open, as if to convey the idea that it was an office rather than a young lady's boudoir—a place of business and not a drawing-room. It was a very pretty room, as Sarrasin saw at a glance when he entered it with a grand and old-fashioned bow, such as men make no more in these degenerate days. It was very quietly decorated with delicate colours, and a few etchings and many flowers; and Dolores herself came from behind her writing desk, smiling and blushing, to meet her tall visitor. The old soldier scanned her as he would have scanned a new recruit, and the result of his impressionist study was to his mind highly satisfactory. He already liked the girl.

'My dear young lady,' he began, 'I have to introduce myself—Captain Sarrasin. I have come to thank you.'

'No need to introduce yourself or to thank me,' the girl said, very simply. 'I have wanted to know you this long time, Captain Sarrasin, and I sent you flowers every morning, because I knew that sooner or later you would come to see me. Now won't you sit down, please?'

'But may I not thank you for your flowers?'

'No, no, it is not worth while. And besides, I had an interested object. I wanted to make your acquaintance and to talk to you.'

'I am so glad,' he said gravely. 'But I am afraid I am not the sort of man young ladies generally care to talk to. I am a battered old soldier who has been in many wars, as Burns says——'

'That is one reason. I believe you have been in South America?'

'Yes, I have been a great deal in South America.'

'In the Empire of Surmer?'

'Yes, I have been in the Empire of Surmer.'

'Do you know that the Emperor of Surmer is staying in this house?'

'My dear young lady, everyone knows *that*.'

'Are you on his side or against him?' Dolores asked bluntly.

'Dear young lady, you challenge me like a sentry.' And Captain Sarrasin smiled benignly, feeling, however, a good deal puzzled.

'I have been told that you are against him,' the girl said; 'and now that I see you I must say that I don't believe it.'

'Who told you that I was against him?' the stout old Paladin asked; 'and why shouldn't I be against him if my conscience directed me that way?'

'Well, it was supposed that you might be against him. You are both staying in this hotel, and, until the other day, you have never called upon him or gone to see him, or even sent your card to him. That seemed to my father a little strange. He talked of asking you frankly all about it. I said I would ask you. And I am glad to have got you here, Captain Sarrasin, to challenge you like a sentry.'

'Well, but now look here, my dear young lady—why should your father care whether I was for the Emperor or against him?'

'Because if you were against him it might not be well that you were in the same house,' Dolores answered with   business-like   promptitude   and straightforwardness, 'getting to know what people called on him, and how long they stayed, and all that.'

'Playing the spy, in fact?'

'Such things have been done, Captain Sarrasin.'

'By gentlemen and soldiers, Miss Paulo?' and he looked sternly at her. The unabashed damsel did not quail in the least.

'By persons calling themselves gentlemen and soldiers,' she answered fearlessly. The old warrior smiled. He liked her courage and her frankness. It was clear that she and her father were devoted friends of the Emperor. It was clear that somebody had suspected him of being one of the Emperor's political enemies. He took to Dolores.

'My good young lady,' he said, 'you seem to me a very true-hearted girl. I don't know why, but that is the way in which I take your measure and add you up.'

Dolores was a little amazed at first; but she saw that his eyes expressed nothing save honest purpose, and she did not dream of being offended by his kindly patronising words.

'You may add me up in any way you like,' she said. 'I am pretty good at addition myself, and I think I shall come out that way in the end.'

'I know it,' he said, with a quite satisfied air, as if her own account of herself had settled any lingering doubt he might possibly have had upon his mind. 'Very well; now you say you can add up figures pretty well—and, in fact, I know you do, because you help your father to keep his books, now don't you?'

'Of course I do,' she answered promptly, 'and very proud of it I am that I can assist him.'

'Quite right, my dear. Well, now, as you are so good in figuring up things, I wonder could you figure *me* up?'

There was something so comical in the question, and in the manner and look of the man who propounded it, that Dolores could not keep from a smile, and indeed could hardly prevent the smile from rippling into a laugh. For Captain Sarrasin threw back his head, stiffened up his frame, opened widely his grey eyes, compressed his lips, and in short put himself on parade for examination.

'Figure me up,' he said, 'and be candid with it, dear girl. Say what I come up to in your estimation.'

Dolores tried to take the whole situation seriously.

'Look into my eyes,' he said imperatively. 'Tell me if you see anything dishonest or disloyal, or traitorous there?'

With her never-failing shrewd common sense, the girl thought it best to play the play out. After all, a good deal depended on it, to her thinking. She looked into his eyes. She saw there an almost childlike sincerity of purpose. If truth did not lie in the well of those eyes, then truth is not to be found in mortal orbs at all. But the quick and clever Dolores did fancy that she saw flashing now and then beneath the surface of those eyes some gleams of fitfulness, restlessness—some light that the world calls eccentric, some light which your sound and practical man would think of as only meant to lead astray—to lead astray, that is, from substantial dividends and real property, and lucky strokes on the Stock Exchange, and peerages and baronetcies and other good things. There was a strong dash of the poetic about Dolores, for all her shrewd nature and her practical bringing-up, and her conflicts over hotel bills; and somehow, she could not tell why, she found that as she looked into the eyes of Captain Sarrasin her own suddenly began to get dimmed with tears.

'Well, dear girl,' he asked, 'have you figured me up, and can you trust me?'

'I have figured you up,' she said warmly, 'and I can trust you;' and with an impulse she put her hand into his.

'Trust me anywhere—everywhere?'

'Anywhere—everywhere!' she murmured passionately.

'All right,' he said, cheerfully. 'I have the fullest faith in you, and now that you have full faith in me we can come straight at things. I want you to know my wife. She would be very fond of you, I am quite sure. But, now, for the moment: You were wondering why I am staying in this hotel?'

'I was,' she said, with some hesitancy, 'because I didn't know you——'

'And because you were interested in the Emperor of Surmer?'

She felt herself blushing slightly; but his face was perfectly serious and serene. He was evidently regarding her only in the light of a political partisan. She felt ashamed of her reddening cheeks.

'Yes; I am greatly interested in him,' she answered quite proudly; 'so is my father.'

'Of course he is, and of course you are—and, of course, so is every Englishman and Englishwoman who has the slightest care for the future fortunes of Surmer—which may be one of the best homes in the world for some of our poor people from this stifling country, if only a man like Ericson can be left to manage it. Well, well, I am wandering off into matters which you young women can't be expected to understand, or to care anything about.'

'But I do understand them—and I do care a great deal about them,' Dolores said indignantly. 'My father understands all about Surmer—and he has told me.'

'I am glad to hear it,' Sarrasin said gravely. 'Well, now, to come back——' and he paused.

'Yes, yes,' she said eagerly, 'to come back?'

'I am staying in this hotel for a particular purpose. I want to look after the Emperor. That's the whole story. My wife and I have arranged it all.'

'You want to look after him? Is he in danger?' The girl was turning quite pale.

'Danger? Well, it is hard to say where real danger is. I find, as a rule, that threatened men live long, and that there isn't much real danger where danger is talked about beforehand, but I never act upon that principle in life. I am never governed in my policy by the fact that the cry of wolf has been often raised—I look out for the wolf all the same.'

'Has he enemies?'

'Has he enemies? Why, I wonder at a girl of your knowledge and talent asking a question like that! Is there a scoundrel in Surmer who is not his enemy? Is there a man who has succeeded in getting any sinecure office from the State who doesn't know that the moment Ericson comes back to Surmer out he goes, neck and crop? Is there a corrupt judge in Surmer who wouldn't, if he could, sentence Ericson to be shot the moment he landed on the coast of Surmer? Is there a perjured professional informer who doesn't hate the very name of Ericson? Is there a cowardly blackguard in the army, who has got promotion because the general liked his pretty wife—oh, well, I mean because the general happened to be some relative of his wife—is there any fellow of this kind who doesn't hate Ericson and dread his coming back to Surmer?'

'No, I suppose not,' Dolores sadly answered. Paulo's Hotel was like other hotels, a gossiping place, and it is to be feared that Dolores understood better than Captain Sarrasin supposed, the hasty and speedily-qualified allusion to the General and the pretty wife.

'Well, you see,' Sarrasin summed up, 'I happen to have been in Surmer, and know something of what is going on there. I studied the place a little bit before Ericson had left, and I got to know some people. I am what would have been called in other days a soldier of fortune, dear girl, although, Heaven knows! I never made much fortune by my soldiering—you should just ask my wife! But anyhow, you know, when I have been in a foreign country where things are disturbed people send to me and offer me jobs, don't you see? So in that way I found that the powers that be in Surmer at present'—Sarrasin was fond of good old phrases like 'the powers that be'—'the powers that be in Surmer have a terrible dread of Ericson's coming back. I know a lot about it. I can tell you they follow everything that is going on here. They know perfectly well how thick he is with Sir Rupert Langley, the Foreign Secretary, and they fancy that means the support of the English Government in any attempt to return to Surmer. Of course, we know it means nothing of the kind, you and I.'

'Of course, of course,' Dolores said. She did not know in the least whether it did or did not mean the support of the English Government; for her own part, she would have been rather inclined to believe that it did. But Captain Sarrasin evidently wanted an answer, and she hastened to give him the answer which he evidently wanted.

'But *they* never can understand that,' he added. 'The moment a man dines with a Secretary of State in London they get it into their absurd heads that that means the pledging of the whole Army, Navy, and Reserve Forces of England to any particular cause which the man invited to dinner may be supposed to represent. Here, in nine cases out of ten, the man invited to dinner does not exchange one confidential word with the Secretary of State, and the day but one after the dinner the Secretary of State has forgotten his very existence.'

'Oh, but is that really so?' Dolores asked, in a somewhat aggrieved tone of voice. She was disposed to resent the idea of any Secretary of State so soon forgetting the existence of the Emperor.

'Not in this case, dear girl—not in this case certainly. Sir Rupert and Ericson are great friends; and they say Ericson is going to marry Sir Rupert's daughter.'

'Oh, do they?' Dolores asked earnestly.

'Yes, they do; and the Surmer folk have heard of it already, I can tell you; and in their stupid outsider sort of way they go on as if their little twopenny-halfpenny Empire were being made an occasion for great state alliances on the part of England.'

'What is she like?' Dolores murmured faintly. 'Is she very pretty? Is she young?'

'I am told so,' Sarrasin answered vaguely. To him the youth or beauty of Sir Rupert's daughter was matter of the slightest consideration.

'Told what?' Dolores asked somewhat sharply. 'That she is young and pretty, or that she isn't?'

'Oh, that she is young and very pretty, quite a beauty they tell me; but you know, my dear, that with Royal Princesses and very rich girls a little beauty goes a long way.'

'It wouldn't with him,' Dolores answered emphatically.

'With whom?' Captain Sarrasin asked blankly, and Dolores saw that she had all unwittingly put herself in an awkward position. 'I meant,' she tried to explain, 'that I don't think his Excellency would be governed much by a young woman's money.'

'But, my dear girl, where are we now? Did I ever say he would be?'

'Oh, no,' she replied meekly, and anxious to get back to the point of the conversation. 'Then you think, Captain Sarrasin, that his Excellency has enemies here in London—enemies from Surmer, I mean.'

'I shouldn't wonder in the least if he had,' Sarrasin replied cautiously. 'I know there are some queer chaps from Surmer about in London now. So we come to the point, dear girl, and now I answer the question we started with. That's why I am staying in this hotel.'

Dolores drew a deep breath.

'I knew it from the first,' Dolores said. 'I was sure you had come to watch over him.'

'That's exactly why I am here. Some of them, perhaps, will only know me by name as a soldier of fortune, and may think that they could manage to humbug me and get me over to their side. So they'll probably come to me and try to talk me over, don't you see? They'll try to make me believe that Ericson was a tyrant and a despot, don't you know; and that I ought to go back to Surmer and help the Empire to resist the oppressor, and so get me out of the way and leave the coast clear to them—see? Others of them will know pretty well that where I am on watch and ward, I am the right man in the right place, and that it isn't of much use their trying on any of their little assassination dodges here—don't you see?'

Dolores was profoundly touched by the simple vanity and the sterling heroism of this Christian soldier—for she could not account him any less. She believed in him with the fullest faith.

'Does his Excellency know of this?' she asked.

'Know of what, my dear girl?'

'About these plots?' she asked impatiently.

'I don't suppose he thinks about them.'

'All the more reason why we should,' Dolores said emphatically.

'Of course. There are lots of foreign fellows always staying here,' Sarrasin said, more in the tone of one who asks a question than in that of one who makes an assertion.

'Yes—yes—of course,' Dolores answered.

'I wonder, now, if you would be able to pick out a South American foreigner from the ordinary Spanish or Italian foreigner?'

'Oh, yes—I *think* so,' Dolores answered after a second or two of consideration. 'Moustache more curled—nose more thick—general air of swagger.'

'Yes—you haven't hit it off badly at all. Well, keep a look-out for any such, and give me the straight tip as soon as you can—and keep your eyes and your senses well about you.'

'You may trust me to do *that*,' the girl said cheerily.

'Yes, I know we can. Now, how about your father?'

'I think it will be better not to bring father into this at all,' Dolores answered very promptly.

'No, dear girl? Now, why not?'

'Well, perhaps it would seem to him wrong not to let out the whole thing at once to the authorities, or not to refuse to receive any suspicious persons into the house at all, and that isn't, by any means, what you and I are wanting just now, Captain Sarrasin!'

'Why, certainly not,' the old soldier said, with a beaming smile. 'What a clever girl you are! Of course, it isn't what we want; we want the very reverse; we want to get them in here and find out all about them! Oh, I can see that we shall be right good pals, you and I, dear girl, and you must come and see my wife. She will appreciate you, and she is the most wonderful woman in the world.'

CHAPTER XIV

A SICILIAN KNIFE

The day had come when the Emperor was to dine with that 'happy warrior,' the Soldier of Fortune.

Captain Sarrasin and his wife lived in an old-fashioned house on the farther fringe of Clapham Common. The house was surrounded by trees, and had a pretty lawn, not as well kept as it might be, for Captain Sarrasin and his wife were wanderers, and did not often make any long stay at their home in the southern suburbs of London. There were many Scotch firs among the trees on the lawn, and there was a tiny pool within the grounds which had a tinier islet on its surface, and on the tiny islet a Scotch fir stood all alone. The place had been left to Mrs Sarrasin years and years ago, and it suited her and her husband very well. It kept them completely out of the way of callers and of a society for which they had neither of them any manner of inclination. Mrs Sarrasin never remained actually in town while she was in London—indeed, she seldom went into London, and when she did she always, however late the hour, returned to her Clapham house. Sarrasin often had occasion to stay in town all night, but whenever he could get away in time he was fond of tramping the whole distance—say, from Paulo's Hotel to the farther side of Clapham Common. He loved a night walk, he said.

Business and work apart, he and his wife were company for each other. They had no children. One little girl had just been shown to the light of day—it could not have seen the daylight with its little closed-up eyes doomed never to open—and then it was withdrawn into darkness. They never had another child. When a pair are thus permanently childless, the effect is usually shown in one of two ways. They both repine and each secretly grumbles at the other—or if one only repines, that comes to much the same thing in the end—or else they are both drawn together with greater love and tenderness than ever. All the love which the wife would have given to the child is now concentrated on the husband, and all the love the husband would have given to the infant is stored up for the wife. A first cause of difference, or of coldness, or of growing indifference between a married pair is often on the birth of the first child. If the woman is endowed with intense maternal instinct she becomes all but absorbed in the child, and the husband, kept at a little distance, feels, rightly or wrongly, that he is not as much to her as he was before. Before, she was his companion; now she has got someone else to look after and to care about. It is a crisis which sensible and loving people soon get over—but all people cannot be loving and sensible at once and always—and there does sometimes form itself the beginning of a certain estrangement. This probably would not have happened in the case of the Sarrasins, but certainly if they had had children Mrs Sarrasin would no longer have been able to pad about the round world wherever her husband was pleased to ask her to accompany him. If in her heart there were now and again some yearnings for a child, some pangs of regret that a child had not been given to her or left with her, she always found ready consolation in the thought that she could not have been so much to her husband had the Fates imposed on her the sweet and loving care of children.

The means of the Sarrasins were limited; but still more limited were their wants. She had a small income—he had a small income—the two incomes put together did not come to very much. But it was enough for the Sarrasins; and few married couples of middle age ever gave themselves less trouble about money. They were able to go abroad and join some foreign enterprise whenever they felt called that way, and, poor as he was, Sarrasin was understood to have helped with his purse more than one embarrassed cause or needy patriot. The chief ornaments and curios of their house were weapons of all kinds, each with some story labelled on to it. Captain Sarrasin displayed quite a collection of the uniforms he had worn in many a foreign army and insurgent band, and of the decorations he had received and doubtless well earned. Mrs Sarrasin, for her part, could show anyone with whom she cared to be confidential a variety of costumes in which she had disguised herself, and in which she had managed either to escape from some danger, or, more likely yet, to bring succour of some sort to others who were in danger.

Mrs Sarrasin was a woman of good family—a family in the veins of which flowed much wild blood. Some of the men had squandered everything early, and then gone away and made adventurers of themselves here and there. Certain of these had never returned to civilisation again. With the women the wild strain took a different line. One became an explorer, one founded a Protestant sisterhood for woman's missionary labour, and diffused itself over India, and Tibet, and Burmah, and other places. A third lived with her husband in perpetual yachting— no one on board but themselves and the crew. A steady devotion to some one object which had nothing to do with the conventional purposes or ambitions or comforts of society, was the general characteristic of the women of that family. None of them took to mere art or literature or woman's suffrage. Mrs Sarrasin fell in love with her husband, and devoted herself to his wild, wandering, highly eccentric career.

Mrs Sarrasin was a tall and stately woman, with an appearance decidedly aristocratic. She had rather square shoulders, and that sort of repression or suppression of the bust which conies of a woman's occupying herself much in the more vigorous pursuits and occupations which habitually belong to a man. Mrs Sarrasin could ride like a man as well as like a woman, and in many a foreign enterprise she had adopted man's clothing regularly. Yet there was nothing actually masculine about her appearance or her manners, and she had a very sweet and musical voice, which much pleased the ears of the Emperor.

Oisin mentioned the fact of his wife's frequent appearance in man's dress with an air of pride in her versatility.

'Oh, but I haven't done that for a long time,' she said, with a light blush rising to her pale cheek. 'I haven't been out of my petticoats for ever so long. But I confess I did sometimes enjoy a regular good gallop on a bare-backed horse, and riding-habits won't do for that.'

'Few men can handle a rifle as that woman can,' Sarrasin remarked, with another gleam of pride in his face.

The Emperor expressed his compliments on the lady's skill in so many manly exercises, but he had himself a good deal of the old-fashioned prejudice against ladies who could manage a rifle and ride astride.

'All I have done,' Mrs Sarrasin said, 'was to take the commands of my husband and be as useful as I could in the way he thought best. I am not for Woman's Rights, Mr Ericson—I am for wives obeying their husbands, and as much as possible effacing themselves.'

The Emperor did not quite see that following one's husband to the wars in man's clothes was exactly an act of complete self-effacement on the part of a woman. But he could see at a glance that Mrs Sarrasin was absolutely serious and sincere in her description of her own condition and conduct. There was not the slightest hint of the jocular about her.

'You must have had many most interesting and extraordinary experiences,' the Emperor said. 'I hope you will give an account of them to the world some day.'

'I am already working hard,' Mrs Sarrasin said, 'putting together materials for the story of my husband's life—not mine; mine would be poor work indeed. I am in my proper place when I am acting as his secretary and his biographer.'

'And such a memory as she has,' Sarrasin exclaimed. 'I assure your Excellency'—Ericson made a gesture as if to wave away the title, which seemed to him ridiculous under present circumstances, but Sarrasin, with a movement of polite deprecation, repeated the formality—'I assure your Excellency that she remembers lots of things happening to me——'

'Or done by you,' the lady interposed.

'Well, or done by me; things that had wholly passed out of my memory.'

'Quite natural,' Mrs Sarrasin observed, blandly, 'that you should forget them, and that I should remember them.' There was something positively youthful about the smile that lighted up her face as she said the words, and Ericson noticed that she had a peculiarly sweet and winning smile, and that her teeth could well bear the brightest light of day. Ericson began to grow greatly interested in her, and to think that if she was a little of an oddity it was a pity we had not a good many other oddity women going round.

'I should like to see what you are doing with your husband's career, Mrs Sarrasin,' he said, 'if you would be kind enough to let me see. I have been something of a literary man myself—was at one time—and I delight in seeing a book in some of its early stages. Besides, I have been a wanderer and even a fighter myself, and perhaps I might be able to make a suggestion or two.'

'I shall be only too delighted. Now, Oisin, my love, you must *not* object. His Excellency knows well that you are a modest man by nature, and do not want to have anything made of what you have done; but as he wishes to see what I am doing——'

'Whatever his Excellency pleases,' Captain Sarrasin said, with a grave bow.

'Dinner is served,' the man-servant announced at this critical moment.

'You shall see it after dinner,' Mrs Sarrasin said, as she took the Emperor's arm, and led him rather than accompanied him out of the drawing-room and down the stairs.

'What charming water-colours!' the Emperor said, as he noticed some pictures hung on the wall of the stairs.

'Oh, these? I am so pleased that you like them. I am very fond of drawing; it often amuses me and helps to pass away the time. You see, I have no children to look after, and Oisin is a good deal away.'

'Not willingly, I am sure.'

'No, no, not willingly. Dear Oisin, he has always my approval in everything he does. He is my child—my one child—my big child—so I tell him often.'

'But these water-colours. I really must have a good look at them by-and-by. And they are so prettily and tastefully framed—so unlike the sort of frame one commonly sees in London houses.'

'The frames—yes—well, I make them to please myself and Oisin.'

'You make them yourself.'

'Oh, yes; I am fond of frame-making, and doing all sorts of jobs of that kind.'

By this time they had reached the dining-room. It was a very pretty little room, its walls not papered, but painted a soft amber colour. No pictures were on the walls.

'I like the idea of your walls,' Ericson said. 'The walls are themselves the decoration.'

'Yes,' she said, 'that was exactly our idea—let the colour be the decoration; but I don't know that I ever heard anyone discover the idea before. People generally ask me why I don't have pictures on the dining-room walls, and then I have to explain as well as I can that the colour is decoration enough.'

'And then, I suppose, some of them look amazed, and can't understand how you——'

'Oh, indeed, yes,' she answered.

The dinner was simple and unpretentious, but excellent, almost perfect in its way. A clear soup, a sole, an entrée or two, a bit of venison, a sweet—with good wines, but not too many of them.

'You have a good cook, Mrs Sarrasin,' the Emperor said.

'I am made proud by your saying so. We don't keep a cook—I do it all myself—am very fond of cooking.'

The Emperor looked round at her in surprise. Was this a jest? Oh, no; there was no jesting expression on Mrs Sarrasin's face. She was merely making a statement of fact. Ericson began to suspect that the one thing which the lady had least capacity for making, or, perhaps, for understanding, was a jest. But he was certainly amazed at the versatility of her accomplishments, and he frankly told her so.

'You see, we have but a small income,' she explained quietly, 'and I like to do all I can; and Oisin likes my cookery—he is used to it. We only keep two maids and this man'—alluding to the momentarily absent attendant—'and he was an old soldier of Oisin's. I will tell you his story some time—it is interesting in its way.'

'I think everything in this house is interesting,' the Emperor declared in all sincerity.

Captain Sarrasin talked but little. He was quite content to hear his wife talk with the Emperor and to know that she was pleased, and to believe that the Emperor was pleased with her. That, however, he assumed as a matter of course—everybody must be pleased with that woman.

After dinner the Emperor studied the so-called autobiography. It was a marvellously well-ordered piece of composition as far as it went. It was written in the neatest of manuscript, and had evidently been carefully copied and re-copied so that the volume now in his hands was about as good as any print. It was all chaptered and paged most carefully. It was rich with capital pencil sketches and even with etchings. There was no trace of any other hand but the one that he could find out in the whole volume. He greatly admired the drawings and etchings.

'These are yours, of course?' he said, turning his eyes on Mrs Sarrasin.

'Oh, yes; I like to draw for this book. I hope it will have a success. Do you think it will?' she asked wistfully.

'A success in what way, Mrs Sarrasin? Do you mean a success in money?'

'Oh, no; we don't care about that. I suppose it will cost us some money.'

'I fancy it will if you have all these illustrations, and of course you will?'

'Yes, I want them to be in, because I think I can show what danger my husband has been in better with my pencil than with my pen—I am a poor writer.'

'Then the work is really all your own?'

'Oh, yes; *he* has no time; I could not have him worried. It is my wish altogether, and he yields to it—only to please me. He does not care in the least for publicity—I do, for *him*.'

The Emperor began to be impressed, for the first time, by a recognition of the fact that an absence of the sacred gift of humour is often a great advantage to mortal happiness, and even to mortal success. There was clearly and obviously a droll and humorous side to the career and the companionship of Captain Sarrasin and his wife. How easy it would be to make fun of them both! perhaps of her more especially. Cheap cynicism could hardly find in the civilised world a more ready and defenceless spoil. Suppose, then, that Sarrasin or his wife had either of them any of the gift—if it be a gift and not a curse—which turns at once to the ridiculous side of things, where would this devoted pair have been? Why, of course they would have fallen out long ago. Mrs Sarrasin would soon have seen that her husband was a ridiculous old Don Quixote sort of person, whom she was puffing and booming to an unconscionable degree, and whom people were laughing at. Captain Sarrasin would have seen that his wife was unconsciously 'bossing the show,' and while professing to act entirely under his command was really doing everything for him—was writing his life while declaring to everybody that he was writing it himself. Now they were like two children—like brother and sister—wrapped up in each other, hardly conscious of any outer world, or, perhaps, still more like two child-lovers—like Paul and Virginia grown old in years, but not in feelings. The Emperor loved humour, but he began to feel just now rather glad that there were some mortals who did not see the ridiculous side of life. He felt curiously touched and softened.

Suddenly the military butler came in and touched his forehead with a sort of military salute.

'Telegram for his Excellency,' he said gravely.

Ericson took the telegram. 'May I?' he asked of Mrs Sarrasin, who made quite a circuitous bow of utter assent.

Ericson read.

'Will you meet me tonight at eleven, on bridge, St. James's Park. Have special reason.—Hamilton.'

Ericson was puzzled.

'This is curious,' he said, looking up at his two friends. 'This is a telegram from my friend and secretary and aide-de-camp, and I don't know what else—Hamilton—asking me to meet him in St. James's Park, on the bridge, at eleven o'clock. Now, that is a place I am fond of going to—and Hamilton has gone there with me—but why he should want to meet me there and not at home rather puzzles me.'

'Perhaps,' Captain Sarrasin suggested, 'there is someone coming to see you at your hotel later on, for whose coming Mr Hamilton wishes to prepare you.'

'Yes, I have thought of that,' Ericson said meditatively; 'but then he signs himself in an odd sort of way.'

'Eh, how is that?' Sarrasin asked. 'It *is* his name, surely, is it not—Hamilton?'

'Yes, but I had got into a way years ago of always calling him "the Boy," and he got into a way of signing himself "Boy" in all our confidential communications, and I haven't for years got a telegram from him that wasn't signed "Boy."'

Mrs Sarrasin sent a flash of her eyes that was like a danger signal to her husband. He at once understood, and sent another signal to her.

'Of course I must go,' Ericson said. 'Whatever Hamilton does, he has good reason for doing. One can always trust him in that.'

Captain Sarrasin was about to interpose something in the way of caution, but his wife flashed another signal at him, and he shut up.

'And so I must go,' the Emperor said, 'and I am sorry. I have had a very happy evening; but you will ask me again, and I shall come, and we shall be good friends. Shall we not, Mrs Sarrasin?'

'I hope so,' said the lady gravely. 'We are devoted to your Excellency, and may perhaps have a chance of proving it one day.'

The Emperor had a little brougham from Paulo's waiting for him. He took a kindly leave of his host and hostess. He lifted Mrs Sarrasin's long, strong, slender hand in his, and bent over it, and put it to his lips. He felt drawn towards the pair in a curious way, and he felt as if they belonged to a different age from ours—as if Sarrasin ought to have been another Götz of Berlichingen, about whom it would have been right to say, 'So much the worse for the age that misprizes thee'; as if she were the mail-clad wife of Count Robert of Paris.

When he had gone, up rose Mrs Sarrasin and spake:—

'Now, then, Oisin, let *us* go.'

'Where shall we go?' Oisin asked rather blankly.

'After him, of course.'

'Yes, of course, you are quite right,' Sarrasin said, suddenly waking up at the tone of her voice to what he felt instinctively must be her view of the seriousness of the situation. 'You don't believe, my love, that that telegram came from Hamilton?'

'Why, dearest, of course I don't believe it—it is some plot, and a very clumsy plot too; but we must take measures to counterplot it.'

'We must follow him to the ground.'

'Of course we must.'

'Shall I bring a revolver?'

'Oh, no; this will be only a case of one man. We shall simply appear at the right time.'

'You always know what to do,' Sarrasin exclaimed.

'Because I have a husband who has always taught me what to do,' she replied fervently.

Then the military butler was sent for a hansom cab, and Sarrasin and his wife were soon spinning on their way to St. James's Park. They had ample time to get there before the appointed moment, and nothing would be done until the appointed moment came. They drove to St. James's Park, and they dismissed their cab and made quickly for the bridge over the pond. It was not a moonlight night, but it was not clouded or hazy. It was what sailors would call a clear dark night. There was only one figure on the bridge, and that they felt sure was the figure of the Emperor. Mrs Sarrasin had eyes like a lynx, and she could even make out his features.

'Is it he?' Sarrasin asked in a whisper. He had keen sight himself, but he preferred after long experience to trust to the eyes of his wife.

'It is he,' she answered; 'now we shall see.'

They sat quietly side by side on a bench under the dark trees a little away from the bridge. Nobody could easily see them—no one passing through the park or bound on any ordinary business would be likely to pay any attention to them even if he did see them. It was no part of Mrs Sarrasin's purpose that they should be so placed as to be absolutely unnoticeable. If Mr Hamilton should appear on the bridge she would then simply touch Sarrasin's arm, and they would quietly get up and go home together. But suppose—what she fully expected— that someone should appear who was not Hamilton, and should make for the bridge, and in passing should see her husband and her, and thereupon should slink off in another direction, then she should have seen the man, and could identify him among a thousand for ever after. In that event Sarrasin and she could then consider what was next to be done—whether to go at once to Ericson and tell him of what they had seen, or to wait there and keep watch until he had gone away, and then follow quietly in his track until they had seen him safely home. One thing Mrs Sarrasin had made up her mind to: if there was any assassin plot at all, and she believed there was, it would be a safe and certain assassination tried when no watching eyes were near.

The Emperor meanwhile was leaning over the bridge and looking into the water. He was not thinking much about the water, or the sky, or the scene. He was not as yet thinking even of whether Hamilton was coming or not. He was, of course, a little puzzled by the terms of Hamilton's telegram, but there might be twenty reasons why Hamilton should wish to meet him before he reached home, and as Hamilton knew well his fancy for night lounges on that bridge, and as the park lay fairly well between Captain Sarrasin's house and the region of Paulo's Hotel, it seemed likely enough that Hamilton might select it as a convenient place of meeting. In any case, the Emperor was not by nature a suspicious man, and he was not scared by any thoughts of plots, and mystifications, and personal danger. He was a fatalist in a certain sense—not in the religious, but rather in the physical sense. He had a sort of wild-grown, general thought that man is sent into the world to do a certain work, and that while he is useful for that work he is not likely to be sent away from it. This was, perhaps, only an effect of temperament, although he found himself often trying to palm it off on himself as philosophy.

So he was not troubling himself much about the doubtful nature of the telegram. Hamilton would come and explain it, and if Hamilton did not come there would be some other explanation. He began to think about quite other things—he found himself thinking of the bright eyes and the friendly, frank, caressing ways of Helena Langley.

The Emperor began somehow to realise the fact that he had hitherto been leading a very lonely life. He was seldom alone—had seldom been alone for many years; but he began to understand the difference between not being alone and being lonely. During all his working career his life had wanted that companionship which alone is companionship to a man of sensitive nature. He had been too busy in his time in Surmer to think about all this. The days had gone by him with a rush. Each day brought its own sudden and vivid interest. Each day had its own decisions to be formed, its own plans to be made, its own difficulties to be encountered, its own struggles to be fought out. Ericson had delighted in it all, as a splendid exhilarating game. But now, in his enforced retirement and comparative restlessness, he looked back upon it and thought how lonely it all was. When each day closed he had no one to whom he could tell all his thoughts about what the day had done or what the next day was likely to bring forth. Someone has written about the 'passion of solitude'—not meaning the passion *for* solitude, the passion of the saint and the philosopher and the anchorite to be alone and to commune with outer nature or one's inner thought—no, no, but the passion *of* solitude—the raging passion born of solitude which craves and cries out in agony for the remedy of companionship—of some sweet and loved and trusted companionship—like the fond and futile longing of the childless mother for a child.

Eleven! The strokes of the hour rang out from Big Ben in the Clock Tower of Westminster Palace— the Parliament House of which Ericson, in his collegiate days, had once made it his ambition to be a member. The sound of the strokes recalled his mind for the moment to those early days, when the ambition for a seat in Parliament had been the very seamark of his utmost sail. How different his life had been from what his early ideas would have constructed it! And now—was it all over? Had his active career closed? Was he never again to have his chance in Surmer—in Surmer which he had almost begun to love as a bride? Or was he failing in his devotion to his South American Dulcinea del Toboso? Was the love of a mortal woman coming in to distract him from his love to that land with an immortal future?

It pleased him and tantalised him thus to question himself and find himself unable to give the answers. But he bore in mind the fact that Hamilton, the most punctual of living men, was not quite punctual this time. He turned his keen eyes upon the Clock Tower, and could see that during his purposeless reflections quite five minutes had passed. 'Something has happened,' he thought. 'Hamilton is certainly not coming. If he meant to keep the appointment he would have been here waiting for me five minutes before the time. Well, I'll give him five minutes more, and then I'll go.'

Several persons had passed him in the meanwhile. They were the ordinary passengers of the night time. The milliner's apprentice took leave of her lover and made for her home in one of the smaller streets about Broad Sanctuary. The artisan, who had been enjoying a drink in one of the public-houses near the Park, was starting for his home on the south side of the river. Occasionally some smart man came from St. James's Street to bury himself in his flat in Queen Anne's Mansions. A belated Tommy crossed the bridge to make for the St. James's Barracks. One or two of the daughters of folly went loungingly by—wandering, not altogether purposeless, among the open roads of the Park. None of all these had taken any notice of the Emperor.

Suddenly a step was heard near, just as the Emperor was turning to go, and even at that moment he noticed that several persons had quite lately passed, and that this was the first moment when the place was solitary, and a thought flashed through his mind that this might be Hamilton, who had waited for an opportunity. He turned round, and saw that a short and dapper-looking man had come up close beside him. The man leaned over the bridge.

'A fine night, governor,' he said.

'A very fine night,' Ericson said cheerily, and he was turning to go away.

'No offence in talking to you, I hope, governor?'

'Not the least in the world,' Ericson said. 'Why should there be? Why shouldn't you talk to me?'

'Some gents are so stuck-up, don't you know.'

'Well, I am not very much stuck-up,' Ericson said, much amused; 'but I am not quite certain whether I exactly know what stuck-up means.'

'Why, where do you come from?' the stranger asked in amazement.

'I have been out of England for many years. I have come from South America.'

'No—you don't mean that! Why, that beats all! Look here—I have a brother in South America.

'South America is a large place. Where is your brother?'

'Well, I've got a letter from him here. I wonder if you could tell me the name of the place. I can't make it out myself.'

'I dare say I can,' said Ericson carelessly. 'Come under this gas-lamp and let me see your letter.' The man fumbled in his pocket and drew out a folded letter. He had something else in his hand, as the keen eyes of the watching Mrs Sarrasin could very well see.

'Another second,' she whispered to her husband.

The Emperor took the letter good-naturedly, and began to open it under the light of the lamp which hung over the bridge. The stranger was standing just behind him. The place was otherwise deserted.

'Now,' Mrs Sarrasin whispered.

Then Captain Sarrasin strode forward and seized the stranger by the shoulder with one hand, and by his right arm with another.

'What are you a-doin' of?' the stranger asked angrily.

'Well, I want to know who you are in the first place. I beg your Excellency's pardon for intruding on you, but my wife and I happened to be here, and we just came up as this person was talking to you, and we want to know who he is.'

'Captain Sarrasin! Mrs Sarrasin! Where have you turned up from? Tell me—have you really been benignly shadowing me all this way?' Ericson asked with a smile. 'There isn't the slightest danger, I can assure you. This man merely asked me a civil question.'

The civil man, meanwhile, was wrestling and wriggling under Sarrasin's grip. He was wrestling and wriggling all in vain.

'You let me go,' the man exclaimed, in a tone of righteous indignation. 'You hain't nothin' to do with me.'

'I must first see what you have got there in your hand,' Sarrasin said. 'See—there it is! Look here, your Excellency—look at that knife!'

Sarrasin took from the man's hand a short, one-bladed, delicately-shaped, and terrible knife. It might be trusted to pierce its way at a single touch, not to say stroke, into the heart of any victim.

'That's the knife I use at my trade,' the man exclaimed indignantly. 'I am a ladies' slipper-maker, and that's the knife I use for cutting into the leathers, because it cuts clean, don't you see, and makes no waste. Lord bless you, governor, what a notion you have got into your 'ead! I shall amuse my old woman when I tell her.'

'Why did you have the knife in your hand?' Sarrasin sternly asked.

'Took it out, governor, jest by chance when I was taking out the letter.'

'You don't carry a knife like that open in your pocket,' Sarrasin said sternly. 'It closes up, I suppose, or else you have a sheath for it. Oh, yes, I see the spring—it closes this way and I think I have seen this pretty sort of weapon before. Well, look here, you don't carry that sort of toy open in your pocket, you know. How did it come open?'

'Blest if I know, governor—you are all a-puzzlin' of me.'

'Show me the knife,' the Emperor said, taking for the first time some genuine interest in the discussion.

'Look at it,' Sarrasin said. 'Don't give it back to him.'

The Emperor took the knife in his hand, and, touching the spring with the manner of one who understood it, closed and opened the weapon several times.

'I know the knife very well,' he said; 'it has been brought into South America a good deal, but I believe it is Sicilian to begin with. Look here, my man, you say you are a ladies' slipper-maker?'

'Of course I am. Ain't I told you so?'

'Whom do you work for?'

'Works for myself, governor.'

'Where is your shop?'

'Down in the East End, don't you know?'

'I want to talk to you about the East End,' Mrs Sarrasin struck in with her musical, emphatic voice. 'Tell me exactly where you live.'

'Out Whitechapel way.'

'But please tell me the exact place. I happen to know Whitechapel pretty well.'

'Off Whitechapel Road there.'

'Where?'

He made a sulky effort to evade. Mrs Sarrasin was not to be so easily evaded.

'Tell me,' she said, 'the name of the street you live in, and the name of any streets near to it, and how they lie with regard to each other. Come, don't think about it, but tell me; you must know where you live and work.'

'I don't want to have you puzzlin' and worritin' me.'

'Can you tell me where this street is'—she named a street—'or this court, or that hospital, or the nearest omnibus stand to the hospital?'

No, he didn't remember any of these places; he had enough to do mindin' of his work.

'This man doesn't live in Whitechapel,' Mrs Sarrasin said composedly. She put on no air of triumph—she never put on any airs of triumph or indeed airs of any kind.

'Well, there ain't no crime in giving a wrong address,' the man said. 'What business have you with where I live? You don't pay for my lodging, anyhow.'

'Where were you born?' Mrs Sarrasin asked.

'Why, in London, to be sure.'

'In the East End?'

'So I'm told—I don't myself remember.'

'Well, look here, will you just say a few words after me?'

'I ain't got no pertickler objection.'

The cross-examination now had passed wholly into the hands of Mrs Sarrasin. Captain Sarrasin looked on with wonder and delight—Ericson was really interested and amused.

'Say these words.' She repeated slowly, and giving him plenty of time to get the words into his ears and his mind, a number of phrases in which the peculiar accent and pronunciation of the born Whitechapel man were certain to come out. Ericson, of course, comprehended the meaning of the whole performance. The East End man hesitated.

'I ain't here for playing tricks,' he mumbled. 'I want to be getting home to my old woman.'

'Look here,' Sarrasin said, angrily interfering. 'You just do as you are told, or I'll whistle for a policeman and give you into custody, and then everything about you will come out—or, by Jove, I'll take you up and drop you into that pond as if you were a blind kitten! Answer the lady at once, you confounded scoundrel!'

The small eyes of the Whitechapel man flashed fire for an instant—a fire that certainly is not common to Cockney eyes—and he made a sudden grasp at his pocket.

'See there!' Sarrasin exclaimed. 'The ladies' slipper-maker is grasping for his knife, and forgets that we have got it in our possession.'

'This is certainly becoming interesting,' Ericson said. 'It is much more interesting than most plays that I have lately seen. Now, then, recite after the lady, or confess thyself.'

It had not escaped the notice of the Emperor that when once or twice some wayfarer passed along the bridge or on one of the near-lying paths the maker of ladies' slippers did not seem in the least anxious to attract attention. He appeared, in fact, to be the one of the whole party who was most eager to withdraw himself from the importunate notice of the casual passer-by. A man conscious of no wrong done or planned by him, and unjustly bullied and badgered by three total strangers, would most assuredly have leaped at the chance of appealing to the consideration and the help of the passing citizen.

Mrs Sarrasin remorselessly repeated her test words, and the man repeated them after her.

'That will do,' she said contemptuously; 'the man was never born in Whitechapel—his East End accent is mere gotten up stage-play.' Then she spoke some rapid words to her husband in a *patois* which Ericson did not understand. The Whitechapel man's eyes flashed fire again.

'You see,' she said to the Emperor, 'he understands me! I have been saying in Sicilian *patois* that he is a hired assassin born in England of Sicilian parents, and brought up, probably, near Snow Hill—and this Whitechapel gentleman understood every word I said! If you give him the alternative of going to the nearest police-station and being charged, or of talking Sicilian *patois* with me, you will see that he prefers the alternative of a conversation in Sicilian *patois* with me.

'I propose that we let him go,' the Emperor said decisively. 'We have no evidence against him, except that he carries a peculiar knife, and that he is, as you say, of Sicilian parents.'

'Your Excellency yourself gave me the hint I acted on,' Mrs Sarrasin said deferentially, 'when you made the remark that the knife was Sicilian. I spoke on mere guess-work, acting on that hint.'

'And you were right, as you always are,' Captain Sarrasin struck in with admiring eyes fixed on his wife.

'Well, he is a poor creature, anyhow,' the Emperor said—and he spoke now to his friends in Spanish—'and not much up to his work. If he were worth anything in his own line of business he might have finished the job with that knife instead of stopping to open a conversation with me.'

'But he has been set on by someone to do this job,' Sarrasin said, 'and we might get to know who is the someone that set him on.'

'We shall not know from him,' the Emperor replied; 'he probably does not know who are the real movers. No; if there is anything serious to come it will come from better hands than his. No, my dear and kind friends, we can't get any further with *him*. Let the creature go. Let him tell his employers, whoever they are, that I don't scare, as the Americans say, worth a cent. If they have any real assassins to send on, let them come; this fellow won't do; and I can't have paragraphs in the papers to say that I took any serious alarm from a creature who, with such a knife in his hand, could not, without a moment's parley, make it do his work.'

'The man is a hired assassin,' Sarrasin declared.

'Very likely,' the Emperor replied calmly; 'but we can't convict him of it, and we had better let him go his blundering way.' The Emperor had meanwhile been riveting his eyes on the face of the captive—if we may call him so—anxious to find out from his expression whether he understood Spanish. If he seemed to understand Spanish then the affair would be a little more serious. It might lead to the impression that he was really mixed up in South American affairs, and that he fancied he had partisan wrongs to avenge. But the man's face remained imperturbable. He evidently understood nothing. It was not even, the Emperor felt certain, that he had been put on his guard by his former lapse into unlucky consciousness when Mrs Sarrasin tried him and trapped him with the Sicilian *patois*. No, there was a look of dull curiosity on his face, and that was all.

'We'll keep the knife?' Sarrasin asked.

'Yes; I think you had better keep the knife. It may possibly come in as a *pièce de justification* one of these days. What's the value of your knife?' he asked in English, suddenly turning on the captive with a stern voice and manner that awed the creature.

'It's well worth a quid, governor.'

'Yes; I should think it was. There's a quid and a half for you, and go your ways. We have agreed—my friends and I—to let you off this time, although we have every reason to believe that you meant murder.'

'Oh, governor!'

'If you try it again,' the Emperor said, 'you will forfeit your life whether you succeed or fail. Now get away—and set us free from your presence.'

The man ran along the road leading eastward—ran with the speed of some hunted animal, the path re-echoing to the sound of his flying feet. Ericson broke into a laugh.

'You have in all probability saved my life,' the Emperor said. 'You two——'

'All *her* doing,' Sarrasin interposed.

'I think I understand it all,' Ericson went on. 'I have no doubt this was meant as an attempt. But it was a very bungling first attempt. The planners, whoever they were, were anxious first of all to keep themselves as far as possible out of responsibility and suspicion, and instead of hiring a South American bravo, and so in a manner bringing it home to themselves, they merely picked up and paid an ordinary Sicilian stabber who had no heart in the matter, who probably never heard of me before in all his life, and had no partisan hatred to drive him on. So he dallied, and bungled; and then you two intervened, and his game was hopeless. He'll not try it again, you may be sure.'

'No, he probably has had enough of it,' Captain Sarrasin said; 'and of course he has got his pay beforehand. But someone else will.'

'Very likely,' the Emperor said carelessly. 'They will manage it on a better plan next time.'

'We must have better plans, too,' Sarrasin said warmly.

'How can we? The only wise thing in such affairs is to take the ordinary and reasonable precautions that any sane man takes who has serious business to do in life, and then not to trouble oneself any further. Anyhow, I owe to you both, dear friends,' and the Emperor took a hand of each in one of his, 'a deep debt of gratitude. And now I propose that we consider the whole incident as *vidé*, and that we go forthwith to Paulo's and have a pleasant supper there and summon up the boy Hamilton, even should he be in bed, and ask him how he came to send out telegrams for belated meetings in St. James's Park, and have a good time to repay us for our loss of an hour and the absurdity of our adventure. Come, Mrs Sarrasin, you will not refuse my invitation?'

'Excellency, certainly not.'

'You can stay in the hotel, dear,' Sarrasin suggested.

'Yes, I should like that best,' she said.

'They won't expect you at home?' the Emperor asked.

'They never expect us,' Mrs Sarrasin answered with her usual sweet gravity. 'When we are coming we let them know—if we do not we are never to be expected. My husband could not manage his affairs at all if we were to have to look out for being expected.'

'You know how to live your life, Mrs Sarrasin,' the Emperor said, much interested.

'I have tried to learn the art,' she said modestly.

'It is a useful branch of knowledge,' Ericson answered, 'and one of the least cultivated by men or women, I think.'

They were moving along at this time. They crossed the bridge and passed by Marlborough House, and so got into Pall Mall.

'How shall we go?' the Emperor asked, glancing at the passing cabs, some flying, some crawling.

'Four-wheeler?' Sarrasin suggested tentatively.

'No; I don't seem to be in humour for anything slow and creeping,' the Emperor said gaily. 'I feel full of animal spirits, somehow. Perhaps it is the getting out of danger, although really I don't think there was much'—and then he stopped, for he suddenly reflected that it must seem rather ungracious to suggest that there was not much danger to a pair of people who had come all the way from Clapham Common to look after his life. 'There was not much craft,' he went on to say, 'displayed in that first attempt. You will have to look after me pretty closely in the future. No; I must spin in a hansom—it is the one thing I specially love in London, its hansom. Here, we'll have two hansoms, and I'll take charge of Mrs Sarrasin, and you'll follow us, or, at least, you'll find your way the best you can, Captain Sarrasin—and let us see who gets there first.'

CHAPTER XV

'IF I WERE TO ASK YOU?'

It is needless to say that Hamilton had never sent any telegram asking the Emperor to meet him on the bridge in St. James's Park or anywhere else at eleven o'clock at night. Hamilton at first was disposed to find fault with the letting loose of the supposed assassin, and was at all events much in favour of giving information at Scotland Yard and putting the police authorities on the look-out for some plot. But the opinion of the Emperor was clear and fixed, and Hamilton naturally yielded to it. Ericson was quite prepared to believe that some plot was expanding, but he was convinced that it would be better to allow it to expand. The one great thing was to find out who were the movers in the plot. If the London Sicilian really were a hired assassin, it was clear that he was thrown out merely as a skirmisher in the hope that he might succeed in doing the work at once, and the secure conviction that if he failed he could be abandoned to his fate. It was the crude form of an attempt at political assassination. A wild outcry on the part of the Emperor's friends would, he felt convinced, have no better effect than to put his enemies prematurely on their guard, and inspire them to plan something very subtle and dangerous. Or if, then, their hate did not take so serious a form, the Emperor reasoned that they were not particularly dangerous. So he insisted on lying low, and quietly seeing what would come of it. He was not now disposed to underrate the danger, but he felt convinced that the worst possible course for him would be to proclaim the danger too soon.

Therefore, Ericson insisted that the story of the bridge and the Sicilian knife must be kept an absolute secret for the present at least, and the help of Scotland Yard must not be invoked. Of course, it was clear even to Hamilton that there was no evidence against the supposed Sicilian which would warrant any magistrate in committing him for trial on a charge of attempted assassination. There was conjectural probability enough; but men are not sent for trial in this country on charges of conjectural probability. The fact of the false telegram having been sent was the only thing which made it clear that behind the Sicilian there were conspirators of a more educated and formidable character. The Sicilian never could have sent that telegram; would not be likely to know anything about Hamilton. Hamilton in the end became satisfied that the Emperor was right, and that it would be better to keep a keen look-out and let the plot develop itself. The most absolute reliance could be put on the silence of the Sarrasins; and better look-out could hardly be kept than the look-out of that brave and quick-witted pair of watchers. Therefore Ericson told Hamilton he meant to sleep in spite of thunder.

The very day after the scene on the bridge the Emperor got an imperious little note from Helena asking him to come to see her at once, as she had something to say to him. He had been thinking of her—he had been occupying himself in an odd sort of way with the conviction, the memory, that if the supposed assassin had only been equal to his work, the last thought on earth of the Emperor would have been given to Helena Langley. It did not occur to the Emperor, in his quiet, unegotistic nature, to think of what Helena Langley would have given to know that her name in such a crisis would have been on his dying lips.

Ericson himself did not think of the matter in that sentimental and impassioned way. He was only studying in his mind the curious fact that he certainly was thinking about Helena Langley as he stood on the bridge and looked on the water; and that, if the knife of the ladies' slipper-maker had done its business promptly, the last thought in his mind, the last feeling in his heart, would have been given not to Surmer but to Helena Langley.

He was welcomed and ushered by To-to. When the footman had announced him, Helena sprang up from her sofa and ran to meet him.

'I sent for you,' she said, almost breathlessly, 'because I have a favour to ask of you! Will you promise me, as all gallants did in the old days—will you promise me before I ask it, that you will grant it?'

'The knights in the old days had wonderful auxiliaries. They had magical spells, and sorceresses, and wizards—and we have only our poor selves. Suppose I were not able to grant the favour you ask of me?'

'Oh, but, if that were so, I never should ask it. It is entirely and absolutely in your power to say yes or no.'

'To say—and then to do.'

'Yes, of course—to say and then to do.'

'Well, then, of course,' he said, with a smile, 'I shall say yes.'

'Thank you,' she replied fervently; 'it's only this—that you will take some care of yourself—take,' and she hesitated, and almost shuddered, 'some care of your—life.'

For a moment he thought that she had heard of the adventure in St. James's Park, and he was displeased.

'Is my life threatened?' he asked.

'My father thinks it is. He has had some information. There are people in Surmer who hate you—bad and corrupt and wicked people. My father thinks you ought to take some care of yourself, for the sake of the cause that is so dear to you, and for the sake of some friends who care for you, and who, I hope, are dear to you too.' Her voice trembled, but she bore up splendidly.

'I love my friends,' the Emperor said quietly, 'and I would do much for their sake—or merely to please them. But tell me, what can I do?'

'Be on the look-out for enemies, don't go about alone—at all events at night—don't go about unarmed. My father is sure attempts will be made.'

These words were a relief to Ericson. They showed at least that she did not suppose any attempt had yet been, made. This was satisfactory. The secret to which he attached so much importance had been kept.

'It is of no use,' the Emperor said. 'In this sort of business a man has got to take his life in his hand.

Precautions are pretty well useless. In nine cases out of ten the assassin—I mean the fellow who wants to be an assassin and tries to be an assassin—is a mere mountebank, who might be safely allowed to shoot at you or stab at you as long as he likes and no harm done. Why? Because the creature is nervous, and afraid to risk his own life. Get the man who wants to kill you, and does not care about his own life—is willing and ready to die the instant after he has killed you—and from a man like that you can't preserve your life.'

Helena shuddered. 'It is terrible,' she said.

'Dear Miss Langley, it is not more terrible than a score of chances in life which young ladies run without the slightest sense of alarm. Why you, in your working among the poor, run the danger of scarlet fever and small-pox every other day in your life, and you never think about it. How many public men have died by the assassin's hand in my days? Abraham Lincoln, Marshal Prim, President Garfield, Lord Frederick Cavendish—two or three more; and how many young ladies have died of scarlet fever?'

'But one can't take any precautions against scarlet fever—except to keep away from where it may be, and not to do what one must feel to be a duty.'

'Exactly,' he said eagerly; 'there is where it is.'

'You can't,' she urged, 'have police protection against typhus or small-pox.'

'Nor against assassination,' he said gravely. 'At least, not against the only sort of assassins who are in the least degree dangerous. I want you to understand this quite clearly,' he said, turning to her suddenly with an earnestness which had something tender in it. 'I want you to know that I am not rash or foolhardy or careless about my own life. I have only too much reason for wanting to live—aye, even for clinging to life! But, as a matter of calculation, there is no precaution to be taken in such a case which can be of the slightest value as a genuine protection. An enemy determined enough will get at you in your bedroom as you sleep some night—you can't have a cordon of police around your door. Even if you did have a police cordon round you when you took your walks abroad, it wouldn't be of the slightest use against the bullet of the assassin firing from the garret window.'

'This is appalling,' Helena said, turning pale. 'I now understand why some women have such a horror of anything like political strife. I wonder if I should lose courage if someone in whom I was interested were in serious danger?'

'You would never lose your courage,' the Emperor said firmly. 'You would fear nothing so much as that those you cared for should not prove themselves equal to the duty imposed upon them.'

'I used to think so once,' she said. 'I begin to be afraid about myself now.'

'Well, in this case,' he interposed quickly, 'there does not seem to be any real apprehension of danger. I am afraid,' he added, with a certain bitterness, 'my enemies in Surmer do not regard me as so very formidable a personage as to make it worth their while to pay for the cost of my assassination. I don't fancy they are looking out for my speedy return to Surmer.'

'My father's news is different. He hears that your party is growing in Surmer every day, and that the people in power are making themselves every day more and more odious to the country.'

'That they are likely enough to do,' he said, with a bright look coming into his eyes, 'and that is one reason why I am quite determined not to precipitate matters. We can't afford to have revolution after revolution in a poor and struggling place like Surmer, and so I want these people to give the full measure of their incapacity and their baseness so that when they fall they may fall like Lucifer! Hamilton would be rather for rushing things—I am not.'

'Do you keep in touch with Surmer?' Helena asked almost timidly. She had lately grown rather shy of asking him questions on political matters, or of seeming to assume any right to be in his confidence. All the impulsive courage which she used to have in the days when their acquaintanceship was but new and slight seemed to have deserted her now that they were such close and recognised friends, and that random report occasionally gave them out as engaged lovers.

'Oh, yes,' he answered; 'I thought you knew—I fancied I had told you. I have constant information from friends on whom I can absolutely rely—in Surmer.'

'Do they know what your enemies are doing?'

'Yes, I should think they would get to know,' he said with a smile, 'as far as anything can be known.'

'Would they be likely to know,' she asked again in a timid tone, 'if any plot were being got up against you?'

'Any plot for my murder?'

'Yes!' Her voice sank to a whisper—she hardly dared to put the possibility into words. The fear which we allow to occupy our thoughts seems sometimes too fearful to be put into words. It appears as if by spoken utterance we conjure up the danger.

'Some hint of the kind might be got,' he said hesitatingly. 'Our enemies are very crafty, but these things often leak out. Someone loses courage and asks for advice—or confides to his wife, and she takes fright and goes for counsel to somebody else. Then two words of a telegram across the ocean would put me on my guard.'

'If you should get such a message, will you—tell *me*?'

'Oh, yes, certainly,' he said carelessly, 'I can promise you that.'

'And will you promise me one thing more—will you promise to be careful?'

'What *is* being careful? How can one take care, not knowing where or whence the danger threatens?'

'But you need not go out alone, at night.'

'You have no idea how great a delight it is for me to go about London at night. Then I am quite free—of politicians, interviewers, gossiping people, society ladies, and all the rest. I am master of myself, and I am myself again.'

'Still, if your friends ask you——'

'Some of my friends have asked me.'

'And you did not comply?'

'No; I did not think there was any necessity for complying.'

'But if *I* were to ask you?' She laid her hand gently, lightly, timidly, on his.

'Ah, well, if *you* were to ask me, that would be quite a different thing.'

'Then I do ask you,' she exclaimed, almost joyously.

He smiled a bright, half-sad smile upon the kindly, eager girl.

'Well, I promise not to go out alone at night in London until you release me from my vow. It is not much to do this to please you, Miss Langley—you have been so kind to me. I am really glad to have it in my power to do anything to please you.'

'You have pleased me much, yet I feel penitent too.'

'Penitent for what?'

'For having deprived you of these lonely midnight walks which you seem to love so much.'

'I shall love still more the thought of giving anything up to please you.'

'Thank you,' she said gravely—and that was all she said. She began to be afraid that she had shown her hand too much. She began to wonder what he was thinking of her—whether he thought her too free spoken—too forward—whether he had any suspicion of her feelings towards him. His manner, too, had always been friendly, gentle, tender even; but it was the manner of a man who apparently considered all suspicion of courtship to be wholly out of the question. This very fact had made her incautious, she thought. If any serious personal danger ever should threaten him, how should she be able to keep her real feelings a secret from him? Were they, she asked herself in pain and with flushing face, a secret even now? After today could he fail to know—could he at all events fail to guess?

Did the Emperor know—did he guess—that the girl was in love with him?

The Emperor did not know and did not guess. The frankness of her manners had completely led him astray. The way in which she rendered him open homage deceived him wholly as to her feelings. He knew that she liked his companionship—of that he could have no doubt—he knew that she was by nature a hero-worshipper and that he was just now her hero. But he never for a moment imagined that the girl was in love with him. After a little while he would go away—to Surmer, most likely—and she would soon find some other hero, and one day he would read in the papers that the daughter of Sir Rupert Langley was married. Then he would write her a letter of congratulation, and in due course he would receive from her a friendly answer—and there an end.

Perhaps just now he was more concerned about his own feelings than about hers—much more, indeed, because he had not the remotest suspicion that her feelings were in any wise disturbed. But his own? He began to think it time that he should grow acquainted with his heart, and search what stirred it so. He could not conceal from himself the fact that he was growing more and more attached to the companionship of this beautiful, clever, and romantic girl. He found that she disputed Surmer in his mind. He found that, mingling imperceptibly with his hope of a triumphant return to Surmer, was the thought that *she* would feel the triumph too, or the painful thought that if it came she would not be near him to hear the story. He found that one of the delights of his lonely midnight walks was the quiet thought of her. It used to be a gladness to him to recall, in those moments of solitude, some word that she had spoken—some kindly touch of her hand.

He began to grow afraid of his position and his feelings. What had he to do with falling in love? That was no part of the work of his life. What could it be to him but a misfortune if he were to fall in love with this girl who was so much younger than he? Supposing it possible that a girl of that age could love him, what had he to offer her? A share in a career that might well prove desperate—a career to be brought to a sudden and swift close, very probably by his own death at the hands of his successful enemies in Surmer! Think of the bright home in which he found that girl—of the tender, almost passionate, love she bore to her father, and which her father returned with such love for her—think of the brilliant future that seemed to await her, and then think of the possibility of her ever being prevailed upon to share his dark and doubtful fortunes. The Emperor was not a rich man. Much of what he once had was flung away—or at all events given away—in his efforts to set up reform and constitutionalism in Surmer. The plain truth of the position was that even if Helena Langley were at all likely to fall in love with him it would be his clear duty, as a man of honour and one who wished her well, to discourage any such feeling and to keep away from her. But the Emperor honestly believed that he was entitled to put any such thought as that out of his mind. The very frankness—the childlike frankness—with which she had approached him made it clear that she had no thought of any romance being possible between them. 'She thinks of me as a man almost old enough to be her father,' he said to himself. So the Emperor reconciled his conscience, and still kept on seeing her.

CHAPTER XVI

THE CHILDREN OF GRIEVANCE

The Emperor and Hamilton stood in Ericson's study, waiting to receive a deputation. The Emperor had agreed to receive this deputation from an organisation of working men. The deputation desired to complain of the long hours of work and the small rate of pay from which English artisans in many branches of labour had to suffer. Why they had sought to see him he could not very well tell— and certainly if it had been left to Hamilton, whose mind was set on sparing the Emperor all avoidable trouble, and who, moreover, had in his heart of hearts no great belief in remedy by working-men's deputation, the poor men would probably not have been accorded the favour of an interview. But the Emperor insisted on receiving them, and they came; trooped into the room awkwardly; at first seemed slow of speech, and soon talked a great deal. He listened to all they had to say, and put questions and received answers, and certainly impressed the deputation with the conviction that if his Excellency the ex-Emperor of Surmer could not do anything very much for them, his heart at least was in their cause. He had an idea in his mind of something he could do to help the over-oppressed English working man—and that was the reason why he had consented to receive the deputation.

The spokesman of the deputation was a gaunt and haggard-looking man. The dirt seemed ingrained in him—in his hands, his eyebrows, his temples, under his hair, up to his very eyes. He told a pitiful story of long work and short pay—of hungry children and an over-tasked wife. He told, in fact, the story familiar to all of us—the 'chestnut' of the newspapers—the story which the busy man of ordinary society is not expected to trouble himself by reading any more—supposing he ever had read it at all.

The Emperor, however, was not an ordinary society man, and he had been a long time away from England, and had not had his attention turned to these social problems of Great Britain. He was therefore deeply interested in the whole business, and he asked a number of questions, and got shrewd, keen answers sometimes, and very rambling answers on other occasions. The deputation was like all other deputations with a grievance. There was the fanatic burning to a white heat, with the inward conviction of wrong done, not accidentally, but deliberately, to him and to his class. There was the prosaic, didactic, reasoning man, who wanted to talk the whole matter out himself, and to put everybody's arguments to the test, and to prove that all were wrong and weak and fallible and unpractical save himself alone. There was the fervid man, who always wanted to dash into the middle of every other man's speech. There was the practical man, who came with papers of figures and desired to make it all a question of statistics. There was the 'crank,' who disagreed with everything that everybody else said or suggested or could possibly have said or suggested on that or any other subject. The first trouble of the Emperor was to get at any commonly admitted appreciation of facts. More than once—many times indeed—he had to interpose and explain that he personally knew nothing of the subjects they were discussing; that he only sought for information; and that he begged them if they could to agree among themselves as to the actual realities which they wished to bring under his notice. Even when he had thus adjured them it was not easy for him to get them to be all in a story. Poor fellows! each one of them had his own peculiar views and his own peculiar troubles too closely pressing on his brain. The Emperor was never impatient—but he kept asking himself the question: 'Suppose I had the power to legislate, and were now called upon by these men and in their own interests to legislate, what on their own showing should I be able to do?'

More than once, too, he put to them that question. 'Admitting your grievances—admitting the justice, the reason, the practical good sense of your demands, what can *I* do? Why do you appeal to me? I am no legislator. I am a proscribed and banished man from a country which until lately most of you had never heard of. What would you have of me?'

The spokesman of the deputation could only answer that they had heard of him as of one who had risen to supreme position in a great far-off country, and who had always concerned himself deeply with the interest of the working classes.

'Will that,' he asked, 'get me one moment's audience from an English official department?'

No, they did not suppose it would; they shook their heads. They could not help him to learn how he was to help them.

The day was cold and dreary. No matter though the season was still supposed to be far remote from winter, yet the look of the skies was cruelly depressing, and the atmosphere was loaded with a misty chill. Ericson's heart was profoundly touched. He saw in his mind's eye a country glowing with soft sunshine—a country where even winter came caressingly on the people living there; a country with vast and almost boundless spaces for cultivation; a country watered with noble rivers and streams; a country to be renowned in history as the breeder of horses and cattle and the grower of grain; a country well qualified to rear and feed and bring up in sunny comfort more than the whole mass of the hopeless toilers on the chill English fields and in the sooty English cities. His mind was with the country with which he had identified his career—which only wanted good strong hands to convert her into a country of practical prosperity—which only needed brains to open for her a history that should be remembered in all far-stretching time. He now excused himself for what had at one moment seemed his weakness in consenting to receive a deputation for which he could do nothing. He found that he had something to say to them after all.

The Emperor had a sweet, strong, melodious voice. When he had heard them all most patiently out, he used his voice and said what he had to say. He told them that he had directly no right to receive them at all, for, as far as regards this country, there was absolutely nothing he could do for them. He was not an official, not a member of Parliament, not a person claiming the slightest influence in English public life. Nor even in the country of his adoption did he reckon for much just now. He was, as they all knew, an exile; if he were to return to that country now, his life would, in all probability, be forfeit. Yet, in God's good pleasure, he might, after all, get back some time, and, if that should be, then he would think of his poor countrymen, in England. Surmer was a great country, and could find homes for hundreds and hundreds of thousands of Englishmen. There—he had no scheme, had never thought of the matter until quite lately—until they had asked him to receive their deputation. He had nothing more to say and nothing more to ask. He was ashamed to have brought them to listen to a reply of so little worth in any sense; but that was all that he could tell them, and if ever again he was in a position to do anything, then he could only say that he hoped to be reminded of his promise.

The deputation went away not only contented but enthusiastic. They quite understood that their immediate cause was not advanced and could not be advanced by anything the Emperor could possibly have to say. But they had been impressed by his sincerity and by his sympathy. They had been deputed to wait on many a public official, many a head of a department, many a Secretary of State, many an Under-Secretary. They were familiar with the stereotyped official answers, the answers that assured them that the case should have consideration, and that if anything could be done— well, then, perhaps, something would be done. Possibly no other answer could have been given. The answer of the unofficial and irresponsible Emperor promised absolutely nothing; but it had the musical ring of sincerity and of sympathy about it, and the men grasped strongly his strong hand, and went away glad that they had seen him.

The Emperor did not usually receive deputations. But he had a great many requests from deputations that they might be allowed to wait on him and express their views to him. He was amazed sometimes to find what an important man he was in the estimation of various great organisations. He was assured by the committee of the Universal Arbitration Society that, if he would only appear on their platform and deliver a speech, the cause of universal arbitration would be secured, and public war would go out of fashion in the world as completely as the private duel has gone out of fashion in England. Of course, he was politely pressed to receive a deputation on behalf of several societies interested on one side or the other of the great question of Woman's Suffrage. The teetotallers and Local Optionists of various forms solicited the favour of a talk with him. The trade associations and the licensed victuallers eagerly desired to get at his views. The letters he received on the subject of the hours of labour interested him a great deal, and he tried to grapple with their difficulties, but soon found he could make little of them. By the strenuous advice of Hamilton he was induced to keep out of these complex English questions altogether. Ericson yielded, knowing that Hamilton was advising him for the best; but he had a good deal of the Don Quixote in his nature; and having now a sort of enforced idleness put upon him, he felt a secret yearning for some enterprise to set the world right in other directions than that of Surmer.

There was a certain indolence in Ericson's nature. It was the indolence which is perfectly consistent with a course of tremendous and sustained energy. It was the nature which says to itself at one moment, 'Up and do the work,' and goes for the work with unconquerable earnestness until the work is done, and then says, 'Very good; now the work is done, let us rest and smoke and talk over other things.' Nature is one thing; character is another. We start with a certain kind of nature; we beat it and mould it, or it is beaten and moulded for us, into character. Even Hamilton was never quite certain whether Nature had meant Ericson for a dreamer, and Ericson and Fortune co-operating had hammered him into a worker, or whether Nature had moulded him for a worker, and his own tastes for contemplation and for reading and for rest had softened him down into a dreamer.

'The condition of this country horrifies me, Hamilton,' he said, when left alone with his devoted follower. 'I don't see any way out of it. I find no one who even professes to see any way out of it. I don't see any people getting on well but the trading class.'

'*But* the trading class?' Hamilton asked, with a quiet smile.

'You mean that if the trading class are getting on well the country in the end will get on well?'

'It would look like that,' Hamilton answered; 'wouldn't it? This is a country of trade. If our trade is sound, our heart is sound.'

'But what is becoming of the land, what is becoming of the peasant? What is becoming of the East End population? I don't see how trade helps any of these. Read the accounts from Liverpool, from Manchester, from Sheffield, from anywhere: nothing but competition and strikes and general misery. And, look here, I can't bear the idea of everything in life being swallowed up in the great cities, and the peasantry of England totally disappearing, and being succeeded by a gaunt, ragged class of half-starved labourers in big towns. Take my word for it, Hamilton, a cursed day has come when we see *that* day.'

'What can be done?' Hamilton asked, in a kind of compassionate tone—compassion rather for the trouble of his chief than for the supposed national tribulation. Hamilton was as generous-hearted a young fellow as could be, but his affections were more evidenced in the concrete than in the abstract. He had grown up accustomed to all these distracting social questions, and he did not suppose that anything very much was likely to come of them—at any rate, he supposed that if anything were to come of them it would come of itself, and that we could not do much to help or hinder it. So he was not disposed to distress himself much about these social complications, although, if he felt sure that his purse or his labour could avail in any way to make things better, his help most assuredly would not be wanting. But he did not like the Emperor to be worried about such things. The Emperor's work, he thought, was to be kept for other fields.

'Nothing can be done, I suppose,' the Emperor said gloomily. 'But, my dear Hamilton, that is the trouble of the whole business. That does not help us to put it out of our minds—it only racks our minds all the more. To think that it should be so! To think that in this great country, so rich in money, so splendid in intellect, we should have to face that horrible problem of misery and poverty and vice, and, having stared at it long enough, simply close our eyes, or turn away and deliver it as our final utterance that there is nothing to be done!'

'Anyhow,' Hamilton said, 'there is nothing to be done by you and me. It's of no use our wearing out our energies about it.'

'No,' the Emperor assented, not without drawing a deep breath; 'but if I had time and energy I should like to try. We have no such problems to solve in Surmer, Hamilton.'

'No, by Jupiter!' Hamilton exclaimed, 'and therefore the very sooner we get back there the better.'

The Emperor sent a compassionate and even tender glance at his young companion. He had the best reason to know how sincere and self-sacrificing was Hamilton's devotion to the cause of Surmer; but he could not doubt that just at present there was mingled in the young man's heart, along with the wish to be serving actively the cause of Surmer, the wish also to be free of London, to be away from the scene of a bitter disappointment. The Emperor's heart was deeply touched. He had admired with the most cordial admiration the courage, the noble self-repression, which Hamilton had displayed since the hour of his great disappointment. Never a word of repining, never the exhibition in public of a clouded brow, never any apparent longing to creep into lonely brakes like the wounded deer—only the man-like resolve to put up with the inevitable, and go on with one's work in life just as if nothing had happened. All the time the Emperor knew what a passionately loving nature Hamilton had, and he knew how he must have suffered. 'I am old enough almost to be the lad's father,' he thought to himself, 'and I could not have borne it like that.' All this passed through his mind in a time so short that Hamilton was not able to notice any delay in the reply to his observation.

'You are right, boy,' the Emperor cheerily said. 'I don't believe that you and I were meant for any mission but the redemption of Surmer.'

'I am glad, to hear you say so,' Hamilton interposed quickly.

'Had you ever any doubt of my feelings on that subject?' Ericson asked with a smile.

'Oh, no, of course not; but I don't always like to hear you talking about the troubles of these old worn-out countries, as if you had anything to do with them or were born to set them right. It seems as if you were being decoyed away from your real business.'

'No fear of that, boy,' the Emperor said. 'What I was thinking of was that we might very well arrange to do something for the country of our birth and the country of our adoption at once, Hamilton—by some great scheme of English colonisation in Surmer. If we get back again I should like to see clusters of English villages springing up all over the surface of that lovely country.'

'Our people are so wanting in adaptability,' Hamilton began.

'My dear fellow, how can you say that? Who made the United States? What about Australia? What about South Africa?'

'These were weedy poor chaps, these fellows who were here just now,' Hamilton suggested.

'Good brain-power among some of them, all the same,' the Emperor asserted. 'Do you know, Hamilton, say what you will, the idea catches fire in my mind?'

'I am very glad, Excellency; I am very glad of any idea that makes you warm to the hope of returning to Surmer.'

'Dear old boy, what *is* the matter with you? You seem to think that I need some spurring to drive me back to Surmer. Do you really think anything of the kind?'

'Oh, no, Excellency, I don't—if it comes to that. But I don't like your getting mixed up in any manner of English local affairs.'

'I see, you are afraid I might be induced to become a candidate for the House of Commons—or, perhaps, for the London County Council, or the School Board. I tell you what, Hamilton: I do seriously wish I had an opportunity of going into training on the School Board. It would give me some information and some ideas which might be very useful if we ever get again to be at the head of affairs in Surmer.'

Hamilton was a young man who took life seriously. If it were possible to imagine that he could criticise unfavourably anything said or done by his chief, it would be perhaps when the chief condescended to trifle about himself and his position. So Hamilton did not like the mild jest about the School Board. Indeed, his mind was not at the moment much in a condition for jests of any kind, mild or otherwise.

'I don't fancy we should learn anything in the London School Board that would be of any particular service to us out in Surmer,' he said protestingly.

'Right you are,' the Emperor answered, with a half-pathetic smile. 'I need you, boy, to recall me to myself, as the people say in the novels. No, I do not for a moment feel myself vain enough to suppose that the ordinary member of the London School Board could at a stroke put his finger within a thousand miles of Surmer on the map of the world—Mercator's Projection, or any other. And yet, do you know, I have odd dreams in my head of a day when Surmer may become the home and the shelter of a sturdy English population, whom their own country could endow with no land but the narrow slip of earth that makes a pauper's grave.'

CHAPTER XVII

MISS PAULO'S OBSERVATION

Miss Paulo sat for a while thoughtfully biting the top of her quill pen and looking out dreamily into the street. Her little sitting-room faced Knightsbridge and the trees and grass of the Park. Often when some problem of the domestic economy of the hotel caused her a passing perplexity, she would derive new vigour for grappling with complicated sums from a leisurely study of those green spaces and the animated panorama of the passing crowd. But today there was nothing particularly complicated about the family accounts, and Dolores Paulo sought for no arithmetical inspiration from the pleasant out-look. Her mind was wholly occupied with the thought of what Captain Sarrasin had been saying to her—of the possible peril that threatened the Emperor.

She drew the feather from between her lips and tapped the blotting-pad with it impatiently.

'Why should I trouble my head or my heart about him?' she asked herself bitterly. 'He doesn't trouble his head or his heart about me.'

But she felt ashamed of her petulant speech immediately. She seemed to see the grave, sweet face of the Emperor looking down at her in surprise; she seemed to see the strong soldierly face of Captain Sarrasin frown upon her sternly.

'Ah,' she meditated with a sigh, 'it is only natural that he should fall in love with a girl like that. She can be of use to him—of use to his cause. What use can I

257

be to him or to his cause? There is nothing I can do except to look out for a possible South American with an especially dark skin and especially curly moustache.'

As she reflected thus, her eye, wandering over the populous thoroughfare and the verdure beyond, populous also, noted, or rather accepted, the presence of one particular man out of the many. The one particular man was walking slowly up and down on the roadside opposite to the hotel by the Park railings. That he was walking up and down Dolores became conscious of through the fact that, having half unconsciously seen him once float into her ken, she noted him again, with some slight surprise, and was aware of him yet a third time with still greater surprise. The man paced slowly up and down on what appeared to be a lengthy beat, for Dolores mentally calculated that something like a minute must have elapsed between each glimpse of his face as he moved in the direction in which she most readily beheld him. He was a man a little above the middle height, with a keen, aquiline face, smooth-shaven, and red-haired. There was nothing in his dress to render him in the least remarkable; he was dressed like everybody else, Dolores said to herself, and it must therefore have been his face that somehow or other attracted her vagrant fancy. Yet it was not a particularly attractive face in any sense. It was not a comely face which would compel the admiring attention of a girl, nor was it a face so strongly marked, so out of the ordinary lines, as to command attention by its ugliness or its strength of character. It was the smooth-shaven face of an average man of a fair-haired race; there was something Scotch about it—Lowland Scotch, the kind of face of which one might see half a hundred in an hour's stroll along the main street of Glasgow or Prince's Street in Edinburgh. Dolores had been in both these cities and knew the type, and as it was not a specially interesting type she soon diverted her gaze from the unknown and resumed attentively her table of figures. But she had not given many seconds to their consideration when her attention was again diverted. A four-wheeled cab had driven up to the door with a considerable pile of luggage on it. There was nothing very remarkable in that. The arrival of a cab loaded with luggage was an event of hourly occurrence at Paulo's Hotel, and quite unlikely to arouse any especial interest in the mind of Miss Dolores. What, however, did languidly arouse her interest, did slightly stir her surprise, was that the smooth-shaven patroller of the opposite side of the way immediately crossed the road as the cab drew up, and standing by the side of the cab door proceeded to greet the occupant of the cab. Even that was not very much out of the way, and yet Dolores was sufficiently interested to lay down her pen and to see who should emerge from the vehicle, around which now the usual little guard of hotel porters had gathered.

A big man got out of the cab, a big man with a blonde beard and amiable spectacles. He carried under his arm a large portfolio, and in each hand he carried a collection of books belted together in a hand-strap. He was enveloped in a long coat, and his appearance and the appearance of his luggage suggested that he had travelled, and even from some considerable distance.

Curiosity is often an inexplicable thing, even to the curious, and certainly Dolores would have been hard put to it to explain why she felt any curiosity about the new arrival and the man who had so patiently awaited him. But she did feel curious, and mingled with her curiosity was a vague sense of something like compassion, if not exactly of pity, for she knew very well that at that moment the hotel was very full, and that the new-comer would have to put up with rather uncomfortable quarters if he were lucky enough to get any at all. The sense of curiosity was, however, stronger than her sense of compassion, and she ran rapidly down stairs by her own private stair and slipped into the little room at the back of the hotel office, where either her father or her mother was generally to be found. At this particular moment, as it happened, neither her father nor mother was in the little room. The door communicating with the office stood slightly ajar, and Dolores, standing by it, could see into the office and hear all that passed without being seen.

The blonde-bearded stranger came up to the office smiling confidently. He had still his portfolio under his arm, but his smooth-shaven friend had relieved him of the two bundles of books, and stood slightly apart while the rest of the new-comer's belongings were being piled into a huge mound of impedimenta in the hall. Dolores expected the confident smile of the blonde man to disappear rapidly from his face. But it did not disappear. He said something to the office clerk which Dolores could not catch; the clerk immediately nodded, rang for a page-boy, collected sundry keys from their hooks, and handed them to the page-boy, who immediately made off in the direction of the lift, heralding the blonde-bearded stranger, with his smooth-shaven friend still in attendance, while a squad of porters descended upon the luggage and wafted it away with the rapidity of Afrite magicians.

Dolores could not restrain her curiosity. She opened the door wider and called to the clerk, 'Mr Wilkins.'

Mr Wilkins looked round. He was a tall, alert, sharp-looking young man, whose only weakness in life was a hopeless attachment to Miss Paulo.

'Yes, Miss Paulo.'

'Who was the gentleman who just arrived, Mr Wilkins?'

Mr Wilkins seemed a little surprised at the interest Miss Paulo displayed in the arrival of a stranger. But he made the most of the occasion. He was glad to have anything to tell which could possibly interest *her*.

'That,' said Mr Wilkins with a certain pride, 'is quite a distinguished person in his way. He is Professor Wilberforce P. Flick, President of the Denver and Sacramento Folk-Lore Societies. He has been travelling on the Continent for some time past for the benefit of the societies, and has now arrived in London for the purpose of making acquaintance with the members of the leading lights of folk-lore in this country.'

Dolores laughed. 'Did he tell you all that just now?' she asked.

'Oh, no,' the young man replied, 'Oh, no, Miss Paulo. All that valuable information I gained largely from a letter from the distinguished gentleman himself from Paris last week, and partially also from the spontaneous statements of his friend Mr Andrew J. Copping, of Omaha, who is now in London, and who came here to see if his friend's rooms were duly reserved.'

'Was that Mr Copping who was with the Professor just now?'

'Yes, the clean-shaven man was Mr Andrew J. Copping, of Omaha.'

'Is he also stopping at the hotel?' Miss Paulo asked.

'No.' Mr Wilkins explained. Mr Copping was apparently for the time a resident of London, and lived, he believed, somewhere in the Camden Town region. But he was very anxious that his friend and compatriot should be comfortable, and that his rooms should be commodious.

'How many rooms does Professor Flick occupy?' asked Miss Paulo.

It seemed that the Professor occupied a little suite of rooms which comprised a bedroom and sitting-room, with a bath-room. It seemed that the Professor was a very studious person and that he would take all his meals by himself, as he pursued the study of folk-lore even at his meals, and wished not to have his attention in the least disturbed during the process.

'What an impassioned scholar!' said Miss Paulo. 'I had no idea that places like Denver and Sacramento were leisurely enough to produce such ardent students of folk-lore.'

'Not to mention Omaha,' added Mr Wilkins.

'Is Mr Copping also a folk-lorist then?' inquired Miss Paulo; and Mr Wilkins replied that he believed so, that he had gathered as much from the remarks of Mr Copping on the various occasions when he had called at the hotel.

'The various occasions?'

Yes, Mr Copping had called several times, to make quite sure of everything concerning his friend's comfort. He was very particular about the linen being aired one morning. Another morning he looked in to ascertain whether the chimneys smoked, as the learned Professor often liked a fire in his rooms even in summer. A third time he called to enquire if the water in the bath-room was warm enough at an early hour in the morning, as the learned Professor often rose early to devote himself to his great work!

'What a thoughtful friend, to be sure!' said Miss Paulo. 'It is pleasant to find that great scholarship can secure such devoted disciples. For I suppose Professor Flick is a great scholar.'

'One of the greatest in the world, as I understand from Mr Copping,' replied Mr Wilkins. 'I understand from Mr Copping that when Professor Flick's great work appears it will revolutionise folk-lore all over the world.'

'Dear me!' said Miss Paulo; 'how little one does know, to be sure. I had no idea that folk-lore required revolutionising.'

'Neither had I,' said Mr Wilkins; 'but apparently it does.'

'And Professor Flick is the man to do it, apparently,' said Miss Paulo.

'If Mr Copping is correct about the great work,' said Mr Wilkins.

'Ay, yes, the great work. And what is the great work? Did Mr Copping communicate that as well?'

Oh, yes, Mr Copping had communicated that as well. The great work was a study in American folk-lore, and it went to establish, as far as Mr Wilkins could gather from Mr Copping's glowing but somewhat disconnected phrases, that all the legends of the world were originally the property of the Ute Indians, who, with the Apaches, constituted, according to the Professor, the highest intellectual types on the surface of the earth.

'Well,' said Dolores, 'all that, I dare say, is very interesting and exciting, and even exhilarating to the studious inhabitants of Denver and of Sacramento. I wonder if it will greatly interest London? Where have you put Professor Flick?'

Professor Flick was located, it appeared, upon the first floor. It seemed, according to the representations of the devoted Copping, that Professor Flick was a very nervous man about the possibility of fires; that he never willingly went higher than the first floor in consequence, and that he always carried with him in his baggage a patent rope-ladder for fear of accidents.

'On the first floor,' said Miss Paulo. 'Which rooms?'

'The end suite at the right. On the same side as the rooms of his Excellency, but further off. Mr

Copping seems to like their situation the best of all the rooms I showed him.'

'On the same side as his Excellency's rooms? Well, I should think Professor Flick would be a quiet neighbour.'

'Probably, for he was very anxious to be quiet himself. But I am afraid the fame of our illustrious guest does not extend so far as Denver, for Mr Copping asked what the flag was flying for, and when I told him he did not seem to be a bit the wiser.'

'The stupid man!' said Miss Paulo scornfully.

'And Professor Flick is just as bad. When I mentioned to him that his rooms were near those of Mr Ericson, the Emperor of Surmer, he said that he had never heard of him, but that he hoped he was a quiet man, and did not sit up late.'

'Really,' said Miss Paulo, frowning, 'this Mr Flick would seem to think that the world was made for folk-lore, and that he was folk-lore's Cæsar.'

'Ah, Miss Paulo,' said the practical Wilkins, with a smile, 'these scholars have queer ways.'

'Evidently,' answered Miss Paulo, 'evidently. Well, I suppose we must humour them sometimes, for the sake of the Utes and Apaches at least;' and, with the sunniest of smiles, Miss Paulo withdrew from the office, leaving, as it seemed to Mr Wilkins, who was something of a poet in his spare moments, the impression as of departed divinity. The atmosphere of the hotel hall seemed to take a rosy tinge, and to be impregnated with enchanting odours as from the visit of an Olympian. Mr Wilkins had been going through a course of Homer of late, in Bohn's translation, and permitted himself occasionally to allow his fancy free play in classical allusion. Never, though, to his credit be it recorded, did his poetic studies or his love-dreamings operate in the least to the detriment of his serious duties as head of the office in Paulo's Hotel, a post which, to do him justice, he looked upon as scarcely less important than that of a Cabinet Minister.

Since the day when Dolores first spoke to Hamilton about the danger which was supposed to threaten the Emperor, she had had many talks with the young man. It became his habit now to stop and talk with her whenever he had a chance of meeting her. It was pleasant to him to look into her soft, bright, deep-dark eyes. Her voice sounded musical in his ears. The touch of her hand soothed him. His devotion to the Emperor touched her; her devotion to the Emperor touched him. For a while they had only one topic of conversation—the Emperor, and the fortunes of Surmer.

Soon the clever and sympathetic girl began to think that Hamilton had some trouble in his mind or in his heart which did not strictly belong to the fortunes of the Emperor. There was an occasional melancholy glance in his eye, and then there came a sudden recovery, an almost obvious pulling of himself together, which Dolores endeavoured to reason out. She soon reasoned it out to her own entire conviction, if not to her entire satisfaction. For she felt deeply sorry for the young man. He had been crossed in love, she felt convinced. Oh, yes, he had been crossed in love! Some girl had deceived him, and had thrown him over! And he was so handsome, and so gentle, and so brave, and what better could the girl have asked for? And Dolores became quite angry with the unnamed, unknown girl. Her manner grew all the more genial and kindly to Hamilton. All unconsciously, or perhaps feeling herself quite safe in her conviction that Hamilton's heart was wholly occupied with his love, she allowed herself a certain tone of tender friendship, wholly unobtrusive, almost wholly impersonal—a tender sympathy with the suffering, perhaps, rather than with the sufferer, but bringing much sweetness of voice to the sufferer's ear.

The two became quite confidential about the Emperor and the danger that was supposed to be threatening him. They had long talks over it—and there was an element of secrecy and mystery about the talks which gave them a certain piquancy and almost a certain sweetness. Of course these talks had to be all confidential. It was not to be supposed that the Emperor would allow, if he knew, that any work should be made about any personal danger to him. Therefore Hamilton and Dolores had to talk in an underhand kind of way, and to turn on to quite indifferent subjects when anyone not in the mystery happened to come in. The talks took place sometimes in the public corridor—often in Dolores' own little room. Sometimes the Emperor himself looked in by chance and exchanged a few words with Miss Dolores, and then, of course, the confidential talk collapsed. The Emperor liked Dolores very much. He thought her a remarkably clever and true-hearted girl, and quite a princess and a beauty in her way, and he had more than once said so to Hamilton.

One day Dolores ventured to ask Hamilton, 'Is it true what they say about his Excellency?' and she blushed a little at her own boldness in asking the question.

'Is what true?' Hamilton asked in return, and all unconscious of her meaning.

'Well, is it true that he is going to marry—Sir Rupert Langley's daughter?'

Then Hamilton's face, usually so pale, flushed a sudden red, and for a moment he could hardly speak. He opened his mouth once or twice, but the words did not come.

'Who said that?' he asked at last.

'I don't know,' Dolores answered, much alarmed and distressed, with a light breaking on her that made her flush too. 'I heard it said somewhere—I dare say it's not true. Oh, I am quite sure it is *not* true—but people always *are* saying such things.'

'It can't be true,' Hamilton said. 'If he had any thought of it he would have told me. He knows that there is nothing I could desire more than that he should be made happy.'

Again he almost broke down.

'Yes, if it would make him happy,' Dolores intervened once again, plucking up her courage.

'She is a very noble girl,' Hamilton said, 'but I don't believe there is anything in it. She admires him as we all do.'

'Why, yes, of course,' said Dolores.

'I don't think the Emperor is a marrying man. He has got the cause of Surmer for a wife. Good morning, Miss Paulo. I have to get to the Foreign Office.'

'I hope I haven't vexed you,' Dolores asked eagerly, and yet timidly, 'by asking a foolish question and taking notice of silly gossip?'

She knew Hamilton's secret now, and in her sympathy and her kindliness and her assurance of being safe from misconstruction she laid her hand gently on the young man's arm, and he looked at her, and thought he saw a moisture in her eyes. And he knew that his secret was his no longer. He knew that Dolores had in a moment seen the depths of his trouble. Their eyes looked at each other, and then, only too quickly, away from each other.

'Vexed me?' he said. 'No, indeed, Miss Paulo. You are one of the kindest friends I have in the world.'

Now, what had this speech to do with the question of whether the Emperor was likely or was not likely to ask Helena Langley to marry him? Nothing at all, so far as an outer observer might see. But it had a good deal to do with the realities of the situation for Hamilton and Dolores. It meant, if its meaning could then have been put into plain words on the part of Hamilton—'I know that you have found out my secret—and I know, too, that you will be kind and tender with it—and I like you all the better for having found it out, and for being so tender with it, and it will be another bond of friendship between us—that, and our common devotion to the

Emperor. But this we cannot have in common with the Emperor. Of this, however devoted to him we are, he must now know nothing. This is for ourselves alone—for you and me.' It is a serious business with young men and women when any story and any secret is to be confined to 'you and me.'

For Dolores it meant that now she had a perfect right to be sympathetic and kindly and friendly with Hamilton. She felt as if she were in his absolute heart-confidence—although he had told her nothing whatever, and she did not want him to tell her anything whatever. She knew enough. He was in love, and he was disappointed. She? Well, she really had not been in love, but she had been all unconsciously looking out for love, and she had fancied that she was falling in love with the Emperor. She was an enthusiast for his cause; and for his cause because of himself. With her it was the desire of the moth for the star—of the night for the morrow. She knew this quite well. She knew that that was the sole and the full measure of her feeling towards the Emperor. But all the same, up to this time she had never felt any stirring of emotion towards any other man. She must have known— sharp-sighted girl that she was—that poor Mr Wilkins adored her. She *did* know it—and she was very much interested in the knowledge, and thought it was such a pity, and was sorry for him—honestly and sincerely sorry—and was ever so kind and friendly to him. But her mind was not greatly troubled about his love. She took it for granted that Mr Wilkins would get over his trouble, and would marry some girl who would be fond of him. It always happens like that. So her mind was at rest about Wilkins.

Thus, her mind being at rest about Wilkins, because she knew that, as far as she was concerned, it never could come to anything, and her mind being equally at rest about the Emperor, because she felt sure that on his part it could never come to anything, she had leisure to give some of her sympathies to Hamilton, now that she knew his secret. Then about Hamilton—how about him?

There are moments in life—not moments in actual clock-time, but eventful moments in feelings when one seems to be conscious of a special influence of sympathy and kindness breathing over him like a healing air. A great misfortune has come down upon one's life, and the conviction is for the time that nothing in life can ever be well with him again. The sun shines no more for him; the birds sing no more for him; or, if their notes do make their way into his dulled and saddened ears, it is only to break his heart as the notes of the birds did for the sufferer on the banks of bonnie Doon. The afflicted one seems to lie as in a darkened room, and to have no wish ever to come out into the broad, free, animating air again—no wish to know any more what is going on in the world outside. Friends of all kinds, and in all kindness, come and bring their futile, barren consolations, and make offers of unneeded, unacceptable service, as unpalatable as the offer of the Grand Duchess in 'Alice in Wonderland,' who, declaring that she knows what the thirsty, gasping little girl wants, tenders her a dry biscuit. The dry biscuit of conventional service is put to the lips of the choking sufferer, and cannot be swallowed. Suddenly some voice, perhaps all unknown before, is heard in the darkened chamber, and it is as if a hand were laid on the sufferer's shoulder, tenderly touching him and arousing him to life once more. The voice seems to whisper, 'Come, arise! Awake from mere self-annihilation in grief; there is something yet to live for; the world has still some work to do—*for you*. There are paths to be found for you; there are even, it may be, loves to be loved by you and for you. Arise and come out into the light of the sun and the light of the stars again.' The voice does not really say all this or any of this. If it were to do so, it would be only going over the old sort of consolation which proved hopeless and only a source of renewed anguish when it was offered by the ordinary well-meaning friends. But the peculiar, the timely, the heaven-sent influence breathes all this and much more than this into a man—and the hand that seems at first to be laid so gently on his shoulder now takes him, still so gently—oh, ever so gently, but very firmly by the arm, and leads him out of the room darkened by despair and into the open air, where the sun shines not with mocking and gaudy glare, but with tender, soft, and sympathising light, and the new life has begun, and the healing of the sufferer is a question of time. It may be that he never quite knows from whom the sudden peculiarity of influence streamed in so beneficently upon him. Perhaps the source of inspiration is there just by his side, but he knows nothing of it. Happy the man who, under such conditions, does know where to find the holy well from which came forth the waters that cured his pain, and sent him out into life to be a man among men again.

Poor Hamilton was, as he put it himself, hit very hard when he learned that Helena Langley absolutely refused him. It was not the slightest consolation to him to know that she was quite willing that their friendship should go on unbroken. He was rather glad, on the whole, not to hear that she had declared herself willing to regard him as a brother. Those dreadful old phrases only make the refusal ten times worse. Probably the most wholesome way in which a refusal could be put to a sensitive young man is the blunt, point-blank declaration that never, under any circumstances, could there be a thought of the girl's loving him and having him for her husband. Then a young man who is worth his salt is thrown back upon his own mettle, and recognises the conditions under which he has to battle his life out, and if he is really good for anything he soon adapts himself to them. For the time the struggle is terrible. No cheapness of cynicism will persuade a young man that he does not suffer genuine anguish when under this pang of misprized love. But the sooner he knows the worst the more soon is he likely to be able to fight his way out of the deeps of his misery.

Hamilton did not quite realise the fact as yet—perhaps did not realise it at all—but the friendly voice in his ear, the friendly touch on his arm, that bade him come out into the light and live once again a life of hope, was the voice and the touch of Dolores Paulo. And for her part she knew it just as little as he did.

CHAPTER XVIII

HELENA KNOWS HERSELF, BUT NOT THE OTHER

Decidedly Surmer was coming to the front again—in the newspapers, at all events. The South American question was written about, telegraphed about, and talked about, every day. The South American question was for the time the dispute between Surmer and her powerful neighbour, who was supposed to cherish designs of annexation with regard to her. It is a curious fact that in places like South America, where every State might be supposed to have, or indeed might be shown to have, ten times more territory than she well knows what to do with, the one great idea of increasing the national dignity seems to be that of taking in some vast additional area of land. The hungry neighbour of Surmer had been an Empire, but had got rid of its Emperor, and was now a Republic and believed to be anxious to make a fresh start in dignity by acquiring Surmer, as if to show that a Republic could be just as good as an Empire in the matter of aggression and annexation. Therefore a dispute had been easy to get up. A frontier line is always a line that carries an electric current of disputes. There were some questions of refugees, followers of Ericson, who had crossed the frontier, and whose surrender the new Government of Surmer had absurdly demanded. There were questions of tariff, of duties, of smuggling, all sorts of questions, which, after flickering about separately for some time, ran together at last like drops of quicksilver, and so formed for the diplomatists and for the newspapers the South American question.

What did it all mean? There were threats of war. Diplomacy had for some time believed that the great neighbour of Surmer wanted either war or annexation. The new Republic desired to vindicate its title to respectability in the eyes of a somewhat doubtful and irreverent population, and if it could only boast of the annexation of Surmer the thing would be done. The new government of Surmer flourished splendidly in despatches, in which they declared their ardent desire to live on terms of friendship with all their neighbours, but proclaimed that Surmer had traditions which must be maintained. If Surmer did not mean resistance, then her Government ought certainly not to have kept such a stiff upper lip; and if Surmer did mean resistance was she strong enough to face her huge rival?

This was the particular question which puzzled and embarrassed the Emperor. He could methodically balance the forces on either side. The big Republic had measureless tracts of territory, but she had only a comparatively meagre population. Surmer was much smaller in extent—not much larger, say, than France and Germany combined—but she had a denser population. Given something vital to fight about, Ericson felt some hope that Surmer could hold her own. But the whole quarrel seemed to him so trivial and so factitious that he could not believe the reality of the story was before the world. He knew the men who were at the head of affairs in Surmer, and he had not the slightest faith in their national spirit. He sometimes doubted whether he had not made a mistake, when, having their lives in his hand, and dependent on his mercy, he had allowed them to live. He had only to watch the course of events daily—to follow with keen and agonising interest the telegrams in the papers—telegrams often so torturingly inaccurate in names, facts and places—and to wait for the private advices of his friends, which now came so few and so far between that he felt certain he was cut off from news by the purposed intervention of the authorities at Surmer.

One question especially tormented him. Was the whole quarrel a sham so far as Surmer and her interests were concerned? Was Surmer about to be sold to her great rival by the gang of adventurers, political, financial, and social, who had been for the moment entrusted with the charge of her affairs? Day after day, hour after hour, Ericson turned over this question in his mind. He was in constant communication with Sir Rupert, and his advice guided Sir Rupert a great deal in the framing of the despatches, which, of course, we were bound to send out to our accredited representatives in Orizaba and in Surmer. But he did not venture to give even Sir Rupert any hint of his suspicions that the whole thing was only a put-up job. He was too jealous of the honour of Surmer. To him Surmer was as his wife, his child; he could not allow himself to suggest the idea that Surmer had surrendered herself body and soul to the government of a gang of swindlers.

Sir Rupert prepared many despatches during these days of tension. Undoubtedly he derived much advantage from such schooling as he got from the Emperor. He perfectly astonished our representatives in Orizaba and in Surmer by the fulness and the accuracy of his local knowledge. His answers in the House of Commons were models of condensed and clear information. He might, for aught that anyone could tell to the contrary, have lived half his life in Surmer and the other half in Orizaba. For himself he began to admire more and more the clear impartiality of the Emperor. Ericson seemed to give him the benefit of his mere local knowledge, strained perfectly clear of any prejudice or partisanship. But Ericson certainly kept back his worst suspicions. He justified himself in doing so. As yet they were only suspicions.

Sir Rupert dictated to Soame Rivers the points of various despatches. Sir Rupert liked to have a distinct savour of literature and of culture in his despatches, and he put in a certain amount of that kind of thing himself, and was very much pleased when Soame Rivers could contribute a little more. He was becoming very proud of his despatches on this South American question. Nobody could be better coached, he thought. Ericson must certainly know all about it—and he was pretty well able to give the despatches a good form himself—and then Soame Rivers was a wonderful man for a happy allusion or quotation or illustration. So Sir Rupert felt well contented with the way things were going; and it may be that now and again there came into his mind the secret, half-suppressed thought that if the South American question should end, despite all his despatches, in the larger Empire absorbing the lesser, and that thus Ericson was cut off from any further career in the New World, it would be very satisfactory if he would settle down in England; and then if Helena and he took to each other, Helena's father would put no difficulties in their way.

Soame Rivers copied, amended, added to, the despatches with, metaphorically, his tongue in his cheek. The general attitude of Soame Rivers towards the world's politics was very much that of tongue in cheek. The attitude was especially marked in this way when he had to do with the affairs of Surmer. He copied out and improved and enriched the graceful sentences in which his chief urged the representatives of England to be at once firm and cautious, at once friendly and reserved, and so on, with a very keen and deliberate sense of a joke. He could see, of course, with half an eye, where the influence of Ericson came in, and he should have dearly liked, but did not venture, to spoil all by some subtle phrase of insinuation which perhaps his chief might fail to notice, and so allow to go off for the instruction of our representative in Surmer or Orizaba. Soame Rivers had begun to have a pretty strong feeling of hatred for the Emperor. It angered him even to hear Ericson called 'the Emperor.' 'Emperor of what?' he asked himself scornfully. Because a man has been kicked out of a place and dare not set his foot there again, does that constitute him its Emperor! There happened to be about that time a story going the round of London society concerning a vain and pretentious young fellow who had been kicked out of a country house for thrusting too much of his fatuous attentions on the daughter of the host and hostess. Soame Rivers at once nicknamed him 'The Emperor' 'Why "The Emperor"?' people asked. 'Because he has been kicked out—don't you see?' was the answer. But Soame Rivers did not give forth that witticism in the presence of Sir Rupert or of Sir Rupert's daughter.

Meanwhile, the Emperor was undoubtedly becoming a more important man than ever with the London public. The fact that he was staying in London gave the South American question something like a personal interest for most people. A foreign question which otherwise would seem vague, unmeaning, and unintelligible comes to be at least interesting and worthy of consideration, if not indeed of study, if you have under your eyes some living man who has been in any important way mixed up in it. The general sympathy of the public began to go with the young Empire of Surmer and against her bigger rival. An Empire for which an Englishman had thought of risking his life—which he had actually ruled over—he being still visible and so the front just now in London, must surely be better worthy the sympathy of Englishmen than some great, big, bullying State, which, even when it had a highly respectable Emperor, had not the good sense to hold possession of him.

So the Emperor found himself coming in for a new season of popularity. One evening he accompanied the Langleys to a theatre where some new and successful piece was in its early run, and when he was seen in the box and recognised, there was an outbreak of cheers from the galleries and in somewhat slow sequence from the pit. The

Emperor shrank back into the box; Helena's eyes flashed up to the galleries and down to the pit in delight and pride. She would have liked the orchestra to strike up the National Anthem of Surmer, and would have thought such a performance only a natural and reasonable demonstration in favour of her friend and hero. She leaned back to him and said:

'You see they appreciate you here.'

'They don't understand a bit about our Surmer troubles,' he said. 'Why should they? What is it to them?'

'How ungracious!' Helena exclaimed. 'They admire you, and that is the way in which you repay them.'

'I know how little it all means,' Ericson murmured, 'and I don't know that I represent just now the cause of Surmer in her quarrel. I want to see into it a little deeper.'

'But it is generous of these people here. They think that Surmer is going to be annexed—and they know that you have been Surmer's patriot and Emperor, and therefore they applaud you. Oh, come now, you must be grateful—? you really must—and you must own that our English people can be sympathetic.'

'I will admit all you wish,' he said.

Helena drew back in the box, and instinctively leaned towards her father, who was standing behind, and who seldom remained long in a box at a theatre, because he generally had so many people to see in other boxes between the acts. She was vexed because Ericson would persist in treating her as a child. She did not want him to admit anything merely because she wished him to admit it. She wanted to be argued with, like a rational human being—like a man.

'What a handsome dark woman that is in the box just opposite to us,' she said, addressing her words rather to Sir Rupert than to the Emperor. 'She *is* very handsome. I don't know her—I wonder who she is?'

'I seem to know her face,' Sir Rupert said, 'but I can't just at the moment put a name to it.'

'I know her face well and I *can* put a name to it,' the Emperor said. 'It is Miss Paulo—Dolores Paulo— daughter of the owner of Paulo's Hotel, where I am staying.'

'Oh, yes, of course,' Sir Rupert struck in; 'I have seen her and spoken with her. She is quite lady-like, and I am told well educated and clever too.'

'She is very well educated and very clever,' Ericson said 'and as well-bred a woman as you could find anywhere.'

'Does she go into society at all? I suppose not,' Helena said coldly. She felt a little spiteful—not against Dolores; at least, not against Dolores on Dolores' own account—but against her as having been praised by Ericson. She thought it hard that Ericson should first have treated her, Helena, as a child with whom one would agree, no matter what she said, and immediately after launch out into praise of the culture and cleverness of Miss Paulo.

'I don't fancy she cares much about getting into society,' Ericson replied. 'One of the things I admire most about Paulo and his daughter is that they seem to make their own life and their own work enough for them, and don't appear to care to get to be anything they are not.'

'Is that her father with her?' Sir Rupert asked.

'Yes, that is her father,' Ericson answered. 'I must go round and pay them a visit when this act is over.'

'I'll go, too,' Sir Rupert said.

'Oh, and may not I go?' Helena eagerly asked. She had in a moment got over her little spleen, and felt in her generous, impulsive way that she owed instant reparation to Miss Paulo.

'No, I think you had better not go rushing round the theatre,' Sir Rupert said. 'Mr Ericson will go first, and when he comes back to take charge of you, I will pay my visit.'

'Well,' Helena said composedly, and settling herself down in her chair, 'I'll go and call on her tomorrow.'

'Certainly, by all means,' her father said.

Ericson gave Helena a pleased and grateful look. Her eyes drooped under it—she hardly knew why. She had a penitent feeling somehow. Then the curtain fell, and Ericson went round to visit Miss Paulo.

'Who has just come into the back of that girl's box?' Sir Rupert asked—who was rather short-sighted and hated the trouble of an opera-glass.

'Oh, it's Mr Hamilton,' his daughter, who had the eyes of an eagle, was able to tell him.

'Hamilton? Oh, yes, to be sure; I've seen him talking to her.'

'He seems to be talking to her now pretty much,' said Helena.

'Oh, the curtain is going up,' Sir Rupert said, 'and Ericson is rushing away. Hamilton stays, I see. I'll go and see her after this act.'

'And I'll go and see her tomorrow,' were the words of his daughter.

In a moment Ericson came in. The piece was in movement again. Helena kept her eyes fixed on Miss Paulo's box. She was puzzled about Hamilton. She had very little prejudice of caste or class, and yet she could not readily admit into her mind the possibility of a man of her own social rank who had actually wanted to marry *her*, making advances soon after to the daughter of a hotel-keeper. But why should she fancy that Hamilton was making advances to Miss Paulo? He was very attentive to her, certainly, and did not seem willing to leave her box; but was not that probably part of the chivalry of his nature—and the chivalry of his training under the Emperor—to pay especial attention to a girl of low degree? The Emperor, she thought to herself with a certain pride in him and for him, had not left his box to go to see anyone but Miss Paulo.

When the curtain fell for the next time, Sir Rupert went round in his stately way to the box where Dolores and her father and Hamilton were sitting. Then Helena seized her opportunity, and suddenly said to Ericson:

'I want you to tell me all about Miss Paulo. Dolores—what a pretty name!'

'She is a very clever girl,' he began.

'But not, I hope, a superior person? Not a woman to be afraid of?'

'No, no; not in the least.'

'Does Mr Hamilton see much of her?' Helena had now grown saucy again, and looked the Emperor full in the face, with the look of one who means to say: 'You and I know something of what happened before *that*.'

Ericson smiled, a grave smile.

'He has to see her now and again,' he said.

'Has to see her? Perhaps he likes to see her.'

'I am sure I hope he does. He must be rather lonely.'

'Are men ever lonely?'

'Very lonely sometimes.'

'But not as women are lonely. Men can always find companionship. Do look at Mr Hamilton—how happy *he* seems!'

'Hamilton's love for *you* was deep and sincere,' the Emperor said, with an almost frowning earnestness.

'And now behold,' she replied, with sparkling and defiant eyes. 'See! Look there!'

Then Sir Rupert came back to the box and the discussion was brought to an end.

Hamilton came into the box and paid a formal visit, and said a few formal words. The curtain fell upon the last act, and Sir Rupert's carriage whirled his daughter away. Helena sat up late in her bedroom that night. She was finding out more and more with every day, every incident, that the conditions of life were becoming revolutionised for her. She was no longer like the girl she always had been before. She felt herself growing profoundly self-conscious, self-inquiring. She who had hitherto been the merest creature of impulse—generous impulse, surely, almost always—now found herself studying beforehand every word she ought to speak and every act she ought to do. She lay awake of nights cross-examining herself as to what precise words she had spoken that day, as to what things she had done, what gestures even she had made, in the vain and torturing effort to find out whether she had done anything which might betray her secret. It seemed to her, with the touching, delightful, pitiful egotism of which the love of the purest heart is capable, that there was not a breathing of the common wind that might not betray to the world the secret of her love. She had in former days carried her disregard for the conventional so far that malign critics, judging purely by the narrowest laws, had described her as unwomanly. Nor were all these harsh and ill-judging critics women—which would have been an intelligible thing enough. It is gratifying to discourage vanity in woman, to set down as unwomanly the girl who has gathered all the men around her. It is soothing to mortified feeling to say that the successful girl simply 'went for' the men, and compelled them to pay attention to her. But there were men not unfriendly to her or to Sir Rupert who shook their heads and said that Helena Langley was rather unwomanly. If they could have seen into her heart now, they would have known that she was womanly enough in all conscience. She succumbed in a moment to all the tenderest weaknesses and timidities of woman. Never before had she cared one straw whether people said she was flirting with this, that, or the other man—and the curious thing is that, while she was thus utterly careless, people never did accuse her of flirting. But now she felt in her own heart that she was conscious of some emotion far more deep and serious than a wish for a flirtation; she found that she was in love—in love—in love, and with a man who did not seem to have the faintest thought of being in love with her. She felt, therefore, as if she had to go through this part of her life masked, and also armoured. Every eye that turned on her she regarded as a suspicious eye. Every chance question addressed suddenly to her seemed like a question driven at her, to get at the heart of her mystery. A man slowly recovering from some wound or other injury which has shattered for the time his nervous power, will, when he begins to walk slowly about the streets, start and shudder if he sees someone moving rapidly in his direction, because he is seized with an instinctive and horrible dread that the rapid walker is sure to come into collision with him. Helena Langley felt somewhat like that. Her nerves were shaken; her framework of joyous self-forgetfulness was wholly shattered; she was conscious and nervous all over—in every sudden word or movement she feared an attack upon her nerves. What would it matter to the world—the world of London—even if the world had known all? Two ladies would meet and say, 'Oh, my dear, do you know, that pretty and odd girl Helena Langley—Sir Rupert's daughter—has fallen over head and ears in love with the Emperor, as they call him—that man who has come back from some South American place! Isn't it ridiculous?—and they say he doesn't care one little bit about her.' 'Well, I don't know—he might do a great deal worse—she's a very clever girl, *I* think, and she will have lots of money.' 'Yes, if her father chooses to give it to her; but I'm told she hasn't a single sixpence of her own, and Sir Rupert mightn't quite like the idea of her taking up with a beggarly foreign exile from South America, or South Africa, or wherever it is.' 'But, my dear, the man isn't a foreigner—he is an Englishman, and a very attractive man too. I think *I* should be very much taken by him if I were a girl.' 'Well, you surprise me. I am told he is old enough to be her father.' 'Oh, good gracious, no; a man of about forty, I should think; just the right age of man for a girl to marry; and really there are so *few* marrying men in these days that even girls with rich fathers can't always be choosers, don't you know?'

Now, the way in which these two ladies might have talked about Helena's secret, if they could have discovered it, is a fair illustration of the vapid kind of interest which society in general would have taken in the whole story. But it did not seem thus to Helena. To her it appeared as if the whole world would have cried scorn upon her if it had found out that she fell in love with a man who had given her no reason to believe that he had fallen in love with her. Outside her own closest friends, society would not have cared twopence either way. Society is interested in the marriages of girls who belong to its set—or in their subsequent divorces, if such events should come about. But society cares nothing whatever about maiden heart-throbbings. It is vaguely and generally assumed that all girls begin by falling in love with the wrong person, and then soberise down for matrimony and by matrimony, and that it does not matter in the least what their silly first fancies were. Even the father and mother of some particular girl will not take her early love-fancies very seriously. She will get over it, they say contentedly—perhaps with self-cherished, half-suppressed recollection of the fact that he and she have themselves got over such a feeling and been very happy, or at least fairly happy, after, in their married lives.

But to Helena Langley things looked differently. She was filled with the conviction that it would be a shame to her if the world—her world—were to discover that she had fallen in love with a man who had not fallen in love with her. The world would have taken the news with exactly the same amount of interest, alarm, horror, that it would have felt if authoritatively informed that Helena Langley had had the toothache. In the illustration just given of a morbid, nervous condition, the sufferer dreads that anyone moving rapidly in his direction is going to rush in upon him and collide with him. But the rapid mover is thinking not at all of the nervous sufferer, and would be only languidly interested if he were told of the suffering, and would think it an ordinary and commonplace sort of suffering after all—just what everybody has at one time or another, don't you know?

Was Helena unhappy? On the whole, no—decidedly not. She had found her hero. She had found out her passion. A new inspiration was breathed into her life. This Undine of the West End, of the later end of the outworn century had discovered the soul that was in her formerly undeveloped system. She had come in for a possession like the possession of a throne, which brings heavy responsibility and much peril and pain with it, but yet which those who have once possessed it will not endure to be parted from. She could follow *his* fortunes—she could openly be his friend—she felt a kind of claim on him and proprietorial right over him. She had never felt any particular use in her existence before, except, indeed, in amusing herself, and, let it be added in fairness to the child, in giving pleasure to others, and trying to do good for others.

But now she had found a new existence. She had come in for her inheritance—for her kingdom—the kingdom of human love which is the inheritance of all of us, and which, when we come in for it, we would never willingly renounce, no matter what tears it brings with it. Helena Langley had found that she was no longer a thoughtless, impulsive girl, but a real woman, with a heart and a hero and a love secret. She felt proud of her discovery. Columbus found out that he had a heart before he found out a new world; one wonders which discovery was the sweeter at the time.

CHAPTER XIX

TYPICAL AMERICANS—NO DOUBT

Up in Hampstead the world seemed to wheel in its orbit more tranquilly than in the feverish city which lay at the foot of its slopes. There was something in its clear, its balsamic air, so cleanly free from the eternal smoke-clouds of London, that seemed to invite to a repose, to a leisurely movement in the procession of life. Captain Sarrasin once said that it reminded him of the pure air of the prairie, almost of the keen air of the cañons. Captain Sarrasin always professed that he found the illimitable spaces of the West too tranquillising for him. The sight of those great, endless fields, the isolation of those majestic mountains, suggested to him a recluse-like calm which never suited his quick-moving temper. So he did not very often visit his brother in Hampstead, and the brother in Hampstead, deeply engrossed in the grave cares of comparative folk-lore, seldom dropped from his Hampstead eyrie into the troubled city to seek out his restless brother. Hampstead was just the place for the folk-lore-loving Sarrasin. No doubt that, actually, human life is just the same in Hampstead as anywhere else, from Peking to Peru, tossed by the same passions, driven onward by the same racking winds of desire, ambition, and despair. People love and hate and envy, feel mean or murderous, according to their temper, as much on the slopes of Hampstead as in the streets of London that lie at its foot. But such is not the suggestion of Hampstead itself upon a tranquil summer day to the pensive observer. It seems a peaceful, a sleepy hollow, an amiable elevated lubber-land, affording to London the example of a kind of suburban Nirvana.

So while London was fretting in all its eddies, and fretting particularly for us in the eddy that swirled and circled around the fortunes of the Emperor, up in Hampstead, at Blarulf's Garth, and in the adjacent cottage which Mr Sarrasin had named Camelot, life flowed on in a tranquil current. The Emperor often came up; whatever the claims, the demands upon him, he managed to dine one day in every week with Miss Ericson. Not the same day in every week indeed; the Emperor's life was inevitably too irregular for that; but always one day, whichever day he could snatch from the imperious pressure of the growing plans for his restoration, from the society which still regarded him as the most royal of royal lions, and, above all, from the society of the Langleys. However, it did not matter. One day was so like another up in Hampstead, that it really made no difference whether any particular event took place upon a Monday, a Tuesday, or a Wednesday; and Miss Ericson was so happy in seeing so much of her nephew after so long and blank an absence, that it would never have occurred to her to complain, if indeed complaining ever found much of a place in her gentle nature.

Whenever the Emperor came now, Mr Sarrasin was always on hand, and always eager to converse with the wonderful nephew who had come back to London as an exiled king. To Mr Sarrasin the event had a threefold interest. In the first place, the Emperor was the nephew of Miss Ericson. Had he been the most commonplace fellow that had ever set one foot before the other, there would have been something attractive about him to Sarrasin because of his kinship with his gentle neighbour. In the second place, he knew now that his brother, the brother whom he adored, had declared himself on the Emperor's side, and had joined the Emperor's party. In the third place, if no associations of friendship or kinship had linked him in any way with the fortunes of the Emperor, the mere fact of his eventful rule, of his stormy fortunes, of the rise and fall of such a stranger in such a strange land, would have fired all that was romantic, all that was adventurous, in the nature of the quiet, stay-at-home gentleman, and made him as eager a follower of the Emperor's career as if Ericson had been Jack with the Eleven Brothers, or the Boy who Could not Shiver. So Mr Sarrasin spent the better part of six days in the week conversing with Miss Ericson about the Emperor; and on the day when Ericson came to Hampstead, Sarrasin was sure, sooner or later, to put in an appearance at Blarulf's Garth, and to beam in delighted approbation upon the exile of Surmer.

One day Mr Sarrasin came into Miss Ericson's garden with a countenance that beamed with more than usual benignity. But the benignity was, as it were, blended with an air of unwonted wonder and exhilaration which consorted somewhat strangely with the wonted calm of the excellent gentleman's demeanour. He had a large letter in his hand, which he kept flourishing almost as wildly as if he were an enthusiastic spectator at a racecourse, or a passenger outward bound waving a last good-night to his native land.

It happened to be one of the days when the Emperor had come up from the strenuous London, and from playing his own strenuous part therein. He was sitting with Miss Ericson in the garden, as he had sat there on the first day of his return—that day which now seemed so long ago and so far away— almost as long ago and as far away as the old days in Surmer themselves. He was telling her all that had happened during the days that had elapsed since their last meeting. He spoke, as he always did now, much of the Langleys, and as he spoke of them Miss Ericson's grave, kind eyes watched his face closely, but seemed to read nothing in its unchanged composure. As they were in the middle of their confidential talk, the French windows of the little drawing-room opened, and Mr Sarrasin made his appearance—a light-garmented vision of pleasurably excited good-humour.

'What *has* happened to our dear old friend?' Ericson asked the old lady as Sarrasin came beaming across the grass towards them, fluttering his letter. 'He seems to be quite excited.'

Miss Ericson laughed as she rose to greet her friend. 'You may be sure we shall not long be left in doubt,' she said, as she advanced with hands extended.

Mr Sarrasin caught both her hands and pressed them warmly. 'I have such news,' he murmured, 'such wonderful news!' Then he turned his smiling face in the direction of the Emperor. 'Good-day, Mr Ericson; wonderful news! And it concerns *you* too, in a measure; only in a measure, indeed, but still in a measure.'

The Emperor's face expressed a smiling interest. He had really grown quite fond of this sweet-tempered, cheery, childlike old gentleman. Miss Ericson drew Sarrasin to a seat opposite to her own, and sat down again with an air of curiosity which suggested that she and her nephew were waiting for the wonderful news. As she had predicted, they had not long to wait. Mr Sarrasin having plunged into the subject on the moment of his arrival, could think of nothing else.

'I have a letter here,' he said; '*such* a letter! Whom do you think it is from? Why, from no less a person than Professor Flick, who is, as of course *you* know, the most famous authority on folk-lore in the whole of the West of America.'

Sarrasin paused and looked at them with an air of triumph. He evidently expected them to say something. So Ericson spoke.

'I am ashamed to say,' he confessed, 'that I have never heard the honoured name of Professor Flick before.'

Mr Sarrasin looked a trifle dashed. 'I was in hopes you might have known,' he said, 'for his name and his books are of course well known to me. But no doubt you have had little time for such study. Anyhow, we shall soon know him personally, both you and I; you probably even sooner than I.'

'Indeed!' said Ericson. 'How am I to come to know him? I am not very strong on folk-lore.'

'Why?' answered Mr Sarrasin. 'Because he is stopping in your hotel. This letter which I have received from him this morning is dated from

Paulo's Hotel, the chosen home apparently of all illustrious persons.'

The Emperor smiled. 'I dare not claim equality with Professor Flick, and I fear I might not recognise him if I met him in the corridors, or on the stairs. I must inquire about him from Miss Paulo.'

'Do, do,' said Mr Sarrasin. 'But he will come here. Of course he will come here. He writes to me a most flattering letter, in which he does me the honour to say that he has read with pleasure my poor tractates on "The Survival of Solar Myths in Kitchen Customs," and on "The Probable Patagonian Origin of 'A Frog he would a-wooing go.'" He is pleased to express a great desire to make my acquaintance. I wonder if he has heard of my brother? Oisin must have been in Sacramento and Omaha and all the other places.'

'I should think he was sure to have met your brother,' said the Emperor, feeling he was expected to say something.

'If not, I must introduce my brother,' Mr Sarrasin said joyously. 'Fancy anyone being introduced to anybody through me!'

Miss Ericson had listened quietly, with an air of smiling interest, while Mr Sarrasin was giving forth his joyful news. Now she leaned forward and spoke.

'What do you propose to do in honour of this international episode?' she asked. There was a slender vein of humour in Miss Ericson's character, and she occasionally exercised it gently at the expense of her friend's hobby. Mr Sarrasin always enjoyed her mild banter hugely. Now, as ever, he paid it the tribute of the cheeriest laughter.

'That is excellent,' he said; 'International Episode is excellent. But, you see,' he went on, growing suddenly grave, 'it really *is* something of an international affair after all. Here we have an eminent American scholar——'

'Who is naturally anxious to make the acquaintance of an eminent English scholar,' the Emperor suggested.

Mr Sarrasin's large fair face flushed pink with pleasure.

'You are too good, Mr Ericson, too good. But I feel that I must do something for our distinguished friend, especially as he has done me the honour to single me out for so gratifying a mark of his approval. I think that I shall ask him to dinner.' And Mr Sarrasin looked thoughtfully at his audience to solicit their opinion.

'A very good idea,' said the Emperor. 'Nothing cements literary or political friendship like judicious dining. Dining has a folk-lore of its own.'

'But don't you think,' suggested Miss Ericson, 'that as this gentleman, Professor——'

'Flick,' prompted Mr Sarrasin.

'Thank you; Professor Flick. That, as Professor Flick is a stranger, and a distinguished stranger, it is your duty, my dear Mr Sarrasin, to call upon him at his hotel?'

Mr Sarrasin bowed again. 'Thank you, Miss Ericson, *thank* you. You always think of the right thing. Of course it is obviously my duty to pay my respects to Professor Flick at his hotel, which happens also to be our dear friend's hotel. And the sooner the better, I suppose.'

'The sooner the visit the stronger the compliment, of course,' said Miss Ericson.

'That decides me,' said Mr Sarrasin. 'I will go this very day.'

'Then let us go into town together,' the Emperor suggested. 'I must be getting back again.' For this was one of those days on which Ericson came out early to Blarulf's Garth and left after luncheon. The suggestion made Mr Sarrasin beam more than ever.

'That will be delightful,' he said, with all the conviction of a schoolboy to whom an unexpected holiday has been promised.

'I have my cab outside,' the Emperor said. Ericson liked tearing round in hansom cabs, and could hardly ever be induced to make use of one of the hotel broughams.

So the two men took affectionate leave of Miss Ericson and passed together out of the gate. There were two cabs in sight—one waiting for Ericson, the other in front of Sarrasin's Camelot Cottage. Two men had got out of the cab, and were asking some questions of the servant at the door.

'These must be your friends of the Folk-Lore,' Ericson said.

'Why—God bless me—I suppose so! Never heard of such promptness. Will you excuse me a moment?

Can you wait? Are you pressed for time? It may not be they, you know, after all.'

'Oh, yes, I'll wait; I am in no breathless hurry.'

Then Sarrasin went over and accosted the two men. Evidently they were the men he had guessed them to be, for there was much bowing and shaking of hands and apparently cordial and effusive talk. Then the whole trio advanced towards Ericson. He saw that one of the men was big, fair-haired, and large-bearded, and that he wore moony spectacles, which gave him something of the look of Mr Pickwick grown tall. The other man was slim and closely shaven, except for a yellowish moustache. There was nothing very striking about either of them.

'Excellency,' the good Sarrasin said, in his courtliest and yet simplest tones, 'I ask permission to present to you two distinguished American scholars—Professor Flick of Denver and Sacramento, and Mr Andrew J. Copping of Omaha. These gentlemen will be proud to have the honour of meeting the patriot Emperor of Surmer, whose fame is world-renowned.'

'Excellency,' said Professor Flick, 'I am proud to meet you.'

'Excellency,' said Mr Andrew J. Copping, 'I am proud to meet you.'

'Gentlemen,' Ericson said, 'I am very glad to meet you both. I have been in your country—indeed, I have been all over it.'

'And yet it is a pretty big country, sir,' the Professor observed, with a good-natured smile, as that of a man who kindly calls attention to the fact that one has made himself responsible for rather a large order.

'It is, indeed,' Ericson assented, without thought of disputation; 'but I have been in most of its regions. My own interests, of course, are in South America, as you would know.'

'As we know now, sir,' the Professor replied, 'as we know now, Excellency. I am ashamed to say that we specialists have a way of getting absorbed right up in our own topics, and my friend and I know hardly anything of politics or foreign affairs. Why, Mr Sarrasin,' and here the Professor suddenly turned to Sarrasin, as if he had something to say that would specially interest him above all other men, 'do you know, sir, that I sometimes fail to remember who is the existing President of the United States?'

'Well, I am sure,' said Sarrasin, 'I don't know at this moment the name of the present Lord Mayor of London.'

'And that is how I had known nothing about the career of your Excellency until quite lately,' the Professor blandly explained. 'I think it wrong, sir—a breach of truth, sir—that a man should pretend to any knowledge on any subject which he has not got. Of course, since I have been in Paulo's Hotel I have heard all about your record, and it is a pride and a privilege to me to make your acquaintance. And we need hardly say, sir, my friend and I, what a surprise it is to have the honour of making your acquaintanceship on the occasion of the first visit we have ventured to pay to the house of our distinguished friend Professor Sarrasin.'

'Not a professor,' said Sarrasin, with a mild disclaiming smile. 'I have no claim to any title of any kind.'

'Fame like yours, sir,' the Professor gravely said, 'requires no title. In our far-off West, among all true votaries of folk-lore, the name of Sarrasin is, sir— well, is a household word.'

'I am pleased to hear you say so,' the blushing Sarrasin murmured; 'I will frankly confess that I am delighted. But I own that I am greatly surprised.'

'Our folks when they take up a subject study it right through,' the Professor affirmed. 'Sir, we should not have sought you if we had not known of you. We knew of you, and we have sought you.'

There was no gainsaying this. Sarrasin could not ignore his fame.

'But you were going to the City, sir, with your illustrious friend.' An American hardly ever understands the Londoner's localisation of 'the City,' and when he speaks of a visit to Berkeley Square would call it going to the City. 'Please do not let us interrupt your doubtless highly important mission.'

'It was only a mission to call on you at Paulo's Hotel,' Sarrasin said; 'and his Excellency was kind enough to offer to drive me there. Now that you are here you have completed my mission for the moment. Shall we not go in?'

'I am afraid I must get back to town,' Ericson said.

'Surely—surely—our friends will quite understand how much your time is taken up.'

'Much of it taken up to very little profit of any kind,' Ericson said with a smile. 'But today I have some rather important things to look after. I am glad, however, that I did not set about looking after them too soon to see your American visitors, Mr Sarrasin.'

'Just a moment,' Sarrasin eagerly said, stammering in the audacity of his venture. 'One part of my purpose in seeking out Professor Flick, and—Mr—Mr Andrew J. Copping—of Omaha—yes—I think I am right—of Omaha—was to ask these gentlemen if they would do me the favour of dining with me on the earliest day we can fix—not here, of course— oh, no—I could not think of bringing them out here again; but at the Folk-Lore Club, the only club, gentlemen, with which I have the honour to be connected——'

'Sir, you do us too much honour,' the Professor gravely said, 'and any day that suits you shall be made suitable to us.'

'Suitable to us,' Mr Copping solemnly chimed in.

'And I was thinking,' Sarrasin said, turning to Ericson, who was now becoming rather eager to get away, 'that if we could prevail upon his Excellency to join us he might be interested in our quaint little club, to say nothing of an evening with two such distinguished American scholars, who, I am sure— —'

'I shall be positively delighted,' Ericson said, 'if you can only persuade Hamilton to agree to the night and to let me off. Hamilton is my friend who acts as private secretary to me, Professor Flick; and, as I am informed you sometimes say in America, he bosses the show.'

'I believe, sir, that is a phrase common among the less educated of our great population,' Professor Flick conceded.

'Quite so,' said Ericson, beginning to think the Professor of Folk-Lore rather a prig.

'Then that is all but arranged,' Sarrasin said, flushing with joy and only at the moment having one regret—that the Folk-Lore Club did not take in ladies as guests, and that, therefore, there was no use in his thinking of asking Miss Ericson to join the company at his dinner party.

'Well, the basis of negotiation seems to have been very readily accepted on both sides,' Ericson said, with a feeling of genuine pleasure in his heart that he was in a position to do anything that could give Sarrasin a pleasure, and resolving within himself that on that point at least he would stand no nonsense from Hamilton.

So they all parted very good friends. Sarrasin and the two Americans disappeared into Camelot, and Ericson drove home alone. As he drove he was thinking over the Americans. What a perfect type they both were of the regulation American of English fiction and the English stage! If they could only go on to the London stage and speak exactly as they spoke in ordinary life they must make a splendid success as American comic actors. But, no doubt, as soon as either began to act, the naturalness of the accent and the manner and the mode of speech would all vanish and something purely artificial would come up instead. Still, he wondered how it came about that distinguished scholars, learned above all things in folk-lore—a knowledge that surely ought to bring something cosmopolitan with it—should be thus absolutely local, formal, and typical of the least interesting and least appreciative form of provincial character in America. 'It is really very curious,' he said to himself. 'They seem to me more like men acting a stiff and conventional American part than like real Americans. But, of course, I have never met much of that type of American.' He soon put the question away, and thought of other people than Professor Flick and Mr Andrew J. Copping. He was interested in them, however—he could not tell why—and he was glad to have the chance of meeting them at dinner with dear old Sarrasin at the Folk-Lore Club; and he was wondering whether they would relax at all under the genial influence, and become a little less like type Americans cut out of wood and moved by clockwork, and speaking by mechanical contrivance. Ericson had a good deal of boyish interest in life, and even in small things, left in him, for all his Emperorship and his projects, and his Surmer, and the growing sentiment that sometimes made him feel with a start and a pang that it was beginning to rival Surmer itself in its power of absorption.

CHAPTER XX

THE DEAREST GIRL IN THE WORLD

Sir Rupert Langley and his daughter had a small party staying with them at their seaside place on the South-Western coast. Seagate Hall the place was called. It was not much of a hall, in the grandiose sense of the word. It had come to Sir Rupert through his mother, and was not a big property in any sense—a little park and a fine old mansion, half convent, half castle, made up the whole of it. But Helena was very fond of it, and, indeed, much preferred it to the more vast and stately inland country place. To please her, Sir Rupert consented to spend some parts of every year there. It was a retreat to go to when the summer heats or the autumnal heats of London were unendurable—at least to the ordinary Briton, who is under the fond impression that London is really hot sometimes, and who claps a puggaree on his chimney-pot hat the moment there comes in late May a faint glimpse of sunshine. The Emperor was one of the party. So was Hamilton. So was Soame Rivers. So was Miss Paulo, on whose coming Helena had insisted with friendly pressure. Later on were to come Professor Flick, and his friend Mr Andrew J. Copping of Omaha, in whom Helena, at Ericson's suggestion, had been pleased to take some interest. So were Captain Sarrasin and his wife. Mr Sarrasin, of Hampstead, had been cordially invited, but he found himself unable to venture on so much of a journey. He loved to travel far and wide while seated at his chimney corner or on a garden seat in the lawn in front of Miss Ericson's cottage, or of Camelot, his own.

The mind of the Emperor was disturbed—distressed—even distracted. He was expecting every day, almost every hour, some decisive news with regard to the state of Surmer. His feelings were kept on tenter-hooks about it. He had made every preparation for a speedy descent on the shores of his Empire. But he did not feel that the time was yet quite ripe. The crisis between Surmer and Orizaba seemed for the moment to be hanging fire, and he did not believe that any event in life could arouse the patriotic spirit of Surmer so thrillingly as the aggression of the greater Empire. But the controversy dragged on, a mere diplomatic correspondence as yet, and Ericson could not make out how much of it was sham and how much real. He knew, and Hamilton knew, that his great part must be a *coup de état*, and although he despised political *coups de état* in themselves, he knew as a practical man that by means of such a process he could best get at the hearts of the population of Surmer. The moment he could see clearly that something serious was impending, that moment he and his companions would up steam and make for the shores of Surmer. But just now the dispute seemed somehow to be flickering out, and becoming a mere matter of formally interchanged despatches. Was that itself a stratagem, he thought—were the present rulers of Surmer waiting for a chance of quietly selling their Empire? Or had they found that such a base transaction was hopeless? and were they from whatever reason—even for their own personal safety—trying to get out of the dispute in some honourable way, and to maintain for whatever motive the political integrity and independence of Surmer? If such were the case, Ericson felt that he must give them their chance. Whatever might be his private and personal doubts and fears, he must not increase the complications and difficulties by actively intervening in the work. Therefore his mind was disturbed and distressed; and he watched with a sometimes sickening eagerness for every new edition of the papers, and was always on the look-out for telegrams either addressed to himself personally or fired at Sir Rupert in the Foreign Office.

He had other troubles too. He was beginning to be seriously alarmed about his own feelings to Helena Langley. He was beginning to feel, whenever he was away from her, that 'inseparable sigh for her,' which Byron in one of the most human of all his very human moods, has so touchingly described. He felt that she was far too young for him, and that the boat of his shaky fortunes was not meant to carry a bright and beautiful young woman in it—a boat that might go to pieces on a rock at any moment after it had tried to put to sea; and which must, nevertheless, try to put to sea. Then again he had been irritated by paragraphs in the society papers coupling his name more or less conjecturally with that of Helena Langley. 'All this must come to an end,' he thought. 'I have got my work to do, and I must go and do it.'

One evening Ericson wandered along outside the gates of the Park, and along the chalky roads that led by the sea-wall towards the little town. The place was lonely even at that season. The rush of Londoners had not yet found a way there. To 'Arry and 'Arriet it offered no manner of attraction. The sunset was already over, but there was still a light and glow in the sky. The Emperor looked at his watch. It wanted a quarter to seven—there was yet time enough, before returning to dress for the eight o'clock dinner. 'I must make up my mind,' he said to himself; 'I must go.'

He heard the rattle of wheels, and towards him came a light pony carriage with two horses, a footman sitting behind, and a young woman driving. It was Helena. She pulled up the moment she saw him.

'I have been down into the town,' she said.

'Seeing after your poor?'

'Oh—well—yes—I like seeing after them. It's no sacrifice on my part—I dare say I shouldn't do it if I didn't like it. Shall I drive you home?'

'It is early,' he said, hesitatingly; 'I thought of enjoying the evening a little yet.'

This was not well said, but Helena thought nothing of it.

'May I walk with you?' she asked, 'and I'll send the carriage home.'

'I shall only be too happy to be with you,' the Emperor said, and he felt what he said. So the carriage was sent on, and Ericson and Helena walked slowly, and for a while silently, on in the direction of the town.

'I have not been only seeing after my poor,' she said, 'I have been doing a little shopping.'

'Shopping here! What on earth can *you* want to buy in this little place?'

'Well, I persuaded papa into occupying this house here every year, and I very soon found out that you get terribly unpopular if you don't buy something in the town. So I buy all I can in the town.'

'But what do you buy?'

'Oh, well, wine, and tongues, and hams, and gloves.'

'But the wine?'

'I believe some of it is not so awfully bad. Anyhow, one need not drink it. Only the trouble is that I was in the other day at the one only wine merchant's, and while I was ordering something I heard a lady ask for two bottles of some particular claret, and the proprietor called out: "Very sorry, madam, but Sir Rupert Langley carried away all I had left of that very claret, didn't he, William?" And William responded stoutly, and I dare say quite truly, "Oh yes, madam; Sir Rupert, 'e 'as carried all that off." Now *I* was Sir Rupert.'

'Yes, I dare say you were. He never knew?'

'Oh, no; my dodges to make him popular would not interest him one little bit. He goes in for charity and all that, and doing real good to deserving poor; but he doesn't care a straw about popularity. Now *I* do.'

'I don't believe you do in the least,' Ericson said, looking fixedly at her. Very handsome she showed, with the west wind blowing back her hair, and a certain gleam of excitement in her eyes, as if she were boldly talking of something to drive away all thought or possibility of talk about something else.

'Oh, not about myself, of course! But I want papa to be popular here and everywhere else. Do you know—it is very funny—the first day I came down here—this time—I went into one of the shops to give some orders, and the man, when he had written them down—he hadn't asked my name before—he said, "You *are* Sir Rupert Langley, ain't you, miss?" and I said, without ever thinking over the question, "Oh, yes, of course I am." It was all right. We each meant what we said, and we conveyed our ideas quite satisfactorily. He didn't fancy that "Miss" was passing off for her father, and I didn't suppose that he thought anything of the kind. So it was all right, but it was very amusing, I thought.'

She was talking against time, it would seem. At least she was probably not talking of what deeply interested her just then. In truth, she had stopped her carriage on a sudden impulse when she saw Ericson, and now she was beginning to think that she had acted too impulsively. Until lately she had allowed her impulses to carry her unquestioned whither they were pleased to go.

'I suppose we had better turn back,' she said.

'I suppose so,' the Emperor answered. They stood still before turning, and looked along the way from home.

The sky was all of a faint lemon-colour along the horizon, deepening in some places to the very tenderest tone of pink—a pink that suggested in a dim way that the soft lemon sky was about to see at once another dawn. Low down on the horizon one bright white spark struck itself out against the sky.

'What is that little light—that spark?' she asked. 'Is it a star?'

'Oh, no,' the Emperor said gravely, 'it is only an ordinary gas-lamp—nothing more.'

'A gas-lamp? Oh, come, that is quite impossible. I mean that star, there in the sky.'

'It is only a gas-lamp all the same,' he said. 'You will see in a moment. It is on the brow of the road— probably the first gas-lamp on the way into the town. Against that clear sky, with its tender tones, the light in the street-lamp shows not orange or red, but a sparkling white.'

'Come nearer and let us see,' she said, impatiently. 'Come, by all means.'

So they went nearer, and the illusion was gone. It was, as he had said, a common street-lamp.

'I am quite disappointed,' Helena said, after a moment of silence.

'But why?' he asked. 'Might not one extract a moral out of that?'

'Oh, I don't see how you could.'

'Well, let us try. The common street-lamp got its opportunity, and it shone like a star. Isn't there a good deal of human life very like that?'

'But what is the good of showing for once like a star when it is not a star?'

'Ah, well, I am afraid a good deal of life's ambition would be baffled if everyone were to take that view of things.'

'But isn't it the right view?'

'To the higher sense, yes—but the ambition of most men is to be taken for the star, at all events.'

'That is, mistaken for the star,' she said.

'Yes, if you will—mistaken for the star.'

'I am sure that is not your ambition,' she said warmly. 'I am sure you would rather be the star mistaken at a distance by some stupid creature for a gas-lamp, than the gas-lamp mistaken even by me'— she spoke this smilingly—'for a star.'

'I should not like to be mistaken by you for anything,' he said.

'You know I could not mistake you.'

'I think you are mistaking me now—I am afraid so.

'Oh, no; please do not think anything like that. I never could mistake you—I always understand you. Tell me what you mean.'

'Well; you think me a man of courage, I dare say.'

'Of course I do. Everyone does.'

'Yet I feel rather cowardly at this moment.'

'Cowardly! About what?'

'About you,' he answered blankly.

'About me? Am I in any danger?'

'No, not in that sense.' He did not say in what sense.

She promptly asked him: 'In what sense then?'

'Well, then,' said the Emperor, 'there is something I ought to tell you, something disagreeable—I am sure it will be disagreeable, and I don't know how to tell it. I seem to want the courage.'

'Talk to me as if I were a man,' she said hotly.

'That would not mend matters, I am afraid.'

They were now walking back towards the Park.

'Call me Dick Langley,' she said, 'and talk to me as if I were a boy, and then perhaps you can tell me all you mean and all you want to do. I am tired of this perpetual difficulty.'

'It wouldn't help in the least,' the Emperor said, 'if I were to call you Dick Langley. You would still be Helena Langley.'

The girl, usually so fearless and unconstrained—so unconventional, those said who liked her—so reckless, they said who did not like her—this girl felt for the first time in her life the meaning of the conventional—the all-pervading meaning of the difference of sex. For the mere sound of her own name, 'Helena,' pronounced by Ericson, sent such a thrill of delight through her that it made her cheek flush. It did a great deal more than that—it made her feel that she could not long conceal her emotion towards the Emperor, could not long pretend that it was nothing more than that which the most enthusiastic devotee feels for a political leader. A shock of fear came over her, something compounded of exquisite pleasure and bewildering pain. That one word 'Helena,' spoken perhaps carelessly by the man who walked beside her, broke in upon her soul and sense with the awakening touch of a revelation. She awoke, and she knew that she must soon betray herself. She knew that never again could she have the careless freedom of heart which she owned but yesterday. She was afraid. She felt tears coming into her eyes. She stopped suddenly, and put her hand to her side and gasped as if for breath.

'What is the matter?' Ericson asked. 'Are you unwell?'

'No, no!' she said hastily. 'I felt just a little faintish for a moment—but it's nothing. I am not a bit of a fainting girl, Mr Ericson, I can assure you—never fainted in all my life. I have the nerves of a bull-dog and the digestion of an ostrich.'

'You don't quite look like that now,' he said, in an almost compassionate tone. He was puzzled. Something had undoubtedly happened to make her start and pause like that. But he could only think of something physical; it never occurred to him to suppose that anything he had said could have caused it.

'Shall we go back to what we were talking about?' he asked.

'What we were talking about?' Already her new discovery had taken away some of her sincerity, and inspired her with the sense of a necessity for self-defence. Already, and for the first time in her life, she was having recourse to one of the commonest, and, surely, one of the least culpable, of the crafts and tricks of womanhood, she was trying not to betray her love to the man who, so far as she knew, had not thought of love for her.

'Well, you were accusing me of a want of frankness with you, and were urging me to be more open?'

'Was I? Yes, of course I was; but I don't suppose I meant anything in particular—and, then, I have no right.'

The Emperor grew more puzzled than ever.

'No right?' he asked. 'Yes—but I gave you the right when I told you I was proud of your friendship, and I asked you to tell me of anything you wanted to know. But *I* wanted to speak to *you* very frankly too.'

She looked at him in surprise and a sort of alarm.

'Yes, I did. I want to tell you why I can't treat you as if you were Dick Langley. I want to tell you why I can't forget that you are Helena Langley.'

This time the sound of the name was absolutely sweet in her ears. The mere terror had gone already, and she would gladly have had him call her 'Helena,' 'Helena,' ever so many times over without the intermission of a moment. 'Only perhaps I should get used to it then, and I shouldn't feel it so much,' she thought, with a sudden correcting influence on a first passionate desire. She steadied her nerves and asked him:

'Why can you not speak to me as if I were Dick Langley, and why can you never forget that I am— Helena Langley?'

'Because you are Helena Langley for one thing, and not Dick,' he said with a smile. 'Because you are not a young man, but a very charming and beautiful young woman.'

'Oh!' she exclaimed, with an almost angry movement of her hand.

'I am not paying compliments,' he said gently. 'Between us let there be truth, as you said yourself in your quotation from Goethe the other day. I am setting out the facts before you. Even if I could forget that you are Helena Langley, there are others who could not forget it either for you or for me.'

'I don't understand what you mean,' she said wonderingly.

'You would not understand, of course. I am afraid I must explain to you. You will forgive me?'

'I have not the least idea,' she said impetuously, 'what I am to understand, or what I am to forgive. Mr Ericson, do for pity's sake be plain with me.'

'I have resolved to be,' he said gloomily.

'What on earth has been happening? Why have you changed in this way to me?'

'I have not changed.'

'Well, tell me the whole story,' she said impatiently, 'if there is a story.'

'There is a story,' he said, with a melancholy smile, 'a very silly story—but still a story. Look here, Miss Langley: even if you do not know that you are beautiful and charming and noble-hearted and good—as I well know that you are all this and ever so much more—you must know that you are very rich.'

'Yes, I do know that, and I am glad of it sometimes, and I hate it sometimes. I don't know yet whether I am going to be glad of it or to hate it now. Go on, Mr Ericson, please, and tell me what is to follow this prologue about my disputed charms and virtues— for I assure you there are many people, some women among the rest, who think me neither good-looking nor even good—and my undisputed riches.' She was plucking up a spirit now, and was much more like her usual self. She felt herself tied to the stake, and was determined to fight the course.

'Do you know,' he asked, 'that people say I am coming here after you?'

She blushed crimson, but quickly pulled herself together. She was equal to anything now.

'Is that all?' she asked carelessly. 'I should have thought they said a great deal more and a great deal worse than that.'

He looked at her in some surprise.

'What else do you suppose they could have said?'

'I fancied,' she answered with a laugh, 'that they were saying I went everywhere after you.'

'Come, come,' he said, after a moment's pause, during which the Emperor seemed almost as much bewildered as if she had thrown her fan in his face. 'You mustn't talk nonsense. I am speaking quite seriously.'

'So am I, I can assure you.'

'Well, well, to come to the point of what I had to say. People are talking, and they tell each other that I am coming after you, to marry you, for the sake of your money.'

'Oh!' She recoiled under the pain of these words. 'Oh, for shame,' she exclaimed, 'they cannot say that—of you—of you?'

'Yes, they do. They say that I am a mere broken-down and penniless political adventurer—that I am trying to recover my lost position in Surmer—which I am, and by God's good help I shall recover it too.'

'Yes, with God's good help you shall recover it,' the girl exclaimed fervently, and she put out her hand in a sudden impulse for him to take it in his. The Emperor smiled sadly and did not touch the proffered hand, and she let it fall, and felt chilled.

'Well, they say that I propose to make use of your money to start me on my political enterprise. They talked of this in private, the society papers talk of it now.'

'Well?' she asked, with a curious contracting of the eyebrows.

'Well, but that is painful—it is hurtful.'

'To you?'

'Oh, no,' he replied almost angrily, 'not to me. How could it be painful and hurtful to me? At least, what do you suppose I should care about it? What harm could it do me?'

'None whatever,' she calmly replied. She was now entirely mistress of herself and her feelings again. 'No one who knows you would believe anything of the kind—and for those who do not know you, you would say, "Let them believe what they will."'

'Yes, they might believe anything they liked so far as I am concerned,' he said scornfully. 'But then we must think of *you*. Good heaven!' he suddenly broke off, 'how the journalism of England—at all events of London—has changed since I used to be a Londoner! Fancy apparently respectable journals, edited, I suppose, by men who call themselves gentlemen—and who no doubt want to be received and regarded as gentlemen—publishing paragraphs to give to all the world conjectures about a young woman's fortune—a young woman whom they name, and about the adventurers who are pursuing her in the hope of getting her fortune.'

'You have been a long time out of London,' Helena said composedly. She was quite happy now. If this was all, she need not care. She was afraid at first that the Emperor meant to tell her that he was leaving England for ever. Of course, if he were going to rescue and recover Surmer, she would have felt proud and glad. At least she would certainly have felt proud, and she would have tried to make herself think that she felt glad, but it would have been a terrible shock to her to hear that he was going away; and, this shock being averted, she seemed to think no other trouble an affair of much account. Therefore, she was quite equal to any embarrassment coming out of what the society papers, or any other papers, or any persons whatever, might say about her. If she could have spoken out the full truth she would have said: 'Mr Ericson, so long as my father and you are content with what I do, I don't care three rows of pins what all the rest of the world is saying or thinking of me.' But she could not quite venture to say this, and so she merely offered the qualifying remark about his having been a long time out of London.

'Yes, I have,' he said with some bitterness. 'I don't understand the new ways. In my time—you know I once wrote for newspapers myself, and very proud I was of it, too, and very proud I am of it—a man would have been kicked who dragged the name of a young woman into a paper coupled with conjectures as to the scoundrels who were running after her for her money.'

'You take it too seriously,' said Helena sweetly. She adored him for his generous anger, but she only wanted to bring him back to calmness. 'In London we are used to all that. Why, Mr Ericson, I have been married in the newspapers over and over again—I mean I have been engaged to be married. I don't believe the wedding ceremonial has ever been described, but I have been engaged times out of mind. Why, I don't believe papa and I ever have gone abroad, since I came out, without some paragraph appearing in the society papers announcing my engagement to some foreign Duke or Count or Marquis. I have been engaged to men I never saw.'

'How does your father like that sort of thing?' the Emperor asked fiercely.

'My father? Oh, well, of course he doesn't quite like it.'

'I should think not,' Ericson growled—and he made a flourish of his cane as if he meant to illustrate the sort of action he should like to take with the publishers of these paragraphs, if he only knew them and had an opportunity of arguing out the case with them.

'But, then, I think he has got used to it; and of course as a public man he is helpless, and he can't resent it.' She said this with obvious reference to the flourish of the Emperor's cane; and it must be owned that a very pretty flash of light came into her eyes which signified that if she had quite her own way the offence might be resented after all.

'No, of course he can't resent it,' the Emperor said, in a tone which unmistakably conveyed the idea, 'and more's the pity.'

'Then what is the good of thinking about it?' Helena pleaded. 'Please, Mr Ericson, don't trouble yourself in the least about it. These things will appear in those papers. If it were not you it would be somebody else. After all we must remember that there are two sides to this question as well as to others. I do not owe my publicity in the society papers to any merits or even to any demerits of my own. I am known to be the heiress to a large fortune, and the daughter of a Secretary of State.'

'That is no reason why you should be insulted.'

'No, certainly. But do you not think that in this over-worked and over-miserable England of ours there are thousands and thousands of poor girls ever so much better than I, who would be only too delighted to exchange with me—to put up with the paragraphs in the society papers for the sake of the riches and the father—and to abandon to me without a sigh the thimble and the sewing machine, and the daily slavery in the factory or behind the counter? Why, Mr Ericson, only think of it. I can sit down whenever I like, and there are thousands and thousands of poor girls in England who dare not sit down during all their working hours.'

She spoke with increasing animation.

The Emperor looked at her with a genuine admiration. He knew that all she said was the true outcome of her nature and her feelings. Her sparkling eyes proclaimed the truth.

'You look at it rightly,' the Emperor said at last, 'and I feel almost ashamed of my scruples. Almost—but not quite—for they were scruples on your account and not upon my own.'

'Of course I know that,' she interrupted hastily. 'But please, Mr Ericson, don't mind me. I don't care, and I know my father won't care. Do not—please do not—let this interfere in the least with your friendship; I cannot lose your friendship for this sort of thing. After all, you see, they can't force you to marry me if you don't want to;' and then she stopped, and was afraid, perhaps, that she had spoken too lightly and saucily, and that he might think her wanting in feeling. He did not think her wanting in feeling. He thought her nobly considerate, generous and kind. He thought she wanted to save him from embarrassment on her account, and to let him know that they were to continue good friends, true friends, in spite of what anybody might choose to say about them; and that there was to be no thought of anything but friendship. This was Helena's meaning in one sense, but not in another sense. She took it for granted that he was not in love with her, and she wished to make it clear to him that there was not the slightest reason for him to cease to be her friend because he could not be her lover. That was her meaning. Up to a certain point it was the meaning that he ascribed to her, but in her secret heart there was still a feeling which she did not express and which he could not divine.

'Then we are still to be friends?' he said. 'I am not to feel bound to cut myself off from seeing you because of all this talk?'

'Not unless you wish it.'

'Oh, wish it!' and he made an energetic gesture.

'I have talked very boldly to you,' Helena said— 'cheekily, I fancy some people would call it; but I do so hate misunderstandings, and having others and myself made uncomfortable, and I do so prefer my happiness to my dignity! You see, I hadn't much of a mother's care, and I am a sort of wild-growth, and you must make allowance for me and forgive me, and take me for what I am.'

'Yes, I take you cordially for what you are,' the Emperor exclaimed, 'the noblest and the dearest girl in the world—to me.'

Helena flushed a little. But she was determined that the meaning of the flush was not to be known.

'Come,' she said, with a wholly affected coquetry of manner, 'I wonder if you have said that to any other girls—and if so, how many?'

The Emperor was not skilled in the wiles of coquetry. He fell innocently into the snare.

'The truth is,' he said simply, 'I hardly know any girl but you.'

Surely the Emperor had spoken out one of the things we ought to wish not to have said. It amused Helena, however, and greatly relieved her—in her present mood.

'Come,' she exclaimed, with a little spurt of laughter which was a relief to the tension of her feelings; 'the compliment, thank heaven, is all gone! I *must* be the dearest girl in the world to you—I can't help it, whatever my faults—if you do not happen to know any other girl!'

'Oh, I didn't meant *that*.'

'Didn't mean even that? Didn't even mean that I had attained, for lack of any rival, to that lonely and that inevitable eminence?'

'Come, you are only laughing at me. I know what I meant myself.'

'Oh, but please don't explain. It is quite delightful as it is.'

They were now under the lights of the windows in Seagate Hall, and only just in time to dress for dinner.

CHAPTER XXI

MORGIANA

Sir Rupert took the Duchess of Deptford in to dinner. The Duke was expected in a day or two, but just at present was looking after racing schooners at Ryde and Cowes. Ericson had the great satisfaction of having Helena Langley, as the hostess, assigned to him. An exiled Emperor takes the rank of an exiled king, and Ericson was delighted with his rank and its one particular privilege just now. He was not in a mood to talk to anybody else, or to be happy with anybody but Helena. To him now all was dross that was not Helena, as to Faust in Marlowe's play. Soame Rivers had charge of Mrs Sarrasin. Professor Flick was permitted to escort Miss Paulo. Hamilton and Mr Andrew J. Copping went in without companionship of woman. The dinner was but a small one, and without much of ceremonial.

'One thing I miss here,' the Emperor said to Helena as they sat down, 'I miss To-to.'

'I generally bring him down with me,' Helena said. 'But this time I haven't done so. Be comforted, however; he comes down tomorrow.'

'I never quite know how he understands his position in this household. He conducts himself as if he were your personal property. But he is actually Sir Rupert's dog, is he not?'

'Yes,' Helena answered; 'but it is all quite clear. To-to knows that he belongs to Sir Rupert, but he is satisfied in his own mind that *I* belong to *him*.'

'I see,' the Emperor said with a smile. 'I quite understand the situation now. There is no divided duty.'

'Oh, no, not in the least. All our positions are marked out.'

'Is it true, Sir Rupert,' asked the Duchess, 'that our friend,' and she nodded towards Ericson, 'is going to make an attempt to recover his Empire?'

'I should rather be inclined to put it,' Sir Rupert said, 'that if there is any truth in the rumours one reads about, he is going to try to save his Empire. But why not ask him, Duchess?'

'He might think it so rude and presuming,' the pretty Duchess objected.

'No, no; he is much too gallant a gentleman to think anything you do could be rude and presuming.'

'Then I'll ask him right away,' the Duchess said encouraged. 'Only I can't catch his eye—he is absorbed in your daughter, and a very odd sort of man he would be if he were not absorbed in her.'

'You look at him long enough and keenly enough, and he will be sure very soon to feel that your eyes are on him.'

'You believe in that theory of eyes commanding eyes?'

'Well, I have noticed that it generally works out correctly.'

'But Miss Langley has such divine eyes, and she is commanding him now. I fear I may as well give up. Oh!' For at that moment Ericson, at a word from

Helena, who saw that the Duchess was gazing at them, suddenly looked up and caught the beaming eyes of the pretty and sprightly young American woman who had become the wife of a great English Duke.

'The Duchess wants to ask you a question,' Sir Rupert said to Ericson, 'and she hopes you won't think her rude or presuming. I have ventured to say that I am sure you will not think her anything of the kind.'

'You can always speak for me, Sir Rupert, and never with more certainty than just now, and to the Duchess.'

'Well,' the Duchess said with a pretty little blush, as she found all the eyes at the table fixed on her, including those that were covered by Professor Flick's moony spectacles, 'I have been reading all sorts of rumours about you, Mr Ericson.'

Ericson quailed for a moment. 'She can't mean *that*,' he thought. 'She can't mean to bring up the marriage question here at Sir Rupert's own table, and in the ears of Sir Rupert's daughter! No,' he suddenly consoled himself, 'she is too kind and sweet—she would never do *that*—and he did the Duchess only justice. She had no such thought in her mind.

'Are you really going to risk your life by trying to recover your Empire? Are you going to be so rash?'

Ericson was not embarrassed in the least.

'I am not ambitious to recover the Empire, Duchess,' he answered calmly—'if the Empire can get on without me. But if the Empire should be in danger—then, of course, I know where my place ought to be.'

'Just what I told you, Duchess,' Sir Rupert said, rather triumphant with himself.

Helena sent a devoted glance at her hero, and then let her eyes droop.

'Well, I must not ask any indiscreet questions,' the Duchess said; 'and besides, I know that if I did ask them you would not answer them. But are you prepared for events? Is that indiscreet!'

'Oh, no; not in the least. I am perfectly prepared.'

'I wish he would not talk out so openly as that,' Hamilton said to himself. 'How do we know who some of these people are?'

'Rather an indiscreet person, your friend the Emperor,' Soame Rivers said to Mrs Sarrasin. 'How can he know that some of these people here may not be in sympathy with Orizaba, and may not send out a telegram to let people know there that he has arranged for a descent upon the shores of Surmer? Gad! I don't wonder that the Surmer people kicked him out, if that is his notion of statesmanship.

'The Surmer people, as a people, adore him, sir,' Mrs Sarrasin sternly observed.

'Odd way they have of showing it,' Rivers replied.

'We, in this country, have driven out kings,' Mrs Sarrasin said, 'and have taken them back and set them on their thrones again.'

'Some of them we have not taken back, Mrs Sarrasin.'

'We may yet—or some of their descendants.'

Mrs Sarrasin became, for the moment, and out of a pure spirit of contradiction, a devoted adherent of the Stuarts and a wearer of the Rebel Rose.

'Oh, I say, this is becoming treasonable, Mrs Sarrasin. Do have some consideration for me—the private secretary of a Minister of State.'

'I have great consideration for you, Mr Rivers; I bear in mind that you do not mean half what you say.'

'But don't you really think,' he asked in a low tone, 'that your Emperor was just a little indiscreet when he talked so openly about his plans?'

'He is very well able to judge of his own affairs, I should think, and probably he feels sure'—and she made this a sort of direct stab at Rivers—'that in the house of Sir Rupert Langley he is among friends.'

Rivers was only amused, not in the least disconcerted.

'But these Americans, now—who knows anything about them? Don't all Americans write for newspapers? and why might not these fellows telegraph the news to the *New York Herald* or the *New York Tribune*, or some such paper, and so spread it all over the world, and send an Orizaba ironclad or two to look out for the returning Emperor?'

'I don't know them,' Mrs Sarrasin answered, 'but my brother-in-law does, and I believe they are merely scientific men, and don't know or care anything about politics—even in their own country.'

Miss Paulo talked a good deal with Professor Flick. Mr Copping sat on her other side, and she had tried to exchange a word or two now and then with him, but she failed in drawing out any ready response, and so she devoted all her energies to Professor Flick. She asked him all the questions she could think of concerning folk-lore. The Professor was benignant in his explanations. He was, she assumed, quite compassionate over her ignorance on the subject. She was greatly interested in his American accent. How strong it was, and yet what curiously soft and Southern tones one sometimes caught in it! Dolores had never been in the United States, but she had met a great many Americans.

'Do you come from the Southern States, Professor?' she asked, innocently seeking for an explanation of her wonder.

'Southern States, Miss Paulo? No, madam. I am from the Wild West—I have nothing to do with the South. Why did you ask?'

'Because I thought there was a tone of the Spanish in your accent, and I fancied you might have come from New Orleans. I am a sort of Spaniard, you know.'

'I have nothing to do with New Orleans,' he said—'I have never even been there.'

'But, of course, you speak Spanish?' Miss Paulo said suddenly *in* Spanish. 'A man with your studies must know ever so many languages.'

As it so happened, she glanced quite casually and innocently up into the eyes of Professor Flick. She caught his eye, in fact, right under the moony spectacles; and if those eyes under the moony spectacles did not understand Spanish, then Dolores had lost faith in her own bright eyes and her own very keen and lively perceptions.

But the moony spectacles were soon let down over the eyes of the Professor of Folk-Lore, and hung there like shutters or blinkers.

'No, madam,' spoke the Professor; 'I am sorry to say that I do not understand Spanish, for I presume you have been addressing me in Spanish,' he added hastily. 'It is a noble tongue, of course, but I have not had time to make myself acquainted with it.'

'I thought there was a great amount of folk-lore in Spanish,' the pertinacious Dolores went on.

'So there is, dear young lady, so there is. But one cannot know every language—one must have recourse to translations sometimes.'

'Could I help you,' she asked sweetly, 'with any work of translating from the Spanish? I should be delighted if I could—and I really do know Spanish pretty well.'

'Dear young lady, how kind that would be of you! And what a pleasure to me!'

'It would be both a pride and a pleasure to *me* to lend any helping hand towards the development of the study of folk-lore.'

The Professor looked at her in somewhat puzzled fashion, not through but from beneath the moony spectacles. Dolores felt perfectly satisfied that he was studying her. All the better reason, she thought, for her studying him.

What had Dolores got upon her mind? She did not know. She had not the least glimmering of a clear idea. It was not a very surprising thing that an American Professor addicted mainly to the study of folk-lore should not know Spanish. Dolores had a vague impression of having heard that, as a rule, Americans were not good linguists. But that was not what troubled and perplexed her. She felt convinced, in this case, that the professed American did understand Spanish, and that his ordinary accent had something Spanish in it, although he had declared that he had never been even in New Orleans.

We all remember the story of Morgiana in 'The Forty Thieves.' The faculties of the handsome and clever Morgiana were strained to their fullest tension with one particular object. She looked at everything, studied everything—with regard to that object. If she saw a chalk-mark on a door she instantly went and made a like chalk-mark on various doors in the neighbourhood. Dolores found her present business in life to be somewhat like that of Morgiana. A chalk-mark was enough to fill her with suspicion; an unexpected accent was enough to fill her with suspicion; an American Professor who knew Spanish, but had no confidence in his Spanish, might possibly be the Captain of the Forty Immortals—thieves, of course, and not Academicians. Dolores had as vague an idea about the Spanish question as Morgiana had about the chalk-mark on the door, but she was quite clear that some account ought to be taken of it.

At this moment, much to the relief of the perplexed Dolores, Helena caught the eye of the pretty Duchess, and the Duchess arose, and Mrs Sarrasin arose, and Hamilton held the door open, and the ladies floated through and went upstairs. Now came the critical moment for Dolores. Had she discovered anything? Even if she had discovered anything, was it anything that concerned her or anyone she cared for? Should she keep her discovery—or her fancied discovery—to herself?

The Duchess settled down beside Helena, and appeared to be made up for a good talk with her. Mrs Sarrasin was beginning to turn over the leaves of a photographic album. 'Now is my time,' Dolores thought, 'and this is the woman to talk to and to trust myself to. If she laughs at me, then I shall feel pretty sure that mine was all a false alarm.' So she sat beside Mrs Sarrasin, who looked up at once with a beaming smile.

'Mrs Sarrasin,' Dolores said in a low, quiet voice, 'should you think it odd if a man who knows Spanish were to pretend that he did not understand a word of it?'

'That would depend a good deal on who the man was, my dear, and where he was, and what he was doing. I should not be surprised if a Carlist spy, for instance, captured some years ago by the Royalists, were to pretend that he did not speak Spanish, and try to pass off for a commercial traveller from Bordeaux.'

'Yes. But where there was no war—and no capture—and no need of concealing one's acquirements——'

Mrs Sarrasin saw that something was really disturbing the girl. She became wonderfully composed and gentle. She thought a moment, and then said:

'I heard Mr Soame Rivers say tonight that he didn't understand Spanish. Was that only his modesty—and does he understand it?'

'Oh, Mrs Sarrasin, I wasn't thinking about him. What does it matter whether he understands it or not?'

'Nothing whatever, I should say. So it was not he?'

'Oh, no, indeed.'

'Then whom were you thinking about?'

Dolores dropped her voice to its lowest tone and whispered:

'Professor Flick!' Then she glanced in some alarm towards Helena, fearing lest Miss Langley might have heard. The good girl's heart was set on sparing Miss Langley any distress of mind which could possibly be avoided. Dolores saw in a moment how her words had impressed Mrs Sarrasin. Mrs Sarrasin turned on Dolores a face of the deepest interest. But she had all the composure of her many campaigns.

'This is a very different business,' she said, 'from Mr Rivers and his profession of ignorance. Do you really mean to say, Miss Paulo—you are a clever girl, I know, with sound nerve and good judgment—do you mean to say that Professor Flick really does know Spanish, although he says he does not understand it?'

'I spoke to him a few words of Spanish, and, as it so happened, I looked up at him, and quite accidentally caught his eye under his big spectacles, and I saw that he understood me. Mrs Sarrasin, I *could* not be mistaken—I *know* he understood me. And then he recovered himself, and said that he knew nothing of Spanish. Why, there was so much of the Spanish in his accent—it isn't *very* much, of course—that I assumed at first that he must have come from New Orleans or from Texas.'

'I have had very little talk with him,' Mrs Sarrasin said; 'but I never noticed any Spanish peculiarity in his accent.'

'But you wouldn't; you are not Spanish; and, anyhow, it's only a mere little shade—just barely suggests. Do you think there is anything in all this? I may be mistaken, but—no—no—I am not mistaken. That man knows Spanish as surely as I know English.'

'Then it is a matter of the very highest importance,' said Mrs Sarrasin decidedly. 'If a man comes here professing not to speak Spanish, and yet does speak Spanish, it is as clear as light that he has some motive for concealing the fact that he is a Spaniard—or a South American. Of course he is not a Spaniard—Spain does not come into this business. He is a South American, and he is either a spy——'

'Yes—either a spy——.' Dolores waited anxiously.

'Or an assassin.'

'Yes—I thought so;' and Dolores shuddered. 'But a spy,' she whispered, 'has nothing to find out.

Everything about—about his Excellency—is known to all the world here.'

'You are quite right, dear young lady,' Mrs Sarrasin said. 'We are driven to the other conclusion. If you are right—and I am sure you are right—that that man knows Spanish and professes not to know it, we are face to face with a plot for an assassination. Hush!—the gentlemen are coming. Don't lose your head, my dear—whatever may happen. You may be sure I shall not lose mine. Go and talk to Mr Hamilton—you might find a chance of giving him a word, or a great many words, of warning. I must have a talk with Sarrasin as soon as I can. But no outward show of commotion, mind!'

'It may be a question of a day,' Dolores whispered.

'If the man thinks he is half-discovered, it may be a question of an hour,' Mrs Sarrasin replied, as composedly as if she were thinking of the possible spoiling of a dinner. Dolores shuddered. Mrs Sarrasin felt none the less, but she had been in so many a crisis that danger for those she loved came to her as a matter of course.

Then the door was thrown open, and the gentlemen came in. Sir Rupert made for Dolores. He was anxious to pay her all the attention in his power, because he feared, in his chivalrous way, that if she were not followed with even a marked attention, she might think that as the daughter of Paulo's Hotel she was not regarded as quite the equal of all the other guests. The Emperor thought he was bound to address himself to the Duchess of Deptford, and fancied that it might look a little too marked if he were at once to take possession of Helena. The good-natured Duchess saw through his embarrassment in a moment. The light of kindliness and sympathy guided her; and just as Ericson was approaching her she feigned to be wholly unconscious of his propinquity, and leaning forward in her chair she called out in her clear voice:

'Now, look here, Professor Flick, I want you to sit right down here and talk to me. You are a countryman of mine, and I haven't yet had a chance of saying anything much to you, so you come and talk to me.'

The Professor declared himself delighted, honoured, all the rest, and came and seated himself, according to the familiar modern phrase, in the pretty Duchess's pocket.

'We haven't met in America, Professor, I think?' the Duchess said.

'No, Duchess; I have never had that high honour.'

'But your name is quite familiar to me. You have a great observatory, haven't you—out West somewhere—the Flick Observatory, is it not?'

'No, Duchess. Pardon me. You are thinking of the Lick Observatory.'

'Oh, am I? Yes, I dare say. Lick and Flick are so much alike. And I don't know one little bit about sciences. I don't know one of them from another. They are all the same to me. I only define science as something that I can't understand. I had a notion that you were mixed up with astronomy. That's why I got thinking of the Lick Observatory.'

'No, your Grace, my department is very modest— folk-lore.'

'Oh, yes, nursery rhymes of all nations, and making out that every country has got just the same old stories—that's the sort of thing, as far as I can make out—ain't it?'

'Well,' the Professor said, somewhat constrainedly, 'that is a more or less humorous condensed description of a very important study.'

'I think I should like folk-lore,' the lively Duchess went on. 'I do hope, Professor, that you will come to me some afternoon, and talk folk-lore to me. I could understand it so much better than astronomy, or chemistry, or these things; and I don't care about history, and I *do* hate recitations.'

Just then Soame Rivers entered the room, and saw that Ericson was talking with Helena. His eyebrows contracted. Rivers was the last man to go upstairs to the drawing-room. He had a pretty clear idea that something was going on. During the time while the men were having their cigars and cigarettes, telegrams came in for almost everyone at the table; the Emperor opened his and glanced at it and handed it over to Hamilton, who, for his part, had had a telegram all to himself. Rivers studied Ericson's face, and felt convinced that the very imperturbability of its expression was put on in order that no one might suppose he had learned anything of importance. It was quite different with Hamilton—a light of excitement flashed across him for a moment and was then suddenly extinguished. 'News from Surmer, no doubt,' Rivers thought to himself. 'Bad news, I hope.'

'Does anyone want to reply to his telegrams?' Sir Rupert courteously asked. 'They are kind enough to keep the telegraph office open for my benefit until midnight.'

No one seemed to think there was any necessity for troubling the telegraph office just then.

'Shall we go upstairs?' Sir Rupert asked. So the gentlemen went upstairs, and on their appearance the conversation between Dolores and Mrs Sarrasin came to an end, as we know.

Soame Rivers went into his own little study, which was kept always for him, and there he opened his despatch. It was from a man in the Foreign Office who was in the innermost councils of Sir Rupert and himself.

'Tell Hamilton look quietly after Ericson. Certain information of dangerous plot against Ericson's life. Danger where least expected. Do not know any more. No need as yet alarm Sir Rupert.'

Soame Rivers read the despatch over and over again. It was in cypher—a cypher with which he was perfectly familiar. He grumbled and growled over it. It vexed him. For various reasons he had come to the conclusion that a great deal too much work was made over the ex-Emperor, and his projects, and his personal safety.

'All stuff and nonsense!' he said to himself. 'It's absurd to make such a fuss about this fellow. Nobody can think him important enough to get up any plot for killing him; as far as I am concerned I don't see why they shouldn't kill him if they feel at all like it—personally, I am sure I wish they *would* kill him.'

Soame Rivers thought to himself, although he hardly put the thought into words even to himself and for his own benefit, that he might have had a good chance of winning Helena Langley to be his wife— of having her and her fortune—only for this so-called Emperor, whom, as a Briton, he heartily despised.

'I'll think it over,' he said to himself; 'I need not show this danger-signal to Hamilton just yet. Hamilton is a hero-worshipper and an alarmist— and a fool.'

So, looking very green of complexion and grim of countenance, Soame Rivers crushed the despatch and thrust it into his pocket, and then went upstairs to the ladies.

CHAPTER XXII

THE EXPEDITION

Every room in every house has its mystery by day and by night. But at night the mystery becomes more involved and a darker veil gathers round the secret. Each inmate goes off to bed with a smiling good-night to each other, and what could be more unlike than the hopes and plans and schemes for the morrow which each in silence is forming? All this of course is obvious and commonplace. But there would be a certain novelty of illustration if we were to take the fall of night upon Seagate Hall and try to make out what secrets it covered.

Ericson had found a means of letting Helena know by a few whispered words that he had heard news which would probably cut short his visit to Seagate Hall and hurry his departure from London. The girl had listened with breath kept resolutely in and bosom throbbing, and she dared not question further at such a moment. Only she said, 'You will tell me all?' and he said, 'Yes, tomorrow'; and she subsided and was content to wait and to take her secret to sleep with her, or rather take her secret with her to keep her from sleeping. Mrs Sarrasin had found means to tell her husband what Dolores had told her—and Sarrasin agreed with his wife in thinking that, although the discovery might appear trivial in itself, it had possibilities in it the stretch of which it would be madness to underrate. Ericson and Hamilton had common thoughts concerning the expedition to Surmer; but Hamilton had not confided to the Emperor any hint of what Mrs

Sarrasin had told him, and what Dolores had told Mrs Sarrasin. On the other hand, Ericson did not think it at all necessary to communicate to Hamilton the feelings with which the prospect of a speedy leaving of Seagate Hall had inspired him. Soame Rivers, we may be sure, took no one into the secret of the cyphered despatch which he had received, and which as yet he had kept in his own exclusive possession. If the gifted Professor Flick and his devoted friend Mr Copping had secrets—as no doubt they had—they could hardly be expected to proclaim them on the house-tops of Seagate Hall—a place on the shores of a foreign country. The common feeling cannot be described better than by saying that everybody wanted everybody else to get to bed.

The ladies soon dispersed. But no sooner had Mrs Sarrasin got into her room than she hastily mounted a dressing-gown and sought out Dolores, and the two settled down to low-toned earnest talk as though they were a pair of conspirators—which for a noble purpose they were.

The gentlemen, as usual, went to the billiard-room for cigars and whisky-and-soda. The two Americans soon professed themselves rather tired, and took their candles and went off to bed. But even they would seem not to be quite so sleepy and tired as they may have fancied; for they both entered the room of Professor Flick and began to talk. It was a very charming 'apartment' in the French sense. The Professor had a sitting-room very tastefully furnished and strewn around with various books on folk-lore; and he had a capacious bedroom. Copping flung himself impatiently on the sofa.

'Look here,' Copping whispered, 'this business must be done tonight. Do you hear?—this very night.'

'I know it,' the Professor said almost meekly.

'What have *you* heard?' Copping asked fiercely. 'Do you know anything more about Surmer than I know—than I got to know tonight?'

'Nothing more about Surmer, but I know that I am on the straight way to being found out.' And the Professor drooped.

'Found out? What do you mean? Found out for what?'

'Well, found out for a South American professing to be a Yankee.'

'But who has found you out?'

'That Spanish-London girl—that she-devil—Miss Paulo. She suddenly talked to me in Spanish—and I was thrown off my guard.'

'You fool!—and you answered her in Spanish?'

'No I didn't—I didn't say a word—but I saw by her look that she knew I understood her—and you'll see if they don't suspect something.'

'Of course they will suspect something. South Americans passing off as North Americans! here, here—with *him* in the house! Why, the light shines through it! Good heavens, what a fool you are! I never heard of anything like it!'

'I am always a failure,' the downcast Professor admitted, 'where women come into the work—or the play.'

The places of the two men appeared to have completely changed. The Professor was no longer the leader but the led. The silent and devoted Mr Andrew J. Copping was now taking the place of leader.

'Well,' Copping said contemptuously, 'you have got your chance just as I have. If you manage this successfully we shall get our pardon—and if we don't we shan't.'

'If we fail,' the learned Professor said, 'I shan't return to Surmer.'

'No, I dare say not. The English police will take good care of that, especially if Ericson should marry Sir Rupert's daughter. No—and do you fancy that even if the police failed to find us, those that sent us out would fail to find us? Do you think they would let us carry their secrets about with us? Why, what a fool you are!'

'I suppose I am,' the distressed student of folk-lore murmured.

'Many days would not pass before there was a dagger in both our hearts. It is of no use trying to avoid the danger now. Rally all your nerves—get together all your courage and coolness. This thing must be done tonight—we have no time to lose— and according to what you tell me we are being already found out. Mind—if you show the least flinching when I give you the word—I'll put a dagger into you! Hush—put your light out—I'll come at the right time.'

'You are too impetuous,' the Professor murmured with a sort of groan, and he took off his moony spectacles in a petulant way and put them on the table. Behold what a change! Instead of a moon-like beneficence of the spectacles, there was seen the quick shifting light of two dark, fierce, cruel, treacherous, cowardly eyes. They were eyes that might have looked out of the head of some ferocious and withal cowardly wild beast in a jungle or a forest. One who saw the change would have understood the axiom of a famous detective, 'No disguise for some men half so effective as a pair of large spectacles.'

'Put on your spectacles,' Copping said sternly.

'What's the matter? We are here among friends.'

'But it is so stupid a trick! How can you tell the moment when someone may come in?'

'Very good,' the Professor said, veiling his identity once again in the moony spectacles; 'only I can tell you I am getting sick of the dulness of all this, and I shall be glad of anything for a change.'

'You'll have a change soon enough,' Copping said contemptuously. 'I hope you will be equal to it when it comes.'

'How long shall I have to wait?'

'Until I come for you.'

'With the dagger, perhaps?' Professor Flick said sarcastically.

'With the dagger certainly, but I hope with no occasion for using it.'

'I hope so too; you might cut your fingers with it.'

'Are you threatening me?' Copping asked fiercely, standing up. He spoke, however, in the lowest of tones.

'I almost think I am. You see you have been threatening *me*—and I don't like it. I never professed to have as much courage as you have—I mean as you say you have; but I'm like a woman, when I'm driven into a corner I don't much care what I do— ah! then I *am* dangerous! It's not courage, I know, it's fear; but a man afraid and driven to bay is an ugly creature to deal with. And then it strikes me that I get all the dullest and also the most dangerous part of the work put on me, and I don't like *that*.'

Copping glanced for a moment at his colleague with eyes from which, according to Carlyle's phrase, 'hell-fire flashed for an instant.' Probably he would have very much liked to employ the dagger there and then. But he knew that that was not exactly the time or place for a quarrel, and he knew too that he had been talking too long with his friend already, and that he might on coming out of Professor Flick's room encounter some guest in the corridor. So by an effort he took off from his face the fierce expression, as one might take off a mask.

'We can't quarrel now, we two,' he said. 'When we come safe out of this business——'

'*If* we come safe out of this business,' the Professor interposed, with a punctuating emphasis on the 'if.'

Copping answered all unconsciously in the words of Lady Macbeth.

'Keep your courage up, and we shall do what we want to do.'

Then he left the room, and cautiously closed the door behind him, and crept stealthily away.

Ericson, Hamilton, and Sarrasin remained with Sir Rupert after the distinguished Americans had gone. There was an evident sense of relief running through the company when these had gone. Sir Rupert could see with half an eye that some news of importance had come.

'Well?' he asked; and that was all he asked.

'Well,' the Emperor replied, 'we have had some telegrams. At least Hamilton and I have. Have you heard anything, Sarrasin?'

'Something merely personal, merely personal,' Sarrasin answered with a somewhat constrained manner—the manner of one who means to convey the idea that the tortures of the Inquisition should not wrench that secret from him. Sarrasin was good at most things, but he was not happy at concealing secrets from his friends. Even as it was he blinked his eyes at Hamilton in a way that, if the others were observing him just then, must have made it apparent that he was in possession of some portentous communication which could be divulged to Hamilton alone. Sir Rupert, however, was not thinking much of Sarrasin.

'I mustn't ask about your projects,' Sir Rupert said; 'in fact, I suppose I had better know nothing about them. But, as a host, I may ask whether you have to leave England soon. As a mere matter of social duty I am entitled to ask that much. My daughter will be so sorry——'

'We shall have to leave for South America very soon, Sir Rupert,' the Emperor said—'within a very few days. We must leave for London tomorrow by the afternoon train at the latest.'

'How do you propose to enter Surmer?' Sir Rupert asked hesitatingly. What he really would have liked to ask was—'What men, what armament, have you got to back you when you land in your port?'

The Emperor divined the meaning.

'I go alone,' he said quietly.

'Alone!'

'Yes, except for the two or three personal friends who wish to accompany me—as friends, and not as a body-guard. I dare say the boy there,' and he nodded at Hamilton, 'will be wanting to step ashore with me.'

'Oh, yes, I shall step ashore at the same moment, or perhaps half a second later,' Hamilton said joyously. 'I'm a great steppist.'

'Bear in mind that *I* am going too,' Sarrasin interposed.

'We shall not go without you, Captain Sarrasin,' Ericson answered with a smile. For he felt well assured that when Captain Sarrasin stepped ashore, Mrs Sarrasin would be in step with him.

'Do you go unarmed?' Sir Rupert asked.

'Absolutely unarmed. I am not a despot coming to recapture a rebel kingdom—I am going to offer my people what help I can to save their Empire for them. If they will have me, I believe I can save the Empire; if they will not——' He threw out his hands with the air of one who would say, 'Then, come what will, it is no fault of mine.'

'Suppose they actually turn against you?'

'I don't believe they will. But if they do, it will no less have been an experiment well worth the trying, and it will only be a life lost.'

'Two lives lost,' Hamilton pleaded mildly.

'Excuse me, three lives lost, if you please,' Sarrasin interposed, 'or perhaps four.' For he was thinking of his heroic wife, and of the general understanding between them that it would be much more satisfactory that they should die together than that one should remain behind.

Sir Rupert smiled and sighed also. He was thinking of his romantic and adventurous youth.

'By Jove!' he said, 'I almost envy you fellows your expedition and your enthusiasm. There was a time—and not so very long ago—when I should have loved nothing better than to go with you and take your risks. But office-holding takes the enthusiasm out of us. One can never do anything after he has been a Secretary of State.'

'But, look here,' Hamilton said, 'here is a man who has been a Emperor——'

'Quite a different thing, my dear Hamilton,' Sir Rupert replied. 'An Emperor is a heroic, informal, unconventional sort of creature. There are no rules and precedents to bind him. He has no permanent officials. No one knows what he might or might not turn out. But a Secretary of State is pledged to respectability and conventionality. St. George might have gone forth to slay the dragon even though he had several times been a Emperor; never, never, if he had even once been Secretary of State.'

Captain Sarrasin took all this quite seriously, and promised himself in his own mind that nothing on earth should ever induce him to accept the office of Secretary of State. The Emperor quite understood Sir Rupert. He had learned long since to recognise the fact that Sir Rupert had set out in life full of glorious romantic dreams and with much good outfit to carry him on his way—but not quite outfit enough for all he meant to do. So, after much struggle to be a hero of romance, he had quietly settled down in time to be a Secretary of State. But the Emperor greatly admired him. He knew that Sir Rupert had just barely missed a great career. There is a genuine truth contained in the Spanish proverb quoted by Dr Johnson, that if a man would bring home the wealth of the Indies he must take out the wealth of the Indies with him. If you will bring home a great career, you must take out with you the capacity to find a great career.

'You see, I had better not ask you too much about your plans,' Sir Rupert said hastily; 'although, of course it relieves me from all responsibility to know that you are only making a peaceful landing.'

'Like any ordinary travellers,' Hamilton said.

'Ah, well, no—I don't quite see that, and I rather fancy Ericson would not quite see it either. Of course you are going with a certain political purpose—very natural and very noble and patriotic; but still you are not like ordinary travellers—not like Cook's tourists, for example.'

'No-o-o,' Captain Sarrasin almost roared. The idea of his being like a Cook's tourist!

'Well, that's what I say. But what I was coming to is this. Your purposes are absolutely peaceful, as you assure me—peaceful, I mean, as regards the country on whose shores you are landing.'

'We shall land in Surmer,' the Emperor said, 'for the sake of Surmer, for the love of Surmer.'

'Yes, I know that well. But men might do that in the sincerest belief that for the sake of Surmer and for the love of Surmer they were bound to overthrow by force of arms some bad Government. Now that I understand distinctly is not your purpose.'

'That,' the Emperor said, 'is certainly not our primary purpose. We are going out unarmed and unaccompanied. If the existing Government are approved of by the people—well, then our lives are in their hands. But if the people are with us——'

'Yes—and if the existing Government should refuse to recognise the fact?'

'Then, of course, the people will put them aside.

'Ah! and so there may be civil war?'

'If I understand the situation rightly, the people will by the time we land see through the whole thing, and will thrust aside anyone who endeavours to prevent them from resisting the invader on the frontier. I only hope that we may be there in time to prevent any act of violence. What Surmer has to do now is to defend and to maintain her national existence; we have no time for the trial or the punishment of worthless or traitorous ministers and officials.'

'Well, well,' Sir Rupert said, 'I suppose I had better ask no questions nor know too much of your plans. They are honourable and patriotic, I am sure; and indeed it does not much become a part of our business here, for we have never been in very cordial relations with the new Government of Surmer, and I suppose now we shall never have any occasion to trouble ourselves much about it. So I wish you from my heart all good-fortune; but of course I wish it as the personal friend, and not as the Secretary of State. That officer has no wish but that satisfactory relations may be obtained with everybody under the sun.'

Ericson smiled, half sadly. He was thinking that there was even more of an official fossilisation of Sir Rupert's earlier nature than Sir Rupert himself had suspected or described. Hamilton assumed that it was all the natural sort of thing—that everybody in office became like that in time. Sarrasin again told himself that at no appeal less strong than that of a personal and imploring request from her gracious Majesty herself would he ever consent to become a Secretary of State for Foreign Affairs.

Sir Rupert had come to have a very strong feeling of friendship and even of affection for the Emperor. He thought him far too good a man to be thrown away on a pitiful South American Empire. But of late he accepted the situation. He understood—at all events, he recognised—the almost fanatical Quixotism that was at the base of Ericson's character, and he admired it and was also provoked by it, for it made him see that remonstrance was in vain.

Sir Rupert felt himself disappointed, although only in a vague sort of way. Half-unconsciously he had lately been forming a wish for the future of his daughter, and now he was dimly conscious that that wish was not to be realised. He had been thinking that Helena was much drawn towards the Emperor, and he did not see where he could have found a more suitable husband. Ericson did not come of a great family, to be sure, but Sir Rupert saw more and more every day that the old-fashioned social distinctions were not merely crumbling but positively breaking down, and he knew that any of the duchesses with whom he was acquainted would gladly encourage her daughter to marry a millionaire from Oil City, Pennsylvania. He had seen and he saw that Ericson was made welcome into the best society of London, and, what with his fame and Helena's money, he thought they might have a pleasant way in life together. Now that dream had come to an end. Ericson, of course, would naturally desire to recover his position in South America; but even if he were to succeed he could hardly expect Helena to settle down to a life in an obscure South American city. Sir Rupert took this for granted. He did not argue it out. It came to his eyes as a certain, unarguable fact. He knew that his daughter was unconventional, but he construed that only as being unconventional within conventional limits. Some of her ways might be unconventional; he did not believe it possible that her life could be. It did not even occur to him to ask himself whether, if Helena really wished to go to South America and settle there, he could be expected to give his consent to such a project.

CHAPTER XXIII

THE PANGS OF THE SUPPRESSED MESSAGE

'By Jove, I thought they would never go!' Hamilton said to Captain Sarrasin as they moved towards their bedrooms.

'So did I,' Sarrasin declared with a sigh of relief. 'They' whose absence was so much desired were Sir Rupert Langley and the Emperor.

'Come into my room,' Hamilton said in a low tone. They entered Hamilton's room, speaking quietly, as if they were burglars. Sarrasin was lodged on the same corridor a little farther off. The soft electric light was sending out its pale amber radiance on the corridor and in the bedroom. Hamilton closed his door.

'Please take a seat, Sarrasin,' he said with elaborate politeness; and Sarrasin obeyed him and sat down in a luxurious armchair, and then Hamilton sat down too. This apparently was pure ceremonial, and the ceremonial was over, for in a moment they both rose to their feet. They had something to talk about that passed ceremonial.

'What do you think of all this?' Hamilton asked. 'Do you think there is anything in it?'

'Yes, I'm sure there is. That's a very clever girl, Miss Paulo——'

'Yes, she's very clever,' Hamilton said in an embarrassed sort of way—'a very clever girl, a splendid girl. But we haven't much to go on, have we? She can only suspect that this fellow knows Spanish—she can't be quite sure of it.'

'Many a pretty plot has been found out with no better evidence to start the discovery. The end of a clue is often the almost invisible tail of a piece of string. But we have other evidence too.'

'Out with it!' Hamilton said impatiently. In all his various anxieties he was conscious of one strong anxiety—that Dolores might be justified in her conjecture and proved not to have made a wild mistake.

'I got a telegram from across the Atlantic tonight,' Sarrasin said, 'that time in the dining-room.'

'Yes—well—I saw you had got something.'

'It came from Denver City.'

'Oh!'

'The home of Professor Flick. See?'

'Yes, yes, to be sure. Well?'

'Well, it tells me that Professor Flick is now in China, and that he will return home by way of London.'

'By Jove!' Hamilton exclaimed, and he turned pale with excitement. This was indeed a confirmation of the very worst suspicion that the discovery of Dolores could possibly have suggested. The man passing himself off as Professor Flick was not Professor Flick, but undoubtedly a South American. And he and his accomplice had been for days and nights domiciled with the Emperor!

'Is your telegram trustworthy?' he asked.

'Perfectly; my message was addressed yesterday to my old friend Professor Clinton, who is now settled in Denver City, but who used to be at the University of New Padua, Michigan.'

'What put it into your head to send the message? Had you any suspicion?'

'No, not the least in the world; but somehow my wife began to have a kind of idea of her own that all was not right. Do you know, Hamilton, the intuitions of that woman are something marvellous—marvellous, sir! Her perceptions are something outside herself, something transcendental, sir. So I telegraphed to my friend Clinton, and here we are, don't you see?'

'Yes, I see,' Hamilton said, his attention wandering a little from the transcendental perceptions of Mrs Sarrasin. 'Why, I wonder, did this fellow, whoever he is, take the name of a real man?'

'Oh, don't you see? Why, that's plain enough. How else could he ever have got introductions—introductions that would satisfy anybody? You see the folk-lore dodge commended itself to my poor simple brother, who knew the name and reputation of the real Professor Flick, and naturally thought it was all right. Then there seemed no immediate connection between my brother and the Emperor; and finally, the real Professor Flick was in China, and would not be likely to hear about what was going on until these chaps had done the trick; whereas, if anyone in the States not in constant communication with the real Flick heard of his being in London it would seem all right enough—they would assume that he had taken London first, and not last. I must say, Hamilton, it was a very pretty plot, and it was devilish near being made a success.'

'We'll foil it now,' Hamilton said, with his teeth clenched.

'Oh, of course we'll foil it now,' Sarrasin said carelessly. 'We should be pretty simpletons if we couldn't foil the plot now that we have the threads in our hands.'

'What do you make of it—murder?' Hamilton lowered his voice and almost shuddered at his own suggestion.

'Murder, of course—the murder of the Emperor, and of everyone who comes in the way of *that* murder. If the Emperor gets to Surmer the game of the ruffians is up—that we know by our advices— and if he is murdered in England he certainly can't get to Surmer. There you are!'

Nobody, however jealous for the Emperor, could doubt the sympathy and devotion of Captain Sarrasin to the Emperor and his cause. Yet his cool and business-like way of discussing the question grated on Hamilton's ears. Hamilton, perhaps, did not make quite enough of allowance for a man who had been in so many enterprises as Captain Sarrasin, and who had got into the way of thinking that his own life and the life of every other such man is something for which a game is played by the Fates every day, and which he must be ready to forfeit at any moment.

'The question is, what are we to do?' Hamilton asked sharply.

'Well, these fellows are sure to know that his Excellency leaves tomorrow, and so the attempt will be made tonight.'

'Suppose we rouse up Sir Rupert—indeed, he is probably not in bed yet—and send for the local police, and have these ruffians arrested? We could arrest them ourselves without waiting for the police.'

Sarrasin thought for a little. 'Wouldn't do,' he said. 'We have no evidence at all against them, except a telegram from an American unknown to anyone here, and who might be mistaken. Besides, I fancy that if they are very desperate they have got accomplices who will take good care that the work is carried out somehow. You see, what they have set their hearts on is to prevent the Emperor from getting back to Surmer, and that so simplifies their business for them. I have no doubt that there is someone hanging about who would manage to do the trick if these two fellows were put under arrest—all the easier because of the uproar caused by their arrest. No, we must give the fellows rope enough. We must let them show what their little game is, and then come down upon them. After all, *we* are all right, don't you see?'

Hamilton did not quite see, but he was beginning already to be taken a good deal with the cool and calculating ways of the stout old Paladin, for whom life could not possibly devise a new form of danger.

'I fancy you are right,' Hamilton said after a moment of silence.

'Yes, I think I am right,' Sarrasin answered confidently. 'You see, we have the pull on them, for if their game is simple, ours is simple too. They want Ericson to die—we mean to keep him alive. You and I don't care two straws what becomes of our own lives in the row.'

'Not I, by Jove!' Hamilton exclaimed fervently.

'All right; then you see how easy it all is. Well, do you think we ought to wake up the Emperor? It seems unfair to rattle him up on mere speculation, but the business *is* serious.'

'Serious?—yes, I should think it was! Life or death—more than that, the ruin or the failure of a real cause!'

Hamilton knew that the Emperor had by nature a splendid gift of sleep, which had stood him in good stead during many an adventure and many a crisis. But it was qualified by a peculiarity which had to be recognised and taken into account. If his sleep were once broken in upon, it could not be put together again for that night. Therefore, his trusty henchman and valet took good care that his Excellency's slumbers should not if possible be disturbed. It should be said that mere noise never disturbed him. He would waken if actually called, but otherwise could sleep in spite of thunder. Now that he was in quiet civic life, it was easy enough for him to get as much unbroken sleep as he needed. The directions which his valet always gave at Paulo's Hotel were, that his Excellency was to be roused from his sleep if the house were on fire—not otherwise. Of course all this was perfectly understood by everybody in Seagate Hall.

'Must we waken him?' Sarrasin asked doubtfully.

'Oh, yes,' Hamilton answered decisively. 'I'll take that responsibility upon myself.'

'What I was thinking of,' Sarrasin whispered, 'was that if you and I were to keep close watch he might have his sleep out and no harm could happen to him.'

'But then we shouldn't get to know, for tonight at least, what the harm was meant to be, or whose the hand it was to come from. If there really is any attempt to be made, it will not be made while there is any suspicion that somebody is on the watch.'

'True,' said Sarrasin, quite convinced and prepared for anything.

'My idea is,' Hamilton said, 'a very simple old chestnut sort of idea, but it may serve a good turn yet—get his Excellency out of his room, and one of us get into it. Nothing will be done, of course, until all the lights are out, and then we shall soon find out whether all this is a false alarm or not.'

'A capital idea! I'll take his Excellency's place,' Sarrasin said eagerly.

Hamilton shook his head. 'I have the better claim,' he said.

''Tisn't a question of claim, my dear Hamilton. Of course, if it were, I should have no claim at all. It is a question of effect—of result—of a thing to be done, don't you see?'

'Well, what has that to do with the question? I fancy I could see it through as well as most people,' Hamilton said, flushing a little and beginning to feel angry. The idea of thinking that there was anybody alive who could watch over the safety of the Emperor better than he could! Sarrasin was really carrying things rather too far.

'My dear boy,' the kind old warrior said soothingly, 'I never meant that. But you know I am an old and trained adventurer, and I have been in all sorts of dangers and tight places, and I have a notion, my dear chap, that I am physically a good deal stronger than you, or than most men, for that matter, and this may come to be a question of strength, and of disarming and holding on to a fellow when once you have caught him.'

'You are right,' Hamilton said submissively but disappointed. 'Of course, I ought to have thought of *that*. I have plenty of nerve, but I know I am not half as strong as you. All right, Sarrasin, you shall do the trick this time.'

'It will very likely turn out to be nothing at all,' Sarrasin said, by way of soothing the young man's sensibilities; 'but even if we have to look a little foolish in Ericson's eyes tomorrow we shan't much mind.'

'I'll go and rouse him up. I'll bring him along here. He won't enjoy being disturbed, but we can't help that.'

'Better be disturbed by you than by—some other,' Sarrasin said grimly.

The tone in which he answered, and the words and the grimness of his face, impressed Hamilton somehow with a new and keener sense of the seriousness of the occasion.

'Tread lightly,' Sarrasin said, 'speak in low tones, but for your life not in a whisper—a whisper travels far. Keep your eyes about you, and find out, if you can, who are stirring. I am going to look in on Mrs Sarrasin's room for a moment, and I shall keep my eyes about me, I can tell you. The more people we have awake and on the alert, the better—always provided that they are people whose nerves we can trust. As I tell you, Hamilton, I can trust the nerves of Mrs Sarrasin. I have told her to be on the watch—and she will be.'

'I am sure—I am sure,' said Hamilton; and he cut short the encomium by hurrying on his way to the Emperor's room.

Sarrasin left Hamilton's room and went for a moment or two to let Mrs Sarrasin know how things were going. He had left Hamilton's room door half open. When he was coming out of his wife's room he heard the slow, cautious step of a man in the corridor on which Hamilton's room opened, and which was at right angles with that on which Mrs Sarrasin was lodged. Could it be Hamilton coming back without having roused the Emperor? Just as he turned into that corridor he saw someone look into Hamilton's doorway, push the door farther apart, and then enter the room. Sarrasin quickly glided into the room after him; the man turned round—and Sarrasin found himself confronted by Soame Rivers.

'Hello!' Rivers said, with his usual artificiality of careless ease, 'I thought Hamilton was here. This is his room, ain't it?'

'Yes, certainly, this is his room; he has just gone to look up the Emperor.'

'Has he gone to waken him up?' Rivers asked, with a shade of alarm passing over him. For Rivers had been meditating during the last two hours over his suppressed, telegram, and thinking what a fix he should have got himself into if any danger really were to threaten the Emperor and it became known that he, the private secretary of Sir Rupert Langley, had in Sir Rupert's own house deliberately suppressed the warning sent to him from the Foreign Office—a warning sent for the protection of the man who was then Sir Rupert's guest. If anything were to happen, diplomacy would certainly never further avail itself of the services of Soame Rivers. Nor would Helena Langley be likely to turn a favourable eye on Soame Rivers. So, after much consideration, Rivers thought his best course was to get at Hamilton and let him know of the warning. Of course he need not exactly say when he had received it, and Hamilton was such a fool that he could easily be put off, and in any case the whole thing was probably some absurd scare; but still Rivers wanted to be out of all responsibility, and was already cursing the sudden impulse that made him crumple up the telegram and keep it back. Now, he could not tell why, his mind misgave him when he found Sarrasin coming into Hamilton's room and heard that Hamilton had gone to arouse the Emperor.

'We have thought it necessary to waken his Excellency' Sarrasin said emphatically; and he did not fail to notice the look of alarm that came over Rivers's face. 'Something wrong here,' Sarrasin thought.

'You don't really suppose there is any danger; isn't it all alarmist nonsense, don't you think?'

'I hadn't said anything about danger, Mr Rivers.'

'No. But the truth is, I wanted to see Hamilton about a private message I got from the Foreign Office, telling me to advise him to look after the—the—the ex-Emperor—that there was some plot against him; and I'm sure it's all rubbish—people don't *do* these things in England, don't you know?—but I thought I would come round and tell Hamilton all the same.'

'Hamilton will be here in a moment or two with his Excellency. Hadn't you better wait and see them?'

'Oh—thanks—no—it will do as well if you will kindly give my message.'

'May I ask what time you got your message?'

'Oh—a little time ago. I feel sure it's all nonsense; but still I thought I had better tell Hamilton about it all the same.'

'I hope it's all nonsense,' Sarrasin said gravely. 'But we have thought it right to arouse his Excellency.'

'Oh!' Rivers said anxiously, and slackened in his departure, 'you have got some news of your own?'

'We have got some news of our own, Mr Rivers, and we have got some suspicions of our own. Some of us have our eyes, others of us have our ears. Others of us get telegrams—and act on them at once.' This was a thrash deeper even than its author intended.

'You don't really expect that anything is going to happen tonight?'

'I am too old a soldier to expect anything. I keep awake and wait until it comes.'

'But, Mr Sarrasin—I beg pardon, Colonel Sarrasin——'

'Captain Sarrasin, if you please.'

'I beg your pardon, Captain Sarrasin. Do you really think there is any plot against—against—his Excellency?' Rivers had hesitated for a moment. He hated to call Ericson either 'his Excellency' or 'the Emperor.' But just now he wanted above all other things to conciliate Sarrasin, and if possible get him on his side, in case there should come to be a question concerning the time of the delayed warning.

'I believe it is pretty likely, sir.'

'In this house?'

'In this very house.'

'But, good God! that can't be. Why don't we tell Sir Rupert?'

'Why didn't you tell Sir Rupert?'

'Because I was told not to alarm him for nothing.'

'Exactly; we don't want to alarm him for nothing. We think that we three—the Emperor, Hamilton, and I—we can manage this little business for ourselves. Not one of the three of us that hasn't been in many a worse corner alone before, and now there *are* three of us—don't you see?'

'Can't I help?'

'Well, I think if I were you I'd just keep awake,' Sarrasin said. 'Odd sorts of things may happen. One never knows. Hush! I think I hear our friends. Will you stay and talk with them?'

'No,' said Rivers emphatically; and he left the room straightway, going in the opposite direction from the Emperor's room, and turning into the other corridor before he could have been seen by anyone coming into the corridor where the Emperor and Hamilton and Sarrasin were lodged.

Soame Rivers went back to his room, and sat there and waited and watched. His thoughts were far from enviable. He was in the mood of a man who, from being an utter sceptic, or at least Agnostic, is suddenly shaken up into a recognition of something supernatural, and does not as yet know how to make the other fashions of his life fit in with this new revelation. Selfish as he was, he would not have put off taking action on the warning he had received from the Foreign Office if he had at the time believed in the least that there was any possibility of a plot for political assassination being carried on in an English country-house. Soame Rivers reasoned, like a realistic novelist, from his own experiences only. He regarded the notion of such things taking place in an English country-house as no less an anachronism than the moving helmet in the 'Castle of Otranto' or the robber-castle in the 'Mysteries of Udolpho.' Not that we mean to convey the idea that Rivers had read either of these elaborate masterpieces of old-fashioned fiction—for he most certainly had not read either of them, and very likely had not even heard of either. But if he had studied them he would probably have considered them as quite as much an appurtenance of real life as any story of a plot for political assassination carried on in an English country-house. Now, however, it was plain that a warning had been given which did not come from the fossilised officials of the Foreign Office, and which impressed so cool an old soldier as Captain Sarrasin with a sense of serious danger. As far as regarded all the ordinary affairs of life, Rivers looked down on Sarrasin with a quite unutterable contempt. Sarrasin was not a man to get in the ordinary way into Soame Rivers's set; and Rivers despised alike anyone who was not in his set, and anyone who was pushed, or who pushed himself, into it. He detested eccentricities of all sorts. He would have instinctively disliked and dreaded any man whose wife occasionally wore man's clothes and rode astride. He considered all that sort of thing bad form. He chafed and groaned and found his pain sometimes almost more than he could bear under the audacious unconventionalities of Helena Langley. But he knew that he had to put up with Helena Langley; he knew that she would consider herself in no way responsible to him for anything she said or did; and he only dreaded the chance of some hinted, hardly repressible remonstrance from him provoking her to tell him bluntly that she cared nothing about his opinion of her conduct. Now, however, as he thought of Sarrasin, he found that he could not deny Sarrasin's coolness and courage and judgment, and it comforted him to think that Sarrasin must always say he had a warning from him, Soame Rivers, before anything had occurred—if anything was to occur. If anything should occur, the actual hour of the warning given would hardly be recalled amid so many circumstances more important. Soame sat in his room and watched with heavy heart. He felt that he had been playing the part of a traitor, and, more than that, that he was likely to be found out. Could he retrieve himself even yet? He knew he was not a coward.

CHAPTER XXIV

THE EXPLOSION

Meanwhile Hamilton came back to his room with the Emperor. The Emperor looked fresh, bright, wide-awake, and ready for anything. He had grumbled a little on being roused, and was at first inclined rather peevishly to 'pooh-pooh' all suggestion of conspiracies and personal danger.

He even went so far as to say that, on the whole, he would rather prefer to be allowed to have his sleep out, even though it were to be concisely rounded off by his death. But he soon pulled himself together and got out of that perverse and sleepy mood, and by the time he and Hamilton had found Sarrasin, the Emperor was well up to all the duties of a commander-in-chief. He had a rapid review of the situation with Sarrasin.

'What I don't see,' he quietly said—he knew too well to try whispering—'is why I should not keep to my own room. If anything is going to happen I am well forewarned, and shall be well fore-armed, and I shall be pretty well able to take care of myself; and why should anyone else run any risk on my account?'

'It isn't on your account,' Sarrasin answered, a little bluntly.

'No? Well, I am glad to hear that. On whose account, then, may I ask?'

'On account of Surmer,' Sarrasin answered decisively. 'If Hamilton here is killed, or *I* am killed, it does not matter a straw so far as Surmer is concerned. But if you got killed, who, I want to know, is to go out to Surmer? Surmer would not rise for Hamilton or me.'

The Emperor could say nothing. He could only clasp in silence the hand of either man.

'They are putting out the lights downstairs,' Sarrasin said in a low tone. 'I had better get to my lair.'

'Have you got a revolver?' Hamilton asked.

'Never go without one, dear boy.' Then Sarrasin stole away with the noiseless tread of the Red Indian, whose comrade and whose enemy he had been so often.

Hamilton closed his door, but did not fasten it. The electric light still burned softly there.

'Will you smoke?' Hamilton asked. 'I smoke here every night, and Sarrasin too, mostly. It won't arouse any suspicion if the smoke gets about the corridor. I am often up much later than this. You need not answer, and then your voice can't be heard. Just take a cigar.'

The Emperor quietly nodded, and took two cigars, which he selected very carefully, and began to smoke.

'Do you know,' Ericson said, 'that tomorrow is my birthday? No—I mean it is already my birthday.'

'As if I didn't know,' Hamilton replied.

'Odd, if anything should happen.'

Then there was absolute silence in the room. Each man kept his thoughts to himself, and yet each knew well enough what the other was thinking of. Ericson was thinking, among other things, how, if there should really be some assassin-plot, what a trouble and a scandal and even a serious danger he should have brought upon the Langleys, who were so kind and sweet to him. He was thinking of Sarrasin, and of the danger the gallant veteran was running for a cause which, after all, was no cause of his. He could hardly as yet believe in the existence of the murder-plot; and still, with his own knowledge of the practices of former Governments in Surmer, he could not look upon the positive evidence of Sarrasin's telegram from across the Atlantic and the sudden suspicions of Dolores as insignificant. He knew well that one of the practices of former Governments in Surmer had been, when they wanted a dangerous enemy removed, to employ some educated and clever criminal already under conviction and sentence of death, and release him for the time with the promise that, if he should succeed in doing their work, means should be found to relieve him from his penalty altogether. When he became Emperor he had himself ordered the re-arrest of two such men who had had the audacity to return to the capital to claim their reward, under the impression that they should find their old friends still in power. He commuted the death punishment in their case, bad as they were, on the principle that they were the victims of a loathsome system, and that they were tempted into the new crime. But he left them to imprisonment for life. Ericson had a strong general objection to the infliction of capital punishment—to the punishment that is irreparable, that cannot be recalled. He was not actually an uncompromising opponent on moral grounds of the principle of capital punishment, but he would think long before sanctioning its infliction.

He was wondering, in an idle sort of way, whether he could remember the appearance or the name of either of these two men. He might perhaps remember the names; he did not believe he could recall the faces. Clearly the Emperor wanted that great gift which, according to popular tradition or belief, always belonged to the true leaders of men— the gift of remembering every face one ever has seen, and every name one has ever heard. Alexander had it, we are told, and Julius Cæsar, and Oliver Cromwell, and Claverhouse, and Napoleon Bonaparte, and Brigham Young. Napoleon, to be sure, worked it up, as we have lately come to know, by collusion with some of his officers; and it may be that Brigham Young was occasionally coached by devoted Elders at Salt Lake City. At all events, it would not appear that the Emperor either had the gift, or at present the means of being provided with any substitute for it. He could not remember the appearance of the men he had saved from execution. It is curious, however, how much of his time and his thoughts they had occupied or wasted while he was waiting for the first sound that might be expected to give the alarm.

Hamilton looked at his watch. The Emperor motioned to him, and Hamilton turned the face of the watch towards him. Half-past one o'clock Ericson saw. He looked tired. Hamilton made a motion towards his own bed which clearly signified, 'would you like to lie down for a little?' Ericson replied by a sign of assent, and presently he stretched himself half on the bed and half off—on the coverlet of the bed as to his head and shoulders, with his legs hanging over the side and his feet on the floor—and he thought again, about his birthday, and so he fell asleep.

Hamilton had often seen him fall asleep like this in the immediate presence of danger, but only when there was nothing that could immediately, and in the expected course of things, exact or even call for his personal attention or his immediate command. Now, however, Hamilton somewhat marvelled at the power of concentration which could enable his chief to give himself at once up to sleep with the knowledge that some sort of danger—purely personal danger—hung over him, the nature, the form, and the time of which were absolutely hidden in darkness. Very brave men, familiar with the perils and horrors of war, experienced duellists, intrepid explorers, seamen whose nerves are never shaken by the white squall of the Levant, or the storm in the Bay of Biscay, or the tempest round some of the most rugged coasts of Australia—such men are often turned white-livered by the threat of assassination—that terrible pestilence which walks abroad at night or in the dusk, and dogs remorselessly the footsteps of the victim. But Ericson slept composedly, and his deep, steady breathing seemed to tell pale-hearted fear it lied.

And other thoughts, too, came up into Hamilton's mind. He had long put away all wild hopes and dreams of Helena. He had utterly given her up; he had seen only too clearly which way her love was stretching its tentacula, and he had long since submitted himself to the knowledge that they did not stretch themselves out to grapple with the strings of his heart. He knew that Helena loved the Emperor. He bent to the knowledge; he was not sorry *now* any more. But he wondered if the Emperor in his iron course was sleeping quietly in the front of danger for him which must mean misery for *her*, and was thinking nothing about her. Surely he must know, by this time, that she loved him! Surely he must love her—that bright, gifted, generous, devoted girl? Was she, then, misprized by Ericson? Was the Emperor's heart so full of his own political and patriotic schemes and enterprises that he could not spare a thought, even in his dreams, for the girl who so adored him, and whom Hamilton had at one time so much adored? Did this stately tree never give a thought to the beautiful and fresh flower that drank the dew at its feet?

Suddenly Ericson turned on the bed, and from his sleeping lips came a murmuring cry—a low-voiced plaint, instinct with infinite love and yearning and pathos—and the only words then spoken were the words 'Helena, Helena!' And then the question of Hamilton's mind was answered, and Ericson shook himself free of sleep, and turned on the bed, and sat up and looked at Hamilton, and was clearly master of the situation.

'I have been sleeping,' he said, in the craftily-qualified tone of the experienced one who thoroughly understands the difference in a time of danger between the carefully subdued tone and the penetrating, sibilant whisper. 'Nothing has happened?'

Hamilton made a gesture of negation.

'It must come soon—if it is to come at all,' Ericson said. 'And it will come—I know it—I have had a dream.'

'You don't believe in dreams?' Hamilton murmured gently.

'I don't believe in all dreams, boy; I do believe in that dream.'

'Hush!' said Hamilton, holding up his hand.

Some faint, vague sounds were heard in the corridor. The Emperor and Hamilton remained absolutely motionless and silent.

The Duchess had disappeared into her room for a while, and called together her maids and passed them in review. It was a whim of the good-hearted young Duchess to go round to country-houses carrying three maids along with her. She had one maid as her personal and bodily attendant, a second to dress her hair, and a third maid to look after her packing and her dresses. She had honestly got under the impression of late years that a woman could not be well looked after who had not three maids to go about with her and see to her wants. When first she settled down at Seagate Hall with her three attendant Graces, Helena was almost inclined to resent such an invasion as an insult. It would not have mattered, the girl said to her father, if it were at King's Langley, where were rooms enough for a squadron of maids; but here, at Seagate Hall, the accommodation of which was limited, what an extraordinary thing to do! Who ever heard of a woman going about with three maids? Sir Rupert, however, would not have a breath of murmur against the three maids, and the Duchess made herself so thoroughly agreeable and sympathetic in every other way that Helena soon forgot the infliction of the three maids. 'I only hope they are made quite comfortable,' she said to the dignified housekeeper.

'A good deal more comfortable, Miss, than they had any right to expect,' was the reply, and so all was settled.

This night, then, the Duchess summoned her maids around her and had her hair 'fixed,' as she would herself have expressed it, and then made up her mind to pay a visit to Helena. She had become really quite fond of Helena—all the more because she felt sure that the girl had a love-secret—and wished very much that Helena would take her into confidence.

The Duchess appeared in Helena's room draped in a lovely dressing-gown and wearing slippers with be-diamonded buckles. The Duchess evidently was ready for a long dressing-gown talk. She liked to contemplate herself in one of her new Parisian dressing-gowns, and she was quite willing to give Helena her share in the gratification of the sight. But Helena's thoughts were hopelessly away from dressing-gowns, even from her own. She became aware after a while that the Duchess was giving her a history of some marvellous new dresses she had brought from Paris, and which were to be displayed lavishly during the short time left of the London season, and at Goodwood, and afterwards at various country-houses.

'You're sleepy, child,' the Duchess suddenly said, 'and I am keeping you up with my talk.'

'No, indeed, Duchess, I am not in the least sleepy, and it's very kind of you to come and talk to me.'

'Well, if you ain't sleepy you are sorrowful, or something like it. So your Emperor *is* going to try his luck again! Well, clear, I just wish you and I could help some. By the way, don't you take my countrymen here as just our very best specimens of Americans.'

'I hadn't much noticed,' Helena said listlessly. 'They seemed very quiet men.'

'Meaning that American men in general are rather noisy and self-assertive?' the Duchess said with a smile.

'Oh, no, Duchess, I never meant anything of the kind. But they *do* seem very quiet, don't they?'

'Stupid, *I* should say,' was the comment of the Duchess. 'I didn't talk much with Mr Copping, but I had a little talk with Professor Flick. I am afraid, by the way, *he* thinks me very stupid, for I appear to have got him mixed up in my mind with somebody quite different, and you know it vexes anybody to be mistaken for anybody else. I meant to ask him what State he hailed from, but I quite forgot. His accent didn't seem quite familiar to me somehow. I wish I had thought of asking him.' The Duchess seemed so much in earnest about the matter that Helena felt inspired to say, by way of consoling her:

'Dear Duchess, you can ask him the important question tomorrow. I dare say he will not be offended.'

'Well, now that's just what I have been thinking about, dear child. You see, I have already put my foot in it.'

'Won't do much harm,' Helena said smiling—'foot is too small.'

'Come now, that's very prettily said;' and the gratified Duchess stretched out half-unconsciously a very small and pretty foot, cased in an exquisite shoe and stocking, and then drew it in again, as if thinking that she must not seem to be personally vindicating Helena's compliment. 'But he might be offended, perhaps, if I were to convey the idea that I knew nothing at all of him or his place of birth. Well—good night, child; we shall meet him anyhow tomorrow.' She kissed Helena and left the room.

When the Duchess had gone, Helena sat in her bedroom, broad awake. She had got her hair arranged and put on a dressing-gown, and sent her maid to bed long before, and now she took up a book and tried to read it, and now and then put it wearily down upon her lap, and then took it up again and read a page or two more, and then put it away again, and went back to think over things. What was she thinking about? Mostly, if not altogether, of the few words the Emperor had spoken to her—the words that told her he must cut short his visit to Seagate Hall. She knew quite well what that meant. It meant, of course, that he was going out to fling himself upon the shore of Surmer, and that he might never come back. He might have miscalculated the strength of his following in Surmer—and then it was all but certain that he must die for his mistake. Or he might have calculated

378

wisely—and then he would be welcomed back to the Emperorship of Surmer, and then he would—oh! she was sure he would—drive back the invaders from the frontier, and she would be proud, oh! so proud, of that! But then he would remain in Surmer, and devote himself to Surmer, and come back to England no more. How women have to suffer for a political cause! Not merely the mothers and wives and sisters who have to see their loved ones go to the prison or the scaffold for some political question which they regard, from their domestic point of view, as a pure nuisance and curse because it takes the loved one from them. Oh! but there is more than that, worse than that, when a woman is willing to be devoted to the cause, but finds her heart torn with agony by the thought that her lover cares more for the cause than he cares for *her*—that for the sake of the cause he could live without her, and even could forget her!

This was what Helena was thinking of this night, as she outwatched the stars, and knew by his tale half-told that the Emperor would soon be leaving her, in all probability forever. He was not her lover in any sense. He had never loved her. He had never even taken seriously her innocently bold advances towards him. He had taken them as the sweet and kindly advances of a girl who out of her generosity of heart was striving to make the course of life pleasant for a banished man with a ruined career. Helena saw all this with brave impartial eyes. She had judged rightly up to a certain point; but she did not see, she could not see, she could not be expected to see, how a time came about when the Emperor had begun to be afraid of the part he was playing—of the time when the Emperor grew acquainted with his heart, and searched what stirred it so—according to the tender and lovely words of Beaumont and Fletcher—and, alas! had found it love. Strange that these two hearts so thoroughly affined should be so misjudging each of the other! It was like the story told in Uhland's touching poem, which probably no one reads now, even in Uhland's own Germany, about the youth who is leaving his native town for ever, accompanied by the *geleit*—the escort, the 'send-off'—of his companion-students, and who looks back to the window which the maiden has just opened and thinks, 'If she had but loved me!' and a tear comes into the girl's deep blue eye, and she closes her window, hopeless, and thinks, 'If he had but loved me!'

'And now he is going!' thought Helena. And at that hour Ericson was waking up, aroused from sleep by the sound of his own softly-breathed word 'Helena!'

'It is now his birthday,' she thought.

Soame Rivers was not in his character very like Hamlet. But of course there is that one touch of nature that makes the whole world kin, and the touch of nature that made Hamlet and Soame Rivers kin tonight was found in the fact that on this night, as on a memorable night of Hamlet's career, in his heart there was 'a kind of fighting' that would not let him sleep. He sat up fully dressed. The one thing present to his mind was the thought that, if anything whatever should happen to the Emperor—and the more the night grew later, the more the possibility seemed to enlarge upon him—the ruin of all Soame Rivers's career seemed certain. Inquiry would assuredly be made into the exact hour when the telegram was sent from the Foreign Office and when it was received at Sir Rupert Langley's, and it would be known that Rivers had that telegram for hours in his hands without telling anyone about it. It was easy in the light and the talk of the dining-room and the billiard-room to tell one's self that there could be no possible danger threatening anyone in an English gentleman's country-house. But now, in the deep of the night, in the loneliness, with the knowledge of what Sarrasin had said, all looked so different. It was easy at that earlier and brighter and more self-confident hour to crumple up a telegram and make nothing of it; but now Soame Rivers could only curse himself for his levity and his folly. What would Helena Langley say to him?

Was there anything he could do to retrieve his position? Only one thing occurred to him. He could go and hide himself somewhere in shade or in darkness near the Emperor's door. If any attempt at assassination should be made, he might be in advance of Sarrasin and Hamilton. If nothing should happen, he at least would be found at his self-ordained post of watchfulness by Hamilton and Sarrasin, and they would report of him to Sir Rupert—and to Helena.

This seemed the best stroke of policy for him. He threw off his smoking-coat and put on a small, tight, closely-buttoned jacket, which in any kind of struggle, if such there were to be, would leave no flapping folds for an antagonist to cling to. Rivers was well-skilled in boxing and in all manner of manly exercises; he took care to be a master in his way of every art a smart young Englishman ought to possess, and he began to think with a sickening revulsion of horror that in keeping back the telegram he had been doing just the thing which would shut him out from the society of English gentlemen for ever. A powerful impulse was on him that he must redeem himself, not merely in the eyes of others—others, perhaps, might never know of his momentary lapse—but in his own eyes. At that moment he would have braved any danger, not merely to save the Emperor, but simply to show that he had striven to save the Emperor. It flashed across his mind that he might even still make himself a sort of second-best hero—in the eyes of Helena Langley.

He thought he heard a stirring somewhere in one of the corridors. He put on a pair of tight-fitting noiseless velvet slippers, and he glided out of his room and turned into the corridor where the Emperor slept. Yes, there surely was a sound in that direction. Rivers crept swiftly and stealthily on.

Soame Rivers belonged to his age and his society. He was born of Cynicism and of Introspection. It would have interested him quite as much to find out himself as to find out any other person. While he was moving along in the darkness it occurred to him to remember that he did not know in the least whither, to what rescue, to what danger, he was steering. He might, for aught he knew, have to grapple with assassins. The whole thing might prove to be a false alarm, an absurd scare, and then he, who based his whole life and his whole reputation on the theory that nothing ever could induce him to make himself ridiculous or to become bad form, might turn out to be the ludicrous hero of a country-house 'booby-trap.' To do him justice, he feared this result much more than the other. But he wanted to test himself—to find himself out. All this thinking had not as yet delayed his movements by a single step, but now he paused for one short second, and he felt his pulse. It beat steadily, regularly as the notes of Big Ben at Westminster. 'Come,' he breathed to himself, 'I am all right. Come what will, I know I am not a coward!'

For there had come into Rivers's somewhat emasculated mind now and again the doubt whether his father, Cynicism, and his mother, Introspection, might not, between them, have entailed some cowardice on him. He felt relieved, encouraged, satisfied, by the test of his pulse. 'Come,' he thought to himself, 'if there is anything really to be done, Helena shall praise me tomorrow.' So he stole his quiet way.

Sarrasin had made himself acquainted with the Emperor's habits—and he at once installed himself in bed. He took off his outer clothing, his coat and waistcoat, kicked off his dress-shoes, and keeping on his trousers he settled himself down among the bed-clothes. He left his coat and waistcoat and shoes ostentatiously lying about. If there was to be a murderous attack, his idea was to invite, not to discourage, that murderous attack, and certainly not by any means to scare it away. Any indication of preparedness or wakefulness or activity could only have the effect of giving warning to the assassin, and so putting off the attempt at the crime. The old soldier felt sure that the attempt could never be made under conditions so favourable to his side of the controversy as at the present moment. 'We have got it here,' he said to himself, 'we can't tell where it may break out next.'

He turned off the electric light. The button was so near his hand that it would not take him a second to turn the light on again whenever he should have need of it. His purpose was to get the assassin or assassins as far as possible into the room and close to the bed. He was determined not to admit that he had thrown off sleep until the very last moment, and then to flash the electric light at once. He would leave no chance whatever for any explanation or apology about a mistake in the room or anything of that kind. Before he would consent to open his eyes fully he must have indisputable evidence of the murderous plot. Once and for all!

Sarrasin kept his watch under his pillow, safe within reach. He wanted to be sure of the exact minute when everything was to occur. He fancied he heard some faint moving in the corridor, and he turned on the electric light and gave one glance at his watch, and then summoned darkness again. He found that it was exactly two o'clock. Now, he thought, if anything is going to be done, it must be done very soon; we can't have long to wait. He was glad. The most practised and case-hardened soldier is not fond of having to wait for his enemy.

Sarrasin had left his door—Ericson's door—unlocked and unbarred. Everybody who knew the Emperor intimately knew that he had a sort of *tic* for leaving his doors open. Sarrasin knew this; but, besides, he was anxious, as has been already said, to draw the assassin-plot, if such plot there were, into him, not to bar it out and keep it on the other side. Now the way was clear for the enemy. Sarrasin lay low and listened. Yes, there was undoubtedly the sound of feet in the corridor. It was the sound of one pair of feet, Sarrasin felt certain. He had not campaigned with Red Shirt and his Sioux for nothing; he could distinguish between two sounds and four sounds. 'Come, this is going to be an easy job,' he thought to himself. 'I am not much afraid of any one man who is likely to turn up. Bring along your bears.' The old soldier chuckled to himself; he was getting to be rather amused with the whole proceeding. He lay down, and even in the lightness of his plucky heart indulged in simulation of deep breathings intended to convey to the possibly coming assassin that the victim was fast asleep, and merely waiting to be killed off conveniently without trouble to anybody, even to himself. He was a little, just a little, sorry that Mrs Sarrasin could not be present to see how well he could manage the job. But her presence would not be practicable, and she would be sure to believe that he had borne himself well under whatever difficulty and danger. So perhaps he breathed the name of his lady-love, as good knights did in the days to which he and his lady-love ought to have belonged; and then he committed his soul to his Creator.

The subtle sound came near the door. The door was gently tried—opened with a soft dexterity and suppleness of touch which much impressed the sham sleeper in the bed. 'No heavy British hand there,' Sarrasin thought, recalling his many memories of many lands and races. He lay with his right arm thrown carelessly over the coverlets, and his left arm hidden. Given any assassin who is not of superlative quality, he will be on his guard as to the disclosed right arm, and will not trouble himself about the hidden left. The door opened. Somebody came gliding in. The somebody was breathing too heavily. 'A poor show of an assassin,' Sarrasin could not help thinking. His nerves were now all abrace like the finest steel, and he could observe a dozen things in a second of time. 'If I couldn't do without puffing like that, I'd never join the assassin trade!' Then a crouching figure came to the bedside and looked over him, and took note, as he had expected, of the outstretched right arm, and stooped over it, and ranged beyond it and kept out of its reach, and then lifted a knife; and then Sarrasin let out a terrible left-hander just under the assassin's chin, and the assassin tumbled over like a heavy lump on the carpet of the floor, and Sarrasin quietly leaped out of bed and took the knife out of his palsied hand and gently turned on the light.

'Let's have a look at you,' he said, and he turned the fallen man over. In the meanwhile he had thrust the knife under the pillow, and he held the revolver comfortably ready at the forehead of the reviving murderer. He studied his face. 'Hello,' he quietly said, 'so it is *you*!'

Yes, it was the wretched Saffron Hill Sicilian of St. James's Park.

The Sicilian was opening his eyes and beginning vaguely to form a faint idea of how things had been going.

'Why, you poor pitiful trash!' Sarrasin murmured under his breath, 'is this the whole business? Are you and your ladies' slipper knife going to run this whole machine? I don't believe a bit of it. Look here; tell us your whole infernal plot, or I'll blow your brains out—at least as many as you have, which don't amount to much. Do you feel that?'

He pressed the barrel of his revolver hard on to the Sicilian's forehead. Under other conditions it might have felt cool and refreshing. The touch *was* cool and refreshing certainly. But the Sicilian, even in his bewildered condition, readily recognised the fact that the cool touch of the iron was evidently to be followed by a distressing explosion, and he could only whine feebly for mercy.

For a second or two Sarrasin was fairly puzzled what to do. It would be no trouble to him to drive or drag this wretched Sicilian into the room where Ericson and Hamilton were waiting. Perhaps if they had heard any noise they would be round in a moment. But was this the plot? Was this the whole of the plot? This poor pitiful attempt at assassination—was this all that the reactionaries of Surmer and of Orizaba could do? 'Out of the question,' Sarrasin thought.

'I think I had better finish you off,' he said to the Sicilian, speaking in a low, bland tone, subdued as that of a gentle evening breeze. 'Nobody really wants you any more. I don't care to rouse the house by using my revolver for a creature like you. Just come this way,' and he dragged him with remorseless hand towards the bed. 'I want to get at your own knife. That will do the business nicely.'

Honest Sarrasin had not the faintest idea of becoming executioner in cold blood of the hired Sicilian stabber. It was important to him to see how far the Sicilian stabber's stabbing courage would hold out—whether there were stronger men behind him who could be grappled with in their turn. He still held to his conviction, 'We haven't got the whole plot out yet. Anybody could do this sort of thing.'

'Don't kill me!' faintly murmured the wretched assassin.

'Why not? Just tell me all, or I'll kill you in two seconds,' Sarrasin answered, in the same calm low voice, and, gripping the Sicilian solidly round the waist, he trailed him towards the bed, where the knife was.

Then there came a flare and splash and blaze of yellowish red light across the eyes of Sarrasin and his captive, and in a moment a noise as fierce as if all the artillery of Heaven—or the lower deep—were let loose at once. No words could describe the devastating influence of that explosion on the ears and the nerves and the hearts of those for whom it first broke. Utter silence—that is, the suspension of all faculty of hearing or feeling or thinking—succeeded for the moment. Sight and sound were blown out, as the flame of a candle is blown out by an ordinary gunpowder explosion. Then the sudden and complete silence was succeeded by a crashing of bells in the ears, by a flashing of furnaces in the eyes, by a limpness of every limb, a relaxation of every fibre, by a longing to die and be quiet, by a craving to live and get out of the noise, by an all unutterable struggle between present blindness and longed-for sight, present deafness and an impatient, insane thirst to hear what was going on, between the faculties momentarily disordered and the faculties wildly striving to grasp again at order. And Sarrasin began to recover his reason and his senses, and, brave as he was, his nerves relaxed when he saw in the instreaming light of the morning—the electric light had been driven out—that he was still gripping on to the body of the Sicilian, and that half the wretched Sicilian's head had been blown away. Then everything was once more extinguished for him.

But in that one moment of reviving consciousness he contrived to keep his wits well about him. 'It was not the Sicilian who did *that*,' he said to himself doggedly.

CHAPTER XXV

SOME VICTIMS

The crash came on the ears of the Emperor and Hamilton. For a moment or two the senses of both were paralysed. It is not easy for most of us, who have not been through the cruel suffocation of a dynamite explosion, to realise completely how the crushed collapse of the nervous system leaves mind, thought, and feeling absolutely prostrate before the mere shrillness of sound. We are not speaking now of the cases in which serious harm is done—of course anyone can understand *that*—but only of the cases, after all, and in even the best carried out and most brutally contrived dynamite attempt—the vast majority of cases in which the intended, or at least the probable, victims suffer no permanent harm whatever. The Emperor suddenly found his senses deserting him with the crash of the explosion. He knew in a moment what it was, and he knew also that for a certain moment or two his senses would utterly fail to take account of it. For one fearful second he knew he was going to be insensible, just as a passenger at sea knows he is going to be sick. Then it was all over with him and quiet, and he felt nothing.

How much time had passed when he was roused by the voice of Hamilton he did not know. Hamilton had had much the same experience, but Hamilton's main work in life was looking after the Emperor, and the Emperor's main work in life was not in looking after himself. Hamilton, too, was the younger man. Anyhow, he rallied the sooner.

'Are you hurt?' he cried. And he trembled lest he should hear the immortal words of Sir Henry Lawrence at Lucknow, 'I'm killed!'

'Eh—what? I say, is it you, Hamilton? I'm all right, boy; how about you?'

'Nothing the matter with *me*,' Hamilton said. 'Quite sure you are not hurt?'

'Not the least little bit—only dazzled and dazed a good deal, Hamilton.'

'Let's see what's going on outside,' Hamilton said. He sprang to open the door.

'Wait a moment,' Ericson said quietly. 'Let us see if that is all. There may be another. Don't rush, Hamilton, please. Take your time.' The Emperor was cool and composed.

'Gunpowder?' Hamilton asked.

'No, no—dynamite. You go and look after Sarrasin, Hamilton; I'll take charge of the house and see what this really comes to.'

And so, with the composure of a man to whom nothing in the way of action is quite new or disturbing, he opened the door and went out into the corridor. All the lights that were anywhere burning had been blown out. Servants, men and women, were rushing distractedly downstairs, those who slept above; those who slept below were rushing distractedly upstairs. It was a confused scene of night-shirts and night-dresses.

Ericson seized one stout footman, whom he knew well by sight and by name: 'Look here, Frederick,' he said quietly, 'don't spread any alarm—the worst is over. Turn on all the lights you can, and get someone to saddle a horse at once—no, to put a bridle on the horse—never mind the saddle—and in the meanwhile guard the house-doors and see that no one goes out, except me. I want to get the horse. Do you understand all this? Have you your senses about you?'

The man was plucky enough, and took his tone readily from Ericson's calm, subdued way. He recognised a leader. He had all the courage of Tommy Atkins, and all Tommy Atkins's daring, and only wanted leadership: only lead him and he was all right. He could follow.

'Yes, your Excellency, I think I do. Lights on; horse bridled; no one allowed out but you.'

'Right,' Ericson answered; 'you are a brave fellow.'

In a moment Helena came from her room, fully dressed—that is to say, fully robed, in the dressing-gown wherein the Duchess had seen her, with white cheeks but resolute face.

'Oh! thank God *you* are safe,' she exclaimed. 'What is it? Where is my father?'

Just at the moment Sir Rupert came out of his room, plunging, staggering, but undismayed, and even then not forgetful of his position as a Secretary of State.

'Here is your father, Heaven be praised!' Ericson exclaimed. 'Sir Rupert, I am an unlucky guest! I have brought all this on you!'

Helena threw herself on her father's neck. He clasped her tenderly, looking over her shoulder to

Ericson as if he were putting her carefully for the moment out of the way. 'It *is* dynamite, Ericson?'

'Oh, yes, I think so. The sound seems to me beyond all mistake. I have heard it before.'

'Not an accident?'

'No—no accident. I don't think we need trouble about *that*. Look here, Sir Rupert; you look after the house and the Duchess, and Sarrasin and everybody; Hamilton will help you—I say, Hamilton! Hamilton! where are you? I am going to have a ride round the grounds and see if anyone is lurking. I have ordered a horse to be bridled.'

'You take command, Ericson,' Sir Rupert said.

'Outside, yes,' Ericson assented. 'You look after things inside.'

'You must order a horse for me too,' Helena exclaimed, stiffening herself up from her father's protecting embrace. 'I can help you, I have the eyes of a lynx—I must do something. I must! Let me go, papa!' She turned appealingly to Sir Rupert.

'Go, child, if you won't be in the way.'

Ericson hesitated, just for a second; then he spoke.

'Come with me if you will, Miss Langley. You can pilot me over the grounds as nobody else can.'

'Oh!' she exclaimed, and they both rushed downstairs together. The servants were already lighting up such of the electric lamps as had been left uninjured after the explosion. The electric engineer was on the spot and at work, with his assistants, as fresh and active as if none of them had ever wanted a rest in his life. Ericson cast a glance over the whole scene, and had to acknowledge that the household had turned out with almost the promptitude of a fire-drill on the ocean. The women-servants, who were to be seen in their night-dresses scuttling wildly about when the crash of the explosion first shook them up had now altogether disappeared, and were in all probability steadily engaged in putting things to rights wherever they could, and no one yet knew the number of the dead.

Ericson and Helena got down to the hall. The girl was happy. Her father was safe; and she was with the man she loved. More than that, she had a sense of sharing a danger with the man she loved. That was a delight to be expressed by no words. She had not the remotest idea of what had happened. She had been sitting up late—unable to sleep. She had been thinking about the news the Emperor had told her—that he was going to leave her. Then came the tremendous crash of the explosion, and for a moment her senses and her thought were gone. Then she staggered to her feet, half blinded, half deafened, but alive, and she rushed to her door and dragged it open; and but for a blue foam of dawn all was darkness, and in another moment she knew that Ericson was alive, and she was able to welcome her father. What on earth did she want more? It might be that there was danger to Hamilton—to Sarrasin—to Mrs Sarrasin—to the Duchess—to Miss Paulo—to some of the servants—to her own maid, a great friend and favourite of hers—to all sorts of persons. She had to acknowledge to her own heart that in such a moment she did not much care. She was conscious of a sense of joy in the knowledge of the fact that To-to had not yet got down from London. There all calculation ceased.

The hall-door was opened. The breath of the fresh morning came into their lungs. Helena drank it in, as if it were a draught of wine—in more correct words, as if it were *not* a draught of wine, for she was not much of a wine-drinker. The freshness of the air was a shuddering and a delight to her.

'Let nobody leave the house until we come back,' Ericson said to the man who opened the doors for Helena and him.

'Nobody, sir?' the man asked in astonishment.

'Nobody whatever.'

'Not Sir Rupert, sir?'

'Certainly not. Sir Rupert above all men! We can't have your father getting into danger, Miss Langley— can we?'

'Oh no,' she answered quickly.

'Which way to the stables?' Ericson asked the man.

'Come with me,' Helena said; 'I can show you.'

They hurried round to the stables, and found a wide-awake groom or two who had a lady's horse properly saddled, and a man's horse with no saddle, but only a bridle on. They had evidently taken the Emperor's command to the letter, and assumed that he had some particular motive for riding without a saddle.

Ericson lifted Helena into her seat. It has to be confessed that she was riding in her already-mentioned dressing-gown, and that she had nothing

395

on her head, and that her bare feet were thrust into slippers. Mrs Grundy was not on the premises, and, even if she were, Helena would not have cared two straws about Mrs Grundy's reflections and criticisms.

'Oh, look here, you haven't a saddle!' she cried to Ericson.

'Saddle!—no matter—never mind the saddle,' he called. The horse was a little shy, and backed and edged, and went sideways, and plunged. One of the grooms rushed at him to hold his head.

The Emperor laid one hand upon his mane. 'Let him go!' he said, and he swung himself easily on to the unsaddled back and gripped the bridle. 'Now for it, Helena!' he exclaimed.

Now for it, Helena! She just caught the words in the wild flash of their flight. Never before had he used her name in that way. He rode his unsaddled horse with all the ease of another Mephistopheles; and what delighted the girl was that he seemed to count on her riding her course just as well.

'Look out everywhere you can,' he called to her; 'tell me if you see a squirrel stirring, or the eyes of an owl looking out of the ivy-bushes.'

Helena had marvellous sight—but she could descry no human figure, no human eyes, but *his* anywhere amid the myriad eyes of the dark night. They rode on and round.

'We shall soon find out the whole story,' he said to her after a while, and he brought his horse so near to hers that it touched her saddle. 'There is no one in the grounds, and we shall soon know all, if we have only to deal with the people who were indoors. I think we have settled that already.'

'But what *is* it all?' she breathlessly asked, as they galloped round the young plantation. The hour, the companionship, the gallop, the fresh breath of the morning air among the trees, seemed to make her feel as if she never had been young before.

'"Miching mallecho; it means mischief," as Hamlet says,' the Emperor replied, 'and very much mischief too,' and he checked himself, pulling up his horse so suddenly that the creature fell back upon his haunches, and then flinging himself off the horse as lightly as if he were performing some equestrian exercise to win a prize in a competition. Then he let his own horse run loose, and he stopped Helena's, and took her foot in his hand.

'Jump off!' he said, in a voice of quiet authority. They were now in front of the hall-door.

'What more is the matter?' she asked nervously, though she did not delay her descent. She was firm on the gravel already, picking up the dragging skirts of her dressing-gown. The dawn was lighting on her.

'The house is on fire at this side,' he said composedly. 'I must go and show them how to put it out.'

'The house on fire!' she exclaimed.

'Yes—for the moment. I shall put that all right.'

She was prepared for anything now. 'We have a fire-escape in the village,' she said, panting for breath. She had full faith in the Emperor's power to conquer any conflagration, but she did not want to give utterly away the resources of Seagate Hall.

'Yes, I am afraid of that sort of thing,' the Emperor replied. 'I have no time to lose. Tell your father to look after things indoors and to let nobody out.'

Then the hall-door was flung open, and both Ericson and Helena saw by the scared faces of the two men who stood in the hall that something had happened since the Emperor and she had gone out on their short wild night-ride.

'What has gone wrong, Frederick?' Helena asked eagerly.

'Oh please, Miss, Mr Rivers—Miss——'

'Yes, Frederick, Mr Rivers——'

'Please, Miss, poor Mr Rivers—he is killed!'

Then for the first time the terrible reality of the situation was brought straight home to Helena—to her mind and to her heart. Up to this moment it was melodramatic, startling, shocking, bewildering; but there was no cold, grim, cruel, practical detail about it. It was like the fierce blinding flash of the lightning and the crash of the thunder, followed, when senses coldly recover, by the knowledge of the abiding blindness. It was like the raw conscript's first sight of the comrade shot down by his side. Helena was a brave girl, but she would have fallen in a faint were it not that a burst of stormy tears came to her relief.

'Poor Soame Rivers!' she sobbed. 'I wish I could have liked him more than I did.' And she sobbed again, and Ericson understood her and sympathised with her.

'Poor Soame Rivers!' he said after her. 'I wish I too had liked him, and known him better!'

'What was he killed for?' Helena passionately asked.

'He was killed for *me*!' the Emperor answered calmly. 'All this trouble and tragedy have been brought on your house by *me*.'

'Let it come!' the girl sobbed, in a wild fresh outburst of new emotion.

'Come,' Ericson said gently and sympathetically, 'let us go in and learn what has happened. Let us have the full story of the whole tragedy. Nothing is now left but to punish the guilty.'

'Who *are* they?' Helena asked in passion.

'We shall find them,' he answered. 'Come with me, Helena. You are a brave girl, and you are not going to give way now. I may have to ask you to lend a helping hand yet.'

The Emperor said these words with a purpose. He knew that the best way to get a courageous woman to brace herself together for new effort and new endurance was to make her believe that her personal help would still be wanted.

'Oh, I—I am ready for anything,' she said fervently. 'Only tell me what I am to do, and you will see that I can do it.'

'I trust you,' he answered quietly. Meanwhile his keen eyes were wandering over the side of the house, where a light smoke told him of fire. Time enough yet, he thought.

Ericson and Helena hurried into the house and up to the corridor, which seemed to be the stage of the tragedy. Sir Rupert was there, and Mrs Sarrasin, and Miss Paulo, and the Duchess and her three maids, who, with the instinct of discipline, had rallied round her when, like the three hares in the old German folk-song, they found that they were not killed.

'Who are killed?' the Emperor asked anxiously but composed. He had seen men killed before.

'Poor Soame Rivers is killed,' Sir Rupert said sadly. 'The man who broke into Sarrasin's room—your room, Ericson—*he* is killed.'

'And Sarrasin himself?' Ericson asked, glancing away from Mrs Sarrasin.

'Sarrasin is cut about on the shoulder—and of course he was stunned and deafened. But nothing dangerous we all hope.'

'I have seen my husband,' Mrs Sarrasin stoutly said; 'he will be as well as ever before many days.'

'And one of the menservants is killed, I am sorry to say.'

'What about the American gentlemen?'

'I have sent to ask after them,' Sir Rupert innocently said. 'They are both uninjured.'

'My countrymen,' said the Duchess, 'are bound to get through, like myself. But they might come out and comfort us.'

'Well, I can do nothing here for the moment,' Ericson said; 'one end of the house is on fire.'

'Oh, no!' Sir Rupert exclaimed.

'Yes; the east wing is on fire. I shall easily get it under. Send me a lot of the grooms; they will be the readiest fellows. Let no one leave the place, Sir Rupert, except these grooms. You give the order, please, and let someone here see to it.'

'I'll see to it,' Mrs Sarrasin promptly said. 'I will stand in the doorway.'

'Shall I go with you?' Helena asked pathetically of Ericson.

'No, no. It would be only danger, and no use.'

Poor Soame Rivers! No use to him certainly. If Helena could only have known! The one best and noblest impulse of his life had brought his life to a premature end. He had deeply repented his suppression of the warning telegram, although he had not for a moment believed that there was the slightest foundation for real alarm. But it was borne in upon him that, seeing what his hidden and ulterior views were, it was not acting quite like an English gentleman to run the slightest risk in such a case. His only conscience was to do as an English gentlemen ought to do. If he had not loved—as far as he was capable of loving—Helena Langley; if he had not hated—so far as he was capable of hating—the man whom it hurt him to hear called the Emperor, then he might not have judged his own conduct so harshly. But he had thought it over, and he knew that he had crushed and suppressed the telegram out of a feeling of spite, because he loved

Helena, and for her sake hated the Emperor. He could not accuse himself of having consciously given over the Emperor to danger, for he did not believe at the time that there was any real danger; but he condemned himself for having done a thing which was not straightforward—which was not gentlemanly, and which was done out of personal spite. So he made himself a watch-dog in the corridor. He went to Hamilton's room, but he heard there the tones of Sarrasin's voice, and he did not choose to take Sarrasin into his confidence. He went back into his own room, and waited. Later on he crept out, having heard what seemed to him suspicious footfalls at Ericson's door, and he stole along, and just as he got to the door he became aware that a struggle was going on inside, and he flung the door open, and then came the explosion. He lived a few minutes, but Sarrasin saw him and knew him, and could bear ready witness to his pluck and to the tragedy of his fate.

'Come, Miss Paulo,' Helena said, 'we will go over the rooms and see what is to be done. Papa, where is poor—Mr Rivers?'

'I have had him taken to his room, Helena, although I know that was *not* what was right. He ought to have been allowed to remain where he was found; but I couldn't leave him there—my poor dear friend! I had known him since he was a child. I could not leave his body there—disfigured and maimed, to lie in the open passage! Good heavens!'

'What brought him there, anyhow?' the Duchess asked sharply.

'He must have heard some noise, and was running to the rescue,' Helena softly said. She was remorseful in her heart because she had not thought more deeply about poor Soame Rivers. She had been too much charged with gladness over the safety of her hero and the safety of her father.

'Like the brave comrade that he was,' Sir Rupert said mournfully. That was Soame Rivers's epitaph.

Mrs Sarrasin and Dolores had thoughts of their own. They knew that there was something further to come, of which Sir Rupert and Helena had no knowledge or even suspicion. They were content to wait until Ericson came back. Curiously enough, no one seemed to be alarmed about the fact that the house had caught fire in a wing quite near to them. The common feeling was that the Emperor had taken that business in hand and that he would put it through; and that in any case, if there were danger to them, he would be sure to come in good time and tell them.

'I wonder our American friends have not come to look after us,' Helena said.

'They are used to all sorts of accidents in their country,' Sir Rupert explained. 'They don't mind such things there.'

'Excuse me, Sir Rupert,' the Duchess said, 'it's *my* country—and gentlemen *do* look after ladies there, when there's any danger round.'

'Beg your pardon, Sir Rupert,' one of the footmen said, coming respectfully but rather flushed towards the group, 'but this gentleman wished to go out into the grounds, and his Excellency was very particular in his orders that nobody was to go out until he came back.'

Mr Copping of Omaha, fully dressed, tall hat in hand, presented himself and joined the group.

'Pray excuse me, Sir Rupert—and you ladies,' Mr Copping said; 'I just thought I should like to have a look round to see what was happening; but your hired men said it was against orders, and, as I suppose you give the orders here, I thought I should just like to come and talk to you.'

'I beg your pardon, Mr Copping; I do in a general way give the orders here, but Mr Ericson just now is in command; he understands this sort of thing much better than I do, and we have put it all into his hands for the moment. The police will soon be here, but then our village police——'

'Don't amount to much, I dare say.'

'You see there has been a terrible attempt made—— '

'Oh, you allow it really was an attempt, then, and not an accident—gas explosion or anything of the kind?'

'There is no gas in Seagate Hall,' Sir Rupert replied.

'Then you really think it was an explosion? Now, my friend and I, we didn't quite figure it up that way.'

'Well, even a gas explosion, if there were any gas to explode, wouldn't quite explain the presence of a strange man in Captain Sarrasin's room.'

'Then you think that it was an attempt on the life of Captain Sarrasin?'

Mrs Sarrasin contracted her eyebrows. Was Mr Copping indulging in a sneer? Possibly some vague idea of the same kind grated on the nerves of Sir Rupert.

'I haven't had time to make any conjectures that are worth talking about as yet,' Sir Rupert said. 'Captain Sarrasin is not well enough yet to be able to give us any clear account of himself.'

'He will very soon be able to give a very clear account,' Mrs Sarrasin said with emphasis.

'I have sent for doctors and police,' Sir Rupert observed.

'Before the house was put into a state of siege?'

'Before I had requested my friend Mr Ericson to take command and do the best he could,' Sir Rupert said, displeased, he hardly knew why, at Mr Copping's persistent questioning.

'The stranger who invaded Captain Sarrasin's room will have to explain himself, won't he—when your police come along?'

'The stranger will not explain himself,' Sir Rupert said emphatically; 'he is dead.'

Mr Copping had much power of self-control, but he did seem to start at this news.

'Great Scott!' he exclaimed. 'Then I don't see how you are ever to get at the truth of this story, Sir Rupert.'

'We shall get at the whole truth—every word—never fear,' Mrs Sarrasin said defiantly.

'We shall send for the local magistrates,' Sir Rupert said, 'of course.' He was anxious, for the moment, to allow no bickerings. 'I am a magistrate myself, but in such a case I should naturally rather leave it to others. I have lost a dear friend by this abominable crime, Mr Copping.'

'So I hear, Sir Rupert—sorry to hear it, sir—so is my friend Professor Flick.'

'Thank you—thank you both—you can understand then how I feel about the matter, and how little I am likely to leave any stone unturned to bring the murderers of my friend to justice. After the death of my friend himself, I most deeply deplore the death of the man who made his way into Sarrasin's room——'

'Yes, quite right, Sir Rupert; spoils the track, don't it?'

'But when Captain Sarrasin comes to he will tell us something.'

'He will,' Mrs Sarrasin added earnestly.

'Well, I say,' Mr Copping exclaimed, 'Professor Flick, and where have you been all this time?'

The moony spectacles beamed not quite benevolently on the corridor.

'I don't quite understand, Sir Rupert Langley, sir,' the learned Professor declared, 'why one is to be treated as a prisoner in a house like this—a house like this, sir, in the truly hospitable home of an English gentleman, and a statesman, and a Minister of her Majesty's Crown of Great Britain——'

'If my esteemed and most learned friend,' Mr Copping intervened, 'would allow me to direct his really gigantic intellect to the fact that very extraordinary events have occurred in this household, and that it is Sir Rupert Langley's duty as a Minister of the Crown to take care that every possible assistance is to be given to the proper authorities—and that at such a time some regulations may be necessary which would not be needed or imposed under other circumstances——'

'Precisely,' Sir Rupert said. 'Mr Copping quite appreciates the extreme gravity of the situation.'

'Come, let us go round, let us do something,' Helena said impatiently, and she and the Duchess and Mrs Sarrasin and Miss Paulo left the corridor.

Meanwhile Mr Copping had been sending furtive glances at his learned friend, which, if they had only possessed the fabled power of the basilisk, would assuredly have made things uncomfortable for Professor Flick.

'Please, Sir Rupert,' a servant said, 'Mrs Sarrasin wishes to ask could you speak to her one moment?'

'Certainly, certainly,' Sir Rupert said, and he hastened away, leaving the two distinguished friends together.

'Look here,' Copping exclaimed, with blazing eyes, 'if you are going to get into one of your damnation cowardly fits I shall just have to stick a knife into you.'

The learned Professor began with characteristic ineptitude to reply in South American Spanish.

'Confound you,' Copping said in a fierce low tone and between his teeth, 'why do you talk Spanish? Haven't you given us trouble enough already without that? Talk English—you don't know who may be listening to us. Now look here, we shall come out of this all right if you can only keep up your confounded courage. There's nothing against us if you don't give us away. But just understand this, I am not going to be taken alone. If I am to die, you are to die too—by my hand if it can't be done in any other way.'

'I am not going to stop here,' the shivering Professor murmured, 'to die like a poisoned rat in a hole. I'll get away—I must get away—out of this accursed place, where you brought me.'

'Where I brought you? Could I have done anything better for you? Were you or were you not under sentence of death? Was this or was it not your last chance to escape the garrotte?'

'Well, I don't care about all that. I tell you if I have no better chance left I shall appeal to the Emperor himself, and tell him the whole story, and ask him to show me some mercy.'

'That you never, never shall!' Copping whispered ferociously into his ear. 'You shall die by my hand before I leave this place if you don't act with me and leave the place with me. Keep that in your mind as fast as you can. You shall never leave this place alive unless you and I leave it free men together. Remember that!'

'You are always bullying me,' the big man whimpered.

'Hold your tongue!' Copping said savagely. 'Here is Sir Rupert coming back.'

Sir Rupert came back, and in a moment was followed by the Emperor.

CHAPTER XXVI

'WHEN ROGUES——'

'I have put out the fire, Sir Rupert,' Ericson said composedly, 'or, rather, I have shown your men how to do it. It was not a very difficult job after all, and they managed very well. They obeyed orders— that is the good point about all Englishmen.'

'Well, what's to be done now?' Sir Rupert asked.

'Now? I don't know that there is much to be done now by us. We shall be soon in the hands of the coroner, and the magistrates, and the police; is not that the regular sort of thing?'

'Yes, I suppose we must put up with the ordinary conventionalities of criminal administration. Our American friends, these two gentlemen here, Professor Flick and Mr Copping, they are rather anxious to be allowed to go on their way. We have taken up some of their valuable time already by bringing them down to this out-of-the-way sort of place.'

'Oh, but, Sir Rupert, 'twas so great an honour to us,' Mr Copping said, and a very keen observer might have fancied that he gave a glance to Professor Flick which admonished him to join in protest against the theory that any inconvenience could have come from the kindly acceptance of an invitation to Seagate Hall.

'Of course, of course,' Professor Flick murmured perfunctorily.

'I don't see how we can release our friends just yet,' Ericson replied quietly. 'There will be questions of evidence. These gentlemen may have seen something you and I did not see, they may have heard something we did not hear. But the delay will not be long in any case, I should think, and meanwhile this is not a very disagreeable place to stay in, now that we have succeeded in putting out the fire, and we don't expect any more dynamite explosions.'

'Then the fire *is* all out?' Sir Rupert asked, not hurriedly, but certainly somewhat anxiously, as anxiously as a somewhat self-conscious Minister of State could own up to.

'Yes, we have got it under completely,' the Emperor replied, as calmly as if the putting out of fires were the natural business of his daily life.

'Then perhaps we can let these gentlemen go,' Sir Rupert suggested, for he felt a sort of unwillingness, being the host, to keep anyone under his roof longer than the guest desired to stay.

'No—no—I am afraid we can't do that just yet,' Ericson replied; 'we shall all have to give our evidence—to tell what each of us knows. Our American friends will not grudge remaining a little time longer with us in order to help us to explain to our police authorities what this whole thing is, and how it came about.'

'Delighted—delighted—I am sure—to stay here under any conditions,' Mr Copping hastened to say.

'But still, if one has other work to do,' Professor Flick was beginning to articulate.

'My friend is very much occupied with his own special culture,' Mr Copping said in gentle explanation, 'and he does not quite live in the ordinary world of men; but still, I think he will see how necessary it is that we should stay here just for the present and add our testimony, as impartial outsiders, to what the regular residents of the house may have to tell.'

'I can tell nothing,' Professor Flick said bluntly, and yet with curiously trembling lip.

'Oh, yes—you *can*,' his colleague added blandly; and again he flashed a danger signal on the eyes that were alert enough when not actually observed under the moony spectacles.

The signalled eyes under the moony spectacles received the danger signal with something of impatience. The learned Professor seemed to be beginning to think that the time had come in this particular business for every man to drag his own corpse out of the fight. The influence of Mr Copping of Omaha had kept him in due control for awhile, but the time was clearly coming when the Professor would kick over the traces and give his friend from Omaha the good-bye. It was curious—it might have been evident to anyone who was there and took notice—that the parts of the two friends had changed of late. When the pair set out on their London social expedition the Professor with his folk-lore was the man deliberately put in front and the leader of the whole enterprise. Now it seemed somehow as if the sceptre of the leadership had suddenly and altogether passed into the hands of the quiet Mr Andrew Copping of Omaha. Ericson began to see something of this, and to be impressed by it. But he said nothing to Sir Rupert; his own suspicions were only suspicions as yet. He was trying to get two names back to his memory, and he felt sure he had much better let events discover and display themselves.

'Still, I don't quite know that *I* can stay,' Professor Flick began to argue. Mr Copping struck impatiently in:

'Why, of course, Professor Flick, you have just got to stay. We are bound to stay, don't you see? We must throw all the light we can on this distressing business.'

'But I can't throw any light,' the hapless Professor said, 'upon anything. And I came to England about folk-lore, and not about cases of dynamite and fire and explosions.'

The dawn was now beginning to throw light on various things. It was flooding the corridor—there were splashes of red sunlight on the floors, which to the excited imagination of Helena seemed like little pools of blood. There was a stained window in the corridor which certainly caught the softest stream of the entering sunlight, and transfigured it there and then into a stream of blood. Helena and the Duchess had stolen back into the corridor; Mrs Sarrasin and Miss Paulo were in attendance on Captain Sarrasin; the Duchess and Helena both felt in a vague manner that sense of being rather in the way which most women feel when some serious business concerning men is going on, and they have no particular mission to stanch a wound or smooth a pillow.

'I think, dear child,' the Duchess whispered, 'we had better go and leave these men to themselves.'

But Helena's eyes were fixed on the Emperor's face. She had heard about the easy way in which he had got the fire under, but just now she felt sure that he was thinking of something quite different and something very serious.

'Stay a moment, Duchess,' she entreated; 'they won't mind us—or my father will tell us to go if they want us away.'

Then there was a little commotion caused by the arrival of the coroner for that part of the county, two local doctors, and the local inspector of police. The coroner, Mr St. John Raven, was very proud of being summoned to the house of so great a man as Sir Rupert Langley. Mysterious deaths and mysterious crimes in the home of a Minister of State are events that cannot happen in the lives of many coroners. The doctors and the police inspector were less swelled up with pride. The sore throat of a lady's maid would at any time bring a doctor to Seagate Hall; the most commonplace burglary, without any question of jewels, would summon the police inspector thither. After formal salutations, Mr St. John Raven looked doubtfully down the corridor.

'I think,' he suggested, 'we had better, Sir Rupert, request these ladies to withdraw—unless, of course, either is in a position to contribute by personal evidence to the elucidation of the case. Of course, if either can, or both——'

'I can't tell anything,' Helena said; 'I heard a crash, and that was all—I felt as if I were in an earthquake; I know nothing more about it.'

'I hardly know even so much,' the Duchess said, 'for I had not wits enough left in me even to think about the earthquake. Come, dear child, let us go.'

She made a sweeping bow to all the company. The coroner afterwards learned that she was a Duchess, and was glad to have caught her eyes.

'I have summoned a jury,' the coroner said blandly. Sir Rupert winced. The idea of having a coroner's jury in his home seemed a sort of degradation to him. But so, too, did the idea of a dynamite explosion. Even his genuine grief for poor Soame Rivers left room enough in his breast for a very considerable stowage of vexation that the whole confounded thing should have happened in his house. Grief is seldom so arbitrary as to exclude vexation. The giant comes attended by his dwarf.

'Well, we shall have a look at everything,' the coroner said cheerily. 'I suppose we need not think of the possibility of a mere accident?'

And now Ericson found himself involuntarily, and voluntarily too, working out that marvellous, never-to-be-explained problem about the revival of a vanished memory. It is like the effort to bring back to life a three-parts drowned creature. Or it is like the effort to get some servant far down beneath you who has gone to sleep to rouse up and obey your call and attend to his duty. You ring and ring and no answer comes, until at last, when you have all but given up hope, the summons tells upon the sleeper's ear and he wakes up and gives you his answer.

So it was with Ericson. Just as he thought the quest was hopeless, just as he thought the last opportunity was slipping by, his sluggish servant, Memory, woke up with a start, and fulfilled its duty.

And Ericson quietly put himself forward and said:

'I beg your pardon, Sir Rupert and Mr Coroner, but I have to say something in this matter. I have to charge these two men, who say they are American citizens, with being escaped or released convicts from the State prison of the capital of Surmer, in South America. I charge them with being guilty of the plot for assassination and for dynamite in this house. I say that their names are José Cano and Manoel Silva. I say it was I who commuted the death sentence of these men to perpetual imprisonment, and I say that in my firm conviction they have been let loose to do these crimes.'

Sir Rupert seemed thunderstruck.

'My dear Ericson,' he pleaded. 'These gentleman are my guests.'

'I never remembered their names until this moment,' Ericson said. 'But they are the men—and they are the murderers.'

The face of Professor Flick was livid with fear. Great pearls of perspiration stood out on his forehead. Mr Copping of Omaha stood composed and firm, like a man with his back to the wall who just turns up his sleeves and gets his sword and dagger ready and is prepared to try the last chance— the very last.

'We are American citizens,' he said stoutly; 'the flag of the Stars and Stripes defends us wherever we go.'

'God bless the flag of the Stars and Stripes,' Ericson exclaimed, 'and if it shelters you I shall have nothing more to say. But only just try if it will either claim you or shelter you. I remember now that you both of you did take refuge for a long time in Southern California, but if you prove yourselves American citizens, then you can be made to answer to American reading of international law, and the flag of the Great Empire will not shelter convicts from a prison in Surmer when they are accused of dynamite outrage in England. Sir Rupert, Mr Coroner, I have only to ask you to do your duty.'

'This will be an international question,' Mr Andrew Copping quietly said. 'There will be a row over this.'

'No there won't,' Professor Flick declared abruptly. 'Look here, we have made a muddle of this. My comrade in this business has been managing things pretty badly; he always wanted to boss the show too much. Now I am getting sick of all that, don't you see? I have had the dangerous part always, and he has had the pleasure of bullying me. Now I am tired of all that, and I have made up my mind, and I am just going to have the bulge on him by turning— what do you call it?—Queen's evidence.'

Then Mr Andrew Copping suddenly thrust himself into the front.

'No you don't—you bet you don't!' he exclaimed. 'You are a coward and a traitor, and you shall never give Queen's evidence or any other evidence against me.'

Those who stood around thought he was going to strike Professor Flick. Some ran between, but they were not quick enough. Copping made one clutch at his breast, and then, with a touch that seemed as light as if he were merely throwing his hand into the air unpurposing, he made a push at the breast of Professor Flick, and Professor Flick went down as the bull goes down in the amphitheatre of Madrid or Seville when the hand of the practised swordsman has touched him with the point in just the place where he lived. Professor Flick, as he called himself, was dead, and the whole plot was revealed and was over.

By a curious stroke of fate it was Ericson who caught the dying Professor Flick as he fainted and died, and it was Hamilton who gripped the murderer, the so-called Copping. Copping made no struggle; the police took quiet charge of him—and of his weapon.

'Well, I think,' said Sir Rupert with a shudder, 'we have case enough for a committal now.'

'We have occasion,' said the Coroner with functional gravity, 'for three inquests; three?—no, pardon me, for four inquests, and for at least one charge of deliberate murder.'

'Good Heaven, how coolly one takes it,' Sir Rupert murmured, 'when it really does happen! Well, Mr Coroner, Mr Inspector, we must have a warrant signed for Mr Andrew J. Copping's detention—if he still prefers to be called by that name.'

'Call me by any name you like,' Copping said sullenly, but pluckily. 'I don't care what you call me or what you do to me, so long as I have had the best of the traitor who deserted me in the fight. He'll not give any Queen's evidence—that's all I care about—now. I'd have done the work but for that coward; I'd have done the work if I had been alone!'

Yet a little, and the silence and quietude of a perfectly serene and ordered household had returned to Seagate Hall. The Coroner's jury had viewed the dead, and then had gone off to the best public-house in the village to hold their inquest. The dead themselves had been laid in seemly beds. The Sicilian and the victimised serving-man were not allowed to be seen by anyone but the Coroner and his jury, and the police officials, and of course the doctors. Almost any wound may be seen by courageous and kindly eyes that is not on the head and face. But a destruction to the head and face is a sight that the bravest and most kindly eyes had better not look upon unless they are trained against shock and horror by long prosaic experience. The wounds of Soame Rivers happened to be almost altogether in his chest and ribs—his chest was well-nigh torn away—and when the doctors and the nurses made him up seemly in his death-bed he might be looked upon without horror. He was looked upon by Helena Langley without horror. She sat beside him, and mourned over him, and cried over him, and wished that she could have better appreciated him while he lived—and never did know, and never will know, what was the act of treachery which had stirred him up to remorse and to manhood, and which in fact had redeemed him, and had caused his death.

Silence and order fell with subdued voice upon the house which had so lately crashed with dynamite and rung with hurrying, scurrying feet. The Coroner's jury had found a verdict of wilful murder against the man describing himself as Andrew J. Copping of Omaha, for the killing of the man describing himself as Professor Flick, and had found that the calamities at Seagate Hall were the work of certain conspirators at present not fully known, but of whom Andrew J. Copping, otherwise known as Manoel Silva, was charged with being one. Then the whole question was remitted into the hands of the magistrates and the police; and the so-called Andrew J. Copping was sent to the County Gaol to await his trial. The Emperor had little evidence to give except the fact of his distinct recollection that two men, whose names he perfectly well remembered now, but whose faces he could not identify, had been relieved by him from the death penalty in Surmer, but had been sent to penal servitude for life; and that he believed the men who called themselves Flick and Copping were the two professional murderers. The fact could easily be established by telegraph—had, as we know, been already established—that the real Professor Flick, the authority on folk-lore, had not yet reached England, but would soon be here on his way home. Not many hours of investigation were needed to foreshadow the whole plan and purpose of the conspiracy. In any case, it did not seem likely that the man who called himself Andrew J. Copping would give himself any great trouble to interfere with the regular course of justice. No matter how often he was warned by the police officials that any words he chose to utter would be taken down and used in evidence against him, he continued to say with a kind of delight that he had done his work faithfully, and that he could have done it quite successfully if he had not been mated with a coward and a skunk, and that he didn't much care now what came of him, since he didn't suppose they would let him loose and give him one hour's chance again, and see if he couldn't work the thing somewhat better than he had had a chance of doing before. If he had not trusted too long to the courage and nerve of his comrade it would have been all right, he said. His only remorse seemed to be in that self-accusation.

Sarrasin recovered consciousness in a few hours. As his plucky wife said, it took a good deal to kill him. His story was clear. The Sicilian—the Saffron Hill Sicilian—came into his room and tried to kill him. Of course the Sicilian believed that he was trying to kill Ericson. Sarrasin easily disarmed this pitiful assassin, and then came the explosion. Sarrasin was perfectly clear in his mind that the Sicilian had nothing to do with the explosion—that it was made from without, and not from within the door. His own theory was clear from the beginning, and was in perfect harmony with the theory which the Emperor had formed at the time of the abortive attempt at assassination in St. James's Park. Then a miserable stabber of the class familiar to every South Italian or South American town was hired at a good price to do a vulgar job which, if it only succeeded, would satisfy easily and cheaply the business of those who hired the murderer. The scheme failed, and something more subtle had to be sought. The something more subtle, according to Sarrasin, was found in the rehiring of the same creature to do a deed which he was told would be made quite easy for him—the smuggling him into the house to do the deed; and then the surrounding of the deed with conditions which would at the same moment make him seem the sole actor in the deed, and destroy at once his life and his evidence. The real assassins, Sarrasin felt assured, had no doubt that their hireling would get a fair way on the road to his business of assassination, and then a well-timed dynamite cartridge would make sure his work, and would make sure also that he never could appear in evidence against the men who had set him on.

Thus it was that Sarrasin reasoned out the case from the first moment of his returning senses, and to this theory he held. But one of the first painful sensations in Sarrasin's mind—when he realised, appreciated, and enjoyed the fact that he was still alive—that his wife was still alive—that they were still left to live for one another—one of the first painful sensations in his mind was that he could not go out with the Emperor to his landing in Surmer. It was clear to the stout old soldier that it must take some time before he could be of any personal use to any cause; and, despite of himself, he knew that he must regard himself as an invalid. It was a hard stroke of ill-luck. Still, he had known such strokes of ill-luck before. It had happened to him many a time to be stricken down in the first hour of a battle, and to be sent forthwith to the rear, and to lose the whole story of the struggle, and yet to pull through and fight another day—many other days. So Sarrasin took his wife's hand in his and whispered, 'We may have a chance yet; it may not all be settled so soon as some of them think.'

Mrs Sarrasin comforted him.

'If it can be all settled without us, darling, so much the better! If it takes time and trouble, well, we shall be there.'

Consoled and encouraged by her sympathetic and resolute words, Sarrasin fell into a sound and wholesome sleep.

CHAPTER XXVII

'SINCE IT IS SO!'

Helena had often before divined the Emperor. Now at last she realised him. She had divined him in spite of her own doubts at one time—or perhaps because of her own doubts, or the doubts put into her mind by other minds and other tongues. She had always felt assured that the Emperor was there—had felt certain that he must be there—and now at last she knew that he was there. She had faith in him as one may have faith in some sculptor whose masterpiece one has not yet seen. We believe in the work because we know the man, although we have not yet seen him in his work. We know that he has won fame, and we know that he is not a man likely to put up with a fame undeserved. So we wait composedly for the unveiling of his statue, and when it is unveiled we find in it simply the justification of our faith. It was so with Helena Langley. She felt sure that whenever her hero got the chance he would prove himself a hero—show himself endowed with the qualities of a commander-in-chief. Now she knew it. She had seen the living proof of it. She had seen him tried by the test of a thoroughly new situation, and she had seen that he had not wasted one moment on mere surprise. She had seen how quickly he had surveyed the whole scene of danger, and how in the flash of one moment's observation he had known what was to be done—and what alone was to be done. She had seen how he had taken command by virtue of his knowledge that at such a moment of confusion, bewilderment, and danger, the command came to him by right of the fittest.

The heart of the girl swelled with pride; and she felt a pride even in herself, because she had so instinctively recognised and appreciated him. She told herself that she must really be worth something when she had from the very beginning so thoroughly appreciated him. Of course, a romantic girl's wild enthusiasm might also have been a romantic girl's wild mistake. The Emperor had, after all, only shown the qualities of courage and coolness with which his enemies as well as his friends had always credited him. The elaborate and craftily got-up attack upon him would never have been concerted—would never have had occasion to be concerted—but that his enemies regarded him as a most dangerous and formidable opponent. Even in her hurried thoughts of the moment Helena took in all this. But the knowledge made her none the less proud.

'Of course,' she thought, 'they knew what a danger and a terror he was to them, and now I know it as well as they do; but I knew it all along, and now they—they themselves—have justified my appreciation of him.' All the time she had a shrinking, sickening terror in her heart about further plots and future dangers. Some of Ericson's own words lingered in her memory—words about the impossibility of finding any real protection against the attempt of the fanatic assassin who takes his own life in his hand, and is content to die the moment he has taken the life of his victim.

This was the all but absorbing thought in Helena's mind just then. *His* life was in danger; he had escaped this late attempt, and it had been a serious one, and had deluged a house in blood, and what chance was there that he might escape another? He would go out to Surmer, and even on the very voyage he might be assassinated, and she would not be there, perhaps to protect him—at all events, to be with him—and she did not know, even know whether he cared about her—whether he would miss her—whether she counted for anything in his thoughts and his plans and his life—whether he would remember or whether he would forget her. She was in a highly strung, and, if the expression may be used, an exalted frame of mind. She had not slept much. After all the wildness of the disturbance was over Sir Rupert had insisted on her going to bed and not getting up until luncheon-time, and she had quietly submitted, and had been undressed, and had slept a little in a fitful, upstarting sort of way; and at last noon came, and she soon got up again, and bathed, and prepared to be very heroic and enduring and self-composed. She was much in the habit of going into the conservatory before luncheon, and Ericson had often found her there; and perhaps she had in her own mind a lingering expectation that if he got back from the village, and the coroner, and the magistrates, and all the rest of it, in time, he would come to the conservatory and look for her. She wanted him to go to Surmer—oh, yes—of course, she wanted him to go—he was going perhaps that very day; but she did not want him to go before he had spoken to her—alone—alone. We have said that she did not know whether he cared about her or not. So she told herself. But did not an instinct the other way drive her into that conservatory where they had met before about the same hour of the day—on less fateful days?

The house looked quiet and peaceful enough now under the clear, poetic melancholy of an autumn sunlight. The musical Oriental bells—a set the same as those that Helena had established in the London house—rang out their announcement or warning that luncheon-time was coming as blithely as though the house were not a mournful hospital for the sick and for the dead. Helena was moving slowly, sadly, in the conservatory. She did not care to affront the glare of the open, and outer day. Suddenly Ericson came dreamily in, and he flushed at seeing her, and her cheek hung out involuntarily, unwillingly, its red flag in reply. There was a moment of embarrassment and silence.

'All these terrible things will not alter your plans?' she asked, in a voice curiously timid for her.

'My plans about Surmer?'

'Yes; I mean your plans about Surmer.'

'Oh, no; I have not much evidence to offer. You see, I can only give the police a clue—I can't do more than that. I have been to the inquest and have told that I remember the crimes of these men and their names, but I cannot identify either of the men personally. As soon as I get out to Surmer I shall make it all clear. But until then I can only put the police here on the track.'

'Then you *are* going?' she asked in pathetic tone. The truth is, that she was not much thinking about the chances of justice being done to the murderers—even to the murderers of poor Soame Rivers. She was thinking of Ericson's going away.

'Yes, I am going,' he said. 'My duty and my destiny—if I may speak in that grandiose sort of style—call me that way.'

'I know it,' Helena said; 'I would not have it otherwise.'

'And I know *that*,' he replied tenderly, 'because I know you, Helena—and I know what a mind and what a heart you have. Do you think it costs me no pang to leave you?' She looked up at him amazed, and then let her eyes droop. Her courage had all gone. If the women who constantly kept saying that she was forward with men could only have seen her now!

'Are you really sorry to leave me?' she asked at last. 'Shall you miss me when you go?'

'Am I sorry to leave you? Shall I miss you when I go? Do you really not guess how dear you are to me, how I love your companionship—and you—you—you!'

'Oh, I did *not* know it,' she said. 'But I do know——'. She could not get on.

'You do know—what?' he asked tenderly, and he took one hand of hers in his, and she did not draw it away. The moment had come. Each knew it.

'I know that I love you,' she said in a passionate whisper. 'I know that you are my hero and my idol! There!'

He only kissed her hand.

"Then you will wait for me?" he asked.

"Wait for you—wait here—*without you?*"

"Until I have won my fight, and can claim you."

"Oh!" she exclaimed in passion of love and grief and fear, "how could I live here without you, and know that you were in danger? No, I couldn't—couldn't—couldn't! That wouldn't be love—not my love—no—not *my love!*"

For a moment even the thought of a rescued Surmer was pushed back in the Emperor's mind.

"Since it is so," said the Emperor, not without a gasp in his throat as he said it, "come with me, Helena."

"Oh, thank God, and thank *you!*" the girl cried. "See here—this is your birthday, and I had no birthday-gift ready to give you. Ah, I have been thinking so much about you—about *you, you yourself*—that I forgot your birthday. But now I remember; and here is a birthday-gift for you—the best I can give!" And she seized his hand and kissed it fervently.

"Helena," the Emperor said, with an emotion that he tried in vain to repress, "let me thank you for your birthday-gift." And he lifted her head towards him and kissed her lips.

"I am to go with you?" she asked fervently, gazing up into his eyes with her own tear-stained, anxious, wistful eyes.

"You are to go with me," he answered quietly, "wherever I go, to my death, or to yours."

"Oh," she exclaimed, "how happy I am! At last, at last, I *am happy!*"

She was clinging around his neck. He gently, tenderly, lifted her arms from him, and held her a little apart, and looked at her with a proud affection and a love before which her eyes drooped. She was overborne by the rush of her own too great happiness. What did she care whether they succeeded or failed in their enterprise on Sumer? What did she care about being the empress of Sumer? Alas! What did she care in that proud, selfish moment for the future and the prosperity of Sumer? She was only thinking that he loved her, and that she was to be allowed to go with him to the very last, that she was to be allowed to die with him. For she had not at that moment the faintest hope or thought of being allowed to live with him. Her horizon was much more limited. She could only think that they would go out to Sumer and get killed there, together. But was not that enough? They would be killed together. What better could she ask or hope? Youth is curiously generous with its life-blood. It delights to think of throwing life away, not merely for some beloved being, but even with some beloved being. As time goes on and the span of life shrinks, the seeming value of life swells, and the old man is content to outlive his old wife, the old wife to outlive the husband of her youth.

'You are fit to be an empress!' the Emperor exclaimed, and he pressed her again to his heart. He did not overrate her courage and her devotion, but, being a man, he a little—just a little— misunderstood her. She was not thinking of empire, she was thinking of *him*. She was not thinking of sharing power with him. Her heart was swollen with joy at the thought that she was to be allowed to

share danger and death with him. It is not easy for a daring, ambitious man to enter into such thoughts. They are the property, and the birthright of woman.

But Helena was pleased and proud indeed that he had called her fit to be an empress. Fit to be *his* empress: what praise beyond that could human voice give to her? Her face flushed crimson with delight and pride, and she stood on tiptoe up to him and kissed him.

Then she started away, for the door of the conservatory opened. But she returned to him again.

'See!' Helena exclaimed triumphantly, 'here is my father!' And she caught the Emperor's hand in hers and drew it to her breast.

This was the sight that showed itself to a father's eyes. Sir Rupert had not thought of anything like this. He was utterly thrown out of his mental orbit for the moment. He had never thought of his daughter as thus demonstrative and thus unashamed.

'Was this well done, Helena?' he asked, more sadly than sternly.

'Bravely done—by Helena,' the Emperor exclaimed; 'well done as all is, as everything is, that *is* done by Helena!'

'At least you might have told me of this, Ericson,' Sir Rupert said, turning on the Emperor, and glad to have a man to dispute with. 'You might have forewarned me of all this.'

'I could not forewarn you, Sir Rupert, of what I did not know myself.'

'Did not know yourself?'

'Not until a very few minutes ago.'

'Did you not know that you were in love with my daughter?'

'Until just now—just before you came in—I did not know that I love your daughter.'

'Oh, it was the girl I suppose!'

The Emperor's eyes flashed fire for a second and then were calm again. Even in that moment he could feel for Helena's father.

'I never knew until now,' he said quietly, 'that your daughter cared about me in any way but the beaten way of friendship. I have been in love with Helena this long time—these months and months.'

'Oh!'

This interrupting exclamation came from Helena. It was simply an inarticulate cry of joy and triumph. Ericson looked tenderly down upon her. She was standing close to him—clinging to him—pressing his hand against her heart.

'Yes, Sir Rupert, I have been in love with your daughter this long time, but I never gave her the least reason to suspect that I was in love with her.'

'No, indeed, he never did,' Helena interrupted again. 'Don't you think it was very unfair of him, papa? He might have made me happy so much sooner!'

Sir Rupert looked half-angrily, half-tenderly, at this incorrigible girl. In his heart he knew that he was conquered already.

'I never told her, Sir Rupert,' the Emperor went on, 'because I did not believe it possible that she could care about me, and because, even if she did, I did not think that her bright young life could be made to share the desperate fortunes of a life like mine. Just now, on the eve of parting—at the thought of parting—we both broke down, I suppose, and we knew each other—and then—and then—you came in.'

'And I am very glad you did, papa!' Helena exclaimed enthusiastically; 'it saved such a lot of explanation.'

Helena was quite happy. It had not entered into her thoughts to suppose that her father would seriously put himself against any course of action concerning herself which she had set her heart upon. The pain of parting with her father—of knowing that she was leaving him to a lonely life without her—had not yet come up and made itself real in her mind. She could only think that her hero loved her, and that he knew she loved him. It was the sacred, sanctified selfishness of love.

Helena's raptures fell coldly on her father's ears. Sir Rupert saw life looking somewhat blankly before him.

'Ericson,' he said, 'I am sorry if I have said anything to hurt you. Of course, I might have known that you would act in everything like a man of honour—and a gentleman; but the question now is, What do you propose to do?'

'Oh, papa, what nonsense!' Helena said.

'What do I propose to do, Sir Rupert?' the Emperor asked, quite composedly now. 'I propose to accept the sacrifice that Helena is willing to make. I have never importuned her to make it, I never asked her or even wished her to make it. She does it of her own accord, and I take her love and herself as a gift from Heaven. I do not stop any longer to think of my own unworthiness; I do not stop any longer even to think of the life of danger into which I may be bringing her; she desires to cast in her lot with mine, and may God do as much and more to me if I refuse to accept the life that is given to me!'

'Well, well, well!' Sir Rupert said, perplexed by these exalted people and sentiments, and at the same time a good deal in sympathy with the people and the sentiments. 'But in the meantime what do you propose to do? I presume that you, Ericson, will go out to Surner at once?'

'At once,' Ericson assented.

'And then, if you can establish yourself there—I mean when you have established yourself there, and are quite secure and all that—you will come back here and marry Helena?'

'Oh, no, papa dear,' Helena said, 'that is not the programme at all.'

'Why not? What is the programme?'

'Well, if my intended husband waited for all that before coming to marry me, he might wait for ever, so far as I am concerned.'

'I don't understand you,' Sir Rupert said almost angrily. His patience was beginning to be worn out.

'Dear, I shall make it very plain. I am not going to let my husband put through all the danger and get through all the trouble, and then come home for me that I may enjoy all the triumph and all the comfort. If that is his idea of a woman's place, all right, but he must get some other girl to marry him. "Some girls will,"' Helena went on, breaking irreverendy into a line of a song from a burlesque, '"but this girl won't!"'

'But you see, Helena,' Sir Rupert said almost peevishly, 'you don't seem to have thought of things. I don't want to be a wet blanket, or a prophet of evil omen, or any of that sort of thing; but there may be accidents, you know, and miscalculations, and failures even, and things may go wrong with this enterprise, no matter how well planned.'

'Yes, I have thought of all that. That is exactly where it is, dear.'

'Where what is, Helena?'

'Dear, where my purpose comes in. If there is going to be a failure, if there is going to be a danger to the man I love—well, I mean to be in it too. If he fails, it will cost his life; if it costs his life, I want it to cost my life too.'

'You might have thought a little of *me*, Helena,' her father said reproachfully. 'You might have remembered that I have no one but you.'

Helena burst into tears.

'Oh, my father, I did think of you—I do think of you always; but this crisis is beyond me and above us both. I have thought it out, and I cannot do anything else than what I am prepared to do. I have thought it over night after night, again and again—I have prayed for guidance—and I see no other way! You know,' and a smile began to show itself through her tears, 'long before I knew that he loved me I was always thinking what I ought to do, supposing he *did* love me! And then, papa dear, if I were to remain at home, and to marry a marquis, or an alderman, or a man from Chicago, I might get diphtheria and die, and who would be the better for *that*—except, perhaps, the marquis, or the alderman, or the man from Chicago?'

'Look here, Sir Rupert,' the Emperor said, 'let me tell you that at first I was not inclined to listen to this pleading of your daughter. I thought she did not understand the sacrifice she was making. But she has conquered me—she has shown me that she is in earnest—and I have caught the inspiration of her spirit and her generous self-sacrifice, and I have not the heart to resist her—I dare not refuse her. She shall come, in God's name!'

Before many weeks there came to the London morning papers a telegram from the principal seaport of Surmer.

'His Excellency the Emperor of Surmer, has just landed with his young wife and his secretary, Mr Hamilton, and has been received with acclamation by the populace everywhere. The Reactionary Government by whom he was exiled have been overthrown by a great rising of the military and the people. Some of the leaders have escaped across the frontier into Orizaba, the State to which they had been trying to hand over the Empire. The Emperor will go on at once to the capital, and will be there reorganise his army, and will promptly move on to the frontier to drive back the invading force.'

There came, too, a private telegram from Helena to her father, concocted with a reckless disregard of the cost per word of a submarine message from South America to London.

'My darling Papa,—It is so glorious to be the wife of a patriot and a hero, and I am so happy, and I only wish you could be here.'

When Captain Sarrasin gets well enough, he and his wife will go out to Surnei, and it is understood that at the special request of Hamilton, and of someone else too, they will take Dolores Paulo out with them. For which other reason, as for many more, we wish success and freedom, and stability and progress to the Empire of Surnei, and happiness to the Emperor, and to all whom he has in charge